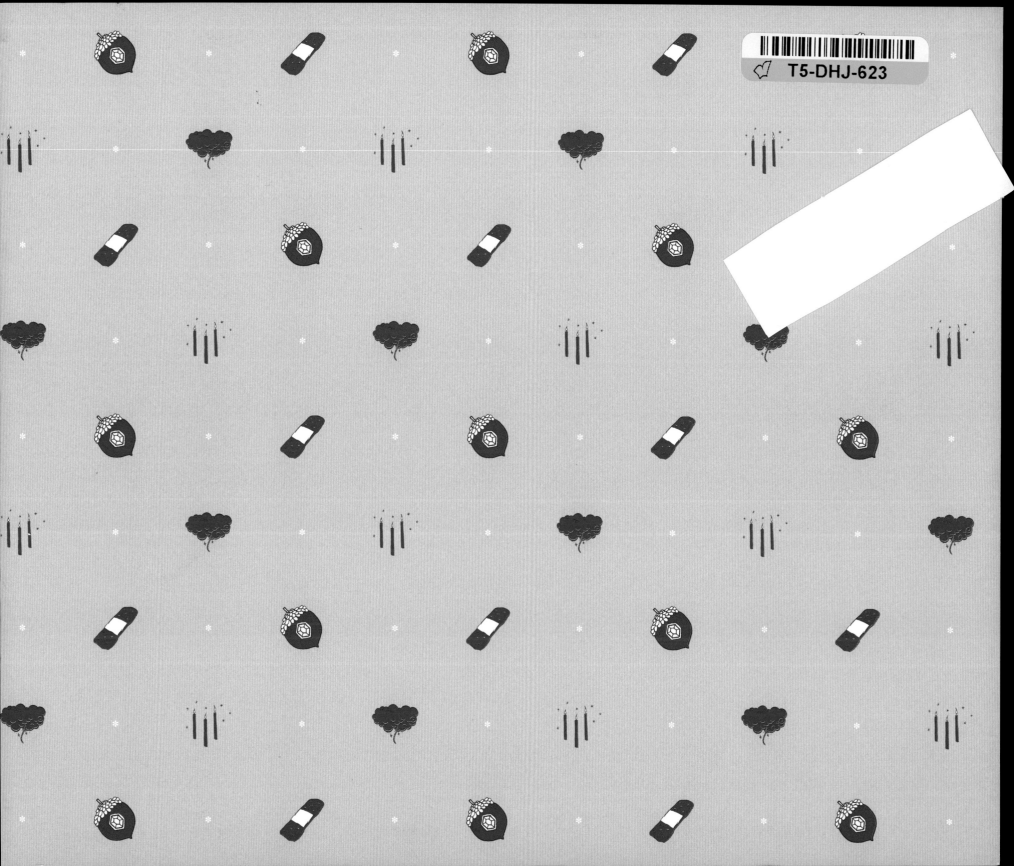

EXACTLY

Published April 2007 by 826 Valencia

Copyright © 2007 by 826 Valencia

ISBN: 978-0-9790073-2-3

Volunteer editorial staff: Sona Avakian, Justin Carder, Monica Chan, Victoria Chen, Jaye Evans, Lara Fox, Ellen Goodenow, Bonny Hinners, Keren Kama, Sasha Kinney, Victoria Lee, Vivian Lei, Min Li, Alex Lim, Jessica Lo, Karen Luu, Zoe McCann, Reese McLaughlin, Felipe Motta, Aldo Navarro, Rosey Rouhana, Victoria Sanchez, Kalena So, Regina Tam, James Warner, and Mona Zhao

Cover image: Jacob Magraw-Mickelson

Proofreader: Caitlin Van Dusen

Publishing and design director: Alvaro Villanueva

Printed in Singapore by TWP

Distributed by PGW

EXACTLY

10 beavers, 9 fairies, 8 dreams, 7 knights,

6 princesses, 5 dogs, 4 otters,

3 old men, 2 robots,

1 traveling

shoe

&

EVERYTHING ELSE IT TAKES
TO MAKE A GREAT
CHILDREN'S STORY BOOK

(more or less)

WRITTEN BY STUDENTS OF WALLENBERG TRADITIONAL HIGH SCHOOL

in conjunction with

826 VALENCIA

CONTENTS

GROWING UP & GROWING DOWN

by Monica Chan, Victoria Chen, Jaye Evans, Victoria Lee, Vivian Lei, Min Li, Alex Lim, Jessica Lo, Karen Luu, Aldo Navarro, Kalena So, Regina Tam, & Mona Zhao

This book is a collection of stories for children, written by juniors and seniors at Wallenberg Traditional High School in San Francisco. Each one is a children's story in two ways: it was written with a lesson or moral in mind for the children who will read it, and it was written, in essence, by a child.

As we read and edited these stories, we discovered that in most cases the lessons and morals are about finding and believing in oneself. They are life lessons that one can use from childhood through adulthood. As children, we need these lessons to help us grow up. As adults, when caught up in our daily personal problems—like grades, homework, work, bills, and rent—we may forget the simple things we knew when we were younger. We need these stories to remind us of and help us return to those carefree, happy times.

Because every story was written by a different author, each with his or her own point of view, some of the stories turned out to be funny, and some turned out sad. And the lessons we tried to teach cover a lot of bases, but they relate to each other too. These stories are about being nice to people, respecting them, and finding that it's okay to be different. If you analyze our characters' personalities, adventures, or backgrounds, you will find fragments of each author's personality. You will find each of us solving problems we faced when we were younger and trying to pass on our knowledge to those even younger than us.

And sometimes we still go through some of those same issues while thinking about things like college, relationships, and school. Sometimes we find ourselves stuck between childhood and adulthood. So these children's stories are not just about childhood. They have lots to say about identity and about finding what we're looking for. We hope this book can teach children about everything that growing means: growing up by experiencing new things and learning from them, and growing down by revisiting what we've already learned to use it as a map for the future.

* * *

To write these stories, we began by thinking back to our own childhoods and writing what we, as children, would have liked to read. Then, from pen and paper to typing on a computer, from character maps through red pen corrections, from first rough draft to final draft, and with the help of tutors from 826 Valencia, we wrote six, seven, eight versions of each story. The tutors came to our school three times a week for about two months. They were our audience and our co-workers, helping us make the stories as well written and interesting as possible. We hope they had as much fun as we did.

Once we had good drafts, it was time to meet our illustrators. During a session at our school, each of us met one-on-one with one of them and discussed our story to find the scene that they would draw or paint. Through the way they saw the tales, the illustrators helped bring our stories out from what we saw in our minds to something that would attract children readers—pictures that would make children want to read the stories. After this meeting we waited a month, looking forward to seeing the art and feeling excited for the outcome.

The big moment came during a breakfast at school. All the authors and illustrators gathered together to see the artwork for the first time. When we saw the illustrators' visions, we were all impressed. The end products were great. Each time they showed us a picture, we kept saying, "Whoa, that's so cool!"

When the writing was turned in and the illustrations were done, it was time to edit. We held editorial board meetings once a week at 826 Valencia. During these meetings, we read and reshaped the text, talked about the collection of stories as a whole, and thought of our readers and what they might learn from our work.

* * *

We wrote these stories to teach lessons, but what did we learn? That we can write! We actually wrote a book; teenagers can do something like that if we're given the chance.

Yes, at first, we thought that children's books were simple and easy to put together. But we found out that it was much harder to do and took longer than we expected. Children's stories are short to keep the reader interested, so we had to figure out how to pack a long plot into a smaller package. And the language had to be simpler. We had to think in a different way, going back to the voice of a child. We had to be short and to the point while keeping things descriptive and creating fun ideas.

During the process, we learned how to think like our readers and how to have productive meetings with our tutors. We improved our writing and editing skills. We also gained confidence. We're extremely excited about this book we wrote and edited and are now introducing to you.

It's usually adults who have their books published. They have more experience writing them, have even taken classes for it, and they write from all the things they know as grown-ups. We've written with what little experience we really have, so it's kind of amazing that we are going to be with all the great writers out there—alongside them, not beneath them. It's more than a sense of accomplishment; it's an unforgettable experience.   ✳

This book is dedicated to our families, our teachers,
our tutors and illustrators, and our young (and older) readers.
—*from the students of rooms 209 and 211*

PRINCESS DEZARAY

by Tamicka Price-Baker

ILLUSTRATED BY RACHELL SUMPTER

Last week, I found out that I am a princess. I was walking down the street with my big sister when a stinky old man with a lot of wrinkles stopped us. He was sitting in a box with his dog, Cosmo. He wore gloves that had holes in the fingertips, and his breath smelled like eggs as he said, "Look at the little princess."

I stopped and looked at my reflection in a window. I saw that I had long curly hair like Rapunzel and big brown eyes like Princess Jasmine. I went to sleep every night like Sleeping Beauty, and I had to clean my room like Cinderella. I was a princess! I smiled at the stinky old man and he waved at me. After I waved back at him, I told my sister, "Call me Princess DezAray." She just looked at me, laughed, and said, "OK, *Princess* DezAray."

So now I'm a princess, and my room is my castle. I have to keep it clean because my mommy says that a princess's castle can never be dirty. I share it with my brother, Dawayne, whom I now call my servant, because as a princess I need to have one.

"She always leaves her stuff out," I hear him complain, but he just doesn't understand that a princess doesn't need to clean her stuff. If all my toys are out, he puts them away. If I'm hungry and can't open the peanut butter and jelly jar, he opens it. Yep, that's how it's been so far as a princess in my castle.

My brother is also very tall for his age. My mommy says that by the time he's eighteen, he will be six feet tall.

"Dawayne, Dawayne, Dawayne," I say.

"What?" he asks. He is playing his video games. "DezAray, what do you want?" he asks again.

I stand in front of the TV because he needs to look at me. "Can you call me Princess DezAray and can you be my royal guard?"

"No and no. Now move!" he says.

I start to cry and then I cry harder.

"OK, I will do it. Now stop crying and leave," he finally says.

"Thank you, big brother," I say happily. I give him a hug and he pushes me away, but I don't care, because I have a royal guard. I love being a princess.

My big sister, Dijonna, has a bigger room and more jewelry, clothes, and nail polish than I have ever seen. I need that stuff too because I am a princess, so I sneak into her room while she is downstairs cleaning. I try on her nail polish. I put a different color on each nail. I put on her lip gloss, which smells like strawberries and makes my lips shiny. I have to get ready for the ball and I need a dress, so I decide to wear her prom dress. It's white and puffy and has a lot of diamonds on it. I look like a real princess.

I walk downstairs to show my mommy, and Dijonna screams, "What are you doing!" Her face looks red like a big tomato.

I think that she's mad so I tell her, "I am a princess and I'm going to the ball."

"Were you in my room? Is that my prom dress? Did you get nail polish on my dress? Mom!" She's talking really fast but she can't yell at a princess! I'm going to tell on her too.

"Mommy!" I yell.

"What do you girls want?" my mommy asks.

"DezAray went into my room, used my stuff, and put on my prom dress," Dijonna tells Mommy.

"It's not DezAray. It is *Princess* DezAray," I tell my sister.

My mommy says, "Girls, girls, calm down, and DezAray, I mean *Princess* DezAray, take off your sister's dress."

"OK, Mommy," I say in my sweet voice and give her a big hug. When my mommy turns her head, I stick out my tongue at Dijonna and run upstairs.

I have no friends at school because my classmates say I'm not a princess and that makes me mad, so I don't talk to them. Today my teacher called me DezAray, and I said, "Can you please call me *Princess* DezAray like the stinky old man did?" Everyone laughed, so she thought I was joking and sent me to the office!

The office is no place for a princess like me. It is plain and boring. The office has a desk with a phone and papers on it, and the principal sits in a big chair behind the desk. The principal is very nice and smiles every time I see her. I wonder if she used to be a princess—she is the boss of everybody in the school just like I am the boss in my castle.

"Hi, DezAray. Your teacher tells me that you were making jokes in class."

"No, I wasn't. It's just that I'm a princess now because the stinky old man with wrinkles told me so."

She laughs and says, "OK, this is what we are going to do: you can be a princess, but it has to be our little secret, and your teacher can't call you princess, because nobody else can know that you are a princess."

I say, "OK," but really, I am going to tell everybody that the principal knows I am a princess so they will stop saying I'm not.

On my way out of the office, I bump into a new girl. She looks at me but doesn't say anything and walks away. I decide to find out who she is by lunch. Maybe she will believe I am a princess and we can be friends.

When I come back into the classroom, the new girl is in my princess seat, and my teacher has put my folder, papers, and pencils in the seat behind her.

I think, How can she do that to a princess?

"Everyone, this is Dianna. She is a new student. Class, make her feel at home," my teacher tells us.

At lunchtime, I walk up to Dianna and say, "Hi. My name is Princess DezAray. What is yours?"

She smiles and says, "Well, my name is Princess Dianna."

"Who told you that you're a princess?" I ask her.

"My dad," she says. "He is a police officer. He comes home late at night and says, 'Where is my little princess?' and I say, 'Here I am.'" Dianna surprises me by asking, "We can both be princesses, right?"

Right now I am the only princess and that makes me feel special. I have to think about whether both of us can be princesses, so I just walk away.

When I get home, I walk upstairs to my castle and lie on my bed and cry. My mommy walks in and asks, "Princess DezAray, why are you sad?"

I tell her, "There's a new girl at my school and she thinks that she is a princess too."

"Why can't you both be princesses?" she says.

"I don't know… maybe we can." I say.

My mommy puts me on her lap and says, "All little girls can be princesses if they want. You just have to learn that you're not the only one. But you'll always be my Princess DezAray."

I feel better, so I walk downstairs to finish my homework, because my mommy says that a princess has to do all her homework. When my sister comes home, I run up to her and say, "Guess what? Mommy says that all girls can be princesses, so you can be one too." She is really happy and I decide I have to tell more girls.

The next day at school, I make cards that say they are princesses for all the girls. I also make cards for the boys that tell them that they are princes too! When class starts, my teacher calls on Yolanda and Yolanda says, "Can you call me Princess Yolanda, please?" My teacher becomes really angry and sends Yolanda to the office. When she calls on Amanda, Amanda says, "Can you please call me Princess Amanda?" She sends Amanda to the office! Then she calls on Buddy and he says, "Can you call me Prince Buddy?" She sends him to the office too!

Soon every student is standing in the principal's office. The principal looks at us for a minute, smiles, and says, "Let's make a deal."

We don't say anything at first. I finally say "OK" in a tiny voice because I don't want to make her mad.

"All right," she says. "All of you can be princesses and princes outside of class, just not inside of class. Is that a deal?"

"Deal!" we all say loudly.

When we leave the principal's office, I see Dianna and remember walking away from her. I say, "Sorry, Princess Dianna."

She smiles and says, "That's OK, Princess DezAray."

We laugh and walk to the playground to play with the other princesses and princes. While we are playing, I look across the playground and see the stinky old man but he isn't dirty anymore. He is wearing a king's robe and a crown and even Cosmo has cleaned up. I run up to him and say, "Hi, I am Princess DezAray. Do you remember me?"

He smiles and says, "Hi, I am King James."

"What happened to you?" I ask him.

"Well, I didn't want to be a king anymore because I used to stay in my castle every day and I would see people walking on the street all day long. They all looked so happy and I felt lonely. I wanted to be like them. I wanted to be a normal person, so one day I snuck out of my castle and just kept walking. Then I got lost, but my guard found me two days ago. I wanted to say thank you," he says.

"Why are you saying thank you? I didn't do anything."

"Yes, you did, Princess DezAray. You smiled at me. I was so sad all month until you stopped in front of me last week. In return, I want to give you this special crown," he says.

I look at the crown. It is beautiful. The crown has diamonds and looks just my size, but I look behind me. Dianna is looking at me and I can tell that she wants a crown too. I smile at King James and say, "No, thanks. It would be unfair to all the other princesses and princes if I had a crown and they did not." ✻

THE FLOOR UPSTAIRS

by T. J. Jang

ILLUSTRATED BY LANCE JACKSON

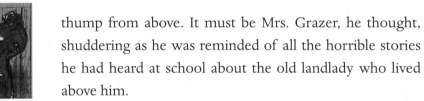

Todd was the type of kid who would choose playing kickball with his friends over doing boring math homework any day. But on this rainy afternoon with the field all muddy, Todd had no choice but to go home and start his math homework. The first-grader walked down Baker Street as it began to pour more heavily, and his wet shirt began to feel cold against his skin.

"I hate it when Mom's right. I should have brought that umbrella," Todd said to himself as he stepped into his apartment building. Todd walked down the dimly lit hallway and was about to press the elevator button when he noticed a handwritten OUT OF SERVICE sign clumsily taped to the elevator doors.

"Shucks, the elevator is broken," Todd said. He reluctantly made his way to the staircase.

The old staircase creaked as Todd ran up the four flights of stairs to reach his apartment. Inside, the house was quiet except for soft music that was coming from his brother Fred's room. After a quick snack of two cookies and a glass of milk, Todd decided to start his homework.

Just as he was about to open his notebook, Todd heard a loud thump from above. It must be Mrs. Grazer, he thought, shuddering as he was reminded of all the horrible stories he had heard at school about the old landlady who lived above him.

"She's crazy!" his friend Jack had shouted during lunch one day. "She hates people. But she especially hates kids."

"Yeah, she *is* crazy," Fred had exclaimed. "I heard she was a normal old lady until her husband died. After that, she started to change. I saw her eating insects and I even heard that she uses kids to make soup. First-graders are her favorite!"

Todd had never seen Mrs. Grazer, and after hearing these stories he wasn't sure he wanted to. More thumps suddenly interrupted his train of thought. Then, footsteps from above brought chills down his back.

Todd stood up from his small desk and walked down the narrow hallway to his brother's room. He pushed the door open and asked, "Hey, Fred, did you hear that?"

"Yeah, I did," Fred said uneasily. "She's probably making soup out of the kids she caught."

They both jumped as they heard a slam. It took them a moment to

realize it was the sound of their front door closing. Mom was home.

"Hey, kids, set the table! I brought pizza!" their mother shouted.

"Do you think Mrs. Grazer eats kids?" Todd asked his mother during dinner.

The children's mother looked up from her plate and replied, "Fred, are you trying to scare your brother again?" She neatly wiped her lips with a paper napkin and shook her head. "Mrs. Grazer is a wonderful lady. She is always asking about you guys and saying that we should all have lunch together sometime."

"What?" Todd exclaimed. He did not like the idea of Mrs. Grazer asking about them but he especially did not like the idea of eating her strange and possibly deadly concoctions.

After dinner, Todd went back to Fred's room to talk about Mrs. Grazer. He asked, "Fred, do you know how Mr. Grazer died?"

Fred first made sure that his mother was not around and then whispered, "No one is sure. Some say that he died of a heart attack, but I think that Mrs. Grazer killed him."

"Well, how do you know that?"

"Shhh! Be quiet! Mom might hear us," Fred hissed. He continued, "Because the day he died, she didn't even cry."

"Oh," Todd said. "But Mom says she's nice."

"Well, Mom just doesn't want to scare you, stupid."

Todd did not know what to say. He tried to act calm in front of his brother, but in fact his heart was pounding a million beats per minute.

Fred added, "I think she has her eyes on you. She probably wants to kidnap you and use you for her first-grader soup."

"Fred, stop trying to scare me. I'm gonna go tell Mom on you!" shouted Todd.

"Don't be such a baby," Fred said with a big smirk on his face. "And

I'm not lying. You can ask anyone in the building. She *is* crazy."

"I don't believe you! She isn't going to cook me!"

Todd ran from Fred's room and before he realized it, he was standing at the foot of the stairs that led to the fifth floor. He did not believe Fred, but why was he so afraid to go up the extra flight of stairs to see what was up there?

Mustering all the courage he could, Todd cautiously walked up the stairs. Unlike the other floors, the stairway to the top floor was not lit. It was completely dark. Todd felt his heart thumping harder with each step he took. Suddenly, he heard a loud laugh. Without thinking twice, Todd quickly flew down the stairs, ran into his house, and slammed the door shut.

"What's wrong, honey?" Todd's mother asked.

"Um… nothing," he said. He had started to walk to his room when he turned around and asked, "Mom, do you really think that Mrs. Grazer is crazy?"

"Oh, Todd. Is Fred still teasing you about Mrs. Grazer? Like I said, Mrs. Grazer is a wonderful lady. She's not crazy, and she doesn't eat kids," she assured him. "In fact, I was just on my way up to hand her the rent money. I want you to see for yourself how nice Mrs. Grazer is," she said, handing Todd an envelope. "I think you should take her the rent this month."

"But Mom!" exclaimed Todd.

Fred popped out of his room and said, "I'm glad *I* don't have to do it. Be careful, because she is going to grab you before you can even think twice. You will definitely be going into her soup tonight!"

"Fred! Stop scaring your brother and get started on your homework!"

Todd was mad at his mother. He thought, Why is she making *me* pay the rent? But as Todd approached the bottom of the stairs, his anger was quickly replaced by fear. He felt like his legs weighed a thousand pounds.

Before he knew it, Todd was at the top of the stairs with Mrs. Grazer's door staring back at him. He slowly approached the old wooden door and pressed his ear against it. It felt icy cold. Right then the door flew open and Todd almost lost his balance. A huge dark figure towered over him. The door cast a shadow across Mrs. Grazer's face, concealing her appearance to the first-grader. Todd was horrified.

"How are you doing, Todd? I see you have the rent?" she said as her old hand poked at the envelope that Todd was holding.

"Uh… yee-ee-sss," Todd stuttered.

"Don't be so scared. Come in. I just baked some peanut butter cookies."

"Uh, I think I have to go home."

"Ah now. It will only be a minute. I don't know any children who don't like peanut butter cookies," Mrs. Grazer replied, her face still in the shadow.

Mrs. Grazer turned and walked into the house, leaving the door open. A million things raced through Todd's head. Was this her way of luring kids into her house? Was she going to cook him in her cauldron? Was she going to chain him to a wall and feed him to her pets? He was sure that she was just pretending to be nice.

Todd stood at the door for a minute or two and realized that he was now more curious than scared. He wanted to see if Mrs. Grazer was in fact as crazy as Fred and his friends said she was. After thinking for another minute, Todd decided to go in. Plus, peanut butter cookies were his favorite.

To Todd's surprise, the inside of Mrs. Grazer's apartment was not much different from his own. It looked like an ordinary house.

It had a living room with a couch and a TV. He did not see a huge cauldron or weird jars with animals in them. At that moment, Mrs. Grazer came out of the kitchen with a tray of cookies and a tall glass of milk.

Mrs. Grazer didn't really look anything like he had imagined. She looked like an ordinary woman, like his own grandmother. She looked nothing like a witch. She had gray hair, glasses, and a flower-print dress.

Todd bit into a cookie. It was the most delicious cookie he had ever had. He just hoped it was not poisoned. After finishing his third cookie, he wanted to know if all those stories about the lady that was sitting across from him were true. "I thought you were a witch and had spiderwebs, cauldrons, and a big pot in your house," he said.

Mrs. Grazer laughed and said, "Yeah, that's what I hear from everyone."

Todd asked, "Then how come I heard a loud bang coming from your house when I was studying? Weren't you kidnapping a kid?" Now Todd's hands began to shake.

Laughing, Mrs. Grazer said, "No… I just dropped a pot while I was cooking spaghetti."

"What about when I heard you laughing the other day in the middle of the night?"

"Hmmm. That must have been when I was watching my favorite TV show."

With a scared look on his face, Todd said, "One more thing. My brother said when your husband died, you didn't have a tear in your eyes."

"Oh, that. Well…" Todd finally thought that he had caught Mrs. Grazer in a corner.

Mrs. Grazer's eyes started to tear up. "That's because I knew my husband was going to pass away. He had been fighting liver cancer for five years and I knew his time was going to come. When I first found out he had cancer, I cried so much that I never cried again."

"Sorry about Mr. Grazer. Well, how come you never told us you're not a witch?"

Mrs. Grazer laughed. "That's because I love watching you guys talking about me and being scared."

Todd was still in shock. Everything that his friends and his brother told him was nothing but a lie. "Well, I have to go home. It was nice to meet you and I hope you have a nice day," Todd said.

Mrs. Grazer said, "Let's keep this secret between us. It's fun watching your friends being scared."

The next day after school Todd and his friends were playing kickball in his backyard until Jack pointed at Mrs. Grazer's window and yelled, "Look, it's Mrs. Grazer spying on us again!" Todd looked up and saw her looking at him from behind the curtains. Everyone dropped what they were doing and ran into the house. As Todd was about to walk in, he stopped and took another look. He caught Mrs. Grazer's eyes and she gave him a wink before disappearing into the dark. ✱

THE MAGIC BAG FROM ABOVE

by Michael Chung

ILLUSTRATED BY JOSHUA GORCHOV

Long, long ago there was a young couple that lived all alone in a deep, mountainous forest. Their only shelter was a two-room wooden hut they had made themselves, but that barely kept them warm. They were so poor that they had to cut two bundles of firewood and carry them on their backs to market every day.

One day, the young couple came back from the mountain carrying the firewood. They put one bundle in the courtyard and planned to sell it at the market the next day to buy rice. The other bundle they kept in the kitchen for their own use. When they woke up the following morning, the bundle in the courtyard had mysteriously disappeared. There was nothing to do but sell the bundle they had kept for themselves to cook food and keep them warm.

That same day, they cut another two bundles of firewood as usual. They put one bundle in the courtyard for market and kept the other bundle for their own use. But the following morning, the bundle in the courtyard had vanished again. The same thing happened on the third and fourth days as well, and the husband began to think there was something strange going on.

On the fifth day, he made a hole in the bundle of firewood in the courtyard and hid himself inside it. From the outside, it looked just the same as before. At midnight an enormous rope came down from the sky, attached itself to the bundle, and lifted it up into the sky with the woodcutter still inside.

The woodcutter became very nervous and confused. He didn't know where he was going or who was pulling the pile of wood up from Earth. When the pile of wood finally stopped moving, the woodcutter climbed out and looked around. The place he was in was full of gold and silver decorations.

The woodcutter became very frightened because he had never seen anything like this place before, but he said to himself, "I have never done anything bad, so nothing bad should ever happen to me!" Seconds later he saw a kindly looking, white-haired old man walking in his direction. The woodcutter thought that the old man must be wise and he hoped to find out where he was from him.

When the old man saw the woodcutter, he asked, "Other people only cut one bundle of firewood a day. Why do you cut two?"

The woodcutter made a bow and replied, "We are penniless. That's why my wife and I cut two bundles of firewood a day. One

bundle is for our own use and the other we carry to market. With it we can buy rice to eat."

The old man said to the woodcutter in a warmhearted voice, "I've known for a long time that you have been a good man leading a hardworking life. I shall reward you with a piece of treasure. Take it back with you and it will provide you with your livelihood."

As soon as the old man finished speaking, seven fairies came out of nowhere and led the woodcutter into a beautiful palace. Inside the palace there were many kinds of rare objects that he had never seen before on display. Moneybags of all shapes and sizes hung in one room.

The fairies asked him, "Which one do you like best? Choose whichever you like, and take it home with you."

The woodcutter was filled with joy. "I'd like that moneybag, the one full of precious things. Give me that round one." He chose the biggest one and took it down.

Just at that moment, the white-haired old man came in with a mean expression on his face. The old man said to the young woodcutter, "You cannot take that one. I'll give you an empty one. Every day you can take only one nugget of silver out of it. Never get greedy and attempt to take more!"

The woodcutter reluctantly agreed. He took the empty moneybag, and, clinging onto the enormous rope, he was lowered back to Earth.

Once home, he gave the moneybag to his wife and told her the whole story. She was very excited. In the daytime, they went as usual to cut firewood. But from then on, whenever they returned home after dark, they would close the door and open the moneybag. Instantly, a nugget of silver would roll out. When they weighed it on the palm of their hand, they found it to be exactly one pound. Every

day one nugget of silver and no more came rolling out of the bag. The wife saved them up one by one.

Time went by slowly, and the couple saved up a significant amount of silver. One day the husband suggested, "Let's buy an ox."

The wife had always wanted to save up money for a needy situation and maybe for a first child with her husband, so she didn't agree.

A few days later, the husband suggested again, "How about buying a few acres of land?"

His wife didn't agree with that either.

A few more days went by, and the wife suggested, "Let's build a little cottage."

The husband was itching to spend all the money they had saved and said, "Since we have so much money on hand, why don't we build a big brick house?"

The wife was concerned about whether it would be wise to spend all their hard-earned savings on a house, but she could not persuade her husband and had no choice but to go along with his idea.

The husband spent the money on bricks, tiles, and timber and on hiring carpenters and masons. From that time on, neither of them went into the mountain to cut firewood.

The day came when their pile of silver was almost gone, and the new house was still unfinished. It had long been in the back of the husband's mind to ask the moneybag to produce more silver. So, without his wife knowing, he opened the bag for a second time that day. Instantly, another nugget of snow-white silver rolled out of the bag onto the ground. He opened it a third time and received a third nugget.

He thought to himself, If I go on like this, I can get the house finished in no time! He quickly forgot the old man's warning. But when he opened the bag for the fourth time, it was empty. This time not one piece of silver came out of it. It was just an old cloth bag. When he turned to look at his unfinished brick house, it was gone as well. There before him was his old hut.

The woodcutter felt very sad and began to wonder why this had happened. He realized that he had become greedy and had forgotten the old man's words.

His wife came over and consoled him saying, "We can't depend on the magic moneybag from heaven. But even though the bag and the treasure are gone, we still have each other. Let's go back to the mountain to cut firewood as we did before. That's a more reliable way of earning a living anyway. We don't need a house and fancy things. We didn't need them before, did we?"

"You are right, wife, I have become greedy," the husband responded.

From that day on, the young couple went up to the mountain to cut firewood, and together they lived on with their worry-free, hardworking life.   ✳

WHAT MAKES YOU SPECIAL?

by Jaye Evans

ILLUSTRATED BY MATT FURIE

In Twinkle Town lived a zebra named Larry. Now, Larry wasn't like the other zebras. He was born without stripes. He liked being all white because he could hide from his parents. For example, when they went skiing he could blend in with the snow until he was tired of playing and wanted to go home.

At school, he would hide on the playground when everyone was supposed to be in class. The other animals hated that. They all wanted to play in the yard too, and when they told their teacher Larry was outside, she would say, "There's nothing there but a white fence."

One day a new family came to Twinkle Town. They were a loving and giving zebra family named the Bakers. They had a daughter named Sally who was caring and respectful, just as her parents taught her to be.

Sally was excited about going to a new school. When her parents dropped her off at the schoolyard, the first thing she noticed was a white zebra by the fence looking at her. When the teacher asked the students to go to class, Larry played longer by hiding near the fence. As class was starting, Sally told the teacher that someone was outside.

The teacher said, "No, there isn't. I don't see anyone."

Sally said, "There, by the fence."

Just then Larry opened his mouth and said, "You're a tattletale." The teacher saw his pink tongue and asked him to come in to class.

"Class, we have a new student today. Her name is Sally and I want you all to say 'hi,'" the teacher said.

"Hi, Sally," said everyone except Larry.

"Sally, I would like you to sit next to Larry."

Sally went to sit down and said, "Hi, I'm Sally."

"So? I don't care what your name is," Larry said.

"That was mean. I just wanted to be your friend," she said.

"I don't care. You told on me when I wanted to play outside. I have magic powers," Larry said with anger.

"No, you don't—you hide in front of white things. Even though you don't have stripes, you're a zebra just like me," Sally stated.

"I don't want to be like you. I want to be special. I am special!" Larry said.

Sally had had lots of zebra friends at her old school. She couldn't understand why Larry was so mean.

Later on that day, Sally was playing on the swings when she met Cindy. Cindy was a light brown polar bear. She saw Sally playing by herself.

"I've never seen you around. Are you new?" Cindy asked.

"Yes," Sally said, still a little sad from Larry's comments.

"Why are you playing by yourself?" Cindy asked.

"I tried to be friends with this boy named Larry, but he was mean to me," Sally said.

"Oh, Larry. Well, he is mean to everyone. He thinks he is better than us because he is all white," said Cindy.

Sally sighed. "I would like to be his friend if he would let me."

"I'll be your friend if you want," said Cindy.

"Sure, I would like that," said Sally.

"Cool, you want to go swimming with me?" Cindy asked.

"Yeah!" said Sally.

After school, Sally and Cindy went off to the swimming pool. At the pool, Sally met all kinds of new animals. She met Louis the moose, Carl the fish, and Tony the bat. Everyone was kind and friendly to Sally.

Larry had been having a great day too, other than Sally showing up and ruining everything. On his way home he found two dollars and bought himself a lettuce-wrapped ice cream. While Larry was walking home eating his ice cream, he ran into Peter the ugly duck.

Peter was homeless and was always hungry. Peter had dirty feathers that would stick out in all directions, his left foot was bigger than his right foot, one of his eyes hung out of its socket, and he had big, yellow, bucked teeth.

Every day Peter would ask Larry if he had any money or food. And every day Larry would play tricks on Peter and never give him anything.

"Can you please spare some change? I am so hungry," Peter quacked.

"I don't have any money, Peter. I spent it all on my ice cream," Larry said.

"Then can I have some of your food, please? I haven't eaten for days," Peter asked.

Larry said to Peter, "Look over there!" When Peter turned around, Larry went to stand next to a white wall. Larry thought Peter couldn't see him.

"Where is my treat?" Peter asked. Larry didn't answer. Peter said, "I can see you near the wall. You have a dirt mark on you. Because you weren't honest with me, I will use my magical power to punish you. You will never hide from anyone again."

At once the duck started to change. His beak turned into a nose, his webbed feet turned into legs. His wings turned into arms. His body was now stretched out and turned into human form. Finally, his head changed into a human face, and on top of the head was a witch's hat.

This scared Larry, and he decided to run. But when he was running, the witch took out her magic wand and turned Larry into his worst wish…

"Ahhh!" Larry screamed. "I have stripes!"

"You weren't honest with me and this is the consequence," the witch said.

"I'm sorry!" Larry cried.

"It's too late. You will have stripes until you learn a lesson."

Once the witch said that, she disappeared. Larry was so sad. Now he was just like everyone else. When he got home his parents didn't recognize him. They thought he was a burglar and were about to call the police when Larry showed them a scar he had from skiing.

The next day when he went to school, everyone was shocked. The animals wanted to know how Larry had gotten stripes. Some were happy because they didn't like it that he hid outside and played longer. Sally was happy too because now Larry was just like everyone else, and, if he wanted to be special, it had to come from inside him.

That day the teacher assigned group projects and Sally and Larry were partners.

"We have to put the words in alphabetical order," Sally said shyly.

"Yeah, whatever," Larry said.

"I don't need your attitude, Larry," Sally said.

"I'm sorry. I'm having a bad day," Larry said.

"Is it because you have stripes?" Sally asked.

"Yes," Larry said in a low voice. "A witch gave them to me. She said I needed to learn a lesson."

"About what?"

"I'm not sure."

"How will you know when you've learned the lesson?"

"I don't know."

There was an awkward silence. Then Sally went on to say, "Well, if you want I can help you find out what the lesson is."

With a slight hesitation, Larry said, "I would like that."

The bell rang and all the animals ran out to the schoolyard for recess except for Larry.

"Hey, Larry, aren't you going to recess?" Sally asked.

"No. I can't hide by the fence anymore," Larry said sadly.

"You could play with me and my friends," Sally said.

"What if they don't like me?" Larry said.

"As long as you are nice to them, like you are to me, they will like you," Sally said.

"OK," Larry said shyly.

So Sally and Larry went off to find her friends.

"I want you to meet my new friend Larry," Sally said.

"Uh… hi," Larry said softly.

"I know you. You're the zebra with no stripes. But now you have them," said Cindy.

"What are you doing over here with us? I thought you liked to play by the fence by yourself and play longer than you're supposed to," said Louis the moose.

"Hey, that's mean. I brought Larry over here to play with us," Sally said.

"Does he want to play with us?" said Tony the bat.

"All right!" said Larry.

"Cool, then let's play," said Carl the fish.

Larry and the gang played for all of recess. Finally the bell rang, and the animals came inside.

"Did you have fun, Larry?" Sally asked.

"Yeah, I did," Larry said.

"I told you. As long as you're nice they're going to like you. They saw that you were nice inside."

"I guess so," Larry said with a smile. "Sally, I want to apologize for how I acted yesterday. I shouldn't have gotten mad at you. You were only trying to be my friend."

"It's OK, Larry. We're friends now and everything is cool," said Sally, smiling too.

A thought came to Larry: Maybe the lesson I need to learn is that what makes you special is what's inside you.

Suddenly the witch appeared. "You got it, Larry," she said, "You realized that how you look doesn't make you special, but you make yourself special. Now I'll take off your stripes again."

With that said, the witch turned Larry white but left one stripe on his tail to remind him that what he looks like isn't what makes him special. He makes himself special. And with a flash of lightning the witch was gone.

"Well, I guess you're back to normal, Larry," said Sally.

"I feel better than normal! Now let's all go back inside to work on our project before we get ourselves in deep trouble," Larry said.

From then on Larry tried to be the best zebra he could be. Instead of hiding by the fence, Larry started to play with the others and be a good friend. And he never played in the yard longer than he was supposed to.   ✻

WHY IS THAT?

by Alex Lim

ILLUSTRATED BY JOEL SMITH

There once was a five-year-old boy named Francis who liked to play outside and to watch cartoons. He was just like any other kid—except for his curiosity… and his stubbornness. He was always asking why things were the way they were and why people did the things they did. People would tell him that he asked too many questions.

One day his mom asked him if he wanted to go to the zoo. Francis said, "No, I don't wanna. Animals are weird. Why don't they just act normal like us?"

"They *are* normal, just different," she said. Francis sighed and crossed his arms in frustration.

Francis's mother hauled him to his car seat and took him to the zoo. He pouted the whole way there. They soon arrived at the zoo and, stubbornly, Francis walked backward until his mother made him turn around. The place was gigantic, stretching farther than the eye could see. Monkeys were swinging, elephants were screaming, and birds were soaring through the never-ending sky.

Struck with awe, Francis now wanted to see every animal, from birds to bears to chameleons and cockroaches. So he and his mother rushed to the hummingbird exhibit. The shiny green hummingbird was zipping and zooming everywhere so fast Francis could barely follow him with his eyes. Francis asked the hummingbird, "Hummingbird, why are you so fast? Slow down like the rest of us, gosh!"

"Faster than your favorite cartoon," the hyper hummingbird said, "because this is how you are when you have too many jellybeans." Francis stared in amazement.

Francis and his mother then rushed to the next animal, the sloth. When Francis got there, the slow, sleepy sloth hung upside down on the big brown branch in boredom. The sloth waved and Francis asked him, "Mr. Sloth, why are you so slow?"

The sloth yawned and answered back, "Because that is what time seems like when you're waiting for recess." Francis suddenly was sleepy and his mom carried him to see the next animal.

Francis rubbed his eyes and awoke staring at the chameleons. He looked and looked into the exhibit and saw a changing blur. He asked the chameleon, "How do you change colors and stand so still?"

The cool, camouflaged chameleon said, "Shhh! You must stay quiet when you are playing hide-and-seek." The chameleon was soon spotted by another chameleon. Feeling like it was his fault, Francis ran away before the chameleon could say anything.

Francis went next door to the hyenas where all Francis could hear was nonstop laughter. "What's so funny?" Francis asked. They just laughed at him. Francis insisted, "No, but really. What is so funny?" They laughed even harder.

One hilarious, happy hyena said, "You said *butt*! Ha-ha-ha-ha-ha!" Francis gave a nervous laugh and held his mom's hand tighter as they left.

After a few minutes they ended up by the gorillas. In all their might, the gorillas stood strong and pounded their chests. Slowly but surely, Francis approached one of the gorillas and asked, "Mr. Gorilla, why did you hit your chest? You're only supposed to do that when you are mad."

The gigantic, grunting gorilla answered, "Hit? I didn't hit my chest. I had to get my cootie shot. Haven't had one in months."

"Ohhh," said Francis.

"Want one?" asked the gorilla.

"Uhh. No thanks. Had mine," Francis said with a smile.

Then his mother took his hand and brought him to the food court. There they had ham and cheese sandwiches. Then a few squirrels came up to Francis and picked up a piece of bread that he had dropped. The squirrel quickly ate it and Francis asked, "What's the rush? Slow down, buddy."

The silly, sneaky squirrel quickly said, "Gotta finish my lunch fast so I can play longer, *duh*." The squirrel darted off into the tree along with the other squirrels. Francis's mother wiped the bread-crumbs off of him and brought him toward the koala bears. They were playing kickball with the kangaroos.

Francis spotted one of the koala bears way high up in the trees and climbed the tree. "Wow, this is pretty high up. Shouldn't you be in the outfield?" he asked.

"I gotta be up here to catch that kickball. That kangaroo's a good kicker," said the climbing koala bear. *Dink,* went the sound of the kangaroo kicking the ball, which climbed higher and higher and ended up right in the koala's grasp. The koala jumped down the tree and went toward home plate to get ready to take his turn kicking for his team.

Looking down toward the ground, Francis saw how high up he was. He wondered and wondered how he would get down, then spotted one of the squirrels. This squirrel looked around and pressed a button on the tree. All of a sudden, a huge door opened. It was an elevator. Francis waited a bit, pressed the button, went in the elevator, and took it down to the ground. Then he snuck back to his mother, who hadn't noticed he was missing. They walked on again, this time to the lemurs.

The lemurs were crowded around one leaping lemur who was jumping in squares painted on the ground while counting, "One, two, three… awww." He fell and had to go back to square one. Francis went into the crowd of lemurs to be a part of the commotion. Then he gave it a try and hopped through all the hopscotch boxes. The lemurs cheered for him. Then his mother tugged him out of the celebration.

"Having fun?" asked Francis's mother.

He nodded his head up and said, "I'm not weird, Mom, and neither are these animals. They're actually kinda cool." He then pointed toward the hippo and pulled on his mother's arm to go over to him.

Splashes of water went everywhere as the hippo opened and closed its jaws. "Whoa! What are you doin'?" asked Francis.

"I'm just one hungry, hungry hippo," said the hippo.

"Well, have this. I'm not that hungry." Francis threw a sandwich toward the hippo, who ate it in one bite.

"Ahhh, delicious! Thanks. Do you have more sandwiches or anything else?" said the hippo.

"Sorry, last one," Francis answered.

"Well, thanks anyway," said the hippo and went below the water. Francis walked away and turned around to see the hippo doing the same thing to another kid. He just shrugged his shoulders and walked on to the next animal.

Francis's walk brought him to the crab tank. He noticed the crabs carefully crawling sideways while pushing a red ball back and forth between each other.

This puzzled Francis, so he asked, "What in the world are you doing walking from side to side like that?"

One of the crabs replied, "What are you talking about? This is *the* best way to play four square."

Francis squinted and the crab said, "What's so weird about that, huh?" Francis was tongue-tied. "Besides, why do *you* walk facing forward?" said the crab. Francis thought, How true! and he noticed his attitude was different.

Just then, Francis heard a loud whine, and a few feet from the sound was a little animal with a very long nose. It was an anteater, digging its nose further into the hole in a chocolate milk box. Puzzled by this, Francis walked up to it and asked, "Ummm, what exactly are you doing?"

The antsy anteater broke his concentration. "No more milk! Rats! They never put enough chocolate milk in these things anymore," said the anteater.

"Yeah I know what you mean. Wait… it might be your lucky day!" Francis replied. He dug in his bag and found a half-empty bottle of chocolate milk. "Here, have this."

"Oh boy, thanks!" said the anteater and walked under a tree to enjoy his little gift.

Francis and his mother walked on down to the penguin section. There, thirty tiny, puffy, playful penguins waddled with their fins at their sides. "Why are you so stiff, penguin?" asked Francis.

"I am doing exercises, human. Now go away, the PE teacher's coming." The little penguins ran in a line around the whole exhibit and slid on their stomachs as soon as the teacher said to. Then the penguin told the teacher Francis was distracting them and pointed to him. Francis tugged his mother to leave quickly.

The blue sky slowly faded to a bright pink. Francis looked up at his mother, who told him, "Well, it's time to go." "Awww," Francis said, but he then realized he was tired and said, "OK." They walked through the zoo to the exit and saw all the animals putting on their backpacks, getting ready to go home.

Francis was shocked by this because he saw that the animals were the same as him… just a bit different. They had feelings too. And they had parents to go home to, homework to do, and friends to play with. In the middle of this, Francis's mother asked him, "So how'd ya like it?"

"I loved it!" replied Francis. "I saw hyper hummingbirds; slow, sleepy sloths; cool, camouflaged chameleons; crawling crabs; hilarious, happy hyenas; gigantic, grunting gorillas; silly, sneaky squirrels; climbing kickball koalas; leaping lemurs; hungry, hungry hippos; antsy anteaters; and puffy, playful penguins. But those crabs, they were right. There is no such thing as weird—just different. I'm just different." ✳

SHADOW FIGHTING

by Monica Chan

ILLUSTRATED BY MATT FURIE

S am was sitting at his desk in his room, working on homework on a Saturday morning, when he got bored and looked at his desk light. He shined it at his younger brother, Jeff, whose long hair lit up. Sam put his finger over the light and made his finger's shadow touch Jeff's face.

"Look! I'm poking you with my finger!" Sam said.

"Ouch! Wait, it doesn't hurt. It doesn't even tickle," Jeff said.

"Of course it doesn't hurt. It's a shadow!" Sam laughed.

Then Sam chased Jeff with his hand's shadow. Jeff dashed around the room but couldn't escape. Sam poked Jeff with his finger's shadow again.

"I saw you poke me," Jeff said, "but how come I don't feel it?"

"It's not really my finger," Sam stated. "I'm controlling it, but it isn't part of me."

"That's weird!" Jeff gasped. "Wouldn't it be cool if it could control itself?"

"No, that's not weird. *You're* weird." Sam looked at Jeff like he was crazy.

Sam went back to doing his homework while Jeff looked for something to play with. He found his yo-yo and practiced new tricks with it. He was trying to concentrate on doing a new yo-yo trick, but from the corner of his eye, he saw Sam's shadow poke his butt. "Stop it, Sam! Leave me alone and do your homework!" Jeff said, annoyed.

The shadow continued poking Jeff. "Quit it!" he said. "You're getting on my nerves!" Jeff turned toward Sam. But Sam had fallen asleep. He couldn't have been using his shadow to poke Jeff. Jeff looked at the shadow and then back at Sam. The shadow was wavy and tall. It floated in the corner of the room by itself. Jeff realized that Sam's shadow had awoken when Sam fell asleep. Jeff was frightened. He watched as the dark, hovering shadow messed up Sam's hair while Sam slept.

Jeff got angry at the shadow for bothering Sam.

"Stop messing up Sam's hair, stupid shadow!" Jeff demanded.

The shadow ignored Jeff.

"Stop!" he yelled. "What is your problem? Could you stop giving him that crazy bed-head hair! No wonder his hair is always so messed up. Go away!"

All of the sudden, the shadow stopped messing up Sam's hair.

Instead, the shadow poked Jeff's head and Jeff felt it. He realized that the shadow could actually touch things. It was alive now.

Jeff got scared. He tried with all of his might to fight the shadow. He kicked it and punched it and jumped on it. This was no use. Jeff's hands just turned gray with each punch as they passed through the shadow.

The shadow watched as Jeff kicked and screamed at thin air. Then it slid up close to Jeff. Jeff fought hopelessly as the shadow ruffled his hair. He jumped up and down and kicked all around. The shadow tried again and again to braid Jeff's hair, but Jeff kept fighting. The slick shadow succeeded in giving Jeff ponytails, but because the boy moved around so much, the shadow began to get frustrated.

So it hugged Jeff. Jeff's body got dark as the shadow sucked him into the shadow world. Jeff didn't know what was happening. He knew he wanted to get out, but he couldn't escape. The shadow stuck to him and pulled him into the shadow room.

Jeff's loud screaming woke Sam up. The shadow should have stuck back onto Sam like it did every morning when Sam woke up, but it was so distracted by Jeff that it didn't notice Sam getting up.

The shadow room was dark, with nothing inside. Jeff felt extremely confused and frightened. Everything was colorless and flat. He wanted to get out, but he was just a useless, wiggly image. He slithered around and around, but he couldn't escape.

"Hold on," the shadow whispered. "I just want to talk to you."

"No!" Jeff said. "Get away from me!"

Meanwhile, Sam looked around the room. "What's going on, Jeff? Jeff?" He rubbed his eyes to make sure he wasn't dreaming.

"Take me back to my brother! Let me get out of here!" Jeff yelled at the shadow.

The shadow sighed. It knew he had no choice but to return Jeff to the human world. It created a slide, which led to an opening. Jeff slid down in his shadow form and landed back in Sam's room, back to his old self.

The shadow stood still in the middle of the room.

"What did it do to you, Jeff?" Sam asked.

"It put me in its shadow room! That place was so weird. Oh, and it messed up your hair when you were sleeping! That's why you always have that crazy bed-head hair!" Jeff cried. "He made me have crazy hair too. Help me beat up this stupid shadow, Sam. We have to get rid of it somehow!" Jeff glared at the shadow.

Sam was still confused, but he wanted to stop Jeff from fighting. He knew that was the right thing to do, so he decided to figure out what was wrong. He wanted to make peace with the shadow.

"Wait, stop fighting!" Jeff and the shadow stopped fighting and looked at Sam. "So, shadow," Sam eyed the shadow suspiciously. "You're the one who always gives me my crazy bed-head, huh?"

The shadow nodded.

"That's so cool! Can you give me a mohawk?"

The shadow nodded and slid through Sam to style his hair into a mohawk.

Sam looked in the mirror and laughed at his new hair.

"Hey, Jeff, wouldn't it be awesome if I woke up every day with a mohawk?" Sam laughed.

Jeff was angry. "Why are you so nice to it? You're supposed to be on my side!"

"Calm down, Jeff. You know you want this stylin' hairdo! Ha ha!" Sam said.

"He fought with me!"

Sam scratched his head. "Can you give Jeff a mohawk, please?"

"No, I want Dragon Ball Z hair!" Jeff complained.

The shadow stood and shook its head. It wanted to give Jeff two big, chunky braids.

"I have an idea." Sam smiled. "Why don't we have a competition to settle this? Jeff, think of the five hardest hand shadows you can make. My shadow has to copy them. If it can't imitate one, then you win. If it can imitate them all, then you lose and you have to get braids."

Jeff made a simple rabbit. The shadow easily imitated it. Jeff made an eagle, an elephant, and a spider. The shadow easily imitated them all.

"C'mon Jeff," Sam said. "Those are easy. Give him something hard to do!"

Jeff thought long and hard. Finally, he had an idea. He made a barking dog. He moved the dog's mouth with his finger and made it bark.

"Arf! Arf! I bet you can't make a barking dog, because you can't bark! Arf! Arf!" Jeff laughed.

The shadow gave up. Jeff was right, the shadow couldn't bark.

The shadow had no choice. It slid through Jeff to go behind him and gave Jeff Dragon Ball Z hair. Jeff looked in the mirror.

He tried to stay angry at the shadow, but he couldn't help but laugh at his hairstyle. His hair looked like it was going to fly off of his head.

"Nice!" Jeff said. "Shadow, you're not as bad as I thought."

The shadow nodded and made the peace sign.

"See, Jeff," Sam said. "If you just gave the shadow a chance, you guys would have been good friends by now."

"Yeah," Jeff said. "I guess I was wrong. I still don't know why it tried to force me to have braids. I was just afraid of it because it is

different, but I shouldn't have been so mean. I'm sorry. Shadow, let's be friends."

Jeff and the shadow high-fived, even though it didn't make the cool slapping noise. Then Jeff and Sam looked at the shadow and smiled.

"Let's go outside to play," Sam said.

Jeff looked at the shadow. The shadow nodded.

"Yay! Let's go! Hey, Shadow, is there any way you could turn us into shadows like you?" Jeff said. "That would be so cool!"

The shadow thought for a while. It pointed at Jeff and Sam and motioned for them to take a quick nap. Jeff and Sam went to sleep for five minutes. When they woke up, they looked at each other and saw that they were shadows. They both slid across the room, around the ceiling, walls, couches, and tables.

"This is so exciting! Hey, I can speak shadow language," Jeff said. "So what's your name?"

"Why, my name is Jessico," the shadow explained. "Listen, I'm sorry for trying to force you to have braids. I just wanted to try out different hairstyles. I want to be able to make Sam's hair extra awesome every time he wakes up. That's all I wanted to say to you."

"Oh," Jeff nodded. "You weren't trying to be mean to me. I should have been more understanding."

"We're all friends now, right?" Sam gleamed. "Let's do something fun!"

As shadows, they raced on the walls of houses and floated up street poles. They attached themselves to the shadows of cars to see who would go fastest. They climbed trees and played a popular game in the shadow world called Squint. When people stopped to rest in the shade of the trees, Jessico, Sam, and Jeff became the shadows of the leaves and acted as the people's shade. Whenever the people looked up, one of them would move his shade a little to try to make the sun go into the people's eyes. Whoever made the most people squint won. They had a lot of fun together.

"Hey, Sam, what time is it?" Jessico asked.

"It's almost five o'clock," Sam said. "We should be home."

"I need to get home quick!" Jessico exclaimed. "If I stay in the dark too long, I'll disappear! I'll get stuck inside this big shade. And I better turn you guys back into humans so you don't disappear with me. When I do that, I'll stick onto you, Sam, so run back home as fast as you can or else I'll disappear. 'Bye, Jeff! 'Bye, Sam!" Jessico winked.

"'Bye, Jessico! It was nice meeting you!" Jeff and Sam yelled.

Sam and Jeff suddenly found themselves in human form again. They ran home as fast as they could. It got darker and darker, and they ran faster and faster. Finally, they were all the way home.

They ran into Sam's room and rushed to the desk to turn the light on.

They looked for Jessico. They looked all around the room, along the walls, the ceilings, the floor, couches, tables, everywhere! But they couldn't find him.

"Jessico is gone," Sam gasped. "Gone! We were too late. Man, I'm going to miss him."

"Yeah," Jeff looked down. "I'm going to miss going into the shadow world and playing Squint with him. It seems like just this morning Jessico and I were fighting and making up."

Sam and Jeff were sad. Sam and Jeff knew they would never see Jessico again. But they would always remember him and the lesson that he taught them. ✳

A DUCK NAMED TEDDY

by Connie Cheung

ILLUSTRATED BY MARTHA RICH

Teddy was a young duck who loved to paddle in the lakes of Duckland, where he lived with his family. His mommy named him Teddy because he looked a little like a bear. He had chubby cheeks and a large bill, and he quacked and squealed when he didn't get what he wanted.

Teddy loved to eat strawberries but his mommy told him not to eat the strawberries from the bushes because they were dirty. She said, "You don't know who has touched them so you shouldn't put them in your mouth or you'll certainly get sick." But when Teddy saw a beautiful bush of juicy strawberries, he ignored his mommy's warning.

One day, he was stuffing strawberries into his mouth so fast that he didn't notice that a red worm, nearly as fat as a pig, was crawling out of one. Almost immediately after he ate the worm-infested strawberry, his tummy began to hurt. His tummy swelled up like a balloon and he quacked loudly for his mommy. She was shocked when she saw Teddy's stomach and immediately rushed him to the doctor.

Doctor Duck wore glasses and combed his white hair back. He was always willing to help ducks with health problems and tend to ducks who didn't listen to their mommies. Doctor Duck had to operate on Teddy to get the worm out so it wouldn't grow. "Don't eat bad strawberries again!" said Doctor Duck.

Two weeks after the surgery, Teddy went for a swim around the lake. When it was noontime, his mouth became as dry as a prune. He saw juicy strawberries out of the corner of his eyes. As his mouth watered, he couldn't resist the temptation. He rushed over to the bush on the side of the lake and ate the strawberries. His mommy and daddy saw him and tried to stop him but Teddy shoved them aside and continued to devour strawberries. When his daddy was finally able to stop him, Teddy was gasping for breath.

His mommy and daddy knew that Teddy couldn't control himself, so they sent him to Ducks With Problems camp, or DWP. A bus came to pick up Teddy the next day. The ride was long and Teddy got bored. He glanced at the girl sitting next to him and then looked away. He glanced at her again and she burst out, "What is your problem?"

Teddy answered, "Nothing… I just wanted to see if you were bored, because I'm very bored." She laughed at Teddy and turned away. Teddy asked her why she was going to camp with question after question, but she ignored him. He finally gave up and simply kept quiet.

The girl, Asia, took out a strawberry lollipop from her backpack and placed it in her mouth. Teddy saw the lollipop and said, "You like strawberries? Me too! But they got me in trouble because I couldn't stop eating them." Asia looked at Teddy. He reminded her of her little brother back home. He loved to talk and would ask Asia a lot of questions. Asia began to talk to Teddy. She tried to comfort him by saying that the camp would help him with his problem. Teddy soon felt assured and knew Asia was there to support him.

Asia told Teddy her story. "I know my parents love me because they told me every day, but they both left me and can't come back." Asia's grandma was worried. Since Asia became involved in numerous fights, her grandma sent her to DWP. Asia knew that fighting was not the answer, but it was difficult to control her anger. By the time they arrived at the camp, Teddy and Asia made a pact to stay together.

When all the campers arrived at DWP, they were assigned to cabins. Teddy was overburdened by his luggage, which blocked his view. As he tried to move it, he bumped into something hard and all his stuff fell to the ground. Teddy, who was exhausted, yelled out, "Get out of my way!" When he looked up, he saw a huge, muscular duck growling at him. Teddy picked up his stuff and shrank away, trying to avoid eye contact.

As he unpacked, the door to his room flew open. There stood the muscular duck. Teddy knew right away that his worst nightmare had come true. The duck walked slowly over to Teddy as Teddy shivered. He told Teddy, "You're going to pay for what you did, little duck." Unfortunately, that duck was Teddy's roommate and would

trip Teddy during lunch and play loud music at night when Teddy tried to sleep.

When Asia met up with Teddy, Teddy burst into tears. But Asia said, "I'm not going to let that duck pick on you. Don't worry, Teddy." At that moment, Teddy felt better and he was not scared anymore.

Asia marched over to the bully and began to yell at him crazily. The bully began to cry. Asia and Teddy were surprised but they soon realized that he was afraid of girls. He never picked on Teddy again.

Later that week, Teddy asked Asia if she could meet him for lunch and Asia agreed. Teddy went off to the lake and began to swim when he saw a hole in the fence of the camp. He wanted badly to know what was on the other side, so he poked his head out of the hole to see. He told himself, "I'm sure I can get back before lunch and no one will know I've been gone," so he squirmed through the hole into the other side of the lake. He saw that it was beautiful and sparkly. The lake was so clear and fresh, he swam happily in the paradise he had discovered.

At lunchtime, Asia went to the cafeteria and waited for Teddy but he never came. Soon she became worried that he had gotten into trouble. She went to his special spot and found it empty, but then she noticed the hole in the fence and knew that curious Teddy would have gone through it.

Meanwhile, Teddy had spotted a bush with red dots and swam toward it. As he got closer to the bush, his eyes glowed and he licked his lips. It was strawberries! He let out a gigantic smile. He felt like he hadn't eaten strawberries in a billion years. He reached for a strawberry and plucked it off the bush.

Just then, Asia spotted Teddy's pale yellow feathers. She swam over to him but he did not notice because he was focused on a strawberry. His chubby cheeks were longing to gobble it up. And when

Teddy was about to eat it, Asia shouted, "Teddy! Don't eat that strawberry!" She swam over to him. "You can do this, Teddy, control yourself. I know you can do it."

Teddy thought for a moment and then he put down the strawberry and turned his back on the bush.

Asia smiled at Teddy and gave him a big high-five. They swam back to the camp and snuck back in without anyone noticing.

During swimming class, Teddy noticed how fast Asia was able to swim and asked her how she did it. She told him, "It's because of these big feet of mine. They make me swim faster but they make me look very ugly too."

Teddy said to her, "It's not ugly at all! And it's so cool how you can swim faster than any other duck! There's a duck race next week. You'll win for sure."

Asia told him that he could swim as fast as he wanted if he practiced. So they spent all their free time practicing for the duck race.

The day of the race, the ducks lined up at the starting line. The duck counselor called, "On your mark, get set, *go!*" All the ducks rushed forward and hustled to win. As Asia gained speed, Teddy struggled to keep up with her. Asia and Teddy were on their last lap when the big bully duck gained on them. In the last stretch of the race, Asia and Teddy leapt toward the finish line. They beat the bully duck by two seconds, with Teddy taking second place.

Asia was glad that Teddy convinced her to join the race. She received a trophy inscribed with the words FIRST PLACE, which made her smile.

During the following weeks, Teddy did really well in his classes. Soon he received permission to go home. Teddy was happy to go home, but he knew he would miss Asia. They met before the bus left. Asia smiled and said to Teddy, "Let's do our secret handshake one more time."

Teddy reached out his wing and said, "We'll always be friends, no matter what." Asia smiled and tried not to show Teddy how sad she felt. When the bus began to move, Teddy waved good-bye to his best friend as Asia waved back until they couldn't see each other any longer. ✳

THE NOTE

by **Ksenia Rakitina**

ILLUSTRATED BY MATT FURIE

Upon entering Gorky Forest, animals passed through a dark canopy of trees with few patches of sunlight shining through dense woodland. Howls echoed throughout the entrance, which was full of broken branches and thorny bushes. It seemed scary until, after passing through it, there was a huge field with birds, butterflies, and animals playing in the sunlight. This is where animal school took place.

English class was in session. Cat, the wise teacher, was explaining to his animal pupils how to read and write. Everyone was listening except for one student, Wolf. Dirty-looking and shoeless, Wolf was big and gray, with yellow teeth, greasy fur, and green-yellow eyes that glowed like two small candles behind the branches of a dark forest. He wore his only shirt, a torn red T-shirt that smelled like garbage that had been sitting in the sun for a few days.

That day, Wolf was disturbing class and not paying any attention to the teacher. He had arrived late, put glue on the teacher's chair, talked during class when he was not supposed to, and argued. The teacher, Cat, told him that if he kept being so disrespectful he would have to stay after class. The thought of staying after school annoyed Wolf. He was frustrated with school, so he decided to drop out.

Then, one day, Wolf was taking a walk in a dark, scary part of the forest that was full of big trees with leaves that even the sun could not get through. Since the day when he dropped out of school, no one had seen Wolf, but that didn't matter, because he hadn't changed. He was still a dirty, unpleasant-looking animal. He still had big ears and sharp teeth, which he never cleaned. When he smiled it was disgusting to look at him! Then, he saw Owl reading in a tree. Wolf thought, Mmm… some good lunch for me…

Owl was the smartest bird in the forest. She was well educated and respectful to others. Everyone liked her. Her feathers were gray and white, and she also had big glasses—twice the size of her head. Owl lived in the hollow of a big tree. Her front door was small and was surrounded by ornaments.

"Be careful, don't ruin your eyes!" said Wolf, laughing.

"I'm reading the story about an Ouch Doctor," Owl said.

"What kind of animal is that?!" wondered Wolf.

"*What?!* You don't know what an Ouch Doctor is?" Owl yelled at him. "You are an ignorant animal, Wolf!"

Of course Wolf didn't know what *ignorant* meant either. He

thought it was some bad word, like *ugly* or *stupid*. *"How can you say words like that to me?! I could eat you right now, but I will give you another chance. Let's play a game! Write a word that is difficult to understand. I bet I can tell you what it means. If you win, I won't eat you, but if I win, I will eat you and your whole family!"* challenged Wolf.

Owl thought for a while and then wrote a few words on a piece of paper and gave it to Wolf. He didn't know any of the words because he hadn't studied at school. But he had an idea. He could make someone else read the paper for him, then he would come back and eat Owl! So Wolf ran off with the note to his neighbor, Rabbit.

Rabbit was small and white. He had long ears and he wore a pink cap. He followed in Wolf's footsteps by dropping out of school after finishing only four grade levels. He didn't have a job. He spent all his time eating carrots, which was the only thing he could grow in his backyard. Even though he was poorly educated, he still knew that everyone should be respectful and nice to each other.

"Hey, what's up, neighbor? Listen, I have a note here, but I can't read it. I forgot my glasses at home. Could you read it for me?" asked Wolf.

"Sure," said Rabbit and began reading, *"The worst animal in the forest is W-Wo-o—"* and than he stopped and looked at Wolf with fear in his eyes. *"I-I c-can't r-read further t-than t-that... I-I don't k-know that l-last w-word. I finished only four grade levels with only average grades."*

"Oh my goodness!" Wolf screamed. *"I'm surrounded by stupid animals!"*

Then he remembered that he had an old friend named Cow. He ran to her house. She should definitely know what those words mean; she is a house-kept animal, and she has lived for so many years with people, Wolf was thinking.

"Listen, Muu-muu!" said Wolf. *"Read this to me please. I forgot my glasses at home."*

Cow took the note and started reading it out loud. *"OK, it says: the worst animal in the forest is—"* Then she stopped and her eyes opened wide.

"So?!" yelled Wolf.

"I can't read the last word, it's weird, it's cursed!"

"Try!" cried Wolf, *"or I will* eat *you."* He started to show his sharp teeth.

"I can't, I swear, I can't!" cried Cow.

Wolf got so angry he couldn't control himself and he tipped Cow over! Cow started to cry. But he didn't pay any attention to that. He just took the message and ran straight to the school where his cousin Fox was teaching. Fox was a teacher in high school and helped young animals to develop their talents.

"Hey, how are you, Orange? Look, I have a note here, and I want to learn the definitions of the words," said Wolf. Fox had many dictionaries so she looked up every single word in the note.

"So," she started, *"I found everything, but I won't tell you the last word. You have to look it up yourself. Here we go, the note says, 'The worst animal in the forest is—'"*

"I knew that without you!" Wolf was so angry that he threw one of the dictionaries at her. He took the message and ran far into the forest.

Sometime later, maybe three or four years later, Wolf was still trying to find out the full meaning of the sentence that Owl had given him, when, while taking a walk in the forest, he suddenly heard a voice.

"Why do you think no one *knows what the last word means?"* someone said from the dark branches.

"I don't know… " answered Wolf. "Who's over there?" But the animal was already gone. Wolf started to think, Why, why does no one know what that word means? Maybe I should go and talk to Owl. She is the one who wrote it, but then I will have to apologize for my behavior, and will have to take back my words about eating her. Then he realized that you have to be nice and respectful to people. If not, you may spend your whole life trying to find out what some word means. He decided to go to Owl and apologize to her.

When he arrived at her house, he saw her playing with her children. One of the little ones saw him and started screaming. Everyone got scared and flew inside the home except for the mother, who was looking at Wolf wisely.

"So I guess you found out the meaning of the sentence, otherwise you wouldn't be here right now," said Owl.

"Actually I came here to apologize," started Wolf. "I'm really sorry for not being nice to you, and if you could help me with my studies I would really appreciate it."

"Well, I'm glad that you understand!" Owl said.

"So, what was the last word, can you please tell me?" he asked.

"I can't tell you the last word because the sentence doesn't make sense now that there are no longer any bad animals in our forest," said Owl, smiling. "And if you have really changed your opinion about being nice, I would strongly recommend you go and say sorry to everyone you ever hurt."

So Wolf went to every animal in the forest to say sorry and now he is friends with everyone. No one is scared of him anymore. ✳

MRZ. G. & ME

by Hector Trasvina

ILLUSTRATED BY JACOB MAGRAW-MICKELSON

My name is Abra. To my father I am a little princess. We live together on Planet Yeeeter. In the morning, the sky is a hot pink, and at night a dark black. I like night here because the stars shine pink and the moon makes them twinkle. They look like sprinkles on a cake, sweet and tasty. The sky is the only thing that's clean around here. Thank goodness.

Our gritty-grumpy trees are a light jungle green. I heard they were once a real forest green but the paint has faded off the leaves. The streets are orange, just like my skin, and they are bumpy with only a car-with-wheels lane, no hover- or flying-car lane. I once heard my teacher saying that's what streets were like way back in the year 2007.

My father has always told me to do my daily chores. I clean every little spot of the house, spick-and-span. I clean the closet and under my bed because my friend Clazer said that's where the human wind monkeys live. My father says, "There is no such thing as a human wind monkey." But I can hear them every time my daddy uses the Flicker-Flacker-Fling-Fangle floor garbage sucker to clean our floor.

My father always gives me five Koo-gives a day for helping to clean our house, so every weekend I go shopping for a toy or two. One weekend, my dad and I went out to find a mingle-mogul music player and buy a toy. My dad drove. Our car has four big wheels and a big motor. My dad calls it "Mr. Big." "Mr. Big is the name of a boss, and a boss runs through a lot of money every day, just like our car," says Daddy. Mr. Big is very, very loud. My dad says Mr. Big roars because it is a beast, but my teacher says beasts only live on Earth, not here on Planet Yeeeter.

My daddy and I drove to the electric-spizzle shop. Along the way, he told me to count the different people at every street corner. I counted one lea-graze, two dragon-dogs, seven lows-lop-leapers, and fourteen of my people, called Yarbons. The store we went to was called Evrrpi. It's the name of the owner. My dad was very sad when we bought our new music player, because it cost a lot of money, three thousand gillion Koo-gives. Then Daddy took me to the Toyz-r-yee to buy a toy. Bahillions and tragillions of toys everywhere—a young Yarbon's dream.

After a few half hourly-hours, my dad told me to hurry up. "Great goodness of Yeeeter!" he said. "Can you choose a toy already?"

I ran and picked the biggest robot I had ever seen. It was bubble pink with mixed sections of different blues. The name of the robot was Mrz. Gragle. She was six-feet-high in the air and I'm only five foot three. Mrz. Gragle could dance, sing, play pianolezy, and help clean around the house. We took her home, and I let Mrz. Gragle clean my closet and under my bed. She made everything twinkle-twinkle like a star in the sky on a dry, dark night. "Mrz. Gragle," I said, "you are wonderful. Maybe I'll buy Mr. Gragle for you since you are so nice." Her metal lips smiled. Every single day, Mrz. Gragle and I cleaned, played, and talked until bedtime. We were best friends! Dad said he fell in love with Mrz. Gragle's cleaning. She was worth every circle-cent, he said.

"Grizle-grazle," Mrz. Gragle said, "it sure is a nice day for a walk."

"Mrz. Gragle," I said, "you don't walk. You roll on wheels."

We both laughed.

"Should we, Little Angel?"

"Yes, let's go for a stroll in the park."

At the park, we saw a dragon-dog boy with a Mr. Gragle. We played in the hurricane tunnel that led to the slide. Mrz. Gragle and I went to the park every day to play with our new friends. My dad said it was nice that we had someone to play with. As days passed, we all became the best of friends. I named my best friends with funny nicknames. I called the dragon-dog Ziker. Ziker named me Abra-Kadabra. Mr. and Mrz. Gragle became Mr. and Mrs. G. I had never had a friend that was a dragon-dog boy, but I thought he and I would be best friends forever. Mr. and Mrs. G. were made for each other. Well, at least that's what it said on the shine-shaz-shingle case they came in.

Ziker's skin color was royal blue, like all dragon-dogs. They are a rare type of people because they breathe fire like a dragon and sniff like a dog. Ziker and I were at the park one day, along with Mr. and Mrs. G., when the sky turned a frigidly foggy green and the wind blew a blue cold breeze. Ziker said it was going to rain.

Ziker, Mr. G., and I ran for cover and hid in the twangle-fun tunnels next to the hyper swings and light laser slide. I hoped Mrs. G. had seen that it was going to rain. Mrs. G! Hmmm, I wondered, where can she be? It started to rain pink raindrops and the sky was a dark green. "Oh, no," Ziker said.

"Where is Mrs. G.? Run, Mrs. G.!" I said. She rolled toward us from the hiding spot she had found when we were playing hide-and-seek. As she rolled toward us through the rain, her wheels turned into feet, and her legs started to run toward the tunnel. "Hurry! Hurry!" Ziker and I yelled. Mrs. G. tripped but got up quickly and made it to the tunnel.

"Are you OK?" I asked.

"Yes, I'll be fine, Abra. Thank you for your concern," she said.

"You are the old model," said Ziker. "They didn't make you water- or weatherproof yet."

"Well, I'll be fine now," said Mrs. G. The rain cleared out and the sun shone bright. "Well, I think your father wants us home, princess," Mrs. G. said. We said our good-byes and went home.

The next morning I woke up and went to eat breakfast. Mrs. G. didn't come to the table. Where can she be? I wondered. I went to the hall closet where she rested and charged her battery. Mrs. G. didn't answer back. She just stood there frozen and had rusty brown spots all over.

"Dad!" I screamed. Daddy ran to me quickly.

"What's wrong, princess?"

"Mrs. G. is sick."

"Oh, no," Daddy said. "The weather got to her." Daddy said the rain had made her rusty.

Daddy took me to school and drove Mrz. G. to the repair shop. I couldn't do any of my work because I was worried about her. Ziker told a few kids what happened. Those kids told a few more kids, then those kids told some other kids. Soon the whole school knew what had happened to my Mrz. G. Even Mr. G. knew what had happened to Mrz. G. He just rolled in circles for hours not saying one word to Ziker or me.

After school, I ran up to Mr. Big to see if Mrz. G. was in the backseat.

"Hi, Daddy, where is Mrz. G.?" I asked.

"She's still at the shop," Daddy said.

"When will she come home, Daddy?"

Daddy told me I would have to wait until next month when his next paycheck came, because Mrz. G. had a lot of damage. Later that night, I cried because I missed Mrz. G. The clock-clank-number displayed 2:00 A.M. when I finally fell asleep.

I woke up sad, so I decided to wear my blurple coat. When I arrived at school, I noticed all the students at the front door. I walked up to them. "Hi, Abra," Ziker said to me.

"Hey," I said. "What's going on?"

"Take a look for yourself," he said.

Everyone walked away from the front door.

"Mrz. G.?"

"Hi, little angel."

"What's going on here?"

"Ziker said he had seen you looking very sad," Daddy said. "He called and I told him what was wrong. Then Ziker called everyone he knew and told them to ask their parents for money to help out."

"Wow! Thank you, everybody. And thank you, Ziker, for everything."

"That's what friends are for," Ziker said.

Mr. G. started talking again and started rolling around with joy instead of sorrow. "She's even weatherproof now," he said.

Now, not only did I have Ziker and Mr. and Mrz. G., I had a whole new group of friends. I smiled. I had people I could play with, and I had Mrz. G. too. I had never been so happy. ✳

THE BUTTERFLY PRINCESS

by Jenny Chung

ILLUSTRATED BY SARAH NEWTON

An incredible insect kingdom existed on the grassland somewhere in the world. Many kinds of insect creatures, including spiders, worms, caterpillars, and others lived peacefully in this kingdom. The Butterfly King and Ladybug Queen lived in the big castle in the middle of the town. The king and queen were nice and considerate, so everyone loved them. They provided every citizen a place to live and food to eat. Everyone helped each other and enjoyed living in the kingdom.

The king and queen had a daughter named Angelina. Angelina was an insect princess, part ladybug and part butterfly. She had gorgeous wings from her father's side. She had an elegant body and face from her mother's side. But beneath the good looks, Angelina was mean, greedy, and spoiled rotten. Everything she wanted had to be the finest in the whole kingdom. She ordered the citizens to help her find or make the things she wanted.

"I want a ring made out of moon rocks," Angelina ordered. But no insects could help her, because none of them could go to another planet.

"I want a dress made out of a bird's feathers," Angelina ordered.

The insect citizens couldn't help her, because no insect would dare to go near a bird.

If the citizens didn't satisfy Angelina, she made fun of them. Angelina was sure of her beauty, so she usually insulted the citizens on their looks. She had never said a single "thank you." The citizens of the kingdom helped Angelina for years without complaints, though, because they feared her parents' power.

As she grew up, Angelina looked in the mirror. It is true that I have the most elegant body, but I still think my wings could be prettier, Angelina thought. Then she called a town meeting. "I, the princess, want my wings to be prettier. Go find different ways to make my wings the prettiest, or you will be kicked out of the kingdom," Angelina ordered.

An artist grasshopper was the first to try. He was one of the most famous artists in the kingdom. He began painting Angelina's wings with more colors. But when it rained the paint came off. "You nasty grasshopper, you made my wings uglier. Go hop yourself back to your house! I never want to see you again!" screamed Angelina.

Next an old lady fly gave it a try. The old lady fly lived in a retirement home. She decorated Angelina's wings with many different things, as if Angelina were a Christmas tree. The decorations were heavy. "You old ugly fly. You have no sense of fashion! Send her away!" yelled Angelina.

A handsome ant named Issac also wanted to try. Issac was a messenger of the king's. He had a great smile that could make others smile. Issac sprayed Angelina's wings with rare glitter. Angelina still didn't like it since the glitter wasn't permanent. "You ants are hardworking, but you have no brains! You might as well keep working for the rest of your life!" Angelina yelled.

One day, a strange young lady came to the castle. She covered herself with black clothing from head to toe. No one knew where she had come from. She told the princess she could make her wings not just the prettiest in the kingdom, but the prettiest in the whole universe. After Angelina heard the young lady's words, she was excited. "Take off your gorgeous wings for just a little while, then I shall start," the young lady said. At first Angelina hesitated, but she decided to give the lady a try. The maids helped the princess take off her wings carefully and gave them to the lady. Then the lady took out a purple potion. She did not pour it on the wings. Instead, she drank it. The princess wondered how that would make her wings prettier. But before Angelina could say anything, the young lady turned into another insect!

The young lady was actually an evil moth who had been banished from the kingdom. Her name was Emily. Emily always got jealous of other pretty insects. She would lock herself in her room to make strange potions to harm the insects she hated. The king and the queen banned her from the kingdom so she wouldn't harm anyone else. As Emily looked at Angelina she laughed and said, "You greedy child, you shall suffer without your gorgeous wings!" Then

green smoke came out. Emily took Angelina's wings and vanished with her evil laughter.

The entire kingdom was in shock and Angelina was furious. The king and queen sent soldiers to capture Emily. But no one knew where she was. Some said Emily ran away with the wings to another kingdom. Some said Emily was not a moth anymore, that she had turned into a butterfly with Angelina's wings.

One day Angelina broke down and cried. "I want my wings back!" The princess was just a plain ladybug without her wings. She ordered her maids to break all the mirrors in the castle so she couldn't see herself. The whole kingdom was filled with the sadness of Angelina's crying.

Some citizens were relieved by what had happened, because Angelina was too sad to order them around. Only the handsome ant, Issac, felt sorry for what others thought of Angelina. He knew Angelina had her good side. When Issac was delivering a letter to the king one day, he accidentally overheard Angelina crying. Angelina was lonely every day because her parents were too busy. And as the days went by, the princess remained sad. The king and queen worried about their daughter very much. The citizens called a town meeting the week before the princess's birthday. They wanted to do something to help her feel better. "We should make her another pair of wings," Issac suggested.

"We could use the petals of flowers," the bumblebees said.

"And we can help with the sewing," the spider and caterpillar said. All the insects agreed and decided to help.

The citizens gathered under a great oak tree and started to make the wings. Some insects flew to the flower fields and picked flower petals. Many of the petals were from different beautiful flowers: roses, lilies, sunflowers, and others. Then the caterpillars spit glit-

tery silk out so the spiders could sew the petals together. Other insects helped prepare food and drink for the workers. Piece by piece, the insects finished making the perfect wings for the princess. They were all very excited.

On the day of Angelina's birthday, there was a big party at the castle. The king and queen had planned it. There were great drinks, food, and decorations. Everyone waited for the princess to come out of her room. Angelina refused to come out because she was ashamed of her body. Issac then went to Angelina's room and tried to convince her to come out. "Princess, we just want you to know, no matter what happens we will still love you as our princess. And we all made a present for you."

Angelina finally came out to the living room. Everyone looked at her. She felt very uncomfortable and naked. She thought of the days she used to make fun of the other insects and regretted it. Issac and two other insects carried the present to the princess. The princess opened the present. She was surprised. Two lady bumblebees helped the princess put on the wings. Angelina finally smiled! Angelina realized there were others that cared about her. After all the horrible times she had given the citizens, they still helped her. She didn't even know how to thank everyone. "I hope you will forgive me for always ordering you around. Also, please forgive me for always making fun of you," Angelina said humbly. Everyone forgave her and was very happy to hear her first thank-you. The citizens then began to dance. The princess enjoyed dancing with Issac. Angelina learned how Issac understood her feelings and helped her. They became best friends and the party continued for the rest of the night.

Then one day, Angelina and her friends went to a picnic in the cherry woods outside the kingdom. The cherry trees smelled good.

It was nice and quiet. They settled under one of the cherry trees and began to enjoy the food they had brought. Then suddenly they heard a loud thump. Someone had fallen from the sky! Angelina and Issac ran up to see who it was. The insect's wings covered its face, but Angelina quickly recognized those wings. Those were her wings.

"It's Emily, who stole your wings!" Issac yelled. Emily tried to fly away, but she was hurt.

Angelina helped Emily up. "We need to get her to the hospital," Angelina said. Others helped Angelina carry Emily to the hospital.

The next morning when Emily woke up, she realized she was in the hospital. She was scared the princess would punish her for stealing the wings, so she tried to leave.

"You still need rest. You want some water?" Angelina asked.

Emily was confused. "Aren't you angry that I stole your wings?" Emily asked.

"At first I was, but not anymore. I realized there are more important things than beauty, like friends," Angelina said. Emily took the wings off and gave them back to Angelina.

"Here, take the wings back," Emily said.

Angelina refused. "Keep them, they look great on you," she said.

Emily finally spoke. "I am really sorry. I stole your wings and you still have the heart to forgive me. I promise I will never harm anyone anymore. Can you please forgive me?" Emily asked sincerely.

"Of course I will forgive you. You should come back to the kingdom to live with us too. It's always great to have friends around you," Angelina said.

"You would accept me as your friend?" Emily asked.

"Of course!" Angelina smiled.

Now, besides their looks on the outside, they were both truly beautiful on the inside.   ✳

THE NAMELESS PANDA

by Jessica Lo

ILLUSTRATED BY MARCI WASHINGTON

One sunny morning at Sunshine Zoo, a nameless baby panda awoke to the smell of sweet bamboo. His mama, Momo, was still sleeping so the baby panda decided to wander around the playpen. He heard Jumpy, the grizzly bear, calling for him. He and Jumpy were best friends and often had a lot of fun together. The sun was just rising above the rocks of his playpen as the baby panda reached the end of his cage. He peeked through the fence and saw Jumpy rolling around in his mud pit. He called Jumpy over.

"Hey, Jumpy! How are you doing today?" the panda asked.

"I'm doing all right, but I heard some of the other animals gossiping. I felt so bad. They were talking about how you don't have a name," Jumpy stated.

"I never thought about it. Aw, I feel sad now. I want my mama," the panda cried.

"Never fear, you'll always have me! I'm going to help you find out your name! I'll just pass the word along to my neighbors and see what names they think of. I'll meet you here at noon," Jumpy reassured him.

The panda went back to his playpen and saw his mama awaken-ing. He ran up to her and asked, "How come I don't have a name?"

Momo replied, "We were waiting to choose your name based on your personality."

The panda cried, "I don't know what a personality is! How am I going to figure out mine?"

"Don't worry, baby, a personality is something that makes you different from everyone else. It's the traits you have that show who you are as an individual," Momo explained.

"Your personality is the way you act or what you show to others of your soul. For example, the new little piggy that was born yester-day was named Noisy because he squeals at all hours of the night."

"Oh, I kind of understand what a personality is now," said the panda.

Then the panda went to meet Jumpy. He saw him running straight toward him and sweating. The panda asked him, "What did you find out?"

"All the other animals have names that are similar to their per-sonalities. Hoppy, the baby frog, likes to hop around a lot. Leapy, the lemur, likes to leap around. Floppy, the penguin, likes to hobble and flop. And I'm named Jumpy because I like to jump around," Jumpy answered.

"Oh, what is my personality then? Am I jumpy or leapy?" The baby panda was confused because he couldn't figure it out. The baby panda and Jumpy decided to go to sleep and discuss the issue the next morning.

The rising sun woke the baby panda. He ran to the end of his cage and saw Jumpy sleeping. He yelled, "Jumpy! Wake up!" Jumpy jumped up with his eyes wide open. He rushed over to the panda, who was hopping with excitement.

"Guess what I dreamt last night!" the panda exclaimed. "I dreamt of a brilliant plan to escape so that we could roam around the zoo and ask the other animals what I should be named. If you create a distraction while Amy, the zookeeper, opens my cage, I can sneak out without her knowing. Once I get out, I will do the same for you."

"Hey, that sounds great!" Jumpy replied. "Let's try it."

When Amy arrived, she went to the baby panda's cage and opened it. Suddenly, Amy heard a strange cry from the grizzly bear cage next door. As planned, when the zookeeper rushed over to see what was happening and forgot to lock the panda's cage the baby panda escaped and hid in a bush. By this time, Amy could see that everything was OK with the grizzly. She was just about to lock the bear cage when she heard another loud wail, but this time it came from the panda cage. Just as they hoped, Amy ran back to the panda's area and left the grizzly cage wide open. Jumpy escaped and ran over to the bush where his friend was hiding.

When the zookeeper discovered that the baby panda had escaped, she hastily locked the panda cage and ran over to the grizzly cage. To her astonishment, a young grizzly had also escaped.

Amy was overwhelmed and decided to keep the escapes quiet so she wouldn't get fired. Next Amy went looking for the baby panda and grizzly bear.

The baby panda and Jumpy crawled out of the bushes and snuck around the zoo, following a dirt path that led from cage to cage. The first animal they reached was the polar bear. Mr. Polar Bear was trying to catch fish in his pond and his forehead was wrinkled with frustration because he couldn't catch his breakfast. They carefully approached.

"Excuse me, Mr. Polar Bear, what do you think my name should be?" the panda asked.

"Well, you look like a Monroe or Harry," Mr. Polar Bear said in his deep, serious voice.

Jumpy chimed in, "Yeah! Yeah! That's a great idea! He looks hairy and small like a… panda!"

"No! No, Mr. Polar Bear, the baby animals in the zoo are named based on their personalities," said the baby panda.

Mr. Polar Bear grumpily dismissed the two babies. "I'm kind of busy. Can't you little kids go and ask someone else?"

Then they hurried away and walked for a long time until Jumpy finally spotted a clearing. They saw a sign for the anteater. They were about to rush in but they stopped suddenly—Amy the Zookeeper was coming toward them. They hid in the bushes hoping that they wouldn't be spotted. After a few minutes, they poked their little heads out of the bush to see if all was clear. Seeing it was safe, they ran over to Mrs. Anteater's cage, where she was doing her chores. She was feeding her baby, cooking ants on the frying pan, and preparing the other kids' lunches all at one time. She was very busy and was in no mood to be bothered by baby animals. But the panda got up his courage and walked up to Mrs. Anteater.

"Excuse me, Mrs. Anteater, what do you think my name should be?" the baby panda asked.

Mrs. Anteater replied in a hurried voice, "Well, sweetie, I think you smell like bamboo and dirt, so your name should be Bamboo! You little animals smell like you haven't had a bath in years! Do you want me to give you a quick lick?"

Jumpy shivered at the thought of the disgusting offer, but the baby panda simply replied, "No, thank you, Mrs. Anteater. As for my name, it's supposed to be based on my personality."

"Well then, darling, maybe you should go ask Mr. Snake. But if you children ever needed a quick bath, you know who to look for!" she said quickly.

Feeling disappointed, he and Jumpy hurried over to Mr. Snake's cage. Mr. Snake was slithering up a tree trying to reach an apple. He was an unusual snake—he was a vegetarian. Seeing that Mr. Snake was very hungry, they didn't want to disturb him for too long. The panda approached Mr. Snake and speaking very quickly asked, "Mr. Snake, what do you think I should be named?"

Mr. Snake complained, "I think you should be named Explosion because you sound so noisy with your loud, heavy stomping."

"Yeah, that sounds like a good name to give to a panda," Jumpy commented.

Mr. Snake, who couldn't see very well, said, "A panda?! I thought you were a lion!"

Jumpy laughed hysterically, but the panda simply replied, "No! No! Mr. Snake, you're supposed to name me based on my personality. Besides, you must be talking about Jumpy, he's the loud one."

The baby panda and the grizzly, disappointed again, proceeded along the dirt path. The next cage they reached was the lion's. They were frightened to go up because they had heard that lions did scary things like roar at little kids passing by, but they went up anyway. The lions were all sitting at the coffee table eating lamb chops. Once the panda gathered his courage, he went up to the cage and asked in a feeble voice, "Excuse me? Mrs. Lion? What do you think I should be named?"

Mrs. Lion growled ferociously and answered, "Well you sort of look like my lunch and I bet you'd taste like it too! I would name you Lamb Chop."

"Eh, well, I'm supposed to be named based on my personality. And I don't think I taste like lamb chop," the baby panda said.

Mrs. Lion roared angrily, "You delicious-looking kiddies better leave soon before I gobble you up!"

Frightened, the panda and Jumpy rushed back to the dirt path. As they ran, they heard loud footsteps following from behind. The panda turned around to see the zookeeper running right toward them. To confuse the zookeeper, the panda and Jumpy split up and ran in two directions. But she was not far behind and she quickly cornered the little animals. They were sure she would hurt them. She was very big, had long, stringy hair and a long nose that made her look like a witch. But to their surprise, Amy the zookeeper did not hurt them. Instead, she held them gently, touched their soft fur, and hushed them quiet. "My oh my! You two have caused me so much trouble today!" she cooed. "But you are so cuddly and soft, I'll let you go this time." So the baby panda and his dearest friend were put safely back into their cages where they were left to deal with their worried mothers.

The baby panda climbed onto his mama's tummy and cried softly. Because she was his mama, she could tell that something big was worrying her baby. "What is the matter, sweetie? And why did you run away?"

The baby panda looked up at his mama and replied, "Mama, I don't have a name! All the other baby animals have names, why am I so different? Do I have a bad personality?"

The mama soothingly replied, "No, dear baby. You have your own special personality and it will show before you know it. But judging by today, I can tell that you are a very curious and sly baby."

He came up with an idea—he would ask his Mama what his name should be. "Mama, what do *you* think I should be named? All the other animals don't really know me that well, but you sure do!"

"Well, dear baby, I think you are many great things. You are loving, smart, and enthusiastic, but most of all you are curious. I think you should be named Curioso." The baby panda, Curioso, clapped and cheered.

"Yay! I have a name now! My name is Curioso! I can feel it's part of me now!"

The next morning, Curioso woke up and ran to Jumpy's fence, eager to tell his good friend his new name.

"Wake up, Jumpy! I have a name now! It's Curioso! It means curious. You like it?" he asked.

"Yes!" Jumpy replied. "I love it! It's so unique!"

The news of Curioso's new name spread through the zoo and all the animals praised it.

Mr. Polar Bear exclaimed, "It's fresh and new, the way your snowy white fur looks!"

Mr. Snake said, "I love it! It sounds quiet."

Mrs. Anteater said, "It's great! It smells like the new spring air."

Mrs. Lion said, "Roar, I still prefer the taste of lamb chop, but Curioso is good also."

And Amy the zookeeper, who was petting Curioso, said, "Wow! Curioso even feels velvety."

Curioso and Jumpy talked for hours in their cages. They lay on their backs and stared at the pretty clouds in the sky. They gossiped about how this new baby elephant was named Nice because after he was born everybody thought he was a very sweet little baby. But now everybody saw that he should have been named Meany because he always picked on the other elephants and made them cry. Curioso and Jumpy thought this was funny and they laughed and laughed. ✳

BECOMING A PIRATE

by Michael Bura

ILLUSTRATED BY JUSTIN WOOD

I am Orlando. Even though I'm just a kid, I am a good sword fighter. I learned how to sword fight because I want to be a pirate. Although some pirates can be cursed because they always want treasure, there are some pirates who save people's lives. Once, I met some pirates.

When I first met a pirate named Captain Jack Sparrow in my class at school, he was very friendly. He had a mustache and beads in his hair, wore a hat with a feather, and had a sword, a pistol, a compass, and a ring.

He said, "How are you doing today?"

I said, "I'm doing really well in school. I'm working hard and making a lot of friends. I'm staying out of trouble. Why are you here?"

He said, "Because I came to visit you and your friends." After that, I was excited. I wanted to meet more pirates.

In the afternoon, I did not get on the school bus after school like I was supposed to. I wanted an adventure. I wanted to go to a pirate cave where there were treasure, gold, jewels, and a skull. I knew it existed because I saw it in a movie. Pirate caves are big. I got on the MUNI bus and gave the fare to the driver.

The bus was very crowded. The first thing I noticed when I got on the bus was the smell of burritos. They smelled especially good because burritos are one of my favorite foods and I was hungry. I found the person with the burrito. It was an old lady in a blue dress. She had a kind face, gray hair, and wore glasses and looked like she would be nice. I moved over to stand by her. I asked her, "May I have a burrito?"

"Yes, you can," she said.

"What does the burrito have in it?" I asked.

"It has cheese, steak, refried beans, and rice," she said to me.

I ate the burrito. It was delicious.

After eating the burrito, I noticed there were lots of teenagers on the bus. Many of them were wearing suits, ties, and dress shoes. They looked really nice. Maybe they were going to a party or an after-school activity. There also were teenagers who were yelling, talking on their cell phones, and listening to their CD players. It was a really busy bus. A man next to me had bad breath—I could smell it. He had yellow teeth because he probably never brushed them. It was too crowded to sit down. I had to stand up and hold on to the railing. The old lady who gave me the burrito was getting off the

bus and accidentally bumped into me. I felt embarrassed. We said good-bye to each other. I also said to her, "Thank you for sharing your burrito with me. Have a nice day."

When a seat became available, I sat down and looked for my stop, but I didn't know where the bus was going. The bus eventually got to the ocean.

In the water there was a pirate ship. The pirate I had met that morning found me. He was sailing the pirate ship.

"I want to be a pirate," I said.

He said, "OK. Come aboard if you dare."

"I need to ask my parents if I can be a pirate," I said.

I got onboard. The ship was so big that I had to climb up on a big rope. When I got onboard, I saw Captain Barbossa. He was wearing a long red wig and a hat with feathers on it. He had yellow teeth and a red mustache and beard. He was wearing big black boots, and he had a sword and gun.

The sails of the ship were black and gray and there was a flag with a picture of a skull and swords on it. The ship had cannons, guns, swords, and lots of food onboard. It was shiny and new and smelled like wet wood. The crew was walking around. I could hear thuds from their boots and I could hear a gunfight happening near-by. When I heard the gunshots, I was scared. I would not have been scared if I had had a gun or sword to defend myself, but I did not have a sword or gun to fight back with so I found a place to hide under the stairs in the hold.

While I was hiding, I saw a big metal cage for locking people up. I was glad it was empty. I found a sword behind me. If the pirates found me, I would fight back.

After a while, it got quiet and I came back up on the deck. The ocean looked really big.

There were different kinds of fish in the water swimming with each other, having fun.

I told my parents that I was saved by a pirate: He said, "Would you love to be a pirate?" and I said, "Yes, I want to be a pirate and go on adventures!"

We sailed away. My parents waved good-bye. They said, "Be careful. We love you." They were happy about it. They knew I would come back in a few years. I would miss them.   *

GRETA, THE COOKIES, & THE EVIL WITCH

by **Cassandra Beutler**

ILLUSTRATED BY PAUL MADONNA

Miles and miles and miles away, in a gigantic forest, there was a tiny house where magical elves made the best cookies ever. The elves would use sugar, spice, eggs, and their secret ingredient to make the cookie mixture. Then they would place the mixture in the oven for fifteen minutes and sprinkle sugary rainbow dust on them.

Far from this tiny house was a small town. The people that lived in the town craved these delicious cookies constantly. Every single day the cookies were delivered at precisely ten o'clock in the morning, and the people of the town would stand in line at the local grocery store to buy them. For years, the people followed this routine.

Not too far from the small town lived an evil witch. She lived in a dark, creepy cave and slept in the mud. The people of the town feared her. Her oversize nose scared them and they cringed at the thought of her green, scaly legs. Every day as the cookies passed the witch's lair she would watch wishfully. The evil witch loved the cookies as much as the townspeople did. Even when she was sleeping, she would have delicious dreams about them. Little did the town know that she was scheming to steal all the cookies for herself.

One day, the cookies were late. They did not arrive until eleven

o'clock. The townspeople were slightly angry, but large smiles came across their faces as they ate the scrumptious cookies. Even the mayor's frustration was overcome as the delicious treats entered his mouth.

The mayor was a large man with white hair. His belly stuck out, and when he ate too much his face turned red, but he thought he was the most handsome man in the world. And he was lazy. He made Greta, his secretary, do everything for him. Greta was smaller than everybody else in the town. Although she had small hands, small feet, and a small head, she had a huge heart. She always put others before herself.

Wondering what could have caused the delay with the cookies, Greta called the baker. "Hello, Mr. Baker. This is Greta," she said as soon as she heard someone pick up the phone.

"Wop dop o ip sop top hop ip sop?" One of the elves had answered the phone.

"Excuse me?" Greta said.

"Top hop ip sop ip sop op nop ey op vop sop," the elf responded.

"Is this the baker?" Greta questioned.

Mr. Baker took the phone from the elf and said, "I'm sorry, one of my elves answered as a joke and they don't speak the same language as us. They speak Elfish."

"Oh, no wonder I didn't understand! Mr. Baker, I was wondering why the cookies were late today," Greta asked.

"One of the elves was missing so the cookie-making process was slowed down one hour," the baker replied.

"I sure hope they'll be on time tomorrow. I don't want the townspeople to get angry again," Greta responded.

"I hope so too. We're worried the witch might have taken the elf," the baker said.

The next morning, the cookies did not arrive until noon! The townspeople were angrier than before. They all went to the mayor and told him that if the cookies were late again they would riot. Greta decided to call the baker once again.

"Hello, Mr. Baker," Greta said.

"Why, hello, Greta. How do you do?" the baker replied.

"Today the cookies were two hours late. If you don't mind my asking, what was the problem?"

"To make a long story short, today two of my elves went missing. That slowed the cookie-making process down by two hours," the baker said.

"How strange. Two workers missing in one day. Well, hopefully they will both be back by tomorrow," Greta responded.

"I hope so, Greta," the baker said.

Greta was really worried now.

The next day, the cookies arrived three hours late because three elves went missing. The day after that, they arrived four hours late because four elves went missing, and, finally, no cookies were delivered because the elves were all missing. Because the cookies didn't arrive, the townspeople became angry and started to riot.

The mayor didn't know what to do so he just went to sleep, but Greta decided that she was going to search for the elves.

"Mr. Mayor, wake up!" Greta shouted as she shoved him awake.

"What do you want?" the mayor answered grumpily.

"The townspeople are still rioting. I want you to go find the workers with me so they can bake the cookies and put an end to this riot," Greta said.

"Why, you're just a small woman. Someone your size can't go on such a dangerous journey! But better you than me. I'm far too handsome to go. People will miss looking at me," the mayor responded.

"If that's how you feel then I will just go alone," Greta snapped.

"Be off, then, I need to get my beauty sleep," the mayor said and fell back asleep.

Greta put some of her belongings in a potato sack and left for her journey. She started walking along the dusty brown dirt road. After about an hour of walking, something odd occurred. The dusty road turned into muddy goop. It squished under the weight of her body, and her shoes started to fill up with the brown mess. She took off her shoes to make the walking easier and the goop went in between her toes as she walked. It was like stepping in a field of pudding. As she kept walking she ran into what seemed to be a cave. Curious about what was inside, she wiped her feet off with a leaf and put her shoes on. Then she went in.

The cave was darker than the night sky. Greta was thankful she had a candle with her, otherwise she wouldn't have been able to see. She could hear water dripping off the top of the cave onto the cold stone floor. Drip, drop, drip, drop, drip, *bang*! Suddenly the evil witch came out of the darkness. The witch looked just like everybody had described her. Greta even cringed at the sight of her green, scaly legs. Behind the witch was a small group of terrified-looking elves. The elves had on orange socks, green coats, red ties, and purple hats. Their pointy ears stuck up and their small noses looked like little magenta buttons. They were quite small, even smaller than Greta.

"What business have you here?" the witch roared.

"The same as yours," Greta said.

"Heh-heh-heh, so you too want to use these magical elves to bake the best cookies ever?" the witch asked.

"Yes, but not for myself. Everybody needs the cookies to make the town peaceful again." Greta glared at the witch.

The witch glared back. She then tried to seize Greta but Greta was too quick for her. Greta threw her candle at the witch and the witch caught on fire, went up in smoke, and disappeared forever.

Greta saw that the cute little elves were all huddled in a corner of the cave. They were happy the witch had died, but were still traumatized from everything that had happened to them for the past few days. Greta looked at them but didn't try to speak, because she didn't speak Elfish.

She used hand motions to tell the elves to follow her. At first they were reluctant, but then they started to trust her. They just wanted to get back to the bakery and she led them there. When they finally arrived, the baker welcomed Greta with a bright smile. As a gift of thanks, the baker gave Greta an enormous gift basket filled with all his finest pastries and treats. She thanked him and started her journey back to her home.

When Greta arrived, the townspeople were still rioting. She announced to them that the cookies would be delivered again on a daily basis at precisely ten o'clock and everybody shouted with joy. Then the people of the town decided that Greta should become the new mayor. After all, she had saved the day and it seemed to the townspeople that she cared more about them than the current mayor did.

Greta then went back to City Hall with the townspeople. As they all entered the mayor's office, they found him sitting in his puffy leather chair gazing out the window. They told him to pack his things so that Greta could move into his office. The mayor refused to move from his seat at first, but finally did after he realized that he had no choice.

He became Greta's secretary and Greta became the mayor of the town and she kept the townspeople safe and satisfied. And the cookies arrived on time every day from that day on. ✳

A BEAR'S JOURNEY

by Addison Chen

ILLUSTRATED BY ADAM McCAULEY

There once was a bear named Nismo who lived in the forest town of Silvia. He had a father, mother, and sister that all lived in a single den. When the family became hungry, someone had to bring food back to the den. One day when Nismo was of age to travel in the woods by himself, he packed some fruit in a bag and decided to go down to the river to retrieve water and catch fish. Before Nismo left, his parents stressed to him that it would be a long and difficult trip by himself, but he shouldn't give up. He walked along Willow Road because his sister told him it would take him to the river.

One mile down the road, Nismo found huge fallen trees blocking the road, so he decided to take a detour through the forest. He walked about ten minutes into the forest until he found another road that he didn't recognize. Nismo was lost.

Nismo saw a creature that was small, black and white, liked to wiggle his tail, and smelled very bad too. He asked it, "Do you know where the river is?"

The creature replied, "I'll help you if you can do two things. First, tell me what animal I am." Nismo thought and thought—an animal that was small and black, and smelled.

"A skunk!" he shouted.

"Good, good," said the skunk. "I'll tell you which way to go if you help me get the berries out from this bush." Nismo dove headfirst into the thorny bush, avoiding most of the thorns, but one snatched hold of him and gave him a scratch across his left leg. He came out the other end of the bush with two handfuls of berries. The skunk thanked him and pointed the way.

Nismo continued with his scraped-up leg until he got to a huge tree, and there the road split into two. "Left or right?" he said. An animal jumped down from inside the tree and said he would tell him which way led to the river if Nismo could tell him what animal he was and do one task as well. Since the animal hung on trees, liked to play games, and was playing in a banana tree, Nismo asked with confidence, "Are you a monkey?"

"You got me," said the monkey, "but I'll only help you if you can also get a banana from the top of the tree." Nismo climbed up and reached for the biggest banana he'd ever seen. He grabbed it with his right paw and fell to the ground. The banana fell onto his belly and bounced into the monkey's paw.

"The river is on the road to your left. Good luck!" the monkey said while leaping back into the tree. Nismo picked up his bruised and scabbed self and continued on his trip.

By now, Nismo was beginning to show fatigue. He thought several times of giving up, taking a break, and returning home, but he kept his mind on his duty to his family and continued walking. He knew this was one of the moments his parents had warned him about, telling him that he shouldn't give up.

Suddenly a big shadow was cast over Nismo. When he looked up to see what it was, he screamed, "Ahhh!" The creature was tall, yellow with black spots, and had an extremely long neck.

The enormous creature replied in a bored tone, "I don't let bears beyond this point!"

Nismo stared straight up into the clouds to see his face. "There has to be something I can do to go by," he said.

The mammal replied, "Tell me what…"

"You're a giraffe!" Nismo interrupted.

"You didn't let me finish! Tell me what the length of my neck is from chin to shoulder and I'll let you pass," the giraffe replied.

Nismo thought, How am I supposed to do that? Then he remembered he was four feet six inches tall, exactly. So he climbed up the giraffe and made a mark next to the top of his head each time he climbed up and found the neck was exactly four markings, so he shouted into the clouds, "Eighteen feet!"

"Eighteen feet and a half inch, but I'll let it go. Get it right next time if you ever come back, but I can't guarantee that I won't grow anymore."

As he continued on his journey, Nismo felt like something was watching him, following him, stalking him. Suddenly another huge animal stopped him and would not let him pass unless he could tell him what animal she was. She had paws the size of Nismo's head, and orange and black stripes.

The animal roared, "I'll give you two chances to tell me what I am. If you can't, I will make you turn back."

"I know, you're a cat!" Nismo roared back.

The beast replied with a snooty purr, "I'm not just a cat. You get one more chance." Now Nismo was scared at the thought of having to turn back, or even worse, being eaten by this creature.

He had several thoughts of giving up and walking back home with empty hands, but he mustered all his courage and screamed, "You must be a lion. Now get out of my way, you bully!"

"Everyone confuses me with my cousin. I'm tired of it!" the beast shouted. "I'm not a lion and you're not getting past!"

"I was just joking. You tigers are so short-tempered," said Nismo.

The tiger was so enraged and offended by Nismo's joke that her eyes turned red, her fur spiked up, and her muscles tightened as if she were going to lunge at Nismo. She even made several gestures trying to scare him away, but Nismo knew he couldn't give up now and wouldn't budge in response to her tactics. The two began to exchange roars. They continued several more times until Nismo got on his hind legs and gave the final verbal blow. The tiger ran back into the forest with her tail between her legs and Nismo kept walking down the road as if nothing had happened.

As he continued on, he knew he was getting closer, the grass was greener than before, the air was fresher, the birds were singing, and the rocky road had become a soft dirt trail. Nismo decided to take a break. He reached into his bag and ate whatever crumbs were left. Nismo was tired and thought many times of lying down with his belly toward the sky and his arms and legs spread out. But his parents had taught him not to give up, so he kept walking.

Shortly after, when Nismo was almost too tired to walk straight, he looked up and saw the most beautiful scene he had ever laid his eyes upon: the river. The water was clear and blue like sapphires, the rocks looked like they were polished, and there were animals replenishing themselves, minding their own business, and not requesting tasks for him to do.

Nismo caught some fish in the river and drank the water from the streams. He later returned with his head held high, his arms full of fish, and his legs marked with a lifetime of bruises and scabs.

And when he saw each of the animals on the way back, he didn't forget to say good-bye to the tiger, the giraffe, the monkey, and the skunk. ✳

THE SMALL BIG KID

by **Ronney Freeman**

ILLUSTRATED BY DAN McHALE

Once upon a time there was a boy named Joey. He lived in a small town that was called Wanomonopia. All of the stores in Wanomonopia were crowded, and so were the main streets. Joey was very small for his age—he was the height of an average man's hip. Joey attended Parkside Elementary School. He loved it there because all of the students were the same height and he didn't feel left out. All of his friends went there too.

One day he came home from school and heard some bad news from his mother. The news was that they were going to move to a bigger city where his mother would make more money for them. Joey started to cry, his tears flowing from each eye. He was leaving all his friends and all the memories he had made at the old school. Joey tried to plead with his mother but there was nothing she could do about it. They were leaving town.

A few days later Joey arrived at his new school, Cordova Elementary. He noticed that he was the smallest of all the kids, and that made him feel left out. He felt awkward and lonely. The school itself was humongous in his eyes. The school had huge window frames which made it a whole lot easier for Joey to see outside. The

doors were like big closets that he had to open up with all his strength. When the school bell rang the students ran to each of their classrooms excited for their first day. When Joey got into his classroom, he saw a lonely seat all the way in the back. While he was walking down the aisle he started sweating because all of the kids were already in their seats looking at him.

The teacher began to take roll call. As she called the students' names they raised their hands, but when she read aloud Joey's name, she couldn't see him raise his, because it was only as high as the person's head in front of him. Just when she was about to mark him absent, Joey jumped into the aisle and said, "I'm here" so loudly that the kids next door could hear him. They started to laugh and that made Joey sad.

As soon as the bell rang, kids ran out of class chanting, "It's lunchtime!" All the kids were happy that they could finally have a break. Joey saw them playing sports and he wanted to play too, so he waited in line to be called on to play basketball. As he expected, Joey was picked last. When he was finally in the game he wanted to use his height as an advantage, so he dribbled the ball and ran under the kids' legs to score. He was extremely fast. He moved around the court like a house mouse, and the other players didn't know how to stop him. Kids in the audience were cheering him on.

While Joey's team was winning the game, this big kid named George from the other team began to take out all of his frustration on Joey. George was a sore loser and he started talking trash to Joey. The other kids started to call George a poor sport, which made George mad. Suddenly he pushed Joey into the grass so hard that the grass had Joey's body print in it when he stood up. Joey began to cry and went home early. He felt ashamed, and all of George's friends were laughing at him.

When Joey got home, Renita, his mother, asked him what he was doing home so early. He said, "Some of the kids don't like me because of my height and because I can do things on the basketball court."

Renita said, "No matter what your size and appearance you are capable of doing something special. These new kids ought to know that." That night Joey went to sleep early so he could begin the next day with a good start.

The next morning he attended all of his classes, but was still hurt from what had happened the day before. The principal talked with George about his actions and decided not to let him play on the playground on certain days, but Joey still felt sad. Later that day, Joey and his teacher were having a discussion about a project that was due in class, when the fire alarm went off. Kids started to panic, running out of the school through every exit. Joey ran with them.

Outside of the building they could see their school burning away. Some of the kids were crying and holding on to their teachers and their friends for support. Meanwhile, Joey saw four gigantic red fire trucks pull up, with loud sirens that could cause a kid's head to ache.

The fire trucks were making the matter even more dramatic with all the noise.

Joey looked at the burning school and noticed that the students on the higher floors hadn't gotten out. Kids tried to tell the fire fighters that their friends were still in the building. The building began to collapse and objects fell in front of the door, barricading it, and there was no way the firemen could get through.

But Joey saw something that the firemen didn't see. There was a small hole between the doors where the firemen thought there was no opening. Joey acted fast and squeezed his way through the hole as the kids started to say, "No, no, you won't come out alive!"

Joey ran up the stairs as if there were a mean dog chasing him. He went to the classroom where the students were locked in. Joey opened the door from the outside and ran in to save two girls. One girl was crying and was able to run with Joey, but the other girl was so stunned that she couldn't move and Joey had to pick her up. She was smaller than Joey, which was helpful. She began sweating and coughing on his arm but he held on to her like a father holding his newborn baby. As the kids began to make their way out of the burning building, objects kept falling. The girl that was running with Joey began to run slower and she told Joey, "I won't be able to make it."

Joey said, "Yes, you will, believe in me."

The fire began to crack and pop, which made the kids more scared, but it didn't stop Joey. The fire began to get hot and the girl in Joey's arms began to throw up on him as she breathed in the smoke. Joey began to feel very weak and his legs started to give up on him. Suddenly he collapsed with the girl in his arms. But just at that moment, the firefighters busted open the barricaded door and carried Joey and the girl back to safety. They also helped the girl that was running with Joey to the ambulance. Joey and the girl he had saved stayed in the hospital overnight.

A week later Joey went back to school. Kids were so proud of his heroism that they gave him goodies that would take him and his mother a whole year to finish eating, and "get well" cards. At a school assembly, the firefighters awarded Joey his own uniform. Renita met her son at school to congratulate him with the rest of the students.

While Joey was being honored, George came up to the stage and said, "I'm sorry for being so hard on you. Thank you so much for what you have done for me and my family."

"What have I done for your family?" asked Joey.

George told him, "That was my sister you saved from the burning building. She was the one in your arms."

Joey accepted the apology and then told the principal to let George play in the playground, since George had said he was sorry and said that it would never happen again. As for Joey being smaller than the others, they never looked at him as different again. ✳

FEELING BLUE

by Erika Tang

ILLUSTRATED BY JOSHUA GORCHOV

Biffy the bunny had lived her whole life in Dittoville, a village where many light blue bunnies lived. Dittoville was full of houses that looked exactly alike, shaped like carrots growing out of the ground. All the animals wore the same outfit and every girl bunny had a pink bow on her right ear.

Biffy's grandmother had been born in Swirlyville, a village far away from Dittoville, but had moved away because Biffy's grandfather got a better job in Dittoville. Grandmother Bunny had always wanted to hop back to Swirlyville one day, but she never got the chance.

Biffy used to ask her grandmother about Swirlyville. "Swirlyville is a wonderful place. It has fun and caring animals. It's a place where you can get help whenever help is needed," Grandmother Bunny would always reply.

"Mommy has always talked about moving there someday in the future. Would I be able to get my own room?" Biffy would say with eager eyes.

"The houses are big and pretty, sweetie, with at least three bedrooms, so you'll definitely get your own room," Grandmother Bunny would answer.

"Yay!" Biffy would reply. Biffy and her grandmother had this same conversation almost every week.

Things changed after Biffy's grandmother died, though. She left Mr. and Mrs. Bunny lots of money, enough to buy a new house. And since Grandmother Bunny had always wanted to go back to Swirlyville, Biffy's parents decided to move there in her memory. They packed all their things in the bunny-mobile and left Dittoville.

As they drove toward their new home, Biffy was excited. She missed her friends most of all, but her grandmother had said that Swirlyville had the best playgrounds around. Biffy had daydreams about playing in the Swirlyville playgrounds with all the new animals she would meet. But then she was afraid she wouldn't be liked in Swirlyville. All of a sudden, she felt like she couldn't breathe. Her parents stopped the bunny-mobile to help her. The fresh air helped calm her down a little, but she was still scared.

"You're just nervous, honey. It's OK to be nervous when you move to a new place. Everything will be fine," said her mother.

When they arrived, she saw that in Swirlyville there were all sorts of different and cute animals. There were plenty of trees and flowers growing everywhere. It was a very clean and pretty place, where everyone played their part in keeping the village spotless, and the sun always shone.

That night, while Biffy and her parents were eating dinner, they began talking about enrolling Biffy in an elementary school.

"How would you like to go to Acorn Academy, Biffy?" her dad questioned.

"Acorn Academy?" Biffy looked confused.

"We've been talking to our new neighbors, Mr. and Mrs. Porcupine, and they said their daughter, Piney, goes to Acorn Academy. We just thought you might like to go to a school where you would know someone already," Mrs. Bunny replied.

"But I don't know her…"

"You can meet her and get to know her, honey," Mr. Bunny said with a big grin.

Biffy stopped listening to what her parents were saying and began to daydream about Piney, what she might be like, and all the things they could do together once they became friends.

The next morning she got up to go with her mom to visit the elementary school. Classes wouldn't start for another two weeks, but the school was open for activities during the summer, so Biffy thought she might see some of her classmates. As her mother drove to the school, Biffy's ears drooped and drooped—she felt shy and scared.

At the school Biffy heard the noise of kids playing and Biffy's ears drooped once more as she stood there, frightened. She saw many purple squirrels, green porcupines, brown prairie dogs, gray chipmunks, and navy blue bunnies running around and having lots of fun. Biffy walked to them and they started introducing themselves, but Biffy was afraid and just stood there saying nothing. Soon the other animals went back to playing among themselves.

Then one of the squirrels noticed that Biffy was a light blue color when all the other bunnies were a navy blue color. The squirrel pointed it out to everyone and they began to whisper about Biffy. They believed someone so different shouldn't be so unfriendly with them.

Biffy was feeling really down, but she remembered her grandmother telling her, "If you try hard enough, you can achieve anything." So Biffy got the courage and introduced herself. "Hi, I'm Biffy." To her disappointment, the other animals went on playing and pretended she wasn't even there.

Biffy sat there for hours with droopy ears watching the others. School was going to start in six days and already everyone thought she was mean and weird.

At home, she locked herself in her bedroom and wouldn't come down for dinner.

The next morning, Biffy was hungry so she went out to buy some food. It was almost lunchtime and Biffy smelled something delicious. She walked toward the smell and ended up at the schoolyard, where there was a big party going on. The little animals were playing on one side of the yard and the adults were on the other side barbecuing.

Biffy stood on the side staring at all the food on the tables. The other children saw her and stopped playing abruptly. When Biffy turned around, they were still staring at her.

"What are *you* doing here?" a brown prairie dog asked.

"Yeeeeah!" everyone else chimed in.

"I'm not trying to cause trouble…" Biffy said softly.

"Then leave, weirdo," a gray chipmunk spat.

With watering eyes and with a lot of courage, Biffy responded, "If you don't want to be near me then you leave!"

"We were here first!" a green porcupine pointed out.

"Yeeeah!" the children yelled again.

From the corner of the yard, a little pink porcupine heard the noise and ran toward the commotion.

"What's happening?" the pink porcupine asked.

"She shouldn't be here, Piney," a purple squirrel said while glaring at Biffy.

"They don't like me because I'm a different color than them," Biffy said sadly.

"That can't be it… they're friends with me and *I'm* a different color," Piney replied in a confident tone.

"No, we just don't like her because she's mean and rude," a navy blue bunny said bitterly.

"Who would want to be friends with her anyway?" argued a gray chipmunk.

As everyone turned to look at Biffy again, tears began rolling down her cheeks. The students knew that the chipmunk had hurt Biffy a lot with that comment and felt that they shouldn't keep trying to hurt her.

"Why don't you want to know her?" Piney asked, finally breaking the silence.

"I'm… not sure anymore…" the chipmunk replied guiltily.

"What's the real reason all of you don't like her?" Piney inquired, deciding she had to help fix the problem.

"She was really mean. When we tried to talk to her, she just ignored us," a squirrel answered.

"No… I wasn't ignoring all of you," Biffy said quickly. "I'm just very shy…"

"I think this has all just been a misunderstanding," Piney said.

"Uh huh!" everyone agreed. Everyone usually agreed with Piney because she was so practical and smart.

By the time everyone had exchanged their apologies and had agreed to be friends, the adults had finished barbecuing and called everyone over to eat. While they were eating, Biffy and Piney began talking.

"So why were you over there by yourself?" Biffy wondered.

"I know other kids really like me and want to become better friends with me, but it's really awkward for me to hang out with them all the time."

"Is it because you're a different color from all the other porcupines?" Biffy asked. Once she had said that, she wished she hadn't—it wasn't exactly the nicest thing to ask when you've just met someone. But soon the barbecue was over and everyone went home.

Biffy and Piney spent the last days before school getting to know each other. They shared their secrets and it was easy for them to talk about anything together. By the time school began, they were already best friends.

On the first day of school, Biffy sat with Piney the whole time, and during lunch break they chatted with all the other animals. After the first day of school was over, they couldn't wait to go back the next day. ✳

THE BABUSHKAS

by Richard McKnight

ILLUSTRATED BY AVERY MONSEN

In a time when dreams became reality and wishes came true, there was a little city in a closet. The city was called Comell-yote. About fifty-thousand little people lived in Comell-yote. The city itself represented all the multicultural aspects of human life thanks to years of migration from closets all over the world. Almost every language ever spoken by man was spoken in the city but the main language was Russian.

In Comell-yote there were buildings made of toothpicks and yarn, and highways built from Hot Wheels tracks and soda cans. The construction workers used the Tonka trucks of the giants to transport things, and they held together their buildings with gum and Play-Doh. Proud and sturdy stood the towers of Comell-yote. Around them lay streets of fur.

The infamous Mayor Mushina had founded the city and was now its head honcho. He had a false smile and a lazy eye and looked at people as if he were about to eat them. Mushina was a mean and greedy man. He was an old soldier born in the lands beyond the Great Gate. He was the bearer of tales of war and battle, sorrow and sadness. He was used to trickery and deception and enjoyed seeing the city he ruled over remain in tip-top shape. The city officials didn't like him very much, and the citizens of Comell-yote stayed away from him in the hope of staying safe.

There was a family in the city known as the Babushkas. Koshka Babushka was the father. He was short and fat with brown skin and spoke Russian. He was a kind man who wouldn't harm a fly. Sabaka Babushka, the mother, was tall and skinny. She spoke Thai and Russian. She had a screechy voice and big green hair with sweet eyes. Devuchka Babushka, the beloved daughter, was a mix of tall and thin, somewhat fat and skinny, and spoke Thai, Russian, and Spanish. Malchik Babushka, their son, was big and strong with dark skin and spoke Thai, Russian, and Arabic. They all lived together happily.

As the mayor watched the progress of the city, he began to feel his greed kick in—he wanted more money. The city was in tip-top shape, as he liked it. There was no need for workers anymore. One day there was a big riot because the mayor decided to cut all the construction workers' salaries by half for his own profit.

Koshka was a master construction worker who trained others with his skills. He was very popular with the people for his work, kindness, and warm heart. He helped fix people's pipes, refrigerators, cars, and roofs and even built someone a garage for free. The people loved Koshka and were close to him and his family. The mayor knew of Koshka's popularity and did not approve. He was jealous of Koshka's skills and the love the people gave him. He feared that Koshka was gaining too much support from the people of the city and thought he might become the new mayor. Worrying about losing his job, Mayor Mushina rudely fired Koshka.

To make matters worse, the mayor exiled Koshka's family to the couch beyond the Great Gates. The couch was far away from the city of Comell-yote. It was said to have no food or water but many earthquakes from the giants that sat on it. Koshka's family had two days to pack and leave for this unpleasant place.

Koshka had no support from the people who loved him, because they too were threatened with losing their jobs and being exiled to the couch. Sad and brokenhearted by the corrupt mayor, Koshka fled with his family to the destitute couch miles away from Comell-yote.

Devuchka asked, "Father, why must we have to deal with things like this? What has our family done to deserve this? You were loved by the people and now we must leave our beloved home."

"Unfortunately, we must. There will be a day when all this will be forgotten, and we will live well again."

On the way to the dreadful couch, they encountered the ant monsters that roamed the wilderness. Malchik asked, "Father, what will we do to protect our things and the women?"

Koshka answered, "We'll have to make spears to kill those dreadful things."

They fought off the ant monsters with rocks and spears, which were actually toothpicks for humans, until they made it the four miles—which was only about four feet—to the couch. When they reached the couch, they saw firsthand why it was such an unlikable place. For starters, it had huge cracks in it where whole families could settle. There were food and crumbs on it as well. The couch was not the best place to live, but the Babushkas had no choice.

Sabaka said, "Koshka, I hate the look of this place. How will we live here?"

"Honey, we just have to find a way to play the cards we have been dealt."

As Koshka and his family settled, they built their houses in the crack of the couch. They used toothpicks left by the giants to make a fire. They used tents to keep warm and built a small protective wall to keep out the ant monsters.

One day, as Koshka's family was just getting used to things, there was a huge earthquake. Koshka saw what made the earthquake happen. It was the giants of the household, legendary creatures from beyond the Great Gate.

A huge white giant with a big bowl of orange chips sat on the couch and shook up everything. The earthquake destroyed most of the work that Koshka's family had done on their wall. They slowly rebuilt the wall and went on living in the couch for a few months, which were only weeks. Still dealing with frequent earthquakes and heat waves, they suffered until the unthinkable happened. There arrived a group of messengers, along with Mayor Mushina himself.

The travelers came with word of a big problem in Comell-yote. The mayor asked for Koshka's family to return.

There had been a huge earthquake in the closet when a four-legged creature with big green eyes came and stomped all over the city, and the mayor needed to retrain construction workers for the job of rebuilding.

Mayor Mushina said, "Koshka, Koshka, Koshka, Koshka, so

these are your dwellings, huh? Not so bad for the best construction worker in the city."

Koshka answered, "Save your lies. Don't try to butter me up after you did what you did to my family and me. Who do you think you are?"

Mayor Mushina said, "OK, I'll tell you what I can do for you. I can give you back your home and position and give you higher wages. And I'll even throw in a complimentary new towel for the sweat I'll need from you when you come back to work."

Sabaka said, "Don't do it, honey. It's wrong and he's not telling the truth, I know it."

Malchik said, "Whatever you do, Dad, I'm right behind you!"

Devuchka said, "Father, I really want to get my nails done."

Koshka said, "What? That's not going to happen right now, Devuchka."

Devuchka said, "Fine, but please let us go home."

Mayor Mushina said, "So is that a deal: you and yours come back to your home, I give you a little more money and a towel, and we call it done?"

Koshka said, "Well, to tell the truth, I do want to be back at my house and live a normal life again."

Mayor Mushina said, "Then it's done."

Koshka said, "Wait, it's not done. That's not all I want. I want the people of the city to have equal rights as I do. No longer should they have to fear you and deal with your meanness! Give them all permanent positions, and give every worker the right to refuse to work. And give them all back their full pay and higher."

Mayor Mushina said, "What! You're kidding, right? Tell me you don't mean that!"

Koshka said, "No sir, I mean it, every word of it!"

Mayor Mushina said, "My money... Ugggh... You're lucky I want my city back. It's a deal."

With this news, Koshka and his family jumped up and packed their things, ready for their life back home.

When the Babushkas arrived in the city, they were sad to see it damaged so badly. In no time, though, Koshka trained the workers, and at the best of their abilities made the city as good as new.

Koshka was happy, and the city was back to normal. The people loved him even more and felt much more confident about themselves. Mayor Mushina learned that life was only hard because he made it hard. With the right mind-set, he could make things better for all.

✳

BUNNIES & BEAVERS VS. JAGUARS & TIGERS

by Roger Chan

ILLUSTRATED BY LISA BROWN

There was once a forest town with tall trees and a big lake where all kinds of animals lived. Its citizens enjoyed the clear sky, the blue lake… and sports. They had enclosed places for basketball, golf, baseball, soccer, volleyball, and swimming, and the whole town was full of active animals.

The squirrels lived in a big tree next to the lake. Father Squirrel was mayor and he was nice to everyone in town. The lake was dammed by a family of beavers. The beavers took good care of the lake and kept it clean. It always looked pretty and they worked as a team to keep it that way. The tigers and jaguars, the big cats feared in the whole forest, lived in their own area just outside of the town because they couldn't get along with the town animals. Finally, the bunnies lived beneath the squirrels' tree. The bunnies were spoiled and selfish, and thought they could do anything anytime they wanted to.

In the summer, all the animals came out to play and have fun. One day, the spoiled bunny twins, Collin and Blake VonStone, who were good players and thought they could beat anyone, were sharing a basketball court with the tigers and jaguars. In the next court over, the beavers were playing. While the tigers and jaguars were rough with their big claws and pawed hard, the beavers were polite players even if they couldn't shoot or dribble very well.

That day, the selfish twins challenged the beavers to a game. The beavers agreed. The twins smiled wide thinking they would win easily. The game started and the twins got the ball. Collin dribbled in and shot. The ball went in with no problem. Collin and Blake continued to make points while the beavers struggled. Then the oldest beaver noticed something. He said to the other two, "They never pass to each other! Just surround the one with the ball." When the game started up again, Collin got the ball and the beavers surrounded him. Collin wouldn't pass, so the Beavers got the ball from him and scored.

Blake yelled at Collin, "Why didn't you pass the ball to me? I was wide open." Collin didn't respond. But when Blake had the ball, he did the same thing. The beavers ended up winning, which made the twins mad. The bunnies had such bad tempers that they went around the town dumping garbage everywhere, destroying lawns, and ruining the whole forest. The tigers and jaguars laughed at the twin brothers.

The twins challenged them, "You can laugh all you want, but we can beat you guys."

"You want a match?" the tigers asked. "If we win, you two will be our servants for a week, and if we lose, we'll be your servants for a month." The twins agreed to the terms and shook on it to close the deal.

That night, they wondered what they had gotten themselves into. They were scared that they might lose to the tigers and jaguars. They also knew that the animals in town would be mad if they didn't clean up the mess—they needed to win so the tigers and jaguars would clean up for them. And they were still three players short of a team.

They decided the beavers would give them their best chance of winning. They had seen the beavers' skills and they wanted to learn from them. The bunnies didn't want to ask the beavers to help but they had no other choice. They hopped to the beavers' dam and knocked on their door. The oldest beaver, Jack, opened the door.

"Mind if we talk to you guys for a moment?" the twins asked. "We think you can help us improve our game and we want to know if you and your brothers can join us on our team against the tigers and jaguars."

Jack looked at them like they were crazy and said no.

The bunnies got on their knees. "Please help us," they begged. "We made a bet that if we lose, we will have to be their servants for a week."

"No!" Jack repeated, then he slammed the door in their faces.

The bunnies wouldn't give up. They kept knocking on the door with their ears, pleading, "Please, please, please, please!"

Jack opened the door and sighed. "Let me get my brothers." Jack called Jacky, the middle brother, and Jackal, the youngest, and told them the situation. The beavers agreed to help and Jack told the twins, "Be at the basketball court in the stadium tomorrow morning at 8:00 A.M. sharp." The twins hopped back home, happy but anxious.

The next morning, the twins were early and the beavers arrived right on time. The beavers told the twins to sit down and just listen. Jack said seriously, "You two have the best skills in the whole forest and you could have beaten us, if you hadn't been so stubborn about not passing." The twins were ashamed. They started practice and spent the morning passing with the beavers guarding. Soon Collin and Blake were tired, but they didn't quit, because they wanted to learn. Finally, they started to get the hang of it.

Jack told them it was time to go three on two. The twins tried their best, but in the end, the beavers still won. The bunnies were frustrated again.

"Don't get mad, it's just a game," said Jack. "Don't worry, you guys did everything right."

Blake said, "But what if we lose? We'll have to be the big cats' servants."

The beavers laughed. "It's not about winning or losing, it's just about having fun." The twins sighed and nodded.

Morning came and the twins and the beavers dressed in their new team jerseys and went to the stadium to wait for the game. When the tigers and jaguars arrived, they laughed at the bunny and beaver team. "Look at those jerseys. You look ridiculous!" they said.

"Just ignore them," said Jack.

The announcer finally called, "First up, Team Flapper and their great twin duo, Collin and Blake VonStone!" The bunnies smiled and walked from their bench to the middle of the court. "And the beaver who laughs for no reason, Jackal!" Jackal came out and laughed.

"Now we have middle beaver, Jacky!" Jacky walked out, expressionless, but everyone clapped because he was known to be so nice. "And now, the brains of the bunch… Jack!" Jack walked out shyly because of the compliments, but the applause continued.

Just as the announcer began to introduce the second team, the big cats ran out and rudely stole the microphone.

"We don't need no stinking introduction. We're Team Stripes, and you know who we are—we're the bad boys of this place. We're going to beat everyone."

Jack held the furious twins back and said, "Take it to the court. We'll beat them. Don't worry."

With that, the ref tossed the ball up in the air and Collin jumped to grab it with no problem. But one of the jaguars pushed him and ran off with the ball. He scored. The audience screamed, *"Booo!"* because the ref hadn't caught the foul but the tigers and jaguars laughed.

"It's fine, just be patient," Jack said to the twins. Sure enough, Team Flapper had the ball again and this time Jacky took it to the hoop. Three jaguars tried to jump him, but Jacky knocked the ball straight up into the air and moved to the side. The jaguars collided and the basketball hit all three of them on its way down. Then Jacky grabbed it and passed it to Blake, who dunked it and made a funny face at the tigers.

The tigers yelled at the jaguars for doing a bad job. The jaguars told the tigers they weren't guarding well. But despite the arguments, the tigers and jaguars were still winning. Jack called for a time out.

He addressed the team, "Guys, they play just like Collin and Blake used to—they don't pass the ball. Just do what we used to do to beat the twins—surround the ball hog and steal it." Team Flapper began to catch up and with two minutes left, Team Flapper went ahead by two. Everyone in the audience cheered.

Eager to score before the game was up, one of the tigers tried a three-point shot. He aimed, shot, and smiled wide, confident he had made it. Everyone stopped cheering as they watched the ball fly toward the hoop, but a few seconds later they started laughing. The tiger turned around and saw that the ball was stuck on the rim and wouldn't come down. The tigers and jaguars panicked; they needed to get it down but they couldn't put a lot of pressure on the ball or they would tear it with their sharp claws. The jaguars and tigers argued and blamed one another. Team Flapper sat down. Jack said, "I told you we would win." And as he predicted, the cats argued until the two minutes ran out. Team Flapper jumped and cheered and celebrated their victory.

The mayor came up to the twins. "I am happy that you guys won, but we do have to settle the matter of you trashing the forest town," he said.

The twins said, "We will have the tigers and jaguars clean it up—they are our servants for the month." The team laughed.

While cleaning up the twins' mess, the tigers and jaguars continued fighting.

Morning came, and the twins checked in on the progress of the cats. They saw that the tigers and jaguars were still not finished. The twins said to the shocked tigers, "We won because we learned teamwork from the beavers. This is our mess too. We can't let someone else clean up for us all the time."

The tigers and jaguars have been kind to the other animals in the forest ever since.　　　　　*

THE EVIL KNIGHT & THE KINGDOM

by Allen Wong

ILLUSTRATED BY BRENDAN MONROE

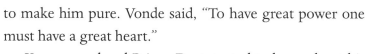

In a wonderful kingdom called Alpha stood a beautiful castle with many gates and small gardens. Many small villages surrounded the castle crossed by rivers that led to wide open farmland of corn and wheat, beyond which were mountains. Every year, knights from different kingdoms would come to the castle and battle for the title of Grand Knight.

One day a prince was born in this kingdom. His father held a great celebration and named him Dart. There were lots and lots of presents for the newborn prince—but the most special gifts arrived at noon.

"Cling, cling, cling," came the sound of heavy armor. Everyone was silent and all their attention went to the grand entrance of the castle, where they saw the five head knights of Alpha. They were the most powerful in the kingdom and each knight gave the prince one of his own traits as a present.

The first knight gave Dart a charming face to make him attractive. The second gave him nerves of steel to make him brave. The third gave him the mind of a coyote to make him exceptionally clever. The fourth gave him the muscles of a tiger to make him powerful. Finally, the head of the five knights, Vonde, gave Dart his heart to make him pure. Vonde said, "To have great power one must have a great heart."

Years passed and Prince Dart started to learn about his special abilities. He was so clever and had so much strength that he won every game he played with other children. Soon they grew tired of playing with him. He couldn't control his powers so he got into a lot of trouble too. He was scolded by the elder council all the time. It wasn't until he was eight years old that he found his first real friend.

On the day of Dart's eighth birthday, a powerful knight came to Alpha from the nearby kingdom of Vivid. He brought his young sister with him. She was around Dart's age, and, like her brother, she was quite strong. Her name was Yupei. She liked to play, so Dart challenged her to try a game he used to play with other children. To Dart's surprise, Yupei outsmarted him and won! Dart was shocked because this was the first time he had ever lost.

Yupei and her brother decided to live in Alpha. Dart was excited. Dart and Yupei became inseparable and went on many adventures.

Eight years passed and Dart was old enough to join the annual Knights' Royale. Yupei was there, screaming and cheering for him.

Dart won all the early rounds. But during the last round he noticed that Yupei wasn't there. That night he found a message on his bedroom table. It was from Yupei and it said to meet her in the forest. Dart was excited to tell Yupei about his victories, so he rushed to see her. When he saw her, before he could say anything Yupei told him she was going to leave Alpha.

"My kingdom is under attack, and they need my brother's help... I might never come back," she said. Then she gave Dart a hug and a kiss on the cheek and ran away. Dart was stunned. This was the first time she had ever hugged him, but it felt cold and sorrowful. He dropped to the ground and stayed there for the rest of the night.

When he awoke, Dart didn't want to go back to Alpha. With Yupei gone, he had no reason to. He didn't know what else to do so he started running. He ran and ran and ended up deep in the forbidden forest.

"Young prince," Dart heard a voice behind him, "I'm here to help you. I can unlock your true power and give you all your desires in the world!" Dart turned around and in the fog making walls in the forest, he saw a knight in black armor.

"Any desire? Even to bring back Yupei?"

"Yes, anything," the knight answered. "Young prince, you have all the power in the world, but you will need my help."

"I don't understand," Dart said.

"Prince Dart, I am Beta, the Dark Knight."

That name sent chills down the prince's spine. Beta was his father's sworn enemy. He had tried to take over Alpha many times. His kingdom, just beyond the forest, was full of sadness and terror. Dart knew all of this, but he didn't care. All he wanted was to get Yupei back. He followed Beta deeper into the forest.

Beta taught Dart how to channel his sorrow and anger into his power. As Dart grew stronger and stronger, he began to challenge other knights for their titles and mightiest weapons. And the more he won, the more he wanted. He became reckless, greedy, and arrogant. He became a different person. After a while, even his desire to bring back Yupei faded.

Years passed and Dart became king of Alpha. Dart ordered his entire citizenry to build a castle of gold and silver just for him. He wanted farmers to give him their entire harvests. He wanted merchants to give him all the great things they had received from other kingdoms. And because everyone feared Dart's power, they obeyed.

After only two years, Alpha had changed. Trees were now stumps and the flowers had all died. The farmland had no more corn or wheat to harvest, and the rivers were polluted. The great knight, Vonde, was so disappointed he left to live in the kingdom of Vivid. Alpha was in chaos at the same time that Dart was in paradise, inside his castle of greed.

When Vonde went to Vivid he met Yupei. He told her what had happened in Alpha. Yupei didn't want to believe it. She was so worried about Dart that she asked Vonde to take her back to Alpha. And there she saw that the once-beautiful Alpha was now in terror. Throughout the kingdom she saw only broken and starving villages. When she arrived at the castle, she rushed to see Dart. As she approached his chamber door, Beta appeared from behind and took her away!

Vonde tried to stop him, but failed. He was too old to stop such a powerful knight. He needed Dart's help. Vonde demanded to be let into Dart's chamber, but the guards wouldn't allow it. Vonde didn't know what else to do so he battled his way in.

"King Dart, what happened? What happened to the good young prince I once knew?"

Dart replied, "This is the prince you knew, only now I have found my true power. I deserved more, and now I have everything!"

"King Dart, you also lost something," Vonde said. "You lost your heart. The purity I once gave you is gone."

"But I have everything—power, fortune, glory," said the prince.

"What about happiness? Do you feel happy?" Vonde asked.

"I… I… "

"Yupei has been kidnapped!" he yelled to Dart. Dart was startled but not discouraged. He asked Vonde to show him where Yupei had been taken. They set off together into the forbidden forest.

Vonde smiled. He knew that the old Dart was still in there.

They made it to a dark and chilly cave. In the shadows of this cave they saw a knight. Dart knew it was Beta.

"After helping me grow so strong, why are you doing this to me?" Dart asked.

"I made you strong and corrupt so you would throw your kingdom into chaos. This way, it would be easy for me to take over!"

"But why did you kidnap Yupei?" Dart asked angrily.

"I took Yupei here as bait. I knew you'd come to get her, and when you did, I would defeat you and make myself king of Alpha!"

He charged at Beta. Beta easily dodged and countered with a slash. Dart reeled, but Vonde defended Dart with his own blade. After a long, furious battle, Vonde and Dart found an open spot and attacked Beta, slashing away his sword and defeating him. They then tied him up and called for reinforcements.

Dart remained confused and scared. Suddenly he could not face

his people or Yupei. He told Vonde to find Yupei, and then ran out of the cave.

As soon as Yupei was untied, she chased after Dart. She finally caught up to him in the forest. They stood there for a moment. When Dart finally had the courage to turn around and face her, Yupei was right there. She slapped him and said, "What are you doing? Are you trying to run away because you made a mistake?"

"I… I… don't know what to do," Dart replied.

"Dart, I always liked you because you were kind and fun to be with. I think the people in the kingdom felt this way too."

Dart smiled bitterly.

"Even though Alpha is in bad shape right now, we could rebuild it. All you have to do is try!"

"You are right," Dart replied. Yupei smiled and hugged him. This was the second time Yupei had ever hugged him—this time it felt warm and joyful.

The next day, Dart returned all gold and foods he had taken from the people and began to rebuild Alpha. Although they didn't forgive him right away, people accepted his help and treated him as king.

He went from village to village to personally repair the damage. His people saw him working so hard and finally decided to forgive him. Dart and Yupei were together again and things slowly came to be like they used to.

At the end of one such day of work, Yupei challenged Dart to one of those games they used to play as children. And, as usual, he lost, but this time he got a kiss. ✳

THE LITTLE BLACK MOOSE

by Janie Ly

ILLUSTRATED BY ZACH ROSSMAN

In Springfield Forest, far from any city, all the animals liked to play baseball except for a little black moose whose name was Toby. He had big antlers, a small body, short hair, and long legs. He also had big white perfect teeth and big black round eyes. He never liked to play any sports—he only enjoyed looking at beautiful scenery. Since Toby never played baseball with the other animals, they thought he was weird.

One day, when Toby came out for recess, he sat by himself. "That moose is weird, he doesn't like baseball," said one of the pigs.

"What, he doesn't like baseball? Then I don't think I want to be his friend!" a bear exclaimed.

After the bear said that, everyone else in the forest agreed with him. Toby took a long walk after school. He felt so lonely and sad that he decided to go out to the city and far from the forest.

When he got there, it was night already. There were a lot of lights, tall buildings, and many food marts that he could go to. Toby was shocked to see how much scenery there was.

"*Wow,* this place is beautiful! This city definitely does not have anything to do with sports. It has lights, buildings, and cars; I could never get bored of it!" he said.

Toby spent a whole night looking at the city. But in the morning, Toby walked back to the forest. He felt a little stronger knowing that he did not need anyone to make him happy. As he was strolling through the woods, he saw a turtle who seemed to have trouble walking because he was as small as a bird, only he couldn't fly. Even small rocks seemed to be in his way. He had a big head, huge hands, enormous feet, a short tail, and a small shell. When Toby saw him, he felt bad, so he decided to ask if he needed some help.

"Hi, I'm Toby, what's your name?"

The turtle replied, "Hi, my name is Squirt."

"Do you want to hop on my back? I can bring you back to the forest."

Squirt said, "Sure, thanks. No one has ever been so nice to me."

"Really? I feel the same," replied Toby. "No one ever wanted to be my friend, because I don't like to play baseball. I like to go to the city and look at beautiful scenery."

"Really? The reason I don't have any friends is because I'm always too *slooow,*" answered Squirt.

"I know… let's be friends," said Toby.

Squirt was so happy that he opened up his arms and gave Toby a big fat hug.

Toby and Squirt headed back to the forest. As they were walking back, a squirrel popped up out of nowhere and asked for directions to the forest. "Um… Hi, excuse me. My name is Spalding and I was wondering if you guys know where the forest is? I got lost when I was looking for food. Could you show me the way back so I can go home?" Spalding was a hairy little squirrel. He had blue eyes and big buck teeth. He got lost very easily because he was never good with directions.

"Of course, if you'd like, you can hop on my back just like my friend here. By the way, my name is Toby and my friend here is Squirt. It's a pleasure to meet you."

"No, the pleasure's all mine," said Spalding. He slowly climbed up Toby's antlers and sat on his back next to Squirt.

As Toby walked along with his friends, a wild fox who had been hungry for the past few days spotted them. The fox was so hungry that he could eat all three of them. He snuck up on them as quiet as an insect. When the fox approached them, they were surprised and shocked.

The fox had wild, crazy hair. He had dirty claws and his clothes were torn and muddy all over. He had sharp brown teeth, a drooling long tongue, and evil looking eyes with red veins popping out. He always carried a side bag full of cookies to lure other animals so he could eat them.

"Oh, gosh, who are you?" asked Spalding. The fox walked around in a circle to see which one of them he should gobble up first.

The fox said in his voice, which was as deep as a cow's, "Well, well, well, what do we have here? A moose, a turtle, and a squirrel. Whom shall I eat first?" Toby ran with Squirt and Spalding on his

back to hide behind the bushes. But Spalding fell off, and when Toby and Squirt reached the bushes they quickly covered their eyes with their hands. The wild fox came up to Spalding and yelled, "Why don't I start with the squirrel. *Haha!*"

He grabbed the squirrel with his bare hands and when he was about to swallow him, the squirrel struggled and flopped around so the fox had trouble putting him in his drooling mouth. Then Spalding whispered, "If you let me go, I'll make you a deal!"

The fox asked, "What kind of deal are we talking about?"

"Well," said Spalding, "if you let me go, I promise to trick the little moose and the slow turtle for you so you can have them for lunch."

The wild, dirty-looking fox agreed and whispered back, "If you don't help me get them by midnight I will come and find you and have you for my dinner."

When Toby and Squirt did not see Spalding, they slowly tiptoed out from the bushes. They were surprised to see Spalding and the wild fox near a small tree. Toby saw them talking, but still he couldn't hear their conversation.

In a slight whisper, Spalding said to the fox, "Yes, sir, I promise. I will get them for you." When they were finished talking, the wild fox ran off into the bushes.

Toby and Squirt could not help but question Spalding. "What did the wild fox say to you? Is he going to come back for us?"

"Don't worry about a thing. It's all under control, OK?" Spalding said.

While they were heading back to the forest, Spalding had his hands on his head. He was wobbling dramatically. He said, "Wait, guys, I'm feeling really dizzy, can we stop for a few minutes so I can take a short rest?"

"Of course… But what's wrong? Are you OK?" asked Toby.

"Yeah, I'm fine, I just need to take a break, that's all," replied Spalding.

Since Toby and Squirt were busy taking care of Spalding, the wild fox quickly made a trail of cookies to try to trick them.

Spalding waited for at least ten minutes and led them to the cookies. He then said, "Hey, look. A trail of cookies. Are you guys hungry? I know I am, maybe that's why I felt so dizzy. Let's dig in."

As Toby and Squirt were following the trail and eating the cookies one by one, Spalding disappeared and the fox suddenly leapt out from the bushes. Toby and Squirt jumped with excitement and tried to run, but the fox caught Squirt. *"Haha*, I got you! It's all thanks to your little friend!"

Toby was shocked and speechless, but he stepped up to the fox and snatched Squirt right back from the wild fox's hand with his antlers. When Spalding saw this, he became so afraid that the fox was going to eat him instead that he decided to get Squirt back from Toby. He slowly approached Toby, tiptoeing like a snail, but as soon as he tried to pull Squirt from Toby's hands, Toby stopped him looking at Spalding with disappointment in his eyes.

He asked, "Why are you doing this? I thought we were friends!"

"I'm sorry, but I had no other choice. He was going to eat me," Spalding sadly explained.

"I'm sorry to tell you this, but we are no longer friends, so beat it!" Toby exclaimed. Toby was so filled with anger that he even scared the wild fox away. The fox tried his best to run as fast as a leopard. When Spalding saw how Toby was acting, he became afraid that Toby might hurt him as well, so he ran off behind the fox.

Toby thought about Spalding. He felt bad for scaring Spalding away. After all, he was trying to save his own life. So Toby and Squirt decided to go back to the woods to look for him. As they were looking around, they saw Spalding and the wild fox behind a bush. The fox was trying to eat Spalding, so Toby pulled Spalding from the fox. The wild fox was so afraid of Toby that he ran away and he was never seen or heard from again in Springfield Forest. Toby then said to Spalding, "I'm really sorry for scaring you away. I forgive you for doing what you did earlier. Can we be friends again?"

Spalding looked at Toby with tears in his eyes and said, "Toby, you are such a nice guy. I'm sorry for what I did and I will promise you that I will not do that again. I learned my lesson. Thank you so much for forgiving me. I also want to apologize to you, Squirt. I didn't mean to trick you. Will you forgive me?"

Squirt looked at Spalding with a serious face and said, "Wait, I thought we were friends already." They all laughed.

Spalding was so happy that he gave both Toby and Squirt huge hugs. Then all three of them decided to go on a long trip far away from foxes. *

HIDDEN IN THE HEART

by Allan Xue

ILLUSTRATED BY LART COGNAC BERLINER

Once, a big family of beavers lived on Woodstick River. Woodstick River had lots of trees and branches that could be used to make homes. Papa Beaver and Mama Beaver had moved here a long time ago and had raised Betty, Billy, Benny, Bobby, and Becky Beaver.

Betty was very greedy, and since she was the oldest, she had power over her siblings. Once, Papa Beaver had found some very shiny rocks and wanted to give them to his children. Betty volunteered to help, so Papa gave her all the rocks. Later when Papa asked, none of the other children had seen the rocks. Betty had hidden them all.

Billy Beaver was the second oldest. Since Billy was the oldest boy, he was supposed to look out for his siblings. If something bad happened Billy was always blamed for it. This made Billy very grumpy.

The third child was Benny Beaver. Benny was shy and quiet and was often left out. Benny was really nice but no one ever tried to get to know him so he was lonely. He hoped that he would find friends one day soon.

Bobby Beaver was the fourth. Bobby was very clever and he loved to play tricks on everyone. The family was so used to his pranks, though, that no one cared anymore. One time, Bobby put rocks in everyone's soup during dinner. When they noticed, the Beavers just picked the rocks out without the slightest shock. Bobby wanted new people to play pranks on.

Becky Beaver was the last of the bunch. Becky was a tiny toddler, but she was loud. Whenever she yelled, one could hear her from miles away.

One summer day, the Beaver family was at home when they heard a knock. Papa Beaver went to the door and saw a group of otters standing there. One big, strong otter walked up to Papa and said, "Hello there! My name is Otto Otter and this is my family. We were wondering if it would be OK if we moved in and became your neighbors." Papa happily said yes. He even offered to help the Otters get settled.

Everyone in the family reacted differently to the news. Betty thought that having more neighbors meant she would get more birthday presents. Billy thought the Otters might cause trouble and he would get blamed for it. Benny thought he might be able to find friends among the Otters. Becky had all sorts of questions to ask about the Otters, such as "Where did they come from?" and "How old are they?" And Bobby just wanted to play pranks on them.

The Otter family had fewer children than the Beaver family. Otto was the dad and Olivia was the mom. Oscar and Oliver were twin boys. The next day the two families decided to hold a big celebration together.

The day of the feast, Mama Beaver was in the kitchen making lots of food. Bobby and Becky peeked in and saw Mama Beaver cooking fish. Bobby saw his chance to play a prank on the Otters. Bobby told Becky to run in and distract Mama Beaver. He knew that otters love to eat fish, so he planned a dirty trick on them.

Becky ran in yelling like crazy. "Mama! Is the food ready yet? What are you making? Mama, it's so hot in here!" Becky went on and on and Mama finally turned to her. While Mama was distracted, Bobby crept up and dumped a bunch of salt on the fish. Bobby was giggling when he met Becky outside.

The feast took place in a big open grassland behind the forest. It was so well hidden, only Papa Beaver knew that it was there. Benny carried a big wooden tray filled with berries in all sorts of colors. When Benny sat the tray down next to the fish dish, he noticed something moving in the trees. It turned out to be Bobby and Becky. They seemed to be secretive so Benny knew something was wrong. As the celebration began, Benny decided to forget about Bobby and Becky and walked to where the Otters were sitting.

Only Oscar sat down because the rest of his family went to talk and get food. Benny was really shy and didn't know what to say. All he could come up with was a weak "Hi." Oscar was much braver than Benny and said, "Hi there! I'm Oscar! Have a seat." Before Benny or Oscar could say another word Oliver had returned with a plate of fish. Oliver didn't notice Benny and dug into the food. Benny was amazed as Oliver cleared his whole plate in just a few moments.

"You're scaring Benny, Oliver," said Oscar.

Oscar replied, "Sorry about that. I have never had fish that tasted and smelled so good! I love the salty taste. Your mom is such a great cook."

Becky's loud voice was then heard exclaiming, "How can he like it? You dumped salt all over it when Mama wasn't looking."

Of course, everyone heard Becky. Papa Beaver was really upset that Bobby and Becky tried to pull such a wicked prank. Papa apologized for Bobby's actions then he made Bobby apologize. After that, Bobby said he wouldn't play tricks anymore. The Otters were just glad nothing really bad had happened.

When the feast was almost over, Betty sat watching Benny and the Otters. Betty was jealous of Benny. She wanted Oscar and Oliver to be friends only with her. Oliver was getting more fish when Betty decided to take action. While Benny and Oscar were talking, Betty walked right into the conversation and started talking to Oscar about Watery Lake. Oscar loved the thought of swimming and started chatting with Betty. Betty noticed that Benny was really quiet, just staring at the floor.

Oscar said, "We should definitely check it out. Do you know where the lake is, Benny?" Betty was shocked. They asked Benny instead of her! Benny looked up happily and said yes. Oliver said, "Great! You can show it to us tomorrow!" Betty was furious and walked away.

The next day, Bobby was in his room thinking about another way to play a prank on the Otters. He had overheard Betty complaining about the Otters going to Watery Lake without her and Bobby had an idea. He said out loud, "I'll dig a hole in the trail to Watery Lake. The Otters won't see it if I cover it with leaves!" Just then, he thought he heard footsteps running out of the wooden house. Thinking he had imagined it, Bobby left for the trail.

Betty was over at the Otters' home trying to think of a way to go to Watery Lake with the Otters without Benny when Benny ran into the house, up the stairs, and straight to Oscar and Oliver. Betty wondered what they could be talking about when she got an idea.

"Papa Otter," she said. "Benny just came over. Why don't you have Benny help you build your new home?" But then Oscar asked, "But who will take us to Watery Lake?" Betty volunteered to do it in Benny's place. Benny didn't say anything, so it was settled. Betty left with the two Otter brothers feeling really good because her plan had worked!

Bobby, on the trail to Watery Lake, had just finished making his trap. He made it without a soft landing because he thought Oscar and Oliver were strong enough to take the fall and because he was too lazy to add leaves for cushioning.

Suddenly, he heard talking in the distance. Bobby hid behind some trees as the voices got closer. Bobby couldn't see who was coming yet but he heard someone say, "What a great day to go swimming!" Bobby saw that it was Oscar Otter heading down the trail. Oliver Otter was a few steps behind him. Bobby was feeling really good until he saw Betty trailing behind the Otters. He thought, What's she doing here? Just then, the two Otters seemed to get very excited and started jumping and skipping. Both of them jumped right over Bobby's trap!

Bobby was shocked. Now he realized that Betty was about to walk right into his trap! He saw no choice but to run out crying, "Betty, stop!" Betty did and looked surprised to see Bobby. She was just one step away from falling into the hole. The two Otters had heard Bobby as well and were coming back.

Betty asked, "Why did you tell me to stop?" Bobby was ashamed and explained his prank. Betty was shocked, but the Otters weren't.

"We knew that you set a trap for us, Bobby!" said Oliver. "Benny overheard you and told us!" So Bobby hadn't imagined hearing footsteps!

Bobby asked, "Then why didn't you tell Betty about it?" Oscar laughed and said that they knew Bobby wouldn't let Betty get hurt. Bobby now understood that he was the one that had ended up being tricked. Not only that but he'd get in a lot of trouble if Papa heard about this. The Otters said that they wouldn't say anything, but Betty was really angry. Sensing Betty's rage, Oscar decided that they all go to Watery Lake together and take a cool swim. With the swim, Betty calmed down and wasn't as mad anymore.

Tired after the swim and on the way back home, the group came back to the trap hole Bobby had made and he filled in the hole with leaves to make it safe. Betty thought that the trap had been cruel and she had almost fallen in, but Bobby had stopped her even if it meant he'd get in trouble.

From then on, Bobby would never play a prank again. He now used his creativity to find better ways to catch fish and to get firewood. Betty started sharing her belongings with others, including the pretty rocks that she had hidden before. And Benny would no longer be alone. He now lived a happy life with his friends Oscar and Oliver Otter.   ✳

IT NEVER WAS ABOUT KARTALINA

by Tenisha D. Miller

ILLUSTRATED BY MICK WIGGINS

Here I am, mighty and strong. It took a long time to figure out where I belong. My name is Kartalina, and I am mixed. I am a car *and* a bug. I wasn't always the prettiest thing in school, but now I am different. I believe in myself.

When I was real young, just a kid in the second grade, I came to a small private school for cars and bugs. We learned about the earth, special insects, and car engines. It was a school that only a few could get into. My first day was cold and rainy and my heart was beating to the same rhythm as the rain. I didn't know anyone and I didn't have any friends. All the kids in class were just one thing, either a car or a bug, and all were so pretty and handsome. I was the ugliest one because I was mixed. I have big spots on my face from my mom, Avis, who is a small ladybug, and I have long, windowlike eyes from my dad, Kinsman, who is a blue Chevrolet.

People teased and talked about me. One day, a girl made fun of my hair. She was a car named Alexis. She pulled my hair and said how hers was prettier and that she would hate to be me. She said I had the ugliest hair she'd ever seen. I just cried, then ran away. Sometimes the kids would act like they were my friends just so that they could eat the snacks that my mom packed for me. I let them. I didn't stand up for myself. I just sat there and watched. That was the only thing I could do. I knew if I stood up and said something they would all get mad.

One time, I was with my old friend Brandun, an Escalade truck. I thought I could trust him so we walked around the school at recess and he said, "So, Kartalina, why do you look so different?"

"Well, I have a mom that's a bug and my dad is car. I think I am really ugly. I hate this school and the kids here who are mean to me."

"Well, don't worry about not having any friends anymore," Brandun said. "I'm going to tell people what a good person you are, and you will have friends very soon."

"Thanks, Brandun, I really appreciate it."

After recess I heard Brandun telling Sofia about how my family wasn't as rich as the other families. He told them that when I came to the school my parents couldn't afford to get the good crayons, the ones with lots of colors and the sharpener at the bottom. Instead I had a ten-pack of crayons that broke if I colored too hard. Sofia laughed in my face. After, everyone asked Brandun why Sofia was laughing and he told them. The whole class laughed in my face. Still, I didn't do anything but cry.

I thought it was my parents' fault I had no friends, because they created me and they sent me to school with normal kids, when they could have homeschooled me. I cried every day when I went home and I told them that it was all their fault. But crying wouldn't solve anything. I was ugly and that wasn't going to change, so each school day there was sadness.

One day a new kid named Cliffardo came to school and he looked like me. He had the same spots on his face and legs as I did. His hair was short with spikes and he had long, window eyes just like mine. He was also a car mixed with a bug. I was so happy to meet him. I felt a little weird, though, when I noticed how he was so happy. I'd see him every day making friends and talking to the other kids. I wanted Cliffardo to be my best friend.

When I told him everyone made fun of me, he said, "Kartalina, that won't happen anymore. I'll help you. I was too scared to stand up for myself and I always let people tease me. But they don't anymore. I have something to give you that will help you out."

He pulled a shiny box out of his backpack. I didn't know what it was but I wondered why he gave it to me. He told me that this gift had been found by his old best friend in Haiti and that he wanted to give it to his new best friend, me! He opened the box and took out a little blue hair tie. It looked brand-new. I turned around, blinked my eyes, and Cliffardo was gone. I didn't see where he went, but later that night I noticed the hair tie was already in my hair, in a high ponytail with lots of pretty rubber bands. I had curls coming out of my ponytail and bangs in the front.

Cliffardo and I played together and ate our snacks together. I felt when I was with him that nothing could go wrong.

One day Cliffardo's friend Ricky, who was a mosquito, came up to us. "Eeew, Cliffardo. Why do you play with her? She is so ugly and stupid nobody wants to be her friend."

With sadness in his voice, Cliffardo said, "Ricky, why did you say that to her? That isn't nice."

I ran the corner, turning around to let out all my tears, but the tears just wouldn't come. I tried to scream at Ricky and tell him that was very mean, but I just couldn't get the courage. Then I turned back around and I noticed my hair was different. It was wrapped up in a bun high in the air, covered up with a spiderweb, and Ricky was caught inside the spiderweb in my hair!

I called Cliffardo that night.

"I was just wondering what happened today. Do you know how Ricky got caught up in that hair tie and the web?"

"No, I really don't know what happened."

"All I remember," I said, "was that I wanted to cry and was going to yell, but I looked up and there he was, all wrapped up."

"You know, maybe you have magical powers to pay back the people that are mean to you."

"No, Cliffardo. I'm not that powerful. It couldn't have been me."

Days passed without Ricky ever coming back to school.

Another day, during recess, Cliffardo and I sat on the bench and ate our snacks. That was when Tenoriea, Wesley, Sterlin, and Stanley, who were all bumblebees, came up to me, took my snacks, and ran away with them. Tenoriea and Sterlin sang a song in my ear while Wesley and Stanley ate my snacks. They kept buzzing…

Kartalina, Kartalina, so dirty and mean.
We eat your snacks and hit you. You're such an ugly thing!
You will never have a real friend. Cliffardo really hates you.

You'll never have a boyfriend and no one will ever date you!"

"Stop it! Don't be mean to her," said Cliffardo.

In a small voice, I said, "You guys give me back my snacks. I want them back now."

I turned around because I didn't want them to see the fear in my face. Cliffardo said, "Don't you understand, Kart? You have so much more power than you know you have. If you just trust yourself, you will see…"

As soon as I turned back around my ponytail was wrapped up in a bun again and the bumblebees were floating in the air screaming, tied up in a spiderweb. It was weird. After, whenever someone teased me I always saw them tied in a web.

I still didn't understand what was going on until the last week of school, when the two biggest and meanest girls, named Nnekarema and Chrislana, came up to me. Nnekarema was a limousine and Chrislana was a butterfly. I was coloring a picture of my sister, my mom, and me all together. It was very pretty. You couldn't help but love it. Nnekarema snatched the picture and Chrislana drew all over it, messing up everything. They ripped up my picture and said, "What is this picture? It looks uglier than your face!" I wanted to punish those girls. Cliffardo wasn't around. I couldn't handle it on my own but I had to.

So I screamed in a loud voice, "Stop it, I won't let you guys mess with me anymore!"

I took my picture and made it look pretty again. I didn't cry, and I didn't run away. I faced the problem. It felt good to do that. They saw how angry I was, and tried to run away, but I didn't let them.

I turned around and then they were tied up! This time they were hanging with two hair ties. I couldn't believe my eyes. I started to think, How could this have happened? But I didn't know.

I thought back to the first time that Cliffardo and I met. Then I remembered how he gave me the hair tie and told me it would keep all my problems wrapped up forever. Every time I turned around it was the hair tie in my ponytail that would tie them up, but it was me who was able to stand up to them by believing in myself. It wasn't long after that Cliffardo had to move again and leave the school. I never got to know why he had to leave, and I never found out why he gave me the hair tie and chose me to become strong like him, but I do know he was my true friend.

Then one day I went swimming and I almost lost the hair tie. I nearly drowned trying to find it and then someone had to pick me up out of the water. To my surprise he looked just like Cliffardo. I couldn't tell if it was him or not because my eyes were filled with water. He had the same spots on his legs, but I cleared my eyes and found out that it wasn't him. It was just my imagination that he was coming to save me again. He even rescued my hair tie, but I learned I didn't need it anymore. I took it off and placed it in a box.

I will keep it on my shelf until I find someone else who needs it. So now here I am, mighty and strong, though it took a long time to figure out where I belong.

Wait a minute… The classroom door opens and here comes a new kid with the same spots that I have. Her name is Tenisha. She is mixed too. She is part caterpillar and part brown BMW. She has long legs and big windowlike eyes that remind me so much of mine. This will be the start of something new. ✳

PAIGE LEARNS A LESSON

by Brenda Chen

ILLUSTRATED BY MARIA FORDE

When Paige was eleven years old and shy, she wanted to make friends at school but didn't know how.

One day, Paige walked home from school, went inside, and said, "Mom, Dad! I'm home!" Her mom and dad were in the living room watching the news. Paige stood near them. They were still watching the TV, not even looking at her.

That's sad that Mom and Dad don't see me, she thought. I'll draw a picture to feel happier. I feel like drawing a small, fuzzy, purple teddy bear with cute ears that stick out on top of his round face. When she finished her drawing, Paige started her homework.

Paige walked to the dinner table and started listening to what the family was talking about.

Her sister, Harmony, said, "I was in the library for three hours today. I wanted to keep studying to get everything correct on my math test next week."

"My day was busier than yours," her mom said. "I was at a meeting for William at school this morning and rushed back to the clothing store to fold at least thirty piles of clothes."

"My office had a mountain of mail to sort through," her dad said.

This is weird, Paige thought. They're not talking to me. Is it *me*? She continued to eat in silence.

One night soon after, Paige was in her room doing math homework when she heard Harmony and her brother, William, yelling at each other.

Harmony said, "At least I get better grades than you!"

William said back, "I don't ever want to be like you!"

Paige sat quietly at the desk in her room and thought, What are they yelling about? I'll just cover my ears.

Suddenly, a teddy bear wearing a top hat with short, fuzzy purple fur appeared out of nowhere and climbed up Paige's chair onto her desk. The bear tapped her on the shoulder. Paige looked up.

"I'm Ernest the Bear," he said in a confident voice. He stretched out his small, soft, and fuzzy paw and shook her hand.

"I'm Paige… Are you really here or am I dreaming?"

Ernest replied, "I am here from Magicalbearland to help you when you need it. You can come to me to tell me anything. I will always care and I will help you to use your courage."

"Huh?" Paige said.

"Courage to do what you want, like, to ask for a sleepover with your friends or learn new things about people." Then Ernest the Bear asked her why she did not talk to her family.

Paige responded, "I want to but I can't. The other day I tried to talk about my day at the dinner table but they just ignored me. I tried leaving them alone and going back to my room, but then I hear William and Harmony yelling. I just want my family to know I'm here and talk to me—it just feels like I'm invisible."

"Does this only happen at home?" Ernest asked.

"Going to school gets me away from home for some of the day, but the kids at school tease me about my long, curly red hair. They say I hide behind it."

"Why do you hide behind your hair?"

"I feel like my hair protects me when it's down."

Ernest smiled. "I think you should try something new with your hair and see what happens… Remember, Paige, I will be here to help you when you need it. My home is beneath your bed—my own bear cave. No one can see me but you."

The next morning Paige's mom knocked hard on her door. "Time to get ready for school, Paige!"

Paige put on her school clothes, ate goopy oatmeal, and waited outside for the yellow bus. When it came she sat next to her best friend, Anna. Paige had been friends with Anna Lark since the first day of kindergarten. Today Anna saw something new about Paige.

She asked, "Did you cut your hair over the weekend? It looks different."

Paige said, "Nah… Today I had the time to make my hair nice. It wasn't easy getting my red curls up in a ponytail. Does it look OK?"

"Yeah! It's so different for you, though."

"Do you think the kids will stop pulling my hair?" Paige asked.

"I really hope so. I mean, I guess we'll see," Anna said.

"Did you do the art homework last night?"

Anna spoke sadly, "You know I'm not as good at art as you are. I need help drawing my tree." Anna pulled out her drawing and handed it to Paige.

"It's not done. Color would make it better. Use my colored pencils, but give them back to me tomorrow," Paige said.

"OK." Anna thanked her.

When they got to school, kids were standing outside playing tag. Paige got off the bus last, after Anna. All the kids stopped playing with each other and looked at Paige.

Paige said, "Anna, they're actually looking at me!"

"They're also not teasing you. Let's get to class and see if they try to pull your hair today."

In class, the teacher said to Paige, "That's a good hairstyle on you! I'm glad you wore it up today."

Throughout the day, boys kept staring at Paige. Paige also collected notes from girls asking her if she'd like to play tag with them during recess.

She brought Anna along with her and they had fun. "We should play tag again tomorrow." Paige smiled.

After school, Paige went home skipping. "Mommy, Daddy! I had a great day at school!" Paige said in a loud voice when she got home.

Mom said, "Paige, we're watching the news right now." Paige walked slowly to her room, looking sad. She found Ernest sitting on the bed close to the window. Paige went over to hug him.

The bear asked, "What is making you feel bad now? Did you have a bad day at school?"

"No, school was good. The other kids liked how I wore my hair today. I don't understand why Mommy and Daddy want me to stay away from them," she said.

"Are you sure this has to do with you?" asked Ernest. "They are just tired from working all day. Don't be afraid to talk to them."

"I can try making them some hot chocolate. Do you think that would help them feel better?" Paige asked.

"That would be nice!" Ernest agreed.

Paige went to the kitchen, opened the cabinet, and took out two big mugs. Then she used a mix to make hot chocolate in the microwave. Paige took one cup at a time to her parents.

"Why, thank you, Paige," her dad said.

Her mom said, "That was sweet of you. What made you want to do something like this?"

"Well I—I hardly talk to you anymore," Paige said.

Her dad said, "I think you might be lonely. Is that right?"

Paige nodded her head. Then her mom said sweetly, "I'm baking peanut butter cookies after dinner. Do you want to help?"

"Yeah, Mom," Paige said. "I miss baking cookies with you."

Later, when it was time for bed, Paige was proud of herself for what she had done that day. She brought Ernest a plate of cookies and milk. She found him under the bed in his cave.

"Ernest, I was looking for you! Wow, it looks nice in here! I just finished baking cookies with my mom, and I brought you some."

"I can't wait to try one. Were you afraid of talking to your parents?" Ernest asked.

"I was scared at first, but after I did I felt proud of myself."

He said, "Are you ready to try talking to your brother and sister?"

"I don't think so. It's scary when I go by their rooms and hear loud music. What should I do?" Paige replied.

"Just knock on their doors and see what happens," Ernest said.

Another day at school went by, and Paige was slowly becoming more confident about talking in class.

That night Paige went to her sister's door and knocked. Harmony opened the door and said, "Is there something you want?"

Paige asked, "Could you help me with my homework?"

"I'm not sure if I can," Harmony replied. "I'm busy studying for my math midterm. It's tomorrow."

Paige frowned. "Oh. All right," she said, turning away.

Then Harmony smiled. "I can help you with your homework later. Come back at nine. I might be done by then."

When Paige went back, Harmony told her to come in and asked, "What homework do you need help with?"

"Math," Paige said.

"My best subject," Harmony said.

Paige looked around and saw the walls were covered in certificates for her achievements in math and for having the best grades every semester.

"You have so many awards!" Paige said.

Harmony told her, "It's because I study all the time. I want to do well on every homework assignment. William is jealous because I do better in school than he does. Have you ever thought about joining the math club?"

"No. I am way better at art than math," Paige answered.

"That's like William," Harmony said, "and how he really enjoys rock music. I try not to listen to music too much, so I can really focus on my homework. But classical music and opera calm me down when I am stressed."

"I want to listen to that!"

"I'll let you borrow one of my classical CDs, but we need to get your homework done first."

When they were finished, Paige asked, "Why do you and William fight so much?"

"Oh. We used to get along well. He used to protect me from bullies, but when I started high school I told him I was OK on my own and he's been angry at me ever since. He thinks I'm weird for studying all the time and I think he needs to care more about school."

"I think you two should talk," Paige suggested.

Then she went back to her room. She told Ernest, "I talked to Harmony and got help with my math homework!"

Ernest responded, "I'm very proud of you."

"Thanks! I'm happy for myself too," she said.

Then Paige decided to try talking to William. She went up to his door and looked at the sign that said KNOCK IF YOU REALLY CARE.

Paige opened the door slowly. She could see nothing but darkness in his room. She went in and turned on the light. William was sitting down facing the wall with his radio on. Though the music sounded nice, what the song was saying made no sense to her. He turned his head and looked at her like he was mad.

"Hi," Paige squeaked out.

"Why do I need to talk to you?" William said.

Paige replied, "Because I am your little sister and I was just wondering what you were doing."

William replied, "I'm just listening to my favorite alternative rock station, which might give a little girl like you nightmares. I'm writing lyrics for a new song too."

"I never hear you sing. I hear people screaming like they're angry about something. Is that you?"

"No, Paige, I don't sing. I just write songs for my band," he said.

"You're in a band?" Paige asked.

"Yeah, I try to write songs all the time." He stood up and pulled out an acoustic guitar. "Did you know I play the guitar?"

Paige stuttered, "No, I—"

"Well, there are actually a lot of things you don't know about. For starters, I like rock music, and there are many kinds of rock. Have you heard of grunge, metal, punk, alternative… ?"

"I've never heard of any of those before… "

"Then you have to listen to one of my songs!" William started to play. It was slow and melodic. Paige liked the sound and the words.

"That's cool!" Paige exclaimed. "How do you play that thing?"

"My guitar? Grab a chair and I'll give you a short lesson—some beginner chords and stuff… "

Paige walked back to her room late that night feeling happy. Ernest the bear told her, "Paige, I am amazed at the work you've done. You've grown so much… You won't need me anymore."

This made Paige sad, but she understood that she was not alone—she had people that cared about her and wanted to teach her things. All she had to do was talk to them.

Ernest said good-bye, giving her one last hug. "I am going back to Magicalbearland now, where I can tell the other bears that I helped a special girl."

"Ernest, you taught me that I shouldn't be afraid to be myself around people. That is true courage… " Paige said and smiled.

Soon Paige made more friends at school with kids that also enjoyed art as much as she and Anna did. They even started their own art club, which Paige became president of. She also started spending time with kids after school. She even had a sleepover at her house.

When the school year ended, Paige went on vacation with her family. Paige and her family took many pictures to remember their vacation, though it was the time they spent with each other that Paige remembered the most. ✳

SUPER LITTLE JIMMY

by Kevin Yu

ILLUSTRATED BY CHRIS PEW

Little Jimmy was eight years old and he didn't like his school at all. He didn't have many friends. The other kids didn't like him and everyone bullied him. He had a bad attitude too. Sometimes Jimmy would bump into other kids without saying sorry. And when teachers asked him questions, he wouldn't answer back if he was in a bad mood, so they would send him to the office. And little Jimmy wasn't patient either. He got mad easily when small problems occurred.

At home, he argued with his dad. They didn't get along very well. Jimmy would never argue with his mom, because Jimmy respected his mom a great deal. She was the one at home all day doing household chores or babysitting the neighbors' kids

Jimmy loved to pretend that he could fly and had super strength. His room was full of cartoon heroes—pictures that he drew when he was bored. His favorite superhero was Superman. He even dressed up as Superman on Halloween. In each of his drawings, Superman was very muscular and strong looking. More than anything, Jimmy wanted to become a superhero himself.

One day at school, he almost got into a fight with another student. When he got home, he asked his mom if she could give him powers. She said, "Each person has his own power, his own unique talent." She told him he had to find his power himself. Jimmy got mad and ran out of the house.

While he wandered around the neighborhood looking at the stars and daydreaming, he saw a shiny little butterfly floating about. Jimmy went after it and accidentally ran into traffic, failing to notice a big truck barreling down the road. The truck blew its horn and screeched to a halt five inches from little Jimmy. But Jimmy didn't notice. He touched the shiny butterfly. As he cupped it in his hands the butterfly read the little boy's thoughts and knew that he wanted the power to be strong and intimidating.

The butterfly told Jimmy, "If you want to be a superhero, you have to earn the power yourself." Jimmy needed to change his attitude and learn to be patient. Jimmy gladly made the promise and thanked the butterfly, then went straight back home.

When he got home, his mom had been crying so much that the rug was wet. Jimmy then made a promise to her that he would never run away from home again. His mom was relieved. She was willing to lose everything but not her family. After this disaster, Jimmy went to his room to sleep.

The next morning, Jimmy woke up feeling really hungry, maybe because he had taken a long walk the night before. He ate breakfast and had to get to school on his own because his mom had gone out to buy groceries. When Jimmy got to the park, the school bus had already left. He decided to run really fast so he wouldn't be late. As he was running he saw cars on the freeway moving slowly, and he felt nothing but wind. Slowly he realized he had a power—super speed. Jimmy couldn't believe his wish was coming true.

On the way to school, he saw a driver going the wrong way down the road. Jimmy tried to stop him from crashing into other cars. He flew into the air, and landed back down with a big stomp. His body had turned into titanium, so heavy that the roads cracked. Jimmy then stopped the cars with his superhuman strength. He was so strong that he lifted a car with one hand to get people out from underneath with the other. Then and there, he didn't know what was going on, but he knew he now had many new powers—speed, strength, and the ability to fly. And these powers were as cool as he imagined them to be.

Then Jimmy ran to school and into his classroom just as the bell rang. During class, he looked out the window and saw smoke coming from his neighborhood. He asked the teacher if he could go to the bathroom so he could actually run to the incident.

Once he got there, he thought of what he could do to help. He broke the fire hydrant and used the water to put out the fire. After the flames were extinguished, he tried to save the people that were trapped inside. He put his arms around them to heal their burn wounds. Jimmy's arms were full of warmth, healing people's cuts from bleeding, and keeping them from panicking about the fire. He hugged everyone, so they could all be healed.

Even though he wanted to use the powers for fun, he remembered what the butterfly had said: "Earn the power yourself." Now little Jimmy was staring to understand. Whenever he helped other people, his powers would pop up. Jimmy became brave and mature—mature enough to become a real hero. Throughout the town, everyone was cheering for Jimmy, shouting, "Yay, little boy! Yay!"

Jimmy had became popular at the age of eight because of the many lives he had saved. He couldn't believe it. He'd become a new person who cared for others and was helpful. And Jimmy was well respected once the news spread. He was someone everyone admired.

In the morning, Jimmy was so proud of what he had done that he fell off his bed. When Jimmy got up, he felt like a regular kid. He jumped, but not too high, and stomped, but not too hard. Nothing happened. As Jimmy woke up, he saw the shiny butterfly again in his room. Slowly, the butterfly flew out the window. Jimmy now remembered what the butterfly had said: "If you are good to others, people will respect you. That's how you will earn your powers."

He realized each power represented something about him. Because of his super speed, he was not late to class. Because he could fly high in the sky, he could easily see and understand things. His titanium body helped him stand up for himself. His super strength helped him take action. And last but not least, his healing arms protected others from getting hurt. Now he understood what his mom had told him earlier: "Each person has his own powers."

Jimmy started talking to his dad that day, and his dad respected him by listening to Jimmy's opinions. They were acting like friends. From then on, Jimmy didn't get mad so easily anymore. Even when someone took his favorite comic book and ripped the cover off, Jimmy just told the person not to do it again. He went to school extremely happy and said hi to everyone. His classmates could tell that there was something different about him too, so they began to respect little Jimmy. His new powers came from the heart. ✳

BAXTER'S TALE OF FREEDOM

by Allison Lee

ILLUSTRATED BY JANE WATTENBERG

Baxter Bam heard the alarm ring. It was time for Baxter, a little six-year-old sea turtle, and all the other sea creatures in the ocean to clean King Eel's castle. Baxter liked the castle because it had floors made out of gold from sunken ships, funny pictures of old eels on the walls, and secret hiding places in all the rooms where Baxter and his best friend, a mermaid named Dora with a beautiful tail of glittery rainbow-colored scales, could hide and play together. Baxter hated cleaning the castle because there were mean bodyguard eels everywhere.

Baxter's mom always told him not to listen to all the mean words the bodyguard eels said to him. "Stop worrying so much about those old eels," said Baxter's mom. "It doesn't matter how big and strong you are. You can be anything you want if you try hard enough."

"I want to be the best dodge shell player in the whole ocean!" said Baxter.

"Then stop worrying and start practicing!"

This morning, Baxter and Dora were in the king's master bedroom fixing the bed and putting the royal robes away. King Eel's bed was made out of sponges and shiny shells. His robes were made out of beautifully colored seed weeds. Even though King Eel had

pictures of her amazing tail all over the castle walls, Dora always made Baxter laugh by pretending to be King Eel. "Hey! Look at me. I'm Mr. King Eel! Go clean that room, you little munchkin! Go wipe the floor, you stinky piece of sponge!" said Dora

When Baxter and Dora had laughed enough, they came out of the hiding place. A bodyguard eel came in the room and said, "Dora, you stinky housemaid! The king would like to have a word with you." Baxter was too worried about Dora to say anything back to the eel and stayed behind as she left.

There was still much work to be done and Baxter was by himself fixing King Eel's bed. He became very tired and decided to take a nap in the comfy bed. A few minutes later, the king's son, Bust, came in and yelled, "What is wrong with you? Who do you think you are sleeping in my father's bed? You have your own small, broken bed to sleep on in your ugly house! Hurry and get up, you dinky fungus!"

Baxter thought it was time to stand up for himself and screamed back at Bust, "I'm not a dinky fungus. You're just a fat old piece of rope! I hope one day you'll know how it feels to be criticized and looked down on! You and your father better watch out because you guys will soon be overthrown if you keep on treating all the sea creatures like sand!"

Bust got mad because no one in his entire life had ever yelled at him like that before. Bust was not intimidated at all because he was so much bigger than Baxter. He was not fat like his father. Bust had muscles that were popping out of his long, slim body. He was six feet long and two feet thick. Bust's dark and large figure scared most of the sea creatures in the ocean because they had never seen an eel that humongous before. So Bust said, "You better take back what you said. I'm gonna tell my dad about what you said to me. He will kick you and your mom out of your house and take all of your family's money!" Baxter stormed out of the castle and swam home crying.

Baxter came home, but he didn't find his mom. Instead, he found all his family's money missing! "Oh no! Now the king has taken all my money! What's next?" Baxter felt so terrible he cried even more. Luckily, Baxter's mom walked in just then to comfort him.

Baxter told her everything. "It's OK, Baxter, honey. Don't listen to those mean eels. And don't worry about the money. Just follow what your heart tells you to do. If you can't take it anymore, we can move to the Indian Ocean, where it's like a small family." Baxter didn't want to run away from the problems, but to solve them.

Baxter marched back to the castle fearlessly. As he got near to the end of the king's hallway, he heard laughing and giggling around the corner. Someone was having fun and eating treats together. Baxter listened carefully, and he thought he heard Dora talking to King Eel. Baxter was confused and whispered to himself, "Dora? She can't be here talking and laughing with King Eel." Baxter got closer to the dining room so that he could get a better view.

"Wow, thanks for the money, Dora. I couldn't have done it without you," said the king.

"No problem. I never thought it was so easy to steal from a stupid little sea turtle. Good golly, he's so annoying! I showed him that you are the boss. And where's my reward?" asked Dora angrily.

King Eel was startled and said, "Oh! That's right! Your new collection of rainbow pearls. Don't worry. You'll get them first thing tomorrow. You are so intimidating and strong! You are so beautiful… I hope you'll never change."

Dora then said with disgust, "Umm… just give me my reward. And don't ever call me that again, you old bag!"

As soon as Baxter knew for sure that Dora was working for King Eel, he was heartbroken. He had lost his best friend and felt like floating around in the ocean freely with no soul, like a jellyfish. He decided to get even with King Eel. When Dora and King Eel left, Baxter snuck into King Eel's bedroom and stole all of his precious jewels.

When King Eel discovered the jewels were gone, he burned up inside. He and Dora stormed out of the castle and went straight to Baxter's house.

"Open up, you dinky fungus! You're really going to get it this time!" yelled the king. King Eel couldn't wait any longer and whipped down the door with his tail.

Baxter got mad and screamed at King Eel, saying, "What are you doing? You can't just come here and break my door. Who do you think you are! We are all equal! How does it feel to lose things that are important to you! Does it feel good? I don't think so!" Baxter yelled so loud that all the sea creatures heard.

They were inspired by a little turtle standing up to an old eel. They never thought anyone would ever stand up to King Eel. "Hey! Leave the poor little boy alone. Why don't you pick on someone your own size? If you want him, you'll have to get through me!" said a shark.

"Ha ha ha ha! That's funny. You really think you can scare me? I've been king of this ocean even before you were born, you stinky piece of sponge!" said King Eel.

"Hey, you guys! Stop yelling at each other. We're not going to get anywhere if we just keep on yelling. I know a way to settle this that everyone can agree on," said Baxter.

"And what do you plan to do, you dinky fungus?" said King Eel.

Baxter had an idea in his head all along and said, "How about a game of dodge shell?" The game of dodge shell was played throughout the ocean for fun and to solve complicated problems. Baxter said, "If you, Dora, and all the bodyguard eels win, all the sea creatures and I will continue cleaning your castle. But if all the sea creatures and I win, you, Dora, and all the bodyguard eels will leave this part of the ocean forever! I've had enough of your attitude, and none of us can take it anymore!"

King Eel thought about the plan carefully and agreed. "Well, that is a good idea, but Dora and I are not going to play with you losers. You forgot one of the most powerful creatures here, my son! Only my strong son, Bust, and the bodyguard eels are going to play. I trained my son for years, and he is the best dodge shell player I have ever seen in my life. I beat your father the first time, and now my son will beat you. This will mark the second generation of the victory of eels over sea turtles."

The game started quickly because everyone was very excited to see who would win. All the sea creatures and Baxter were on one side, and Bust and the bodyguard eels were on the other side. Bust threw the shell first and knocked a blowfish out. The blowfish was hit so hard that his round body flew ten feet away. When Bust threw the ball with his tail, everybody could see the bulging muscles popping out of his tail. One by one, the sea creatures got out. Baxter

was the only one left, and there were only a few bodyguard eels left including Bust.

Baxter got scared, and his mind went blank. Baxter saw his mom and the rest of the sea creatures cheering for him, and the strategies of dodging and throwing the shell quickly came to his mind. Baxter felt the spirit of everybody and threw the shell hard like a gun shooting a bullet. Soon only Bust was left. It was up to Baxter and Bust to see who would win.

"Let's go, son. You can beat this stupid turtle easily. How hard is it to beat a six-year-old?" said King Eel. Bust flung the shell to Baxter, but Baxter swam away quickly. He swam as fast as he could to get a nice throw, but he tripped on his foot! The shell rolled on slowly over to the other side.

"Ha ha ha. It's over now, you dinky fungus!" said Bust. The shell that rolled out of Baxter's hand did not bounce off the wall, so the shell was still in play. If a player from the opposing team picked it up, he would be out. Bust picked it up, and everybody started shouting and cheering for Baxter. "Ha, you foolish eel. The shell was still in play, and you picked it up. You're out now!" shouted Baxter with joy.

"Jiminy Crickets! I can't believe you guys won. All the eels, Dora, Bust, and I will leave this kingdom forever. You will never see us again, for we are going to live deep down on the ocean floor. Are you happy now, you scrawny shrimps?" said the king with fury. All the creatures celebrated while the old king left. Baxter was sad to see Dora leave, but he didn't want a friend that he couldn't trust.

As years passed by, all the creatures in the ocean knew Baxter Bam. All the children looked up to him because he stood up for what was right and he was considered the dodge shell champion because he won everyone freedom from King Eel.　　　＊

CHEWS CAREFULLY

by Victoria Chen

ILLUSTRATED BY RACHELL SUMPTER

There was once a tooth named Pearl who lived with her mom in a small village called Incisorville. Pearl was extremely white and smooth and really tiny. She was a shy tooth but always wore a smile.

One day, Pearl and her mom moved to another village, Molarville. There, Pearl started fourth grade at a new school. On the school bus the first day, Pearl saw other teeth, cookies, chocolate, apples, tomatoes, and many other kids. Pearl was different from any other tooth there. They all had their own groups of friends, so Pearl sat alone.

When the bus stopped in front of the school, all the kids ran to their classes. Pearl stood outside looking at the school. Finally, she walked into the noisy hallway, feeling scared and nervous. She didn't know what the students would think of her and was afraid she wouldn't make any friends. In her classroom, she saw some kids from the bus, but she sat down without saying anything.

The teacher, Ms. Skip, introduced Pearl, saying, "Everyone be nice to Pearl and show her around the school when you have time."

Pearl smiled and softly said hello to the class.

At recess, Pearl sat alone and watched the others play. She hummed to herself and ate the cereal her mom had packed for her snack. Then two kids walked over to Pearl and introduced themselves. They were a cookie named Bites and a chocolate named Darkman. Bites was a huge cookie with a deep voice. Wherever he walked, a trail of crumbs followed him. Darkman was a tiny chocolate with a pointed head and a babylike voice.

"New here in school, are ya? You'll have a lot of fun here. Come play with us whenever you want," said Bites. He looked down at Pearl's bag of cereal and then turned toward Darkman and said, "I'm hungry. Darkman, are you hungry? Do you have any food with you right now?"

Darkman said, "I'm hungry too, but I don't have any food today." Pearl offered them some of hers. Bites gobbled down almost the entire bag.

Pearl said, "You two must be really hungry!"

Bites responded, "Yeah… you could say that."

Then Bites and Darkman talked with Pearl about school and how she was adjusting. They also played kickball together. After that, the three sat together in class every day.

One day, Pearl wondered why no other kids ever talked to her. Whenever she talked to anyone, they acted as if they were afraid of her and walked away.

Pearl asked Bites and Darkman, "How come nobody talks to me besides you two? Is it because I'm different and nobody likes me?"

Bites said, "No, of course not. You are different in a way—you're a lot whiter than the other teeth in the school. Maybe that's why they don't talk to you."

Darkman said, "We're not like the others. We don't mind that you're a little different." His eyes glinted, "And besides, you also bring the biggest lunches!"

Pearl smiled and said, "You two are the greatest friends ever."

The next day, Pearl arrived at school earlier than usual. She heard Bites's and Darkman's voices in the hallway. She wanted to know what they talked about with other kids, so she hid and watched. She saw a little grape whose legs were shaking. Bites stood right in front of the grape, holding him up by his shirt.

Bites said, "Give me your lunch money, kid! And all the food you have!" And he shoved the grape against the wall. Darkman was standing beside Bites with a smirk on his face.

The little grape threw the money and food on the floor and quickly ran away. Pearl was shocked to see her two friends act that way. She became angry and jumped out, scaring Bites and Darkman.

Pearl asked, "Why did you guys take money from the little kid? How can you be so mean?"

Bites answered, "We were only playing with him, we weren't being mean at all."

Pearl got angrier and said, "Did you see the look on that grape's face? I don't think you guys were playing! I can't believe you guys are so mean and then you lie to me about it."

Bites said, "So what if the kid was scared? He's a chicken. He's afraid of everything."

Pearl said, "You're the chicken! I'm not going to be friends with you guys anymore. You're both horrible. I'm going to tell Ms. Skip what you two have been doing to other kids."

Bites responded, "If you dare to tell the teacher anything, you're going to be sorry."

Darkman said, "Did you think we really liked you? We were only nice because we saw how much food you brought to school."

Pearl's eyes filled with tears. She ran to the bathroom and burst into tears. She thought about everything that had happened and decided to tell Ms. Skip. When she did, Ms. Skip went to talk to the principal, who called Bites and Darkman into his office.

The principal said angrily, "If I ever hear of you two bullying other kids again, you guys are going to be kicked out of school!"

Darkman and Bites responded, "We're sorry! We won't do it again."

"During recess and lunch, you two can only play where Ms. Skip can see you. I will not tolerate this behavior in this school. Now, get back to class," the principal boomed.

As the two walked back into class, Bites stared at Pearl with mean, squinting eyes. When Pearl saw him, she was scared and looked away.

During recess the next day, Pearl sat alone. An apple named Bright and a celery named Stick sat down and offered Pearl some snacks. Bright was a chubby, short, red apple with huge eyes. Stick was a skinny, tall celery stick who talked really fast. Stick and Bright knew what had happened between Pearl, Bites, and Darkman.

Bright asked, "Are you OK? Don't be sad about Bites and Darkman. They're bullies and have always been. They are part of the

'junk' food group. Forget them and come play kickball with us."

"I can't believe I ever thought they were my friends. They are so mean, and I thought they were nice," responded Pearl.

Sticks told Pearl that she could be friends with them and play with them whenever she liked.

But Pearl was afraid of the same thing happening again. She didn't know whom to trust anymore.

Several days passed, and Pearl didn't talk to anyone. Bright and Stick asked her every day if she wanted to play, but she would just shake her head and look away.

One day, Pearl's mom asked her how school was going, and Pearl told her that she was afraid to trust anyone.

Mom said, "I know it's really hard to trust somebody, especially after what you've gone through. But do you want to have friends? You don't want to continue sitting alone every day, do you?"

"Of course not, but what can I do? I can't be friends with just anyone who talks to me," responded Pearl.

"That's true, but you can talk to your classmates first. You can begin by saying hi or talking about schoolwork. Get to know your classmates a little better. Then you won't choose the wrong friends," said Mom.

"Yeah, that's a good idea," said Pearl.

Mom kissed her and said, "Just remember, you'll never know what kind of person someone is until you try to get to know them."

"I know, Mommy. Thank you," Pearl said.

The next day, Pearl asked other students in the class what they thought about Stick and Bright. Everyone said how helpful and nice the two were.

At lunch, when Bright and Stick again asked Pearl if she wanted to play with them, Pearl decided to try being friends with them. As the three got to know each other, they found out that they loved similar things. Pearl loved to sing, Bright knew how to play the piano, and Stick knew how to dance. During lunch they would get together in the music room with Bright playing the piano, Stick dancing, and Pearl singing.

One day, Pearl bumped into Bites and Darkman on the playground.

Bites said, "We're going to beat you up for telling on us!"

Pearl was nervous but responded, "I'm not scared of you two."

At that moment, Bright, Stick, and some other kids walked over and told the boys to stop bothering Pearl. Pearl had so many friends now and Bites and Darkman knew they were outnumbered. They slid away.

That night, Mom asked Pearl about school.

"Bites and Darkman tried to scare me during recess, but Bright and the others were there to support me. They are really nice. You were right, Mommy. Getting to know someone is really important. Now I have the coolest friends ever!" ✳

XINDERELLA

by Mona Zhao

ILLUSTRATED BY JACOB MAGRAW-MICKELSON

In a small town there lived a group of hardworking people. Everyone liked to help out in this community, except for two girls and their brother. These spoiled brats never worked a day in their lives—they just lived off their father's money. As the father got old and sick, he promised to split his fortune among his daughters and his son. He also had a third daughter, whom he loved, but not as much as the others. She would not inherit any of his money.

I am that man's third daughter and my name is Xinderella. My mother died giving birth to me so I have always been thought of as a sin to the family. Lolitia and Addiena, my two mean sisters, nicknamed me Xin because it sounds like "sin." It's unfortunate because Xinderella sounds so pretty.

Lolitia and Addiena have always talked down to me but my older brother, Ian, used to be nice to me. One year, he got me a present for Christmas. My sisters told him if he continued being nice to me he would be sorry. After that, Ian didn't treat me nicely. I had never felt like more of an outsider in my own family.

At first, I thought my father, like my siblings, didn't love me. Every night when I brought his supper, milk and pecan cookies, he would continue reading his newspaper and tell me to go back to my room.

But one time my father came home early from work and saw me roasting a chicken, doing my sisters' laundry, and cleaning the kitchen, all at the same time. He thought I needed a helper, and I did hope to have another person in the house. Maybe he or she could be my friend since I didn't have any. So Father kindly gave Lolitia and Addiena each two hundred dollars to hire a servant. But they were greedy and took the money to buy clothes and CDs.

Father didn't do anything about it. Every time he was about to defend me, perhaps even show me love, he thought of his beloved wife. He looked at me, his eyes sparkled, then dulled. He remembered how he and Mother met, got married, and had their first child. But he was also thinking about how she passed away, how she might still be alive if I hadn't been born. He blamed his unhappiness on me.

I had to wash, scrub, and cook while my sisters went to dances, parties, and malls. Lolitia and Addiena wanted the mansion spotless, especially their own rooms. They forced me to use cleaning products that would burn my hands, even when I used gloves. The toilet bleach smelled so bad I almost passed out when I used it.

My sisters wouldn't let me wear their hand-me-downs so once a month I would go to a thrift shop in the darkest alley of town. I found peace in the alley. I couldn't hear Addiena and Lolitia bragging and laughing about the newest dresses they bought or the fun parties they were invited to.

I was happiest from nine in the morning to three in the afternoon, when my sisters were at school. I got to read my favorite books like *Snow White*, *Sleeping Beauty*, and *The Little Mermaid*. My very favorite was story was "Cinderella." I couldn't understand some of the words because I never went to school, so I would guess the meaning of the story by looking at the drawings. In my room I could laugh, sing, and dance, without anyone making fun on me.

As time passed, Father aged and weakened. One morning he coughed nonstop. He asked Ian and Lolitia and Addiena to get him water and medication. Ian said, "Pop, I'm sort of late for band practice, so tell Addiena or Lolitia to get it." He ran out the door like an ant on a hot pan.

Father then called for Addiena and Lolitia. "Sorry, Daddy, we have to go to school or we'll be late," they giggled. Father thought they went to school, but I knew they were going to a party.

I was the only one left so I cared for him as I had my whole life. I brought him water and medication constantly, fluffed his pillow day and night, and gave him sponge baths. In those days, he finally realized how wrong he had been about me. I was not a sin but a blessing. Mother gave up her life so that I could take care of my father. It seemed too late, though, to make up for the hatred he had seemed to have for me. But on his deathbed I stood next to him and he told me this:

"My daughter, though I didn't love you as I was supposed to, I indeed feel guilty about it. Don't be afraid to grab hold of true love if it comes your way. Free yourself and love yourself. I gave all my money to your siblings but I know you deserve more than money could buy. Here is a necklace I gave to your mother when we first met." The necklace was made of shining silver and had a crystal bead on it. "She told me to pass it on to my most beloved child." He took his last breath, and passed away.

After Father died Ian moved out of the house to go to college. He couldn't stand Addiena and Lolitia. Every time he tried to be nice to me, Lolitia and Addiena would glare at him.

Now it was just Addiena and Lolitia, and I had to follow their rules. One day I went out to buy salad and steak for their dinner and wheat bread with a slice of Spam for myself. In the supermarket I overheard a woman talking about a prom at her daughter's school. She spoke of a supercute, sweet boy who was the captain of the basketball team. I suddenly remembered Father's last words. "Don't be afraid to grab hold of true love if it comes your way." Though I didn't have the slightest idea what true love felt like I was eager and curious to meet this boy.

The following night I asked my sisters about prom. Addiena grinned and said she knew nothing about it. Lolitia said I couldn't go because I didn't attend the school and because I needed to be pretty to get in. That night, while Addiena and Lolitia slept, I sat in front of the little window in my room praying that I could go to the prom and meet my prince.

To prepare for the dance Addiena and Lolitia went shopping for dresses, some of which they would never wear. They also bought shoes, diamond necklaces, and matching earrings. The night of the prom Addiena wore a long black dress with white beads sewn in the shape of snow flowers and a shimmery necklace, beautiful earrings, and a diamond bracelet.

Lolitia wore a short white dress with black roses around her head. She didn't wear jewelry because she thought it looked too normal—she wore jewelry every day. I decided to sneak into the dance. The problem was, I didn't have a beautiful dress or jewelry. I had nothing but leftover roses from Lolitia and beads from Addiena. But I made a necklace out of what I had.

By the time I left the house wearing an old, dirty dress, it was almost midnight. I ran ten blocks to the hotel where the prom was being held. I couldn't wait to meet the boy the lady at the grocery store had been talking about. But who was he? What did he look like? Did he have a girlfriend? I knew when our eyes met on the dance floor that he would invite me to dance. The whole world would watch us with admiration.

But when I stood in front of the Kitop Hotel, the security guards thought I was homeless and wouldn't let me in. I didn't give up. I snuck into the hotel through the back door, which led through a garden to the dance. I climbed the fence to meet my prince.

The garden had roses and carnations, red and pink ribbons, and there were fountains everywhere. It was absolutely amazing. I turned and looked toward the end of it, where there stood the most handsome man I had ever seen. It was the man I had been waiting for my whole life. I wanted to scream, but my voice got stuck in my throat. All I could do was stand still and stare, like a fan to her idol.

Suddenly he turned and spotted me. He yelled, "Guards, who let this dirty, repulsive girl into the prom? Her feet are dirtying up the ground and her breath is contaminating the air!" From behind the water fountain came a guard. I pushed him aside and ran, my mind blank. I was not sure how long I ran or where I went. I had thought that if I met the boy we would fall in love and live happily ever after, like Cinderella.

Instead of praying and crying, I thought about who I was. After that night, I would be different. The prince and the prom were gone, but I still had the necklace my father had given me, the one with the crystal bead. This is what mattered.

The next morning at breakfast, Addiena and Lolitia talked about how fun the prom had been and how handsome the boys were, hoping it would make me jealous. But I had seen how handsome the boys were, and how beautifully the prom was decorated. I had never thought about abandoning my sisters, but I knew it was time to leave, even if it meant I would be alone.

I headed to a new town. I walked for many days. When I rested, I dreamed about the future. I saw that Ian and his band would become famous. I envisioned that Addiena and Lolitia would spend all the money Father left for them and that they would end up scrubbing store windows at the mall where they used to shop. They would even use the same cleaning products they made me use.

At last, I saw Father. "Don't be afraid to grab hold of true love if it comes your way." I could feel wetness on my cheek, and I heard words come out of my mouth. "Father, I never blamed you for not loving me enough. My whole life I haven't loved myself. I understand why you wanted me to find true love. It would set me free from the family. But, Father, I don't need to find true love. I can set myself free. I am not Xin any more. I am Xinderella. The name Xinderella means happiness and living with joy and freedom. This is how Mother would want it." I felt a sudden warmness on my face and when I woke up, the tears on my cheek had dried. I saw a big orangey sun rising. I smiled and kept walking toward the bright sun, following the road to a new city, and a new life ahead. ✳

A JOURNEY OF HOPE:
HOW ONE MAN'S DREAM BECAME A REALITY

by **Kurtis Wong**

ILLUSTRATED BY HANNAH STOUFFER

Guy wasn't the richest or best looking but he was a boy of pride. Guy was thirteen years old and living in the city of Canton, China. Growing up, Guy was full of laughter and energy.

One day, Guy went for a walk. As he passed a toy store, something shiny caught his attention: it was a toy-size battleship, with an American flag on it.

"Wow, I can't believe this was made over in America!" he exclaimed. Guy was captivated by all things American because in Guy's opinion, that's where all the new technology and new inventions were. Guy even dreamed of going to America to live when he grew up. He didn't want to spend the rest of his life in China. He wanted to make something of himself, and in America he could make it happen. America was the place to make a good living and to fulfill his dreams of a successful life. Excited by his new plan, Guy ran all the way home to speak to his father.

He said, "Father, I know I am only thirteen but I must ask you a serious question: may I go to America to find a better life?"

"Why, Guy? You can have a successful life here," said his father. "How will you pay for the trip? It costs a lot to go to America."

"I think America is the place for me," Guy said with confidence. "I heard that you can have nothing and make it into something. If you let me borrow five hundred dollars, I will have enough to buy a ticket. I can use the leftover money to make even more when I am in America and with that, I will pay you back."

"All right Guy, you can go to America. I don't want to see you suffer. I will loan you some money and you will live with your uncle in Boston," his father said.

"Thank you for giving me this opportunity, Father," Guy said. "I will make you proud."

A week later, Guy set sail. It was not a boat of comfort or luxury, but it was the boat that would get him to America. It traveled slowly and it was so crowded that Guy had no room to roam. No matter where he was, he felt like he couldn't really stretch or move his arms, so he spent most of his time crammed in his sleeping quarters.

After twenty-five grueling days at sea, the boat arrived in the port of Boston. Guy had finally made it to America. He got off the boat and started to look around. He had never seen such beautiful, tall buildings before. He saw steaming factories everywhere, and also things rolling on wheels, carrying humans—cars! And compared to Canton, the streets of America were clean and there was less pollution. Guy was thrilled—everything was different, even the people. For the first time ever, he was in a place populated by Caucasians and he was amazed at the number of them. Even the clothes that these Caucasians wore were different. They wore "Western" pants and jackets and dresses, and nothing like what most of the people in Canton wore.

But what was most amazing of all were the ships. They were just like the toy Guy had seen back in China but here they were humongous and real. He was so excited. He felt like he could spend the rest of his life in America.

Finally, Guy was composed enough to start off for his relative's house. Though his father had written out the directions for him, when he looked at them, he realized that he couldn't read the English street signs so none of it made any sense. When he tried to get help, all the Caucasians looked at him funny. Eventually, he saw someone who looked Chinese, but dressed in Westernized clothes. He got up the courage to approach him and asked the man for directions. "Excuse me, sir, do you know this address?"

"It is right around that corner," the man said, pointing. "Turn left at the second street and you will find it. Good luck!"

"Thank you," Guy said. He followed the man's directions until he came upon a Chinese restaurant. "This is strange," said Guy, "this should be where Uncle's house is." He entered the restaurant to ask for further directions and inside, he saw his father's brother.

"Uncle!" Guy said with surprise.

"Guy!" replied his uncle. Uncle could tell by the look on Guy's face that he was disturbed. He said, "This is where we live, Guy. We work *and* live here so get used to it."

Guy had never pictured living in a restaurant. He had been expecting the "American dream"—lots of money and a nice house. But he had to wake up to reality. He would live in the back of the restaurant with the rest of his relatives.

Guy worked at the restaurant twelve hours a day, every day, washing dishes. Guy was getting used to life in America, but he also realized that living there wasn't as easy or pleasurable as he had thought. "Go back to your old country! No outsiders allowed here!" the Caucasians said to Guy. These comments hurt Guy. Guy wondered if it was simply because he was not the same skin color as them. He told Uncle about the incidents and that they made him feel inferior to the Caucasians. "Everything will get better, Guy, trust me," his uncle said.

One of the good things about America was that Guy was able to attend English school and he picked up the language quickly. It was exciting that he could speak English and he soon learned enough to get around in the big city of Boston. With his new language, Guy felt more confident in his ability to survive in America. Still, he missed his family.

After a little while, Guy's homesickness became too much. He thought a long time about all his efforts to get to America but one day he finally decided that it was time to go back to China. On that evening, he called his uncle into the back room and told him his decision. After telling Uncle about leaving, he sobbed, "Thank you for all you've done, Uncle. I really appreciate the home and all the opportunities you gave me."

Wiping his tears, Uncle said, "Just don't forget to come back and visit me." Guy wrote a letter to his family informing them of his return and with the money given to him by his uncle, Guy bought a ticket for the next boat back to Canton.

On the return, the trip took twenty days. Guy finally reached his homeland and in addition to his family, a surprise awaited him at the dock. His father introduced him to the most beautiful girl that he had ever seen.

"Son, this is your bride, May."

Guy was shocked. Finally, he stammered, "Hi, May, it is a pleasure to meet you."

"It is my pleasure," May replied.

Two weeks later, they had a beautiful wedding with both families and many friends attending. At the end of the night, Guy asked May if she would live in the United States.

"I'd love to, Guy," May answered. "America will be a start in the right direction."

Guy and his wife moved to America but this time they moved to the city of San Francisco. The city was far more beautiful than Boston and Guy and May settled in Chinatown as soon as they got there. Six years later, Guy and May had three children and they were very happy. Guy's family received a good education and all the opportunities they needed to fulfill the American Dream. And when Guy bought his first car, he felt even more proud; he now owned a small piece of the technology that first drew him to America.

Ten years later, as a successful man, Guy looked back on his life with pride and amazement. He had never given up or stopped believing in himself and because of that, he and his family prospered. America and all of Guy's hard work and dreams had paid off in prosperity and happiness. ✳

SAY MY NAME

by Min Li

ILLUSTRATED BY JACOB MAGRAW-MICKELSON

In a beautiful orphanage there lived a special eight-year-old boy. His name was Say My Name.

On the first day of school the teacher, Ms. So What, started by taking attendance. She called out, "Say My Name!"

The class replied, "So What!"

The teacher asked, "What?"

The students said, "You said to say your name, so we did."

"Oh no, not me. Who is Say My Name?"

"That's me! My name is Say My Name, So What," Say My Name explained.

"What did you say? Don't give me that attitude, mister," said Ms. So What.

"I was just saying your name, So What," Say My Name said.

"Oh, OK," said Ms. So What, feeling embarrassed.

The teacher and the class stared at him. Everyone was wondering what kind of name it was. Japanese? Korean? Spanish, German, or Alien? No one knew. Say My Name stared back at the teacher wondering what kind of name hers was too. Her cheeks turned red like a tomato, so she looked away and continued with attendance.

After school, while walking to the bus stop, one of Say My Name's classmates politely said, "Hi, my name is Wow and this is my mommy!"

"Why did you say 'Wow'? Did you see something interesting?" Say My Name asked.

"Wow is my name," he said.

"Oh, sorry. My name is Say My Name!" he said.

"What kind of name is it? If you don't mind my asking," Wow's mother said.

"I don't mind. It's a… it's… to tell you the truth, I don't know," Say My Name said as they reached the bus stop.

"No problem. Do you go home and go to school by yourself every day?" Wow's mother asked.

"Yeah," Say My Name said.

"Wow!" said Wow.

"Why did you say your name?" Say My Name asked.

"No, I was really amazed, that's all," Wow said.

"Um, OK, if you say so," Say My Name said.

The two boys talked and laughed all the way. Say My Name went home to the orphanage and started on his homework. He kept thinking about his classmate Wow and his mommy; how they held hands and went home together. Say My Name wanted to feel that warmness too, but in the orphanage there were only nuns, no parents. Say My Name hoped that someday he would get adopted and be able to live in a real home with parents.

At the same time, Say My Name was happy living with his orphan friends. The orphanage looked old from the outside, but the inside looked like an art museum. It had three floors, a kitchen, a living room, lots of bedrooms, a backyard full of flowers and grass, a swing, a seesaw and a slide, and a fence surrounding it so that nobody could climb in. Inside the house, all the orphans' baby pictures hung on the wall. Looking at those photos always brought back memories. Say My Name never wanted to leave them, but what about getting adopted?

The second day in school Wow saw Say My Name and ran up to him and said, "Hi, remember me? I'm Wow!" Wow was really excited to see Say My Name and was eager to play with him. The two boys grew closer each day and became good buddies.

One day Wow came to class with a sad, hanging face. Say My Name asked him what had happened but Wow didn't want to talk about it. Say My Name wondered how he could cheer his friend up and finally thought of something. He grabbed some food from the cafeteria and started putting it on himself. He taped lettuce behind his ears, tomato slices on his mouth, eggs over his eyes and a long noodle hanging from his nose. He walked up to Wow and showed it to him. Wow stared at him for a minute and then laughed really hard.

After school, Say My Name asked Wow why his mom hadn't picked him up that day. Wow said he had told his mom not to come anymore because he wanted to take the bus with Say My Name.

"Aw, thanks!" Say My Name said. After a while, Say My Name asked again why Wow had been sad earlier, but Wow really didn't want to say.

"You will feel better if you talk to someone about it," Say My Name said. Wow started wondering.

Then Wow told him how his parents argued a lot when his father got back from work. His father was a busy man and didn't eat dinner and it made his mother worried. Wow's mom tried everything she could to help but Wow's dad never listened, but continued to work. Say My Name understood how Wow felt and gave him some advice. He told Wow to tell his parents that their arguments make him feel sad and that they affected his relationship with them and his mood in school.

The next day, Wow ran up to Say My Name, gave him a hug, and thanked him for the advice. "It worked really well!" Wow said.

They both continued to have a lot of fun with each other no matter where they went or what they did. And at night they talked on the phone.

On the phone one time, Say My Name had told Wow that he wanted to help anyone who had difficulties. So the next day of school, Wow secretly told all the students that Say My Name could solve many problems. After school, lots of students came up to Say My Name and asked him for advice. After Say My Name was done with all his classmates' problems, he walked up to Wow and thanked him.

"It's no big deal. You helped me too, right? Besides, we're best friends!" said Wow.

Say My Name's classmates treated Say My Name to some ice cream for giving them such great advice. After eating the ice cream and saying good-bye to his classmates, he went home.

Say My Name walked in the gate of the orphanage and saw two

adults, a woman and a man. The supervisor smiled at Say My Name and told him, "These are your new adoptive parents."

Say My Name didn't know what to say. His body was frozen and his mouth was open as wide as a tiger's yawn. The day had finally come, and he was excited, but at the same time he was wondering whether he should stay with his friends or leave with his adoptive parents.

"Say My Name! Say My Name, wake up," the supervisor said.

"We are awake, Mr. Supervisor, but why do you want us to say your name?" asked Mrs. and Mr. I Don't Know.

"No, not my name. Here, let me introduce you," the supervisor said. "This boy's name is Say My Name."

"Oh! Hi, Say My Name. I am Mrs. I Don't Know," she said.

"You don't know your name?" Say My Name asked.

"No, my name is I Don't Know," Mrs. I Don't Know said.

"Oh, I see, ha ha!" Say My Name said.

The supervisor told both parents to come with him to sign the adoption forms for Say My Name, so they followed. While they were in the office all the children from the orphanage came up to him and congratulated him. Then the supervisor and the two parents came back out. The supervisor said that he could leave with his adoptive parents and told him to get his luggage, so he did. But while packing his belongings, Say My Name thought about the happy memories he had in the orphanage. He thought about how every one of his friends looked after one another and how he felt the warmness of a family there even without parents. He stopped packing and ran down the stairs to the supervisor and asked if he could stay in the orphanage.

"But why, Say My Name?" the supervisor and Mr. I Don't Know asked.

"Because I want to stay here with my friends and go to school with Wow, and, especially, I don't want to leave this home after I promised to be the orphanage's counselor," Say My Name said. "It's really fun helping my classmates and I really like doing it."

"You can still do the same thing with your adoptive parents," the supervisor said.

"But it's different. I, I really don't want to leave. This is my family," Say My Name said.

Every one of his friends, even the supervisor and both Mr. and Mrs. I Don't Know, cried as he spoke.

"It's OK if Say My Name wants to stay. We respect his decision," Mrs. I Don't Know said to the supervisor.

Say My Name gave them a big hug and thanked them.

"Well, we should be going now," Mrs. I Don't Know said.

"No, wait, why don't you both stay here and have dinner with us and spend some time with Say My Name?" the supervisor asked.

"That's a great idea!" Mr. I Don't Know said.

"Great!" I will prepare the dinner!" the supervisor said.

"I'll help too!" Say My Name offered.

When the food was cooked, Say My Name brought it all out. It all smelled so good and tasty. After everyone was done eating Mrs. I Don't Know said, "'Bye, everyone, we will come back next week and visit, if that's OK?"

"Yay!" the children yelled.

Say My Name walked both of his adoptive parents to the door and gave them both another big hug and Mrs. and Mr. I Don't Know gave him a kiss on the cheek. He went back inside the house and everyone gave him a big hug and the supervisor gave him a high-five.

The next day on the way to school, Wow came up to Say My Name and said hi. Say My Name didn't say anything.

"What's wrong?" Wow asked.

"I got adopted," Say My Name said quietly.

"Really?" Wow said. "Are you living with your new parents?"

"No, I'm not living with them," Say My Name said. "I made a promise to the supervisor that I would be the orphanage's counselor and… " Say My Name stopped.

"And what? Come on, say it," Wow asked anxiously.

"I don't want to leave, um, you," Say My Name said finally.

"Really, Say My Name?" Wow asked.

"Yes, I really don't want to leave you because you said we are best friends, and it's true. I just didn't want to leave without my best friend," Say My Name explained with tears in his eyes.

Wow didn't know what to say. He hugged Say My Name and said, "Thank you!"

Even though Say My Name knew every one of his friends in the orphanage was going to leave one day, he didn't care. All he wanted was to help them solve their problems and be with them every day until they got adopted.

Say My Name became the counselor of the orphanage and Wow stayed by his side to help him as an assistant. They both took care of the problems that people had, then they would go to the park and play every day, like they used to after school.   ✱

MY MOM IS A WITCH!

by Barry Au

ILLUSTRATED BY JON ADAMS

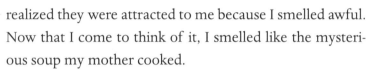

Before I went to middle school, I would sit in my room every day reading books about sorcerers. I did not read them because everybody else in the world was reading them. I read them because I had started to wonder about the scary things in my house, like the frogs hanging in the freezer. The boiling pot in the middle of my mother's bedroom, the wands positioned flat in my mother's drawer, the many bottles of potions in the cupboard, even my mother, all terrified me. And our pitch-black cat gave me chills every time it passed by me. I came to wonder if my family used witchcraft. That was the only assumption I could make about it—that it was all closely related to the things in the sorcerer books I had read.

My name is Alexander Lee and when I was a fourth-grader, I would eat alone in the cafeteria away from all the other kids. Everybody at school stayed far away from me. During class, the other students would move their desks to the corners, isolating me from the rest of the class. The only friends I had at school were the flies that hovered around my head. The flies did not bother me. They were the only company I had and they had been with me forever. I counted exactly five flies around my head daily. In the third grade, I realized they were attracted to me because I smelled awful. Now that I come to think of it, I smelled like the mysterious soup my mother cooked.

I lived with Father, Mother, and my older sister, Jamie, in a small apartment in Chinatown. My building stood thirteen stories high. The hallway and elevator lights were dim. I started to believe that my mother chose this creepy building because she wanted to distract Jamie and me from her own creepiness.

My mother was skinny and tall and had hideously long fingernails. She had a scratchy and high-pitched voice, and was loud. She had all the power in the family. She made us do all of the work in the house while she sat, watched television, and ate. She was truly a cantankerous and venom-tongued old lady. She even shouted at us when we brushed our teeth for less than one minute and fifty-nine seconds—she expected us to brush our teeth for exactly two minutes.

My father had a stumpy and plumpish body. I pitied his appearance. Whenever we played basketball, I wouldn't jump, because he was too short to shoot the ball over my head. He was bucktoothed and powerless compared to my mother. And his voice was meek and quiet when he spoke, and he only spoke twenty words a day! Fa-

ther was not like the fathers I saw at the parent-teacher conference. All of the other dads I saw stood taller than their kids. As for me, I was taller than my father.

Jamie was an eighth-grader with great wisdom and curiosity. Despite her great wisdom, she was lazy in school and never did her work. Jamie did not like school, because she also had no friends. Perhaps she smelled awful too. She would get disgracefully bad grades at school, then get yelled at by Mother.

One day, while I sat quietly in my room and read my sorcery book, Mother entered the room and disrupted me. "Alexander Lee, why are you reading this book?" she said with her wicked voice.

"Mom, it's part of my homew—" Before I could finish my sentence, she snatched the book away from my hands and waved so I could not reach it.

"You know reading is bad for you. It gives you all sorts of ideas. Now go clean the bathroom." She pointed to the bathroom and I went slowly.

As I walked into the bathroom, Jamie came into the house. I closed the bathroom door behind me to work. As I was cleaning the bathroom, Jamie and my mother argued about school. Mother said her report card was bad. Then, a green light flashed through the cracks around the door. I opened the door quickly and found that Jamie and her possessions were gone. Her Mickey Mouse clock was gone. Her shoes on the shoe rack vanished, and her clothes in our room too. I had the chills. I wanted to tell Father about what happened, but I knew he was powerless to Mother.

Days passed, but Jamie never came back. Not only did I have no friends at school, I no longer had an older sister. I went home every day and hoped that Jamie would come back so I would not be alone any longer.

The following day there was someone new at school. Her name was Kawai. She was just like me, smelly and friendless. She told me she had transferred from a wizard school far away—in England. And she told me that she did not know she was a wizard until her parents told her. To find out, I tried a couple of her wizard tricks. I found out that I was a wizard too! Kawai told me the only way I could be a wizard was if my father or mother were a wizard, witch, or warlock.

When my father picked me up from school, I was afraid to ask him about wizardry, but fear would not stop me from asking. Kawai walked with me. We entered the car and I sat in the passenger seat.

"Father, I have a question." I was eager to find an answer, whether or not it was the one I was looking for.

"What is it, Alex?" he said with effort, as if he had lost his voice.

"Are you a wizard?" He remained silent.

"Keep asking him," Kawai whispered softly into my right ear from the backseat.

"Father, you know there are weird things in the house." I saw sweat run down his cheeks. He was as uncomfortable as I was.

"I have magic powers." I lied to see if he would answer me.

"There are things that I did not want to tell you until you were older," he said, "but I think you are old enough now to know who we really are." That was the longest sentence I had ever heard from him. He told me that Jamie had been banished into another dimension because she had found out that Mother was a witch. All this time, I thought she had moved out because of her bad grades.

The next day, Kawai took me to her house because I wanted her to teach me some magic, especially the basic spells that would turn my mother good. As we practiced, I feared that Father would also be banished into another dimension because he had told me about Mother's secret.

Later that day, Kawai and I went to my apartment. We found out that my father had indeed been banished. My legs were shaking violently because I never thought I would rebel against Mother. I thought about the consequences. Would I be grounded for the rest of my life? Would I have to live in another dimension? We knocked on Mother's door and it opened. She stood there and before she could lift up her wand to cast a spell, I quickly said, "Kumaza Kuku," and froze her on the spot.

Kawai and I cast another spell. "Haza Mutootoo, let the power of evilness leave you!" This spell was not a special spell to banish her into another dimension, but a spell to turn her good.

She twitched and woke up immediately. "What a nice shirt, Alex," she said. That was the nicest comment I had ever heard from her! Then she noticed that everybody was gone, and she realized the evilness she had caused.

"Jabba Dee Doo, bring back the lost at no price and no cost."

Suddenly, Jamie and Father appeared, standing in the position they had been in when Mother had banished them.

I was happy that they came back. I had a sister again to teach me new things every day. And a father to attend the parent-teacher conference at school and play basketball with me.

As for me, I now live a better life—a normal life. My family is now whole and nothing can separate us. Mother no longer yells at us. Instead, she encourages us to read. I no longer smell like the soup my mother used to make with the big pot in her room. And without the awful smell, I made new friends at school. In fact, the pot is gone, the bottles of potion have disappeared, the old books were burned and never seen again, the wands were broken in half, and our cat ran away during the duel between Mother and me. We agreed not to use our magic.

Well, except me. I use my magic whenever the bus is late, or if it rains too long. ✳

MY HAIR FRED

by Jonathan Jeung

ILLUSTRATED BY SETH MATARESE

My name is Asklepios, and as if I'm not made fun of enough for that, my hair is always going in funny directions. I can never control it. I'm in the third grade, and it's hard getting a good reputation at school with hair looking like a cat's hairball. But I still try.

I'm just an average student at school. Well, I think I'm average. I'm not so sure anymore because my dad talks about baseball averages and I don't play baseball. And math has averages too but I'm not good at math. Maybe I'm not average. Maybe I'm just ordinary.

My hair, on the other hand, is far from ordinary. Ever since I can remember, it has looked like an explosion on top of my head. Even my cousin's dog is more controllable. I think it's because they gave him a name. Now every time they say his name, he listens. That's why I named my hair. I call it Frederic Hairican III—Fred for short. But he still doesn't listen to me. We've had a few adventures though.

Once I was running around and pretending that I was on a spaceship heading for Mars. Fred was on my head, so I made him into a helmet. As usual, I couldn't control Fred, and he covered my face. I couldn't see that we were going to crash. Fred fell into my face, I fell into the laundry, and my brother fell into laughter.

My brother has really different hair than I do. His hair is a little straight and a little shiny with some curls at the end. I always wonder how such good hair can belong to someone so bad. But my mom says that bad people become bald. I hope that his hair falls out for good when he grows up. Dad's bald too. Was he bad when he was a child?

Fred, that uncontrollable mess that sits on my head, always keeps me warm, and he always scares my aunt when she touches him. She thinks there's something living in him. I just think her hands are so wrinkly that she is actually touching her own hand.

Sometimes when I wake up and go to the bathroom to wash my face and brush my teeth, I use my mom's comb and try to make Fred look good. It never works. The only time I remember having nice hair was during my cousin's wedding. My mom put this gooey stuff in my hair. It was so cold that Fred straightened like magic. I couldn't stop looking at it. My older brother said, "Stop or you're going to break a mirror with your face."

I told him, "Well, I can't break any, because you already broke all the mirrors in the world." He got so mad that he gave me a noogie, and next thing I knew, my hair was messy again.

At the wedding, Uncle George fell asleep, and the cat ate his hair. I was shocked. My mom told me it was a *"to-pay."* "How much did the cat have *to pay* to get to eat that?" I asked. My mom laughed at me. I think my mom knows something that I don't.

My mom says that I should be happy for my hair. She told me that I should love my hair because Daddy lost all of his. I think it just moved down to his back. He took off his shirt once when he was lying down on our carpet, and I almost walked on him. You would have thought he was the carpet too if you were there.

I see my dad shaving sometimes. Every time he goes into the bathroom to shave, he comes out with funny pieces of paper all over his chin. They look like little daisies sprouting out of his skin. I wonder if I'm going to get pieces of paper growing on my face when I grow up.

Every day at school, my friends' hair is always the same, while Fred always looks like a war zone.

I used to think girls had cooties, but in school I have three girlfriends. They say that I dress funny, but they always play with my hair. I went home with a ponytail once. My older brother made fun of me for weeks!

In school we learned about this Greek guy with the same name as me. Asklepios was the Greek god of healing and his father, Apollo, was the Greek god of the sun. One of my classmates said, "If you're the god of healing, why don't you heal your hair?"

"Haha," I said. "I tried, but Apollo blew it up again." Everyone started to laugh.

I even dream about my hair. Once I dreamt that Fred got so big that he became a jungle. I was cutting through my hairs like they were vines until they grabbed me. I tried to kick my way out, but I ended up falling off my bed and waking up.

That morning, I noticed that my alarm clock hadn't gone off yet. I had another thirty minutes to make Fred look good before the bus arrived. I had all the tools I needed—a comb, a brush, hair spray, gel, mousse, a blow dryer, and even superglue.

My mom brushes her hair all the time. She uses a big, round brush, so I decided to use it too. I started out at the tips of my hair. Then I tried brushing it up, down, and all around, but it made Fred look fuzzier. "That didn't work," I said to myself. "Sorry, Fred."

I used the comb then. Oop… Ee… Ah… Ugh… *Snap!* Oops, I broke the comb in half. It looked like my older brother wasn't going to be combing his hair that day. Maybe Fred would like something a little stickier, I thought. The gel and mousse poured out like jelly and foam and were really gooey. Now Fred looked like a birthday hat. Nothing was working! Maybe I'll use the superglue…

"Hold on a second! Superglue smells funny and doesn't come off for a long, long, long time," I said. "What am I doing? Am I really going to do this to Fred? He's my buddy. We've had tons of fun together. If I change him, will we still have as much fun? Fred is fine just the way he is. Sorry again, Fred. You are perfectamundo!"

Besides, why would I want to have neat hair? I'm only eight years old. I don't have to look cool. It's not like I'm ten or anything.

Oh my, the bus is here. I have to go. Maybe my girlfriends will give me ponytails again. They really have talent and Fred could go for a massage… Huh, Fred? ✳

THE PICTURE OF HEAVEN

by Leha Dang

ILLUSTRATED BY JON ADAMS

Once upon a time, in a small town, there lived an only child named Jason. Jason had a gift from God. He could draw anything he saw. His drawings were colorful and lively. He drew pictures of his friends going to school, playing in the grass, or fishing by the river. After going to the beach with his parents, he would draw things he had seen and done there. His drawings looked so real that when people saw them, they could imagine themselves at the beach. They could feel the waves moving, the wet sand on their feet, and the wind blowing in their hair.

Jason also had many friends, but his best friend was Mike. Mike's parents had divorced when he was two. Since then, Mike had lived with his grandma, who was very weak. She sold flowers and fruits in front of her doorstep. When Mike went fishing, he sold the fish to help pay for school and books. Many people helped Mike and his grandma. But Mike had a very tough childhood, so he grew up to be one of the toughest kids in the neighborhood. He thought that he couldn't trust people. However, Mike was close to Jason. They told each other every secret and shared everything they had. They were the opposite of each other, but they clicked so well together, enjoying each other's company, always there for each other. Jason was satisfied with his happy life.

But one day, Jason noticed that his mother seemed weak. She stayed in bed for many days and often coughed.

His father called doctors from every town, but it seemed like his mother was not doing well. Jason didn't know what to do to make her feel better.

When he found out that his mother wouldn't be with him much longer, Jason was sad. He stayed by her bed every day after he came home. He told his mom what had happened at school and read her many stories. Jason wanted to spend as much time with her as he could. He drew a picture of heaven for his mom and told her that he would see her every day in that picture. He called his mom an angel.

His mother passed away not long after. Jason didn't want to be around anybody or do anything. He just sat on the desk looking out the window. He never went out anymore. Most of the time he locked himself in his room.

Jason also stopped drawing for a while. When he started again, his drawings were dark and blue, and depressing. Everyone who saw them knew they weren't the same anymore. They didn't have any people in them or any lively colors.

Jason became quiet. He often looked at the picture of heaven he had drawn for his mom. He treasured it very much. Every time Jason looked into the drawing, he felt like he had a magic power. He could see the future inside that drawing. He saw the town and the people that he talked to and the places he went by each day. And sometimes Jason saw something in the painting, and days later it would happen in real life.

One time when Jason was cleaning the picture, he looked deep inside it and saw a big fire. Jason recognized the place and the people where it happened. He was scared that he was beginning to see things. He never told anyone, hoping that the fire would never come true. But he began drawing the future after he saw it in the picture.

In town, many accidents and bad things began to happen. There were floods, houses collapsed, and people argued more often. The town was messier and there was litter almost everywhere. It was a bad time for everyone, which made a lot of people mad.

One day, Jason was hanging out with his friends in his living room and Mike noticed his drawings. He saw that most of Jason's drawings were bad things that could happen in real life so he asked Jason why he drew these scary things. Jason didn't answer and went back to playing games.

Not long after, there was a fire in the next town. Everyone went to see it except Jason and his father. Jason knew that the fire was going to happen sooner or later. But he never told anyone because he was afraid people would turn around and question him.

What Jason didn't know was that Mike's grandmother had been in the house where the fire happened, visiting a friend. Luckily, both Mike's grandmother and her friend got out and were not injured.

But people were spreading rumors that Jason was psychic and could see things before they happened.

Jason knew Mike had seen his painting of the fire. He must have told people. Jason was scared. He didn't want to be a weirdo that everyone talked about in town.

Now no one wanted to hang out with Jason anymore. He ate lunch alone. He walked home instead of taking the bus. He stopped drawing and was always by himself. Even Mike was mad at Jason for not telling him about the fire, which could have been serious and could have injured his grandmother. However, Jason hadn't had the guts to talk to Mike about it.

Jason felt lonely. He cried every night about losing his mom and now he had no friends to talk to. He felt like no one loved him in this world. Jason's father knew what was going on but he didn't know how to help.

One night, Jason dreamt of his mother. She told him how much she loved him. Jason cried and told his mom that everyone in town hated him. His mother told him to think of all the fun times they spent together and all the good memories they had. She said that even though she was gone, she would always protect him and she would always love him.

When Jason woke up, he was smiling. He realized that even though his mom was gone, she would be watching over him. Jason went to school and ignored all the talking and whispering as he passed by in the hallway.

He found Mike and told him he could prove that he wasn't the one causing all the bad things to happen. He drew a picture of Mike living in a rich house with lots of money. Jason said that if that drawing did not come true in a week, it would mean he wasn't the one causing the trouble in town.

A week passed by and nothing happened. Mike still had some doubts but he knew that Jason wasn't lying to him. They started to hang out again. Jason admitted to Mike that he felt guilty about the things that had happened in town. He knew they were going to happen but didn't want to tell anyone because they would have thought he was a freak. Mike now understood why Jason had been alone and had acted weird.

Time passed, and the rumors stopped. People at school understood that Jason's drawings had nothing to do with things happening, and everything went back to normal after a while. The town was happy; there was no more arguing, no more floods or houses on fire. It was the good season again.

Now, every time Jason looked into the picture of heaven, he saw happy things in town and people that he loved. He started to draw again. His drawings were full of life and color like before. He realized that it had just been his thoughts that had made things feel bad. He saw that, no matter how bad the situation, he could learn a lot from it. He thought that all the things that he had gone through had only made him stronger.

Jason grew up to be a famous artist and his drawings sold everywhere in the world. Sometimes, he still looked into the picture of heaven and he thanked his mother for the motivation that she had given him. She had taught him that even though things could get tough, he should be strong and find a way to overcome them. He would always remember the heaven picture, and his mom would always be the angel in it. ✱

YUFFIE & THE MAGIC BAND-AID

by Molly Chu

ILLUSTRATED BY DETH SUN

My name is Yuffie Angel. My real name is Yvette but Yuffie sounds so much cooler. My goal in life is to be a spy for the United States. Ever since I was six years old, I have been training to become one. Now I am eight years old and I am becoming *pretty* stealthy, if I do say so myself.

It was Saturday morning, October 13. I looked at my calendar to see what my mission was for this week, and written for this day in big red letters was "Stay in the library for two hours without getting spotted." I stomped around my room looking for my spy clothes. I found them, put them on, and was buckling the waist pouch that carried my spy gear, when Mom barged in.

"Yuffie, could you please not shake the house at eight in the morning?" asked Mom as she examined my room. My mom is a tall, magical woman with beautifully long, dark, flowing hair. She is also kind—most of the time. "Yvette Angel! How many times do I have to tell you to clean your room? Why can't you be more like your sister?" Mom shouted. She likes using my full name when she's mad.

"*Because* Hope does not have missions like I do, Mom! I swear I'll clean up afterward!"

"You say that *every* week. One day you're going to hurt yourself in that jungle you call your room."

"No, I have great stealth! A little mess will never stop the Great Spy Yuffie!" and then I tripped over a week-old Coca-Cola can. I fell and cut my knee on a puzzle piece that I lost a month ago. The cut began hurting a lot. Turns out, I wasn't nearly as stealthy as I thought I was. Mom just shook her head and left the room.

I was looking at my cut when Mom reentered my bedroom. She was holding a Band-Aid that was glittery and had a picture of a mouse on it. It was for little kids, not for a spy like myself. Why was she putting it on me?

"That Band-Aid is so girly," I mumbled.

But Mom ignored my comment and said, "Cleaning up your room wasn't such a bad idea after all, huh? You should go back to sleep and rest your knee, Yuffie. You can clean up later."

"But *Mom,* I have a mission to complete!" I complained.

"It's Saturday! Your only mission for today is to rest. Am I understood, Spy Yuffie?" Mom asked.

"Yes, madam," I mumbled while climbing back into bed. Just

before Mom left the room, I saw her smile mysteriously. Suddenly this weird feeling came from my knee, and before I knew it, I had fallen asleep.

I woke up two hours later and felt something heavy on top of me. I looked up and saw an enormous blanket! I crawled out from under it to find that my room was gigantic. My bed was bigger than a soccer field! I looked around, walked over to the sneaker that was on my bedside table, slid down a shoelace, and landed on the floor. I walked around watermelon-size marbles and bus-size Rollerblades. What had happened to me? How had I become so small? I walked up to the Coca-Cola can. From its size, I guessed I was about three inches tall. I sat down next to it and looked around my room. I saw my Band-Aid gleam brightly from my knee and realized that it had shrunk me. But before I could ponder this any longer, I saw a gray mouse. I quickly jumped up and ran after him.

I shouted to him, "Hey, stop! Can you please tell me what's going on?" He stopped and turned around. He was about four inches tall and wore a tiny polo shirt and shorts.

"Who's there?!" he shouted back.

"Um, Yuffie," I replied.

"Yuffie? The princess of this land?" he asked.

"Well, I guess… since this *is* my room," I answered.

"So you *are* the princess! I'm Vincent Mouse! Princess, why are you so small? Legend has it that you're so big that your head touches the heavens! What are you doing out here alone? It's dangerous! Oh, I can't believe I'm meeting you. My friends will be so jealous!" he said.

"Whoa! Vincent, slow down! I don't know why I'm so small… And why do you say it's dangerous here?" I asked.

"Let's walk and talk at the same time. We shouldn't be out here alone for so long," he said. Then we talked about the recent invasion of the cockroaches.

"Papa wouldn't tell me much about the invasion other than the fact that it started when you stopped cleaning your room, and that I should not go out alone," Vincent told me.

"Whoa, if I wasn't so messy, this would have never happened," I said sadly.

"Don't blame yourself!" said Vincent. "It's not your fault. Let me bring you to my father. He would agree with me."

I followed Vincent as he walked under my bed and toward an old Barney videotape that was up against the wall. "I always wondered where this had gone!" I said as Vincent pushed the tape aside to reveal a small door.

The door was ancient and golden with flower carvings. It was no bigger than five inches tall and ten inches wide. I stared in amazement before following Vincent inside.

Inside was a long hallway filled with light from a small lightbulb. Along the walls of the hallway were pictures of me at different ages. Where did they get these pictures of me? I wondered. At the end of the hallway was another door, a replica of the one in my bedroom! Through the door was a big city made of many different objects, from stationery to hardware. In front of us was a sign that said WELCOME TO ANGELTOPIA. Vincent led me down the street and we took a windup toy taxi car.

During our taxi ride, we passed by a papier-mâché statue of a mouse. "That's Papa! He owns this city!" Vincent said proudly, pointing at the statue.

"This city is amazing! How long has it been here? I can't believe that mice built this place on their own," I said, smiling at Vincent.

Vincent smiled back while I looked around the city. Each house was made from half a shoe box. I giggled out loud. "So that's where all Dad's shoe boxes went!"

The taller buildings were made of cereal boxes. There was a grocery store in the center of the city that held the food scraps they found in our house. There were thin, tall candles used as streetlamps for nighttime. I looked up and saw a lightbulb being used as the sun. We then came to a stop in front of a building that was made out of a big cardboard box. It was the tallest building in Angeltopia.

Vincent and I entered the building and took the elevator to the top floor. The elevator was made out of Popsicle sticks with two hair rollers and one long rope to operate it with. When we reached the top, we walked to an office. By the window was an old mouse. Vincent approached him and said, "Papa! Look who I brought to meet you!" Papa Mouse turned around and stared at me. He was three and a half inches tall and wore a tiny green suit.

"Can it really be you… Princess?" he said, squinting at me through his glasses.

I nodded and replied, "Hello, Mr. Mouse. I met Vincent by my bed and he told me about the cockroaches. Please tell me, what is going on with the conflict between the mice and the cockroaches?"

"Vincent! Why did you tell her? We should not bother her with our problems," Papa told Vincent.

"No, I want to know! Tell me what's going on. I want to help the mice out! It is my fault for not cleaning up my room," I responded. Papa Mouse looked at me and sighed.

"The mice have lived peacefully within the walls of your home for many decades. We only come out of our city to get food. We try our best to stay out of view from you and your family, but you might have seen signs of us once in a while," Papa said.

"Oh, I think I have! But I have never had the time to wonder if there are mice in my house with all my missions and homework," I said, and laughed.

"Yes, I understand. You are a busy girl." Papa cleared his throat and continued, "Two months ago, our peace ended when the cockroaches moved in. They have been taking our crumbs, our territories, and leaving a horrible smell wherever they go. We barely have enough food for the city now. We do not know what we can do," Papa finished, frowning.

"OK, we have to make a plan! Let's attack and force the cockroaches to leave!" I said.

"But we do not have the supplies to do that," Papa replied.

"But I do! My spy gear shrunk with me!" I said. I began going through my waist pouch to look for my walkie-talkies. I threw out my rope, climbing hook, plastic hook gun, black gloves, head lamp, and binoculars.

We made a plan to trap the cockroaches. We covered some food scraps in White-Out and left it for the cockroaches to eat. They would be poisoned by it and would want to leave the house. Vincent brought five mice. The seven of us quickly left the building and headed for my room. When we exited the golden door, we quietly ran to my bedside table. Vincent and I climbed up the table while the rest of the mice waited at the bottom. When we reached the top, Vincent and I pushed the White-Out over the ledge to the others. We climbed back down and helped carry it back to Angeltopia. In under an hour, with the help of the city, we were able to cover all of the food necessary in White-Out. The seven of us carried the food to the center of my room.

At sunrise, the cockroaches smelled the food. We watched nervously from the top of my dresser as they did. But they stopped sniffing the crumbs and looked around suspiciously.

"Hey! We're not dumb enough to fall for a food trap!" one of the cockroaches shouted. "Come out and show yourself!"

"Yuffie, we should ignore them. We don't know what they'll do!" Vincent whispered, but I was already climbing down the drawer. I waited as Vincent climbed down too.

"Who are you? Why are you trying to do this to us?" asked a cockroach.

"I'm Yuffie and I own this room. The mice have lived here for decades before you moved in. They barely have enough food for themselves, so I was hoping that maybe you and the other cockroaches would find another place to live. It is only fair since the mice were here first," I said.

"We did not know that we had caused trouble for the mice. Cockroaches are not as bad as everyone thinks. We just want to live in peace. We're extremely sorry and we're going to be moving now," the cockroach replied.

"No problem! Thank you for understanding!" I said, smiling.

All the cockroaches began walking toward the open bedroom window. They left for good.

I stared at the window before shouting, "We won!"

A roar of cheers responded from the walkie-talkie as Vincent and I smiled at each other. We walked back to Angeltopia, where they had a celebration for us in Papa Mouse's lobby. I had never felt so happy in my life.

Papa Mouse came up to me in tears of joy and said, "We could never thank you enough, Princess."

I yawned and replied, "No problem! It's all in a day's work for the Great Spy Yuffie."

"You must be tired from not sleeping this whole day! Please go and have a rest on one of the lobby couches," Papa said.

I took his advice and soon fell asleep. When I awoke, I was back in my bed and I was no longer small. I jumped up and looked around. "What… how?" I went to the mirror hanging on my door. The Band-Aid on my knee was gone and the cut was healed.

"Was it all a dream?" I asked out loud. I slowly looked under my bed and spotted my old Barney tape. I pushed it aside and it revealed the small golden doors that led to Angeltopia.

I wanted to talk to Vincent again but the mice probably needed rest. Still happy from being able to help them, I began to clean my room. I took my full garbage can and walked to the bins out in the front yard. While I was walking, I made a secret promise to the mice that I would never forget to clean up my room ever again. I passed Mom in the hall on the way out, and she still wore that mysterious smile.   ✳

NANA'S SECRET

by La Shanna Smith

ILLUSTRATED BY CARLA CALETTI

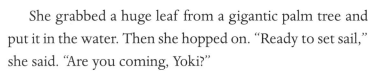

In a far-off island village called Tropicana, there lived an eight-year-old girl named Yukiko. She was no ordinary girl; she was a princess. She lived with her nana and her brother, Yoki, who was ten years old. As weird as it may sound, the whole village—women, men, and children—was bald. No hair at all. In fact, the village people were called the Baldarians.

One day Yukiko and Yoki were in the jungle, by the river, playing a game called "find the rainbow fish." And, as usual, Yoki won and even though he was a boy, he called himself a man. Yukiko just looked at him like he was crazy.

After their game, something amazing caught Yukiko's attention from across the river. It was a flower.

"Yoki, do you see that?!" asked Yukiko.

"You're such a girl! Who cares about flowers?" Yoki said.

"I do, and I'm going to go look at it!" Yukiko said with attitude.

"No, you're not!" shouted her brother. "You know we're forbidden to go across the river. Nana wouldn't allow it!"

"Whatever, Yoki—there's something about that flower, and I'm going to see it!"

She grabbed a huge leaf from a gigantic palm tree and put it in the water. Then she hopped on. "Ready to set sail," she said. "Are you coming, Yoki?"

"No, I'm OK. There's no telling what's over there. Plus, I'm not in the mood for being a curious little monkey." Yukiko just ignored him and set out across the river.

When she reached the other side she looked back across the river and could not see her brother at all. It didn't bother her, though. All she was worried about was the flower. She spotted it and when she went over to it, she didn't just see one; she saw a whole tree of them. They were all the different colors of the rainbow—red, orange, yellow, green, blue, and purple. There were big ones, little ones, skinny ones, and thick ones.

Being a curious girl, she picked one up. Then she went toward the river, knelt down, placed the flower behind her ear, and looked at her reflection. "Now I really feel like a princess, not a bald-headed girl." As she was admiring herself, something weird started to occur. Part of her head, where the flower was touching it, started to itch. In her reflection in the water, she saw a patch of black specks growing. Within minutes, the specks grew into hair. Yukiko was shocked

and let out a loud scream. Birds flew from the trees in reaction to her shriek.

After that patch of hair grew to its full length, she started to realize that it wasn't a bad thing. All her life she had wanted hair. Now was her chance. Yukiko wondered, If I rub more flowers on my head, will hair grow in all the other hairless spots? So Yukiko ran over to the flowers, picked up two handfuls, and rubbed them on her head. Minutes later, Yukiko had a whole head full of long, beautiful, silky hair.

"This is what a princess should look like," she told herself. After dancing around the flowers, she plunged into the river and watched as her hair flowed in the water. When she came out, she looked across the river and decided not to tell anyone about her discovery.

When she returned to the village, all the Baldarians, who usually greeted her after a day's play, just stood still and stared at her. She stood still with a straight face too, but then began to smile and everyone ran up to her to touch her hair. Yukiko liked the attention for a moment, but then she shouted, "Now that's enough!" Everybody suddenly stopped and knelt in front of her.

Even though she had promised herself that she would tell no one, she explained her discovery, but didn't tell where she found it. Her nana then walked through the crowd of people and told Yukiko she wanted to have a word with her. Yukiko was focusing too much on the attention she was receiving from her tribe to notice, but Nana didn't like how she was acting, so she pulled her by her hair and into the hut.

"What did I tell you?! Why would you disobey my orders?!" Nana shouted.

"I don't know what you're talking about, Nana," said Yukiko.

"Yoki told me what you did, and I can see it," Nana said.

"I don't see what I did wrong," replied Yukiko.

"It's been years since this happened, and I don't know what to do," said Nana.

"What are you talking about, Nana?" asked Yukiko.

"Tell me, Yukiko, how you grew the hair, and tell me the truth." Yukiko was quiet.

"Fine, then," said Nana. "Since you don't want to tell me, I'll tell you a story of my own. A long time ago, when I was a little girl, this village went through a huge change because of me. You see, Baldarians weren't always bald. We actually had long, beautiful hair that one could make a tight braid with. Then there was a terrible spell put on this village that caused all of us to lose our hair, and it was all because of me."

"What are you trying to say, Nana?" asked Yukiko.

"One day, I found a flower, and an old wise man of the village told me it was very rare and not to touch it. At that time, I thought he was a crazy old man, but it turned out that I was wrong. 'It's there for a reason,' he told me. I didn't listen, though. That night I went back to where the flower was and I picked it. When I did, the clear sky turned to gray and started pouring down heavy water. When I looked up, all I could see was that old man staring at me with disgrace. I ran for home, but the sound of thunder struck me to the ground. When I looked up, all I could see was the old man standing over me, saying, *'Akko dejie mi yon zina, ayay pusha, evro prumo evro pracka, ayay pusha.'* When I woke up, I thought it was a dream, but when I looked in the mirror my hair was gone. Not just my hair—the whole village was bald. And the old man was nowhere to be found."

"Nana, why didn't you tell me this before?!"

"I was too hardheaded to admit I'd done such a terrible thing!"

"We could have prevented this from happening. Some secrets

just aren't worth keeping secret. Now we don't know what's going to happen, not even to me!"

Then Yukiko started to itch. Out of nowhere millions of bumps and rashes started to appear all over her body. Her eyes bubbled up like they were going to burst out of her face. "Ahhh!" Yukiko screamed. "Nana, what's happening to me?!"

"The magic has begun," Nana whispered.

Nana looked over to where the people of the village were, as they started to experience the same symptoms. Nana called Yoki over to where they were and he too had the symptoms, but for some reason Nana didn't.

"Why is this happening to us?" the villagers asked. They were covered in bumps and their bodies itched terribly.

Yukiko looked at Nana. Neither of them wanted to tell the villagers that she had caused them such terrible pain. Suddenly Yukiko got an idea. "Nana, we must admit to the villagers what we have done. Maybe then the curse will be lifted. Maybe the curse goes on because it is a secret."

"But what can we do?"

"You have to repeat exactly what you told me you did that day so that the villagers know how it all happened!"

As fast as she could and as old as she was, Nana ran through the jungle and across the river to get the flower. By the time she got back, the entire village had grown hair. Not black and beautiful, but gray and thin. Nana didn't want to find out the worst that could happen, so she had to act quickly. She called everybody to come crowd around her, but she especially needed Yukiko at her side.

Then Nana had Yoki got rainwater from the barrel, and had him bring it to her. With the water, she made an *X* across everyone's forehead. She also made sure everybody made contact with the flower she had picked. Then she started to repeat the lines, *"Akko dejie mi yon zina, ayay pusha, evro prumo evro pracka, ayay pusha."*

Yukiko joined in with her, *"Akko dejie mi yon zina, ayay pusha, evro prumo evro pracka, ayay pusha."* The sky started to pour down heavy rain, while thunder roared. Nana felt the old man's presence. Then Nana heard a voice, the same voice that once cursed her, saying, *"Rewolf dekcip eht,"* then repeating the old curse.

The rain and thunder then stopped and the old man was gone. Everybody rose to their feet. Everybody's bumps and itching symptoms were now gone. But surprisingly, they had all grown new hair. It was long, black, and beautiful just like Yukiko's hair. Yukiko and Yoki ran to Nana and gave her a huge hug. The villagers were jumping for joy now that they had hair.

As for Yukiko and Yoki, they eventually cut their hair off to be bald again. They felt they didn't need hair. Being bald reminded them of their Nana, whom they never saw again after that night. She was gone, just like the river and the tree of mysterious, beautiful flowers.   ✳

THE TOWN OF NO SMILES

by Regina Tam

ILLUSTRATED BY LARK PIEN

There was a sensible little girl of eight named Lori who lived with her sensible parents in a straight, upright little house on a spotless street lined with identical houses. In this sensible town under constant gray skies, every little house was the same: a dark brown roof, white walls, two square windows, and one rectangular door.

Lori was content with her school and town. As a sensible little girl she never thought her life had to have fun in it, anyway. To her, there was no such thing as fun. No one ever smiled and no one ever laughed. Everyone went around doing their sensible everyday things. The adults worked hard and the children went to school.

Lori went to the school where all the other children in town went. The school was gray and the windows were square. The teachers were strict and the children never misbehaved. During recess the children had sensible things to do: they sat on gray benches, walked about the spotless schoolyard, and that was all. There was no running, no laughing, no talking loudly, and, most of all, no fun. Lori woke up every morning and walked on a spotless street to school, where every child in her class spent the whole day reading history books, doing countless math problems, and writing vocabu-

lary words over and over. Then Lori walked home and did homework. She ate dinner with her sensible parents and slipped off to a dreamless sleep.

No one ever had dreams in this town. And Lori spent every day of her sensible life feeling neither happy nor sad, just like all the people in the town.

It was another gray day in town and Lori was going to school like always. She walked fast and efficiently. Suddenly, as her foot caught on something, she tripped. This had never happened to Lori before and she turned to look at what had tripped her. It was a small picture in a frame—a simply drawn face made of two dots for eyes and a line curving upward for a mouth. Lori had never seen anyone make this face before.

Being the sensible little girl that she was, she did not want the spotless street to have litter and so she put the picture in her pocket to throw away later. Lori went on with her day at school as usual, forgetting about the picture in her pocket. At home, Lori put her jacket on the tidy little dresser next to her neat little bed. She went downstairs to do her homework and then ate a sensible dinner with her parents. When it was time to go to bed, Lori climbed into her

neat little bed and went to sleep right away, expecting to slip off into another dreamless sleep.

Lori opened her eyes, rubbing the sleep away and expecting to see her mother waking her as usual, but instead she saw a dog dressed in a blue suit and top hat looking back at her. Lori sprang up in surprise as if the bed had just burned her. "Where is my mother?"

The strange dog stood on its hind legs looking at her and bowed. "You are in the wonderful Dream Town, where everyone goes when they dream."

But Lori was as confused as if the dog had told her that pigs could fly and asked, "What are dreams?"

"How silly! Dreams are places where people go when they sleep! Don't you know that?" the dog exclaimed in surprise. Lori thought hard for a second and shook her head, then turned to look at the light coming into her room. She got out of bed and walked to the window. It was the same town, but there was something funny about it. A bright yellow ball that hurt her eyes was floating in the sky lighting up everything. Even the clouds were barely present in the big blue sky as if gray skies didn't exist.

Lori turned to the dog and asked, "What is that thing in the sky?"

The blue-suit dog wagged his tail. "The sun. Haven't you ever seen the sun before? It's a wonderful thing!"

Lori turned, looked at him solemnly, and replied, "We don't have one in my town."

The dog stopped wagging its tail and studied Lori as if she was the strangest little person he had ever seen. As he stared, loud, upbeat music drifted in through the bedroom window. The dog's ears pricked up and his face suddenly looked interested. He took hold of Lori's hand with his paw and dragged her to the door of the room.

"Come! Come!"

"Wait! Where are we going? Who are you?" Lori asked.

"My name is Toby and I am your dream guide, Lori," he replied. "A dream guide is your company in a dream and everyone has one. I have been waiting eight years for you to dream. Didn't you know that? Oh, and the beautiful music from the window means the circus is in town. We must go! It is what everyone looks forward to in Dream Town."

"Cir-cus?" Lori allowed herself to be pulled out to the street. A sun, blue skies, talking dogs, dream guides, and a circus? What in the world was going on? Lori's head felt like it was spinning.

As Toby tugged Lori down the street toward the sound of the loud music, she noticed the town she knew so well was very different. People, dressed in bright and colorful clothes that she had never seen, were moving about strangely. A lady in a purple-frilled dress spun by her. A round man wearing pink pants and a green overcoat walked and jumped at the same time. A boy her own age was not quite walking but moved quickly through the crowd. "Toby, what's wrong with these people? Are they sick? They keep jerking about!"

"No, silly, it's called skipping and running. It's normal. In fact, you stand out more than they do," Toby told Lori. Lori realized she was still in her nightgown while everyone else wore clothes of different colors and sizes. She noticed that most of the people had their mouths turned upward and let out a funny sound that sounded like they couldn't breathe right.

"Oh, I'm so excited. The circus is in town!" a woman in pink said to her friend all dressed in yellow.

"I know! It's going to be fun! Look! The smiling gate." The man dressed in yellow pointed to an archway formed by balloons with faces drawn on them—two dots for eyes and a line curving upward for a mouth drawn. Lori wanted to ask what this face was, but the crowd pushed her through the gate. Inside, colorful booths were lined up next to one another. One booth sold cotton candy and popcorn, while another had games to play to win prizes. Lori, in her plain white nightgown, stood overwhelmed by the colors and noises surrounding her.

"Over here! Over here!" Toby started tugging her to the right. He guided her into an enormous tent. Other people were pouring into the tent. Inside, rows and rows of seats surrounded a large ring in the center.

Toby and Lori sat near the front. It was very noisy and full of chatter. All of a sudden, the whole place went dark with the only light shining on the stage ring. Silly people with paint on their faces walked out. They wore ridiculously baggy clothing and oversize shoes of every color.

Lori gasped, "Their faces are different colors! Are they sick?"

"No, no, they are clowns who paint their faces to look funny," Toby reassured Lori. "Just watch them." Lori watched the clowns as they ran around the ring doing silly things. They squirted water on each other, played tricks, and did somersaults. One clown threw a pie at another. Then ten of them tried to fit in a car but fell out of it instead. Lori noticed that everyone had their mouths turned up and was letting out that funny sound she heard at first. Even Toby was doing it.

"Toby, what is that thing everyone is doing with their mouths?" Lori asked.

"What a silly thing to ask! You don't know what a smile or laughter is? It's when you feel happy inside," Toby said while laughing. Lori felt funny inside when she thought about what he said. Soon she heard her own voice making laughter too.

Lori whispered to herself, "It's happiness." Looking around, she realized people were fading away and when she looked at her hands she could see through them!

Toby smiled. "It's time for you to go. May we meet again soon, silly one." Lori closed her eyes and the circus and everything else faded away.

In the morning Lori opened her eyes expecting to see Toby standing there looking at her, but she saw her own mother this time telling her to wake up. Lori opened her hand, which was holding something, and saw the smiley-face picture that she had found on the sidewalk. "How silly," she said. Then Lori smiled.   ✻

THE WORLD OF RAGILAN

by Gia Truong

ILLUSTRATED BY PAUL MADONNA

A long time ago, a rumor spread telling of a magical book that existed. The book was the gateway to a mystical world with mountains, deserts, oceans, dragons, ogres, dinosaurs, and monsters. People said that a legendary wizard created the book to escape from the tragedies of his world. Many people sought after the book, but it remained undiscovered. Eventually they gave up searching, and the book was forgotten.

In San Francisco not too long ago, there lived a ten-year-old boy named Roy Rin. Roy was a very shy boy who didn't have many friends. But Roy had a big imagination and it often led him to fantasize about adventuring in a strange new world. During recess, he read about fantasies instead of playing with his classmates. His classmates considered him a real bookworm.

One day Roy was happily reading as he sat at the table in the schoolyard when Ed approached him. Ed was a tall and bulky boy who was known as the school bully because he always picked on the smaller students at school.

"Hey, nerd, since you're just sitting there, you wanna do my homework for me?"

"I don't want to," Roy replied quietly.

"Well, too bad 'cause you're going to do it anyway, got it?" Ed said as he raised his fists.

"B-b-but you should be doing your own homework," Roy said.

Ed grabbed Roy's shirt collar and said, "Look here, Roy, you better do my homework or else, got that?" Ed shoved Roy onto the ground as he walked away laughing.

After school Roy liked to read for a few hours at the library before his mother picked him up. As Roy walked to the library day, he felt angry from the bullying. He hated Ed for what he did but he looked forward to a shipment of books that had arrived that day. He walked faster to the library, eager to look through them.

He ran through the big wooden doors and rushed up to the librarian, Miss Mia Fey. She had wild, frizzy, shiny orange hair that went everywhere, and she was wearing her usual mismatched clothes and long polka-dot socks.

"Why, hello, Roy," she said.

"Good afternoon, Miss Fey."

"Are you here for that new shipment of books?" she asked.

Roy nodded.

"They're in the back."

Roy quickly said thanks and ran off to look for the books.

Roy smiled as he saw the stack labeled NEW BOOKS. He pulled a couple of interesting books on monsters and fairy-tale creatures from the shelf. Then his hand ran over an unusual book that gave him a funny tingling feeling in his finger, so Roy took the book and walked to the far corner of the library. He sat at a table that was blocked by bookshelves on all sides and lit by a single chandelier. No one but Roy ever sat in that corner of the library. He liked the seclusion because he could read his books in peace and quiet.

When he touched the cover, the tingling feeling came back, and he trembled with excitement. As he looked over the book he couldn't find a title or author. And when he opened the book he found only blank pages. The pages began to turn by themselves and shone with a bright white light that illuminated Roy.

The next thing he knew, Roy found himself inside a huge forest with thick trees that towered over him. Fear filled him as he stood in this new, strange place and questions ran through his mind. He looked down and saw that the book was gone. A strange ring had placed itself on his finger. He examined the ring and the sky flashed a bright orange-red color.

"I wonder what that was," Roy said.

Suddenly Roy heard a rustling sound in the bushes and he jumped. He turned toward the sound and saw a small blue dinosaur. Roy turned around and ran… right into a tree. He fell on his back and the strange dinosaur approached him.

"Oh my, are you OK? That was quite a hit," said the creature. Roy sat up and scooted back until his back was to the tree.

Roy asked, "W-w-what, who are you? Where am I?"

"Well, my name is Po, and you're in Ragilan," he answered.

"Ragilan? Hmm, are there more of your kind here?" Roy asked.

"There sure are and many other kinds of creatures too. Why don't you just look around and see?" Po said with a smile.

Roy started to notice everything around him. Dragons, birds, even gryphons flew above him. Teensy miniatures of all sorts of dinosaurs and animals crawled below him. And all sorts of animals and creatures walked and talked around the trees.

"What am I going to do? How am I going to get home?" Roy yelled as he ran in circles.

Po looked at him with a freaked-out expression and said, "Umm, I'm not sure how you can get back but maybe you can leave the way you came."

"How I came here… oh! The book! What happened to it?" Roy responded.

"Umm, well, I have no idea what book you're talking about, but why don't you stay here awhile and check out our world?" asked Po.

"Well, as long as I'm here, I might as well enjoy it. I can finally explore the lands of a fantasy world," Roy responded happily. Roy and Po smiled at each other.

Po said, "C'mon, I'll show you around."

"Hey, Po, when I first came here, I saw this bright orange-red flash in the sky. What was that?"

"That was probably Arch doing another experiment."

"Who is Arch?"

"Arch is an evil wizard who likes to trick other creatures into fighting each other for his entertainment."

Roy became enraged. He remembered how Ed had bullied him to do his homework and knew how it felt.

"There are some monsters who say that a long time ago Arch

wasn't a bad person at all, that he was even kind. Nobody believes them, though. It's hard to believe that someone like Arch could've been good."

Suddenly, they heard loud thumping and screeching and a huge apelike creature charged straight for Roy and Po from the bushes. The ape looked like it had gone berserk. Po leapt at the ape to protect Roy, but the ape smacked Po into a tree.

Seeing this reminded Roy of what had happened between him and Ed, and he yelled out to Po. The ring shone and Po started to glow too as he changed and grew into a bigger and stronger version of himself.

Po attacked the ape, knocking it away from Roy, who was shocked by Po's newfound power. Po had knocked some sense into the ape and he seemed to calm down.

Po asked, "What's gotten into you? Why did you attack us?"

The ape said, "What happened? How did I get here? You said I attacked you?"

"You don't remember?" asked Po.

The ape said, "The last thing I remember was that I was sitting in my hut in the trees relaxing and eating some nice coconuts. Then a white light hit me. The next thing I know, I'm here with the two of you."

Roy and Po decided to confront the evil sorcerer Arch. Roy felt good about himself because he had been able to help someone.

The pair made their way up to the top of the castle and up to Arch's room.

"There you two are. I've been waiting for you," said Arch.

"Why did you have that ape attack us?" asked Roy

"That ring is a threat to my quest for power!"

Po and Arch started fighting and it seemed like Po was going to

lose, but the ring on Roy's finger shone and Po became even stronger. He hit Arch really hard and knocked him out.

"We did it!" yelled Roy.

"Ugh, what happened to me? What have I done?" asked Arch as he awoke.

"He's waking up," said Po.

"I'm really sorry about all this," said Arch.

Roy asked, "What happened to you?"

Arch replied, "Well, I was trying to make this new potion that would be able to heal every wound but it made me go crazy instead." Roy's and Po's eyes widened.

Roy asked, "Since you're back to normal, do you want to be friends now?"

Arch replied with a big "Yes!"

The ring started to glow again and this time the ring changed back into the book. Then another flash enveloped Roy.

Roy woke up to a slight tap on his shoulder. He found himself sitting in his secluded spot in the library and Miss Fey was smiling down at him.

"Your mother is here, Roy. She's waiting for you outside," said Miss Fey. Roy rubbed his eyes, still confused about his dream.

"Oh, OK, thank you, Miss Fey. Can I borrow these new books?" asked Roy.

Miss Fey replied, "Of course." She noticed the book that Roy was reading. "Hmm, I don't remember this being cataloged into the library."

"Really?" asked Roy.

"Well, I'll tell you what, since you are such a nice boy, how about I let you borrow this book for an extended period, but you can't tell anyone. OK?" Miss Fey said with a wink.

"OK! I promise," Roy exclaimed.

When Roy and his mother arrived home, it was bedtime and Roy went straight to sleep from exhaustion.

The next day at school, Roy was studying and Ed confronted him again.

"Hey, pipsqueak, you got my homework?" Ed asked as he walked up to Roy.

Roy said, "No, I didn't do it, because I don't need to! Why don't you just get out of here? Stop bullying people around and do your own work!"

Ed was shocked that the quiet little Roy had suddenly become so defiant. Roy's tone of voice scared Ed so much that he ran away. Roy smirked to himself because he felt proud that he had finally stood up to the bully.

Roy went to his room that night and brought out the Ragilan book from his backpack. He started to feel that tingle in his fingers again as he opened it. The pages turned on their own and the white light light covered Roy. He instantly found himself back in the town, wearing the ring. Po and Roy were so happy to see each other again that they smiled and hugged.

From then on, Roy would visit Ragilan and go on numerous adventures with Po. They helped other creatures and met new friends. Roy eventually had to return the book to the library, but he still borrowed it every now and then to see Po. ✳

THE BRAVE LITTLE FISH

by Vivian Lei

ILLUSTRATED BY SCOTT BARRY

Down in the ocean there was a little fish with shiny scales named Phil. Phil loved his big family with hundreds of cousins and aunts and uncles, but there was one family member missing and that made Phil very sad: his dad. Phil loved his father because he would take Phil out to play all the time and was very good to him. Phil's father was taken one day by fishermen so Phil's mother always kept Phil inside and away from danger: she worried he would be taken away.

Phil was a little fish and wasn't very good at anything. Phil went to school like normal fish but went straight home to his mother. Because Phil was scared of making friends at school, everyone picked on him and called him names like *loner, scaredycat,* or *nerd.* Phil knew they were teasing him but he didn't stop them. Phil believed that he couldn't do anything except homework.

One day at school, one of Phil's classmates, Mark, came up to him. Mark wasn't that big of a fish himself but he liked to pick on Phil because it made him feel bigger. "Ha ha," Mark said, making fun of Phil. "You don't do anything well but sit and listen to other fish." All the little fish swimming behind Mark laughed.

Phil got really mad and puffed up. He said, "Well, let me tell you one thing! My mom said I am better than you because I don't make fun of fish!" The other fish laughed even harder at Phil. After they laughed, Phil swam to the corner and cried.

Their teacher, Ms. Swimmers, saw Phil crying and was worried. After school, she took Phil aside and had a little talk with him. Ms. Swimmers didn't know what had happened so she asked Phil to tell her everything. When Phil was done, Ms. Swimmers asked if he felt better after talking. Phil replied, "A little better." Ms. Swimmers took Phil home to his mother and asked to talk to her about Phil. Ms. Swimmers told his mother what happened at school and asked if there was anything that they could do at home that would make Phil feel better.

The next day at school Ms. Swimmers watched the class during break time. She watched Phil especially to see if he got picked on. Sure enough, Mark cornered Phil again and he made scary faces at him. Ms. Swimmers told Mark to stop. When Ms. Swimmers left, Mark got mad at Phil.

"Did you tell on me?" asked Mark.

Phil was surprised but he blurted out, "Yes! Because you *do* pick on me!" Mark made Phil pick up his books as punishment.

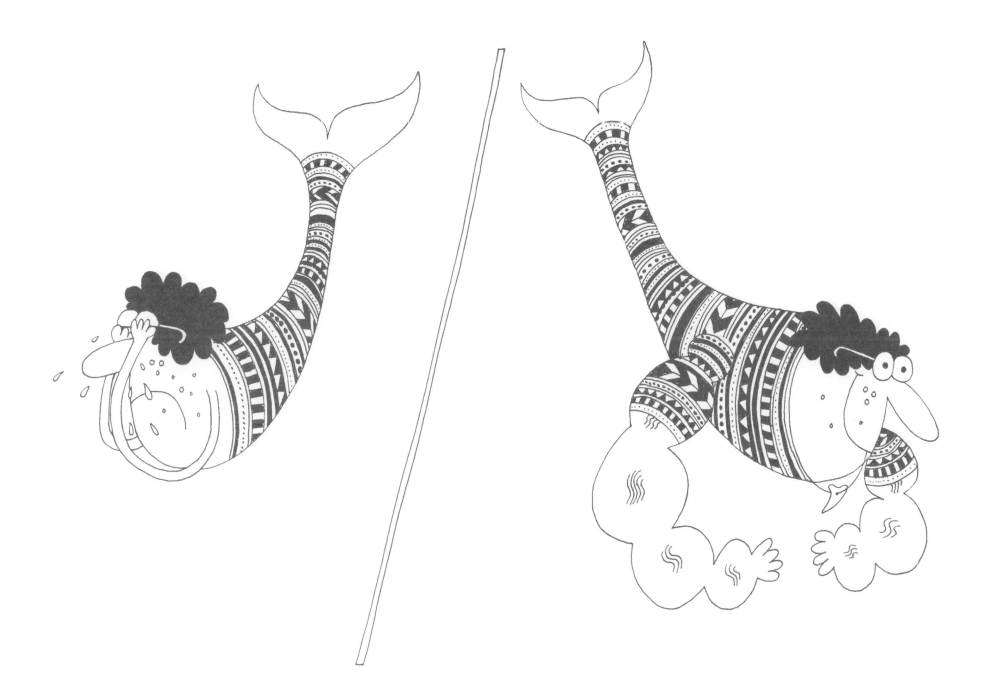

After school, Phil returned home crying because he felt he couldn't do anything right.

"Oh, my baby! What happened?" Phil's mother asked.

"I'm fine, Mom," replied Phil.

The next day on his way to school a giant hook dropped in front of Phil. He feared that the hook might take him like it had his father so he swam around it. But Phil still continued toward school. As Phil swam, a hungry piranha popped up out of nowhere and scared him so much that he shook till he got to school.

At school, Ms. Swimmers asked why Phil was shaking. Phil couldn't say a word. Ms. Swimmers tried to comfort Phil but he just stayed quiet in the corner. Mark saw Phil shaking and started to laugh. The whole class joined in when Phil began to cry.

"*Quiet!*" Ms. Swimmers yelled to the class. Everyone stopped.

Ms. Swimmers took Phil home. When Phil got home, he went upstairs while Ms. Swimmers talked to his mother. Ms. Swimmers thought Phil should talk about what had happened so Phil's mother called him down. They found out that Phil had had a frightening day and that he had faced a hook just like his father had—now they understood. Phil's mother hugged Phil. Ms. Swimmers thanked him for telling his story.

The next day, he told his teacher that he was still shaky but he could stay calm enough to return to school. Ms. Swimmers was surprised at how fast he recovered from such a scary incident and she realized he was actually a very brave and strong fish. She told him so. Phil was not used to getting any compliments so he denied it and said he needed to go home. When Phil got home he told his mother that there had been only a little bit of bullying and that it wasn't too bad. Phil's mother wondered if her son was hiding something important and she swam as fast as she could to Phil's school.

When Phil's mother arrived, she excitedly asked Ms. Swimmers about Phil's day.

"I told your son that I believe he is a very strong fish and that he can overcome any problems that are thrown his way, because of the very fact that he returned to school today," Ms. Swimmers replied. Phil's mother thanked Ms. Swimmers but she secretly wondered why Phil hid his teacher's comment from her.

One week later, on the way to school, Phil encountered a snoring, sleeping shark. When it snored, it showed its *gigantic,* sharp white teeth. Phil was scared so he swam away. But the shark woke up at the sound of Phil. And as Phil was swimming away, the shark sneaked up and attempted to take a big bite. Luckily, Phil saw the shark and swam away as fast as he could, screaming, "Ahhh!" Phil turned around and saw the shark swim back to where it had come from. After a rest, Phil finally remembered that he was on his way to school so he went on, even though he was still shaking.

After school, Phil asked Ms. Swimmers if she could take him home. Ms. Swimmers agreed and when they were on their way, Phil spotted the shark again. Scared, they swam for their lives. Because they were both pretty small, they swam through a little hole inside a rock and when the shark followed she was too big for the little hole so she got stuck. Phil, curious, turned and asked the shark, "Why do you eat little fish like us?"

The shark answered, "There is nothing else in this sea that tastes as good." Ms. Swimmers and Phil talked to the shark and found out her name was Shelly. Ms. Swimmers and Phil decided to help Shelly.

When Phil arrived home, his mother noticed that he seemed so calm. She asked him why and he told her everything about Shelly. Phil's mother was very proud of Phil and how he treated other animals even when he was scared.

Phil continued to meet up with Shelly almost every day and they became friends.

One day, Phil asked Shelly, "Why do you eat meat but you don't eat any vegetables?"

Shelly replied, "I've never tried vegetables before. I was raised to eat little fishes like you." Phil got an idea and dared Shelly to eat some vegetables. Shelly took the dare and ate some seaweed. Smiling, Shelly told Phil how good the food tasted. From that day on, all Shelly wanted to eat was seaweed.

One day, while Phil was at school, he started to think about all the good times he had had with Shelly. Then he saw all of his classmates swimming as fast as they could away from school. Shelly was swimming toward the school. Phil was so excited to see his friend that he swam straight to her. As Phil approached the shark, Ms. Swimmers watched. When Phil met up with Shelly, he asked her, "What brings you here?"

"I came by to thank you, my good friend," she replied.

"Thank me? Thank me for what?" asked Phil.

"Well, thank you for introducing me to vegetables."

"Why?" asked Phil.

"Can't you tell? I am much bigger and stronger now."

During this conversation, Mark and his friends hid in the corner, terrified. Mark wondered out loud why the shark was not trying to eat Phil. Phil explained that Shelly was his friend. At that moment, Shelly said, "I'm going to go now." Phil turned around and waved to his friend Shelly.

Days passed and Phil was sitting at his desk. Mark watched him. Mark asked Phil, "Why aren't you in the corner like you used to be?"

Ms. Swimmers, who was standing nearby, replied, "I've been trying to figure that out too." Ms. Swimmers took Mark and they sat down next to Phil. Ms. Swimmers asked, "Why do you think you changed?"

Phil started to think back on the past few months and with a happy face he shouted out, "Shelly!"

Ms. Swimmers smiled and said, "Because of Shelly, you have gained self-confidence and you are not afraid of anything anymore."

Mark looked at Phil smiling and decided that Phil was a very cool guy. From then on, Mark started to hang out with Phil.

That night, Phil went home with a big smile. "Why are you smiling, sweetie? Did something good happen at school today?" his mother asked.

Phil nodded and answered "Yes! I'm not as scared of everything anymore!"

Phil's mother smiled at him and said, "That's great!" and gave him a big hug.   ✳

SIR FINKLE & CHIPOTLE

by Aldo Navarro

ILLUSTRATED BY EIZABETH GÓMEZ

Once upon a time in a far-off land, there lived a retired knight named Sir Finkle. He was a simple man with simple features and a slight gut who kept to himself on his farm. People would often ask him for help with bandits.

"No, sir," he would answer. "I am a *retired* knight. I'm just a farmer now." And he would go back to plowing his fields. One day a beggar came by with important information.

"Sir, I have lost my farm," he said. "A bandit named Chipotle has stolen it. I have nothing left. Please help me and the other farmers."

This stirred Sir Finkle's memory. Chipotle was a dreadful man. He was tall, dark, and handsome, but he was still a bandit. He often stole from farmers and burned their houses. Sir Finkle remembered when they first met. Sir Finkle had been hired in his glory days to rid the farmers of a group of bandits called the Horribly Hot Habañeros. He had spent years tracking and trapping the leader, Chipotle! A burning spread through Sir Finkle's body, willing him to have his revenge. Sir Finkle would once again rid the land of evil!

However, he needed to find his armor and sword first. He searched his house—up and down and all around and even under-

ground! Finally, he gave up looking and just went to bed.

The next day, he was walking under a tree and accidentally hit his head on a branch. The branch was actually a secret switch that opened up a hidden stair, where Sir Finkle happened to be standing. He fell down five hundred steps and hit the bottom with a loud *crash*! He shakily got up and looked at a chest next to him. It had a note that read:

Sir Shminkle,

This is for all those years of chasing me around. I've hidden your sword and armor in this chest and even if you find it you won't find the key! Muahahahahahahahahaha!

But seeing as how I'm a fair chap, I'm just going to give you an obstacle to overcome. What do you say? Go back down the stairs. Behind the chest is a secret room with spikes on the bottom and monkeys on the top. The key is inside. Don't just stand there! Get to it!

Sir Finkle walked inside the room and was greeted by monkeys throwing explosive bananas! He started to climb up, but the monkeys threw more explosive bananas at him, so he jumped off. But when the bananas hit the wall and exploded, the wall crumbled. Sir Finkle found the key on a pedestal inside and was able to retrieve his sword and armor.

Sir Finkle was then ready for his noble quest to catch Chipotle and his men. He set out on his horse, Fickle, down a long road. They met many people who told horrifying tales of bandits stealing, burning, and smashing, which reminded Sir Finkle of what it meant to be a knight.

Then a large roadblock stopped him. It was a dragon! A huge red one, with spikes running along his back and sharp fangs jutting from his jaw. Sir Finkle had never seen a dragon and was shaking in his armor when a small elderly man stepped out next to the dragon.

"Bad, Fido!" the man scolded. "Scaring that poor knight… What have I told you? Don't worry, sir, he's harmless." The man scratched Fido's belly and Fido began to scratch the ground.

"Wh-what are you doing with a dragon?" squeaked Sir Finkle.

"Oh, he's my pet," replied the old man. "But we've hit on some hard times, haven't we, boy? I can barely take care of him, you know? Dragons are really expensive to keep. I'd hate to lose the old boy, but I might just have to sell him."

"Sell him?" inquired Sir Finkle

"Why, yes. I think I have to. Are you looking to buy?"

"I could always use a dragon. I'm hunting bandits."

"Oh, Fido loves doing that. He does it for fun, you know. You can have him for five hundred gold pieces."

"Five hundred? For a dragon? That's a deal! I'll take him."

Sir Finkle set out with Fido and Fickle to take on the bandits. They continued along the road up the mountain. The trio marched on until they came upon a sign that read TURN BACK OR ROT IN A DUNGEON FOREVER!

"We must be getting close," said Sir Finkle, reading the sign. Finkle and Fickle marched on and found a giant gate around the corner, but Fido stretched out in the trees for a rest. Suddenly a group of bandits jumped out and stopped Finkle.

"You should have listened to the sign!" they cried. "Now you'll rot in a dungeon forever!"

They threw nets over Sir Finkle and Fickle but they didn't notice the dragon napping behind the trees. He awoke, came out, and yawned a great yawn. The bandits ran in fright but it was too late. Fido saw the bandits and the only thought that crossed his mind was: habañero-flavored bandit. He jumped in front of Sir Finkle and tried to breathe fire… but nothing came out.

The bandits began to laugh and said, "What dragon can't breathe fire? What a weakling!"

This of course didn't sit well with Fido. He started rampaging, throwing rocks and bandits everywhere. He rammed down the wall guarding the fort and stopped their attack. Then he freed Sir Finkle and Fickle. It looked like the bandits, were done for good.

"You can't breathe fire?" exclaimed Sir Finkle. "What good are you? Well, at least you got rid of the bandits so you're not entirely useless…"

Fido looked sad, and was very sorry. He trotted sullenly toward a cave with a sign that said: DANGER, NO FIRE BEYOND THIS POINT.

Wanting to stop the bandit boss Chipotle once and for all, Sir Finkle didn't pay attention to Fido. Instead, he ran beyond the ruined walls and into the castle searching for Chipotle.

"Chipotle! You will pay for this!" screamed Sir Finkle when he found Chipotle in the throne room.

"I think not," returned Chipotle. "My guards will make short work of you even if my army was destroyed by your lizard."

The two guards rushed at Sir Finkle and he got ready to fight them...

* * *

Meanwhile, Fido had sadly walked farther into the cave, where he discovered a huge factory. Normally he wouldn't care, but he saw vats filled with hot sauce, his favorite sauce. He was eating it with gusto when some bandits spotted him.

"Hey! Stop that, you dragon!" they screamed.

Fido didn't need to be told twice. The hot sauce was *hot*! He ran around in circles looking for water and knocking things over. Soon Fido lost all control and opened his mouth to roar, but instead of a roar, fire came out. Fido was so shocked and happy! He tried to toast the bandits and breathe out fire, but accidentally lit the hot sauce instead. Then came the explosion... *Boom!*

* * *

Up in the castle, the explosion threw Chipotle, Sir Finkle, and the two guards around. Chipotle fell unconscious next to Sir Finkle, who wasted no time and tied him up. Sir Finkle had no idea what had exploded but he aimed to find out. He walked to the edge, looked down the hole in the ground, and saw a large factory of some sort, in ruins. There, he saw a sign that used to read: CHIPOTLE'S HOT SAUCE. SO HOT THAT IT EXPLODES. PLEASE, FOR BADNESS SAKE, DON'T SET IT ON FIRE!"

Amid the burning timbers, ashes, and charbroiled bandits, Sir Finkle saw Fido smiling.

"I guess I was too hard on the guy," he said.

As Sir Finkle took Chipotle to jail, he thought about the hot sauce, trying to understand why bandits would want a factory of it.

He reached Fickle, who was eating from a barrel with an odd label that said: CHIPOTLE'S SAUCE, CAUTION—IT'S HOT. USE ONLY FOR FLAVOR AND BURNING FARMS." The answer clicked in Sir Finkle's mind. Chipotle was making explosive hot sauce!

Sir Finkle tied Chipotle to Fickle, and they traveled toward the city and told people on the road the good news. Soon a parade came out to meet the hero Sir Finkle, but it wasn't all that it seemed to be. Out of nowhere bandits ambushed the procession and attacked Sir Finkle. Fido raged again, throwing rocks and bandits left and right. Sir Finkle fearlessly fought off multiple bandits by swinging his sword, but just as suddenly as they attacked, the bandits ran away.

"Are you all a bunch of cowards?" challenged Sir Finkle.

"Why no," answered Chipotle. "They were just a diversion! While you were fighting, I used my secret hot sauce to burn through the ropes. Now you'll never catch me!"

Just then Fido really acted like a dragon. He flapped his wings and flew over the bandits intending to breathe fire on them. However, Fido mis-flapped and fell from the sky on top of them instead. This caused enough confusion to give Sir Finkle a chance. He chased after Chipotle, across fields and woods. They ran far, and Sir Finkle was clearly out of shape. But just when Finkle would have caught him, Chipotle fell from sight. Sir Finkle couldn't believe his eyes! Chipotle had just disappeared! Then a voice came from out of the ground.

"What the...?" said the muffled voice of Chipotle. "*Oh no*! How could I have fallen *here*? This was the pit I dug for Sir Finkle. Now what am I going to do?"

Sir Finkle walked over to the pit, looked down, and smiled.

"Finally!" Sir Finkle laughed. "I knew you couldn't escape three times. Now it's time for you to go to jail."

And Chipotle did go to jail, where he stayed forever more. ✳

PRINCESS MICHELLE

by Brittany Rhynea Jones

ILLUSTRATED BY EVAH FAN

O nce upon a time there was a princess named Michelle. Everyone in the village of Rocklington liked Princess Michelle because she was nice to everyone. Unlike other princesses, Princess Michelle didn't have servants who helped her get dressed every morning. She didn't wait for people to bring her her clothes or run her bathwater. She did all these things by herself.

Princess Michelle lived in a very big palace. The palace had ten floors, fifty bathrooms, one hundred guest rooms, and ten master bedrooms. Princess Michelle lived on the tenth floor in the master bedroom of the palace, while the king and queen also lived on the tenth floor but in guest rooms.

There weren't many things that got on Princess Michelle's nerves, but one thing that did was when people were joking around and having fun when they were supposed to be working. This made Princess Michelle mad.

Princess Michelle was like any other princess except for one thing. She had a lot of responsibilities around the palace because her parents, the king and queen, had become very ill. Princess Michelle had to step in and do their job.

When Princess Michelle was born, her mother and father had arranged for her to marry Prince Troy. When she was sixteen years old, her mother said, "You will be getting married in one month."

Princess Michelle was confused. She said, "How can I be getting married when I have never seen this person before?"

But her mother responded, "This marriage was arranged when you were born and set for this date."

So Princess Michelle and Prince Troy finally met and they agreed to get married. Princess Michelle thought that everything would be great, but that wasn't the case. She started to realize that her husband would spend hours standing in front of the mirror staring at his long black hair and handsome face, which he was always complimented on. She felt that she shouldn't have to beg people to do things. But since she couldn't depend on her husband, she was forced to do it all on her own.

All the people in the village felt that it was wrong for Princess Michelle to do all of the work on her own. They felt that Prince Troy should have been helping her do some of it. The children tried to talk to their father and get him to help, but the prince was too

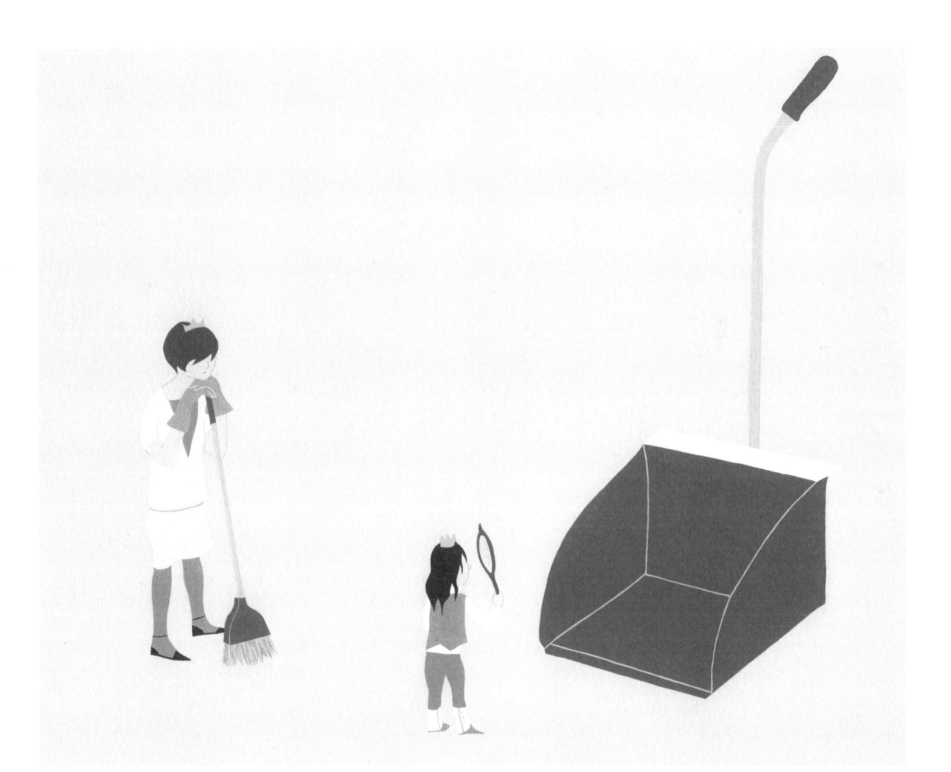

cocky. He didn't listen to anybody because he thought that he was the god of the palace, and therefore felt that it was his job to tell the people of the village what to do.

Princess Michelle got up every morning at six o'clock. She would take her morning walk, get her children ready for school, and then start her day of work in the palace. Prince Troy had an entirely different routine in the morning. He would wake up and have one of his servants run his bathwater. The water had to be a certain temperature or he would make the servant start all over. He would soak in the tub for two hours while looking at himself in the mirror and then he would do his daily pampering. He would get his massage, pedicure, and facial while looking at himself in the mirror. Then he would take his nap.

Around five o'clock in the evening, he would get dressed and go to dinner and then after dinner it was back to his mirror until he went to bed.

Princess Michelle didn't want to kick Prince Troy out of the palace, but she felt like she had no other choice. She was tired of doing all the work by herself and she needed a prince who was going to help run the palace.

Her first job of the day was to check on the king and queen and make sure that they had their breakfast and medicine. Then she would go and meet the servants and assign them their daily tasks. But unfortunately, Princess Michelle didn't have any servants who were willing to go out of their way to help her.

Once finished with their daily jobs they would go off and do whatever they wanted to do. Even though Princess Michelle was able to get help from the few servants that she had, there was still a lot of work to be done because her husband was obsessed with himself and wouldn't step away from the mirror. Princess Michelle

had to pick up the children, do the grocery shopping, and clean their portion of the palace. After that, Princess Michelle had to make sure that her children ate dinner, took their baths, and prepared for the next day of school. She also had to make sure that her parents had dinner and that they were properly prepared for bed. She did all of this on her own and without the help of her lazy husband, leaving her completely tired at the end of each day.

One day, an unhappy Princess Michelle went to her parents and asked, "What am I supposed to do when my husband refuses to help out around the palace?"

Her parents told her, "We're sorry. We didn't know he would act this way, and if you want to get rid of him, then you may. Do what is best for you."

So Princess Michelle went to Prince Troy and said, "I don't want you living in the palace anymore, because the only person you care about is yourself."

Prince Troy said, "What are you talking about? I always help out around the palace."

Princess Michelle, scolding the prince, said, "You have *never* helped out around the palace. The only thing you've done since you've been here is stand in front of the mirror as if you were some kind of model!"

Prince Troy then decided that he was going to compromise with Princess Michelle and said to her, "If you can find someone who can beat me in a duel, then I will leave and never cause you any more problems."

Princess Michelle then went to her parents and asked, "Do you think that I should find someone to fight Prince Troy in a duel?" They agreed and then a message was sent to all the princes in the nearby land.

The message said:

I am looking for a strong prince who can defeat Prince Troy. The first person to defeat Prince Troy in a duel will become the new prince of Rocklington.

With the message sent out to all the princes, it became a race to see who was going to get to Princess Michelle first. There was a tie between Prince Darryl and Prince Pierre. Prince Darryl was given the privilege of going first, because she decided to let them go in alphabetical order. If Prince Darryl couldn't defeat Prince Troy, then Prince Pierre would be given a chance.

Everyone gathered for the duel, which began with Prince Troy and Prince Darryl arguing. Prince Troy laughingly said, "Do you really think that this man can beat me?"

Prince Darryl responded, "I know for a fact that I can beat you. You are nothing but a pretty boy who doesn't know anything about fighting." So Prince Troy became very angry with Prince Darryl and he threw a punch. The punch broke Prince Darryl's nose and the duel was over.

The next day everyone gathered for the second duel, between Prince Pierre and Prince Troy. For some weird reason the duel began with Prince Troy and Prince Pierre arguing. Prince Troy said, "Do you really think that this man can beat me?" and then he began to laugh.

Prince Darryl then said, "I know for a fact that I can beat you. You are nothing but a pretty boy who doesn't know anything about fighting." Everyone in the village was whispering about how the duel yesterday had started off the same exact way. They wondered if Prince Pierre was trying to copy Prince Darryl.

So Prince Troy and Prince Pierre began to fight. They both wrestled around for a few minutes and then Prince Troy punched Prince Pierre in his jaw and broke it and the duel was over.

Everyone in the village was upset because Prince Troy had defeated both challengers and was still the prince, but no one was nearly as upset as Princess Michelle.

Everyone thought that Princess Michelle was going to call for another duel, but she didn't. She said, "I have decided that I don't want anyone to be my prince, because I don't need a man to help me. I can be strong all by myself." The people in the village cheered and cheered because they were happy that Prince Troy was no longer going to be their prince.

Princess Michelle walked over to Prince Troy and said, "I hope that you learned your lesson. In order to be an authority, you have to work hard for it. It is not going to just come to you."

So Princess Michelle decided that she was going to tell all the women in the village that there was nothing wrong with being independent. They didn't need a man to help them. They could be strong for themselves and they could take care of themselves if they wanted to. ✻

THE ANTEATERS & WALTER, THE MISUNDERSTOOD WIZARD

by Leslie Franco

ILLUSTRATED BY RACHEL LYON

Kenny Anteater lived in a tropical forest in Costa Rica with his family and his friends. He was loving, sweet, curious, and young. He had a best friend named Archie who was just as great as he. The two anteaters went on many adventures together.

One day, Kenny was unable to spend the day with Archie, but that didn't stop Archie from going on an adventure. After his breakfast he went on a walk along the river. It was very peaceful, but when he reached the end of his walk Archie saw an ugly, green wizard wearing all black. His name was Walter.

Walter walked toward Archie with a frightening look. In a blink of an eye, Walter turned Archie into a frog! Archie didn't know what to do so he hopped all the way back to Kenny's front steps and waited for Kenny to come back home.

When Kenny came home that evening he was surprised to see his best friend had turned into a frog. But he saw the situation was an opportunity to go on a quest to help his best friend. He said, "Hey, Archie, I'm going to get a potion to turn you back into an anteater."

"But it's too dangerous out there!" said Archie. He knew of all the dangers in the forest.

"Archie, you're my best friend," answered Kenny. "I love you and nothing you say can change my mind." In a matter of minutes Kenny was on his quest to find Walter the wizard.

As Kenny walked, a man came up to him and said, "I know you. You're Kenny. I am Wise William and if you want to find Walter Wizard you'll have to follow me."

"O-OK," responded Kenny in a frightened voice. Wise William then led Kenny to the darkest, coldest part of the forest. Kenny was scared because the old man seemed to be just as evil as Walter.

William took Kenny to the shack where he lived. To Kenny's surprise the house was made of one hundred percent pure, delicious milk chocolate with all different types of candy adorning it. Kenny loved chocolate. "Whatever you do, *do not* eat my chocolate house *or* my colony of chocolate-covered ants," Wise William said. And although the man appeared to be evil Kenny knew he was just misunderstood. William said he had to go do laundry at the river so he left Kenny alone in the living room, reading magazines. While waiting for Wise William to return, he thought he heard a voice.

"Kenny… Oh, Kenny," he heard over and over. "You can go

ahead and eat the back door of my house if you want." Kenny was suspicious that William would suddenly allow him to eat the house after he'd told him not to, but he believed the voice because there'd be no reason for anyone to lie about something like that. Kenny had no clue that the person who had told him it was OK to eat the chocolate house was not Wise William but, in fact, Sniper the Chameleon, Walter Wizard's sidekick. Nevertheless, in just a matter of hours, Kenny had eaten the whole house. He left nothing.

When William returned, he was furious. He scolded Kenny for eating the house. "I am no longer willing to help you. It's up to the lemurs to help you get to Walter now." Kenny was disappointed in himself for giving in to temptation so easily. He had let Archie down, but he didn't give up. Instead he took William's advice and decided to look for the lemurs.

When he finally arrived at the lemurs' house he was surprised they were so kind. "I know you, you're Kenny. I am Lindsay Lemur," said the head Lemur. "If you want to find Walter Wizard you have to follow me." Lindsay led Kenny to a beautiful garden where the lemurs were having a party.

The party was being held to honor a sacred fruit found only in that part of the forest. It was the juiciest, tastiest fruit known to the animals. Lindsay asked Kenny to guard the fruit for the rest of the lemurs, then she'd lead him to Walter the next day.

As he was guarding the fruit he noticed a small, sneaky little animal nibbling off a small amount of the fruit. "Hey," Kenny shouted.

"Oh, excuse me, is this yours?" the small little animal said. "My name is Sniper, and I'm a chameleon," he informed Kenny as he changed colors.

That chameleon was sneaky. Sniper told Kenny that he'd keep Kenny company all through the night while the lemurs were out

partying. Then Sniper said to Kenny, "Go have fun with the lemurs. I will watch the fruit for you. Nothing will happen to it. I promise." And sure enough, Kenny believed him. When he walked down the hill to the party, the lemurs yelled at him and rushed him back to the top of the hill where he was supposed to be. Then Kenny realized Sniper had fooled him. He had eaten every last bit of fruit.

The lemurs were furious! Lindsay was especially disappointed in Kenny. She said to him, "Kenny, I trusted you with the sacred fruit and you betrayed me. If you want to find Walter you're going to have to go to Sinister the Serpent."

Kenny felt like once again he had let his best friend down. But without hesitation he went down the path in search of Sinister the Serpent. As he was walking he heard "Sssss, you're stepping on me."

"Oh my goodness!" Kenny cried, looking down.

"Hello, Kenny. Lindsay Lemur told me about you. I am Sinister Serpent and if you want to find Walter Wizard, come with me."

Kenny was frightened. Sinister looked like an evil serpent. He had fiery red eyes and a long, narrow body. He led Kenny to a dark cave where two hundred different snakes lived. He noticed two snakes were stuck on a tree branch as if they had been tied up into a knot. Kenny was so afraid he didn't bother asking Sinister about it. Then Sinister led Kenny to a small room where he was to rest the whole afternoon because his task would begin at midnight.

Shortly before midnight, Sinister called for Kenny and explained his task. He was to untie the good snake from the tree branch, leaving the bad one up there while Sinister and the other snakes went egg hunting.

When he went to untie them, two snakes were asleep so Kenny had no clue how to determine which one was good. He closely observed the serpents. One was all black, and had huge yellow eyes, a long forked tongue, and a scaly body, while the other snake was a yellow-spotted white python. Unlike the other snake, there was something serene about the python.

Then the python woke up and said, "Just free me already. You're so lazy."

Kenny went up to the other snake, woke it, and said, "How do you feel about the situation?"

"I think you should follow your heart. That's the only right thing to do." Finally, Kenny released the black, scaly serpent.

When the snakes came back with eggs for their breakfast they were very proud of Kenny. "You have succeeded with your mission. I will take you to the wizard tomorrow," said Sinister.

Like Sinister promised, he led Kenny to Walter's front gate the next day. There were no animals or flowers near Walter's house, only huge trees. Sinister said, "OK, Kenny, my work here is done. Just knock on Walter's door and he'll be out shortly." Kenny nodded and watched as Sinister slithered away.

When Kenny knocked on Walter's door, the chameleon opened it and Kenny heard someone crying inside. The chameleon was scared that Kenny would squash him for tricking him so many times, so he camouflaged himself into the color of the door. But Kenny didn't hurt the chameleon. Instead he gathered his strength and walked into the living room. There he saw Walter crying. He

was so surprised he didn't know what to do. He tapped Walter on the shoulder and said, "Are you OK?"

"Ahhh, what are you doing here?" Walter cried. "Get out of here! Get out!"

"But Walter, you turned my best friend into a frog. I just want Archie back to normal, I've come a long way," Kenny said as Walter cried more and more.

"I don't understand," Walter said. "Why doesn't anyone care about me? Why can't I be loved and have friends the way you and Kenny do?"

"Walter, do you think you're going to have friends if you put spells on people and have your sidekick trick them just because you feel like it?" Kenny asked.

"Well, honestly, I just do it because no one gives me a chance. They think just because I'm green and ugly I don't have any feelings. But I do, Kenny, and I want friends too," Walter complained.

Kenny finally decided to give Walter a chance. The two walked back to Kenny's house and Walter turned Archie back. Walter really was just misunderstood. Talking about everything that had happened, the three got along surprisingly well and became friends. In the end, Walter built a house down the street from Archie and Kenny, and he was welcomed into the community. As for Sniper, he stayed evil and lived unhappily forever and ever. ✷

THE STORY OF GUS THE BUS

by Abe Jue

ILLUSTRATED BY CHRIS PEW

A long time ago, in the mid-nineties, San Francisco was like a big jungle, and only buses could take you from place to place. The city had everything you could imagine. Whatever you wanted to do, there was a place for it. There was a beach that stretched for miles and miles, a park with endless grass, a baseball field, skyscrapers, luscious gardens, and other interesting places. But there was a place called the Danger Zone, and it was the worst part of the city. Animals roamed the streets looking for food. People seemed to disappear from there quite often. No one wanted to be there. Even the people who lived there said they wanted a change, but the politicians were too scared to take action, and it seemed as if the place would rot until everyone moved out.

The one bus that would go all over the city was Gus Monterey. He was the oldest of the buses and was grumpy. He was a mix of three colors: black, orange, and white. But he was so old that he had graffiti all over him, like a blob of colors. Whenever he started up, piles of smoke would come from his exhaust and cause everybody to cough.

One night after a baseball game, Gus and his brothers had the job of driving all the fans from the stadium. In his cockiness he said, "I bet I can drive faster than anybody else!"

His brothers were angered and one of them said, "Just because he's the oldest doesn't mean he's the best!"

Busload by busload, Gus began taking people home at an amazing rate, but on his fourth trip, he was stopped at a stoplight when, out of nowhere, his engine died. The baseball fans were already angry that their team had lost, and if they were stalled any longer, chaos would have erupted. Gus tried for minutes to start back up, but he couldn't move an inch. The passengers found out that it would take an hour for another bus to come and they were furious. They yelled and kicked him. He felt horrible that he had let the people down.

A newspaper columnist who rode Gus that night wrote about his breakdown. The whole city read the paper and the bus family was embarrassed. The article caused many people to shy away from riding buses. Apparently, the buses were getting older and less reliable. People got fed up and they demanded better service. Still, the service remained the same so the riders went to the bus yard to protest.

For three months, people stopped riding the buses. They rode bikes and walked, anything to avoid Gus and his brothers. And they got to work on time without having to pay. People started to question why they had paid the bus company all along.

Gus and his brothers were in bad shape. They were underfed and they started to complain. "We want to be fixed, we need new parts!" But their boss was a mean old man who only cared about how much money he made. He told the buses that they needed to work harder, so the buses worked longer, but still they were mostly empty.

After three months of losing money and respect, the boss told the buses he had to sell his company and that they would be sold or turned into junk metal. The boss mentioned Gus in particular, citing how many times he was late and how none of the riders liked him. Gus decided that he needed to stick up for himself and the buses and take charge of the situation. Gus said, "Sir, this is untrue! We can still work and we have feelings. I will show you how strong we are! I will work until my engine dies or falls apart!"

At first, nobody rode Gus, but after seeing him drive old people and the disabled, people gained confidence in him. More and more people started to ride. Gus woke up at sunrise and did his job, driving all the people throughout the city. He even worked late at night for people who couldn't buy a car. He became well respected again and known all over the city as the hardest-working bus in the world. Riders finally said, "I want to ride Gus the Bus." He became a symbol of hard-working public transportation and a role model to all buses. Everyone had forgotten about the time he broke down.

After a month, though, Gus became tired. His engine gave out at times, his metal body was rusting, and his tires were on their last legs. Late one night Gus was in the Danger Zone. That day had been unusually long because he had woken up early to help kids who needed a ride all the way across town for a field trip. That night he was driving a group of nuns home from church when all of a sudden he slipped on the pavement, drove over some broken glass, and his back right tire blew out. *Poof!* Gus was left there helpless in the middle of the dark streets. He tried desperately to move on three tires, but he couldn't. After a couple of minutes in the street, some bad people noticed Gus. "Hey, guys, it's Gus the Bus. Remember how he always left us standing there in the cold to wait for the next bus? Let's make him pay for all the things he's done to us!"

Gus pleaded with the bad people by saying, "Please, don't hit me, I've changed. Now I'll drive you anywhere." But the people ignored him and charged at him. They kicked him and called him bad names. They thought of how, years ago, they had waitied for Gus for an hour and when Gus came by he had driven right past them. The nuns stood there helpless and all they could do was scream out for help. The people hit and kicked Gus for fifteen minutes and all Gus could do was try to start his engine to drive away, but he couldn't. Finally, Gus's brothers came to the rescue. They scared off the evil people and helped Gus to the bus hospital.

Gus's story was on the six o'clock news everywhere and the whole country knew his story. The bus doctors weren't sure if he was going to make it, but his brothers pleaded for them to try. For sixteen hours, the bus surgeons worked as hard as they could to repair Gus. He got a new body, new headlights, windshield wipers, and even a new engine. In the end, Gus looked better than he had in his prime.

After Gus's repair, there was a party with the people and buses to celebrate and renew peace between the two. It was the best day of Gus's life. He even got a medal of honor for his bravery. During his speech, he said, "I just did what I had to do!" ✳

JACK & HIS QUEST FOR JACK

by Julian Merino

ILLUSTRATED BY MARIA FORDE

Matt and Jack lived in the great, big, bustling city of San Francisco and they were the kindest, most polite brothers there could be. But like the diverse city they lived in, they were different from each other.

Jack was seven years old and he was four feet tall. He needed a stool to brush his teeth. Every morning, Jack would walk to school, even though he didn't like it there. He hardly talked to anyone. At recess, Jack stayed in the corner of the yard while everyone else played. Jack was never wanted on a team. He would always get picked last.

One time, when Jack was playing kickball, he had been the last one up to kick, with his team down by one run. Jack kicked the ball short, the other team caught it, and he lost the game. He felt that he was never good enough.

Matt, on the other hand, was the coolest guy in school. He was taller than Jack by at least a foot and a half. He went to the local high school across the street from Jack's school and everyone who was anyone knew him. "Matt? Yeah, I know him, he drives that shiny black car." "Matt? Oh, he's got straight As." "Matt? He's got everything going for him."

Recently, Matt had stolen the ball from the other team and hit a three-pointer just before the buzzer. He'd made his team number one in the city! He was everything his little brother, Jack, wanted to be.

Without Matt, Jack would feel helpless. If Jack needed help on his homework, Matt would be there. If Jack wanted to go to the park, Matt would take him. If Jack was late to school, Matt would drive him.

One day, Matt took Jack to the park to teach him how to shoot. "Here," Matt said, passing the ball. "Shoot up and out."

Jack tried it, but missed. "I'll never make it, Matt," he mumbled.

Matt tried to reassure him. "It takes practice but you can do it." Jack thought about it and tried it again. He shot out and up, the way Matt had told him to. *Boing.* Jack missed.

After playing for a while, Matt told Jack he was going to get water. "OK," said Jack, as he sat under the basketball hoop. Jack noticed how hot it was and wished he had brought a drink from home. Maybe I'll go with Matt, he thought. Jack walked over to the fountain but Matt was not there. As Jack took a sip from the fountain he thought, He'll be back soon. But a long time passed and Matt never

returned. Jack asked people who were around. No one knew where his brother was.

Jack frantically yelled, "Matt! *Matt!* Where are you?! I wanna go home now! This is not funny!" Jack started to search the playground. He looked by the swings and under the merry-go-round. Jack even stood on top of the tallest slide but he could not see Matt. Jack walked back to the water fountain crying. He wiped the tears off with his sleeve, making a wet ring on his long-sleeved T-shirt, and sat against the water fountain. Just then, Jack noticed a folded piece of paper next to him.

Dear Jack,

If you ever want to see Matt again, you'll have to pay a price. Find all the items on this list and bring them back to this water fountain by sundown tomorrow. All the items must be found or else Matt will not be returned.

- *The Goblet of Hope in the sands of Ocean Beach*
- *The Sword of Courage on top of the north tower on the Golden Gate Bridge*
- *The Rings of Friendship at the bottom of the San Francisco Bay*
- *The Pendant of Love in the cellars of the Ghirardelli Square*
- *The Crown of Knowledge in the statue at Union Square*

You have until sundown tomorrow.

Amazed by the letter, Jack said, "Who wrote this letter? How do they know my name?" Jack looked at the letter again and was shocked that he had to find five items! "It's already noon! I won't find them all in time." Jack slumped down and started to cry again. Jack ran back to the basketball court and with his basketball, shot the ball. *Swish*. Jack made it. "I *can* do it." With that in mind, Jack raced home to start his quest.

At his house he put on his hoodie and emptied out his piggy-bank. Jack looked around the room and saw his backpack. He put a shovel, a snorkel, his goggles, and a rope in it to take with him. You never know what an adventure can bring you.

When Jack was ready to go, he looked at the location of all the items on the list. Since it was easiest to get to, he decided to start at Ocean Beach with the goblet.

When Jack reached the beach, he took out the shovel and looked for a place to dig. "It might be over here by this wall," Jack said. He dug a deep hole that went up to his chest. "I don't think the goblet would be that deep down. Maybe it's closer to the water," he said. Jack moved closer to the water and dug there, but again no luck. Jack moved around all over the beach. He had dug about twenty big holes and still could not find the goblet. It was beginning to get a little dark and Jack felt hopeless. The night would make everything harder to see.

I can't find it. How will Matt come back if I can't even find the first thing on the list?! he thought.

But then Jack saw that in the dark, some of the sand was glowing yellow, as if in daylight. Wondering, Jack began to dig right where the glow was. He dug and dug and kept on digging. Then he heard a thud when the shovel hit something. He picked out an object that was glowing. "This must be the goblet," Jack yelped. "I found it!"

Jack was so happy that he began to jump up and down and do cartwheels. Now he could look for the next item on the list.

Jack decided to go to the Golden Gate Bridge next. When Jack arrived, he saw a staircase that lead him to the top of the north tower. It scared him. If I tie the rope around the railing, I won't fall, he thought. Jack tied his backpack to the rail and climbed. "It won't be that bad," he told himself. He opened his eyes and felt a rush of wind. Then, Jack saw an orange glow ahead. "Here it is!" He found the sword!

"I'm tired," Jack said, yawning. He used his backpack as a pillow and fell asleep quickly. When Jack woke up, he saw the sun shining. From the bridge, he looked at his hometown, San Francisco. The buildings covering the hills and the sun shining on the bay amazed Jack. "Wow. Home looks so different from up here. When I get Matt back, I will bring him up here.

"The list says the Rings of Hope are at the bottom off the bay and this is the bay right here." Jack gulped. "Looks like I have to jump." Jack changed into his swimming shorts and took out his snorkel and goggles. He put them on and looked below. He moved closer to the edge, held his breath, and swan-dove off the tower. Jack's heart beat quickly. Jack yelled as his stomach swirled. "Oh no! This is gonna hurt!"

All of a sudden, a *phffit* came from behind him. The wind had caught Jack's backpack and opened it up like a parachute. He hit the water softly and swam down into the bay.

"It's pretty creepy down here," he said, as he passed a forest of seaweed. Jack played with colorful fish and saw a whale. After a while he saw a blue glow in the distance. Squinting, Jack saw a couple of circular objects on the top of a mound of rocks. "The rings! That's the third item."

Jack tried to swim to the rings but he saw something blocking him. "A shark! Help!" Jack swam round and round the rocks. I have the sword, I can use that, he thought. Jack unhooked the sword from his backpack and led the shark closer to the rocks. Reaching out, he scooped the rings onto the sword. Then he quickly swam ashore.

"The Pendant of Love is close by at Ghirardelli Square," Jack said, running. He headed down Fisherman's Wharf with seaweed on his head, and tourists snapped pictures of him as he ran. Jack made his way to Ghirardelli Square and walked into one of the chocolate factories. The shelves were full of different kinds of chocolate.

A growl came from Jack's stomach. He hadn't eaten since yesterday. While gazing at the mountain of chocolate, a man in a white apron came up to Jack. "You're making my store wet. Out with you!" He took a broom and tried to hit Jack. Frightened, Jack dashed behind an unmarked door and locked it.

Jack looked behind him and saw a stairwell. "This must be the way to the cellar." Jack walked down the stairs and along a long hallway. At the end, Jack could see a door. He opened it to find a castle made of chocolate. A reddish glow came from the tallest tower of the chocolate castle.

"Yay! I'm so hungry!" Jack loaded chocolate into his mouth, eating and eating, until he reached the pendant. Feeling sickly, Jack mumbled, "I got it," and placed it in his backpack.

The last item Jack had to retrieve was the Crown of Knowledge at the statue in Union Square. Jack was having so much fun that he hadn't noticed that it was six o'clock already and sundown came in an hour. "It's just one last thing," he said. Jack looked around and in the middle of the square was a statue of a man in a weird position with an engraving at the bottom. Jack read it to himself, "Begin Every Labor Implementing Endlessly Vast Efforts."

Worrying about the time, Jack shook the statue, saying, "Where's the crown?" When nothing happened, Jack got frustrated. "Come on, statue. I only have until sundown to save my brother!" Jack shook and shook the weird man, knocked it on the head, and punched its chest. Still, nothing happened. Jack paused and looked down at the bottom of the statue. He looked at the engraving and thought that it seemed to spell out something.

"I've got it. The first letter of every word spells B-E-L-I-E-V-E." Jack said to himself, "Believe," and the statue began to move its hand and open up. Inside, there was a green glow. "The crown! It's the last piece of the puzzle!" Quickly putting the crown into his backpack, Jack ran back to the park.

Jack ran to the water fountain where he'd lost his brother and took out all the items in his backpack. He then placed them in a line. But it was already sundown—Jack thought he hadn't returned in time. "OK, whoever you are! I brought back all the things you wanted, just like you said. Tell me where my brother is!" All of a sudden, Matt came up behind him.

"Matt, you're back!" Jack yelled. Jack hugged him tightly. "Wait, who took you? Where'd you go? Are you OK?"

Matt replied, "Slow down! I'm just so proud of you."

"Proud of me? What are you talking about? You were gone for two days!"

"No, I wasn't. I set you up," Matt said.

Surprised, Jack said, "Set me up? What do you mean?"

"Well, you needed some faith in yourself. So I went around and hid the items for you to find, so that you could save me. I wanted you to realize your true colors."

"So I just went all over town, believing that I was saving my brother from never coming back, when you were safe all along?"

Matt tried to reassure Jack, "I want you to believe in yourself. You don't always need me. You can do things for yourself."

Jack thought about his journey. He had done amazingly by himself. He had climbed the Golden Gate Bridge, which took a lot of courage. He had hoped that after digging most of the day, he could find the goblet. He had used knowledge to discover the crown. Jack had even eaten a whole castle of chocolate!

Knowing that he had achieved so much, Jack said, "Yeah, I guess I did!" With that, Jack and Matt walked home, talking and laughing about Jack's adventure. ✳

THE LADY & THE INVISIBLE BOY

by Kai-Fan Tsang

ILLUSTRATED BY DETH SUN

A long time ago, there was an old mansion with lots of rooms and the biggest yard you ever saw. The occupants, Stan and his grandfather, lived very happily together in this giant mansion. They played games, watched movies, and tended to the giant garden. The coolest thing of all was Stan's grandfather's science lab. Eventually, Stan's grandfather grew old and passed away. Stan, having no one else to turn to, lived in the mansion all by himself.

One day, while snooping around in the old science lab, Stan came upon a potion he'd never seen before. As he picked it up, some spilled on his hand. All of a sudden, he began to disappear. This potion was his grandfather's most secret invention of all, the invisibility juice.

One day the house came up for sale. A lady came along to buy the house and her name was Ms. Mole. She was an old lady with puffy round hair, some small-heeled shoes, and a long dress.

"I would like to have a tour of this house," said Ms. Mole to the salesman.

"Certainly," said the salesman, Mr. Winkles.

"Can you tell me the history of this house?" asked Ms. Mole.

"It belonged to a rich old man. He passed away and I was ordered to sell this beautiful mansion. Would you like to buy it?"

"I'd be happy to. I am thinking of making it into an amusement park," said Ms. Mole. So Ms. Mole went back to Mr. Winkle's office, signed the contracts, and the mansion was hers. When she moved in, she tore down the mansion and started to build an amusement park.

After the park construction was finished, Stan stayed around because there was nowhere else to go. He watched as the amusement park's business started to do really well. The lines on the rides were long but the rides were worth the wait.

When the weather was nice and sunny, the water rides were fun and cooled down kids and adults. Fun was never-ending, until the park closed at night.

But soon, things started to get weird.

One night when Ms. Mole was closing and locking up the park late at night, she heard a loud rattle on the gate. She thought there was someone still inside so she walked back to the gate and looked all around.

"Is anybody there?" said Ms. Mole.

"No," said the ghost in a tiny, giggling voice. Ms. Mole left thinking the rattling and the voice were in her imagination after her long, hard day. Then she heard the rattling noise again. There was still no sign of people, but she decided to double check. So she returned, unlocked the gate, and went inside. She walked toward the center of the park and saw a stuffed bear that had fallen off the prize shelf near the carousel. She walked toward the bear to put it back on the shelf. Suddenly, the carousel turned on and played its music while spinning. Ms. Mole thought she had gone crazy! What she had seen couldn't be real. She decided to go to the restroom to wash up so she could wake herself up a little more. In the restroom, she splashed a handful of water onto her face. Then, as she wiped her face dry, she saw two white gloves juggling three colorful balls right in front of her. She fell and fainted.

Stan started to giggle again. He saw that she had fainted so he locked her in the restroom.

The next day, everybody thought Ms. Mole was missing, because the park had not been opened. Every person there was muttering and talking quietly but you could hear things like, "Where is Ms. Mole?" or, "Hmm, I don't know, but where could she be?"

And you could hear the police saying, "Ten-four, I think she's in the restroom. I repeat, I think she is in the restroom." The police had the whole amusement park closed while searching for her. They finally found her inside the restroom, fast asleep. Then they questioned her.

"Are you OK, ma'am?" asked an officer.

"Yes," replied Ms. Mole.

"What happened?" the policeman asked.

"I was closing up and heard a sound, so I opened up the gate again, and the next thing I know I was in here, all locked up!" said Ms. Mole.

The policeman wrote up a report and then replied, "Ma'am, we will have this place searched to find out what really happened. Don't worry, everything is under control. Why don't you just go home and take a nap?" Then Ms. Mole heard the police mutter, "Hey, I think we might have a ghost on our hands and everybody knows the only way to defeat a ghost is with a laser."

But before the police could do anything, Stan decided to play with them. He grabbed one of the officers and put him on an active roller coaster ride. All that the others could see was a floating officer landing on a roller coaster. Stan decided to give another officer a face painting so he picked up the brush and the paint and turned the officer into a clown. He then painted another officer like a cat and made cat noises while moving the officer's lips.

Stan then tied up the rest of the officers on the carousel and squirted them with the water guns from the water booth as they spun around. Ms. Mole was scared so she went to hide in the foggy laser tag room. Stan ran around looking for her while chanting, "Ms. Mo*oole*, where are you? I want to pla*aay*. Ehh Ehh *Ehh*? Come out, Ms. Mo*oole*, I want to play."

Ms. Mole heard his voice though the fog. She didn't know what to do. Stan tried to grab her by the arm, but Ms. Mole dodged him. There was a laser gun next to her on the floor. She decided to pick it up and try it on the ghost. Stan said, "Ehh Ehh Ehh… I want to pla*aay*…"

So Ms. Mole said, "Let's play laser tag, then."

Stan shouted, "OK!"

Ms. Mole put on her laser tag glasses, loaded her laser, zipped up her laser tag vest, and was ready. She shot a couple times. Stan said,

"Ha ha! You missed!" Stan tried to grab the laser shooter out of her hands but couldn't. Ms. Mole suddenly tripped over the laser gun and dropped it. Suddenly the laser went *beewl*. Stan was hit by the laser, which made him feel sleepy, and he went to find a place to rest.

Ms. Mole noticed that Stan was gone, so she untied the police officers. When they were free, they told her to go home.

After a couple of weeks Stan was back again. Ms. Mole heard him and said, "I thought I finished you last time… "

Stan said, "The laser only made me tired. So I decided I had to go to bed."

Ms. Mole said, "What do you want from me now?"

Stan said, "I want to play laser tag with you again."

Ms. Mole said, "I'll play with you but promise not to scare away the customers."

Stan said, "OK, I promise, but you have to play with me when I want to."

Ms. Mole said, "Agreed."

So they became laser tag–playing buddies. Every day she would close the park a little early so she could play laser tag with Stan.

Then one day the potion's effect ran out and Stan became visible again. He realized that he now knew the meaning of friendship, and he and Ms. Mole never stopped playing laser tag.   ✳

THE ADVENTURES OF DRAKE THE DINOSAUR

by Tiffany Lee

ILLUSTRATED BY AVERY MONSEN

My name is Drake Dino and I am a Tyrannosaurus rex. I am light green, like my Papa Dino, with yellow spots that I got from my Mama Dino. I am currently eight years old and attend St. Dino and St. Saur Elementary. We don't have to wear uniforms at school, so I always wear my favorite CatDino T-shirt with red pants and sneakers. I live with my Papa Dino, my Mama Dino, and my older brother, Chester, in a city called Dinoville. Papa Dino and Mama Dino usually have a lot of work and Chester has a lot of friends because he's so cool. I'm thankful that they try to make me happy all the time, because, you see… I was born different.

All dinosaurs have holes in their heads to hear, but I have huge elephant ears. The other dinosaurs look at me weirdly and I usually play by myself in a corner but it gets very lonely after a while. I wish I could look normal like the other kids. I admire my brother, Chester, for being so outgoing. I also envy him because he's so normal. I don't understand why I am the only one with weird ears.

One day I decided to ask my mama about my ears.

"Mama Dino, why are my ears so weird?" I asked while covering them with my hands. I looked at her with tears in my eyes. Mama Dino immediately stopped what she was doing and pulled me into a big hug.

"My little baby, you look very handsome with those ears," Mama Dino said while patting my head. When Papa Dino tries to comfort me, I usually end up feeling worse. Chester tries too, but he's not very good at it either. After all, they can't understand what I go through daily.

I still love school, even though other kids stare at me, and I like my teacher, Mrs. Dranny. She encourages me to play with the other kids every day.

"Go and play. I'll be here to help," Mrs. Dranny said one day, smiling. I nodded and looked around our play yard.

There were some kids playing catch around the four square. I walked toward that group and tapped the dinosaur that didn't look too mean.

"Can I play?" I asked a dino named Lexi. I hoped she heard me, but I was too nervous to repeat myself.

"Sure! You can stand here," a dinosaur named Wilson said while pointing to a spot next to him. I stood on that spot and waited for the game to begin.

Lexi tossed the coconut first. It was passed around for a while but it never came in my direction. I was worried that they didn't want me to play.

"Look out, Drake!" Lexi called. I turned my head around real fast, and accidentally knocked Wilson in the face with my ears.

"Ouch!" Wilson started crying. The coconut landed in my hands, but I dropped it immediately. Everyone ran toward Wilson. Mrs. Dranny was walking toward us too.

"What happened?" Mrs. Dranny asked.

"Drake hit Wilson with his *big* ears! We shouldn't have let him play!" Bono said. I started to cry.

"Go and get some ice, Wilson," Mrs. Dranny ordered. Wilson nodded and walked off.

"I want to go home," I whispered to Mrs. Dranny. I thought about running away to a place where people were weird, just like me. Mama Dino finally arrived and took me home, where I immediately ran to my room.

I jumped onto my bed and thought about running away some more. "I want to go to a place where all dinosaurs are accepted, where all animals look like me," I whispered and fell asleep.

"Hey! Wake up! You're blocking my way home, you know," a little thing buzzed in my ear. I shook my head and wished my ears would hit this annoying thing.

"Watch the ears!" the thing buzzed again. I slowly opened my eyes and saw a purple and green bug staring at me. "Now move so I can get home," it said.

"A bee!" I said. "But aren't bees supposed to be black and yellow, not green and purple?"

"Where have you been? In the Jellotine Forest, everyone is different! Now move." I got up and the bee flew to its hive.

"Where am I?" I asked and looked around. The grass was pink instead of green. The flowers were green in the middle with brown petals. The trees had gold leaves while the trunks were silver. The sun wore sunglasses, the clouds were blue, and the sky was all the colors of the rainbow. I stepped into the field and the grass started to giggle.

I called out to my mama in fear but my mama was nowhere to be seen. Tears started to fall from my eyes. Each one came out in different patterns and colors. The first few drops were circles, then squares, and then rectangles. I sat down and started to cry harder.

"Hey! Watch the waterworks, would you! I'm trying to do my laundry here!" I looked down and saw a blue bug wearing a green T-shirt and red pants.

"What are you?" I asked, sniffling.

"I'm an ant! How can you not know me? I'm Francis Ant, the Second!" the bug yelled, patting its chest.

"It is not obvious! Ants are brown!" I said.

"Not in the Jellotine Forest! We are all different here!" Francis said, wringing out his clothes.

"Jellotine Forest? I've never heard of it! How far is that away from home? I want my mama and my papa and my brother, Chester." I started crying again.

"Hey! Stop crying! I'll help you find your family. Just please stop crying!" Francis yelled. I looked down at him in hope.

"How are you going to help me?" I asked. Francis scratched his head and looked at me.

"I don't know… " Francis pondered. My eyes started to tear up again. "But, I have a friend named Owl who is very wise." Francis took his laundry and disappeared into a hole. He came out a few minutes later with a red bag with white polka dots.

"Come on! Let's go." I stood up to my full height and Francis stared at me.

"Why are you staring at me? Is it because of my ears?" I asked, trying to cover them.

"No. Of course not. It's just that you're so big and tall!" Francis yelled.

"Really?" I asked excitedly. "My brother, Chester, always calls me a shrimp because I am so small. Where are we going, by the way?"

"Toward the forest, of course. Owl cannot stand the daylight. You're not afraid of the dark, are you? A big thing like you," he tried to comfort me.

I swallowed and nodded. I knew Francis would protect me. We continued walking again.

"Where are you from, anyway?" Francis asked.

"Dinoville," I said proudly. Francis stopped walking and looked at me strangely.

"I never heard of that place before. Maybe I'm not as well traveled as I thought," Francis said to himself and started walking again. We walked for a while. To me it seemed like forever.

"Since I'm such a small bug it usually takes me days before I reach the forest," said Francis.

I turned pale. Days? I wanted my mama right away!

"How about I carry you then, Mister Ant? Just tell me where to go," I said.

"I don't know about that idea. I'm sort of afraid of heights," Francis said.

"Please, Mister Ant! I really want to go home," I begged. Francis gave in, and jumped onto my hand. We arrived at the forest in minutes.

I walked into the forest and it was actually pretty on the inside.

I was so absorbed with my surroundings that I didn't notice something was coming toward me until it hit me in the face.

"Ouch!" I said falling back. A red dog repeated what I said. The dog's fur was long; it covered his eyes and even his mouth. His ears were really long too, longer than any dog's ears I had ever seen.

"I should have watched where I was going too," the dog barked.

"Clipper, is that you?" Francis said.

"Francis! I knew I smelled something familiar," Clipper said, wagging his tail.

"Aren't you supposed to be in Cupcake Field performing with your circus?" Francis asked. Clipper's ears drooped at the question. "What's wrong, Clipper?"

"I was tired of Chimpanzee making fun of my ears, so… I left," Clipper replied.

"There's nothing weird about your ears, Mister Dog!" I yelled. Clipper shook his head at me and stretched his ears out. Suddenly he started floating and eventually flying around.

"Whoa!" I yelled and followed his movements. Clipper landed in front of us again. "That's really cool, Mister Dog. I wish I could do that with my ears. My ears are useless," I said.

"Not true! I bet you can hear really well with those ears," Clipper said.

"Well, Mama Dino always said I have very good hearing," I smiled.

Then Clipper asked Francis, "What are you doing in the forest?"

"We're going to ask Owl to help Drake find his way home," Francis explained.

"Mind if I come along? I wouldn't mind having someone to talk to," Clipper said and started flying again.

"Sure!" I said. Then we continued walking until we came across a pink bunny walking on its ears.

"Lula!" Francis and Clipper cried. The pink bunny stopped walking and turned around.

"Why are you guys in the forest with a dinosaur?" Lula asked and tilted her head with curiosity.

"His name is Drake and we're trying to help him find his way home," Francis explained. Lula looked me up and down.

"Nice to meet you, Drake! I'm Lula Shine," Lula chirped.

"Where are you heading to, Lula?" Clipper asked.

"To teach Chimpanzee a lesson! He was making fun of my ears again," Lula said.

"I'm tired of that chimp. He's always going around making fun of others just because he thinks his ears are normal," Clipper said.

"I think your ears are very cool," I whispered. Lula smiled and clapped.

"Thank you! You are a cool dinosaur. How about I give you some tips on karate," Lula said, doing a back flip with her ears.

"That's OK. I just want to go home right now," I explained.

"I'm coming, then! I'll protect you guys from any villain that might come along," Lula said.

"It's great to finally have some friends. Back home I hardly have any," I said. "Because of my weird ears, no one wants to play with me. My ears are so ugly! I wish I could get rid of them." I sighed.

"Your ears are very useful! Don't ever put yourself down because of what other people say," Lula said.

"Yeah! I used to think my ears were worthless too, but one day I saved a kitten from a tree by using my ears to fly up to her. I was so proud of myself," Clipper woofed.

"Besides, like Clipper said, your ears might be very good for hearing," Francis said. I nodded and smiled at my newfound friends. We continued our journey in comfortable silence. Suddenly I heard a strange noise. It sounded like evil laughter.

"I hear something, you guys," I whispered. Everyone stopped walking and listened.

"Right when they're near enough, I'll throw bananas at them!" I heard the voice say.

"It's Chimpanzee! That rotten monkey is picking on people again!" Clipper barked angrily.

"He's over there in that tree!" I yelled and pointed. A purple chimpanzee came out holding bananas.

"So, Big Ears here has found me," Chimpanzee said.

"Try and say that here, in front of me!" Lula said and punched the air. Clipper flew toward Chimpanzee, who dodged and jumped into another tree.

"You can't catch me!" Chimpanzee said, jumping again to another tree. Chimpanzee was so caught up in taunting Clipper that he didn't notice Owl was sitting in the tree that he was about to jump to.

"Bad Chimpanzee," Owl said. He whacked Chimpanzee with his wings. "Stop making fun of the other animals, or they might make fun of you someday." Chimpanzee got up and started running away.

"Whatever! You weird-looking bird," Chimpanzee yelled before he faded away.

"Good job, Drake! You saved us from getting hurt by bananas!" Clipper cheered.

"If you hadn't been here we wouldn't have known about Chimpanzee's plan!" Lula said, patting me on the foot.

Owl flew down from his tree and landed in front of us.

"My friend is lost and he wants to go home," Francis explained.

"You know why you are here?" Owl asked. I shook my head. "You wished to be here," he hooted.

"I didn't really want to run away! I just wanted everyone to accept me and to fit in. I don't want to lose Mama Dino, Papa, or Chester either," I cried, tears falling from my eyes. Francis, Clipper, and Lula came over to comfort me.

"I want my mama! I want my papa! I want my brother!" I yelled.

"You will see them again soon," Owl hooted. I wiped my eyes and looked at him hopefully. "You were sent here to learn a lesson. Do you understand what that lesson is now?"

I looked at him and nodded. "I need to accept myself. My ears make me special. And I shouldn't think about running away, because my family is important," I said.

"You have learned a lot from this journey. It makes me very happy. Go to sleep and when you wake up, you'll find yourself at home," Owl hooted and smiled. The last thing I heard before I fell asleep was Lula, Francis, and Clipper saying good-bye.

I slowly woke up and looked at my surroundings. "I'm home," I whispered. My door opened and Mama Dino stuck her head in

"Are you feeling better, Drake?" Mama asked. I nodded. She walked in holding a plate of cookies. Papa and Chester came in right behind her. They all sat down on my bed.

"Are you feeling better, kiddo?" Chester asked.

"Yep! Starting tomorrow I'm going to make a lot of friends," I said.

"That's my boy!" Papa Dino said and smiled.

"My baby brother is growing up!" Chester said and started to tickle me. Mama and Papa Dino joined in. I laughed and tried to get them to stop. ✳

WHERE'S CARLOS?

by Jasmine Criss

ILLUSTRATED BY MARIA FORDE

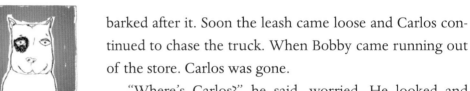

Bobby lived with his mom in a big blue house in San Francisco. Bobby was an eight-year-old with green eyes and long brown hair. He talked a lot, mostly about his dog, Carlos, who was a very playful white pitbull with a big black spot on his eye. Bobby's mom was a sweet lady with hazel eyes and light brown skin. Her voice was soft and smooth, as if she used to be a jazz singer. Carlos barked really loudly and wagged his tail when he was happy. If he was sad, his bark got really soft and his eyes got watery. He loved to walk around the house biting shoes and playing tug-of-war with Bobby.

One day Bobby's mom asked him to go to the store with Carlos and get a carton of milk so she could make him a cake for his birthday, which was the next day. Bobby was really happy. All his friends were coming over for a party, so he couldn't wait to get back home and help his mom make the cake.

When they got to the store, Bobby tied Carlos to a pole and then went in. But, rushing to get back home, Bobby forgot to make sure the leash was tight enough. As Carlos waited he smelled a meat truck. He began barking and pulling toward the truck to get a big juicy steak. When the truck started, Carlos began running and barked after it. Soon the leash came loose and Carlos continued to chase the truck. When Bobby came running out of the store. Carlos was gone.

"Where's Carlos?" he said, worried. He looked and looked and called his name but Carlos was nowhere to be found. As Bobby walked home, tears began to fall from his eyes. When his mother opened the door she yelled, "Where have you been?" Then Bobby looked up at her with red, watery eyes.

"What's wrong?" she said.

Bobby mumbled, "Carlos ran away."

She gave him a hug. "It's going to be all right," she said, trying to cheer him up

Meanwhile, Carlos had chased the truck all the way to the meat factory. As he walked around, he began to remember Bobby and how fun and warm his house was. "I've got to get home," Carlos barked. "Where am I?"

Carlos was walking down the street when he heard a voice saying, "Where are you going?" Then from behind a trash can came a little brown, furry collie named Paulina. It was Carlos's friend from down the street. She was also lost. She had just moved to San Francisco and talked like a nine-year-old girl from Brooklyn.

"What are you doing here?" Carlos said.

"Well, the mailman came to my house today and I chased him all the way over here," said Paulina.

"Wow, did you catch him?" said Carlos.

Paulina said, "No, he ran into a building and stayed there."

"Man, I sure wish you had caught him. I'm sick of him slipping papers into my house," said Carlos.

Carlos looked around. It was dark with huge old buildings everywhere. "I think we should start asking people to help us get home," said Carlos.

"Yeah, but who? There's no one around," said Paulina.

"Hey, look over there," said Carlos. They began to walk toward a big brick building with music coming out of it.

Paulina walked in first, then Carlos. It was loud and colorful. There were dogs everywhere dancing, singing, and just hanging around. There were big dogs, small dogs, blue dogs, red dogs, furry dogs, and dogs with spots.

Carlos and Paulina ran to the middle of the dance floor and began to dance while a Chihuahua was singing everything—from reggae to R&B and hip-hop.

After they danced they began to ask the other dogs in the club how to get home. First, they asked a small, furry red Pomeranian named Aimée.

"Excuse me. Can you help us get home?" said Paulina.

"Oh, no, I can't help you. Besides, even if I could, I just had my paws done and I'm not getting them dirty," she said in a snobby French accent.

Then they asked a big dog named La'Sean. He was wearing a black-and-white cap, a white T, and black jeans, and had a toothpick in his mouth. "Excuse me, can you help us get home?"

"No, I can't. I'm busy trying to talk to that pretty pink dog with the white spots," he said in a deep street-like voice.

After asking most of the dogs for help and being turned down, Carlos and Paulina started to cry. Then a big black Great Dane named Lucky asked them in a smooth country voice, "What's wrong? Why are y'all crying?"

Carlos and Paulina said, "We're lost."

Lucky, feeling sorry for them because he knew how it felt to be lost, said, "I'll help you get home. Let's go!" So Lucky, Carlos, and Paulina started home.

They followed him down a small dark alley. Carlos barked, "Look, food."

They started eating, and then they heard, "Meow, meow." When they looked up, they just one little alley cat with a scary, raspy voice.

He hissed, "Get out of here. Stop eating my food." But because they were hungry and there was only one cat they just kept eating.

Then about fifteen alley cats slowly began to creep toward them, hissing with their sharp claws out, ready to pounce. The cats looked wild and dirty and had sharp teeth.

Carlos looked up and started to bark at them while saying, "They're just cats. We can take them." But the cats looked at each other and then ran toward him. They jumped on Carlos, hissing.

Paulina and Lucky ran over to Carlos to help. "Let's get out of here! I know a shortcut!" yelled Lucky, and they ran.

Meanwhile, at his house, Bobby wouldn't play with his friends when they came over to celebrate his birthday.

He ended the party early and sat in his room without even eating cake. His mother walked upstairs and sat next to him on the bed.

"Hey, honey, how are you doing?" she said in a soft voice.

"Mom, why did Carlos run away?" Bobby said, trying to hold back his tears.

"Well, I don't know, but I bet he's thinking of you right now and when he's ready, he'll come home."

Running from the cats, Carlos, Lucky, and Paulina came to a big gray building. Lucky got nervous. "This is the pound and none of us have tags on." Lucky looked around. "I used to live here before I ran away."

"Why did you run away?" Carlos and Paulina asked Lucky at the same time.

"Well, I was lonely, the food was bad, there were always bugs in my water, and I had to sit and a small dark cage all day. So one day I got sick of it and when the guard opened my cage to give me my food I jumped on him and growled. After I scared him I began to run down the long hallway that led to the exit. Once I was out, I was happy, but I still had no place to go. I've been hoping one day I'll find a real home," Lucky said.

"Hey, when we get to my house maybe Bobby will let you live with us," said Carlos.

All of a sudden, they heard a voice. "Hey, Lucky, is that you?" It was the dogcatcher!

"Where did you think you were going? I didn't say you could leave," he said. Just as he was about to grab them, Lucky ran behind him and bit him once on his butt.

"Awww!" screamed the dogcatcher. Lucky looked toward Carlos and screamed, "Run!" Then he freed all the dogs by hitting a big red button that opened every cage door.

The dogcatcher tried to stop some of them by blocking the door but the dogs just ran over him. After all the dogs were out, Carlos, Paulina, and Lucky began to walk until they got to Bobby's house.

After that night Carlos never got lost again. He would still go to the dance club with Lucky and Paulina but they always came straight home.   ✳

MAGICAL WISH

by Karen Luu

ILLUSTRATED BY MARCI WASHINGTON

Janella was a friendly, bighearted girl who was always helping her friends and family. And she loved to read. She was always at the library reading fantasy books.

One day at the library, she found a book called *The Magical Wish*. When she pulled it from the shelf, a secret door leading down to a hidden stairway opened up. Janella was shocked.

She carefully peeked in. The stairway was lit with floating blue candles and it led to a tunnel. She walked down the stairs farther and farther until she saw an orange light. She then skipped the rest of the way and found herself in a forest.

The forest was bright and had trees of all different sizes with leaves shaped like stars and moons. There were also many colorful flowers. Janella ran around exploring the forest.

Suddenly, Janella tripped and fell near the tallest and leafiest tree. She saw that there was a big pink sign on it that read: THIS IS THE HOME OF KAY, FAIRY OF MAGICAL WISHES. Janella had never seen a fairy before. She called out, "Fairy! Oh fairy! Can you come out, please?" Nothing happened. Janella called out again, but there was silence. Janella called out once more. Then *boom*! A big poof of glittery powder puffed out of the tree and a tiny green magical fairy appeared with pink hair and purple wings. It was Fairy Kay!

She asked Janella, "What is wrong, my child?"

Janella's words came out in a rush. "Fairy, I have a best friend who has the chicken pox and they won't go away! She's miserable and itchy and I really miss her. I want to ask you to help her so she can play with me again."

The fairy said, "Janella, since you came all the way to the hidden magical forest and because you are so kind to care about your friend, I will help you!"

"Thank you so much, fairy!" she said, jumping up and down.

The fairy then said, "Oh, but wait, if I help you and Tiffany, you have to return the favor."

Janella agreed, but was a little worried. The fairy gave Janella a pouch filled with blue glittery fairy dust and told Janella to sprinkle it around Tiffany three times and give her a great big hug. "Her chicken pox will disappear one by one," she said.

The fairy then added, "Janella, once Tiffany is healed, you and she must come back and look for me, or her chicken pox will return *forever*!"

"OK, fairy, I promise to come back," said Janella.

Janella ran all the way, holding the pouch tightly. When Janella got to Tiffany's house, she pulled Tiffany out of bed and made her stand, sprinkled the blue fairy dust around her three times, and gave her a great big hug. They looked on as the chicken pox disappeared one by one.

"Janella, it really worked! You are such a great best friend!" Tiffany said.

The two began to play hide-and-seek right away and played until it was dark and they were exhausted. Janella was so excited that Tiffany was all better that she forgot to tell her about going back to the fairy.

The next morning when Janella woke up, she remembered the promise and hurried to call Tiffany, thinking that her chicken pox had returned.

"Tiffany! Wake up! Look in the mirror," said Janella

"Hey, Janella. Is something wrong?" Tiffany said. When Tiffany reached the mirror she screamed, "I got all the chicken pox back!"

Janella told Tiffany that she'd forgotten to tell about a promise she'd made to go back to the fairy. They both ran out of their house and met up at the library. When Janella went to the section where the book was, it was missing! But there was a note there saying:

To Janella,

You did not keep your promise! Tiffany will have the chicken pox forever!"

Janella and Tiffany searched everywhere for the book, but couldn't find it. They asked the librarian what had happened to the book, and the librarian said that the book was old and that they were ordering a new one, which would be here soon.

For a couple of days, Janella continued to go to school and to play by herself. After a few days, they went back to the library. When Janella and Tiffany approached the fantasy bookshelf, Janella spotted the book! She took it out and the shelf opened. Tiffany was shocked to see what happened. They both went in and Janella led Tiffany to the biggest, tallest, and most leafy tree in the forest.

There, Janella called out to the fairy, "Fairy, oh Fairy, please come out. I am so sorry I forgot my promise." Silence covered the forest. Janella then said, "Fairy, please, oh please come out. We will do anything you say!" Then fairy dust came out of the tree and Fairy Kay appeared again.

The fairy said, "I am disappointed in you! But I do have a favor to ask you two." Janella and Tiffany were anxious to hear what the fairy wanted. She said, "I am lonely here in the magical forest, and I want to see the real world. Could you let me stay with you two for a while? I will be invisible to everyone else. And I will take Tiffany's chicken pox away."

"Yes," the girls said, "we will let you come to the real world and play with us."

The three then walked past the tunnel and to the door that led to the library. Fairy Kay was nervous but Tiffany held her hand and they walked out through the shelf. Janella smiled to Tiffany and the fairy. Then they ran all the way to Tiffany's house while the fairy followed, flying. Janella first sprinkled the fairy dust around Tiffany three times, gave her big great big hug, and the chicken pox all disappeared again

The fairy was amazed at the real world and asked the two girls many, many questions. She asked Janella and Tiffany what the name of the place was that they'd come out of. The girls answered that it was a library.

"What is a library?" Kay asked

Janella responded, "A library, it's a place where you go to borrow and read books."

"What was that big rectangle on the four black things? What was this gray hard thing on the floor? What were those big triangles with a square under them?" Kay asked.

Janella and Tiffany laughed but answered, "The big rectangle is a bus. It picks people up and takes them where they want to go. The four black things are called tires. They help the bus move. The gray hard thing is called a road. And those triangles with squares are called houses. Houses are where humans live."

Janella and Tiffany then taught the fairy how to play hide-and-seek, and they played until they were too tired. The next day, Janella and Tiffany went to school and the fairy followed. The fairy had so much fun playing with the girls that she didn't want to go back to the magical forest.

But the next day, after Janella and Tiffany played some games, the fairy got homesick. Janella and Tiffany decided to take the fairy back to the magical forest. All three went into the library and took the book out once again. The shelf opened and the fairy was excited to get back home. Janella and Tiffany skipped to the forest while the fairy flew in front of them. When the three got to the fairy's tree, the fairy said, "Home sweet home!" Janella and Tiffany giggled. The fairy thanked the two girls for bringing her out to the real world and teaching her all about it, especially how to play all the fun games.

The girls had so much fun with Kay that they didn't want her to leave. Fairy Kay then came up with the idea that Janella and Tiffany should come visit her once a week. The two girls then smiled with joy and thought that was a great idea! Fairy Kay made Janella and Tiffany promise.

Kay said, "So, Janella and Tiffany, I hope to see you two once a week from now on." To make a promise, you have to keep the promise! Or there will be consequences!"

Janella and Tiffany said, "We promise!"

All three of them smiled and hugged each other.   ✳

THE PRINCESS OF FUN LAND

by **Sandra Ortega**

ILLUSTRATED BY LART COGNAC BERLINER

Everyone loved Fun Land. It was a city with a lot of clubs, parks, and other places to entertain yourself. It was beautiful with flowers—all you could see were colors—and it was clean.

But this city had problems that needed to be solved. It was run by a committee that worked with a princess who helped make all the decisions. When they needed a new change, the people of the city voted and picked a new princess.

One of the problems was that the grades of schoolkids were dropping dramatically. Also, a lot of people worked too much and they were too stressed out. So they thought it was time for a new princess.

The city had two candidates. One of them was Angelina. She was willing to do all it took to solve the problems. She was a pretty, tall girl, and sensitive, with long hair and nice brown eyes. She volunteered a lot in the community. The other candidate was Jasmine. She was also tall, but with long black hair. She was straightforward and aggressive, and did not help out unless she needed to. Jasmine wanted to shorten school hours to have more time to play and goof off.

There were five days to get everything prepared and to pick a princess, so both girls went everywhere in the city to convince the people to vote for them. The girls had totally different opinions about how they were going to do their changes.

When the day came to vote for a princess a lot of people showed up to vote. Everyone was excited to see the results.

Jasmine obnoxiously said, "I'm going to be the winner!"

Kathy, Jasmine's best friend, said, "Angelina's not fun enough to be a princess!" Kathy was just like Jasmine—they liked to talk about people and put them down.

Angelina ignored them, telling herself, "Let the best person win."

While people were voting the girls went ice skating. At the rink, Angelina fell and Jasmine and Kathy laughed really hard. They both mocked her, "Like, she totally doesn't even know how to skate. What a loser!" Angelina tried to ignore them but it was making her mad.

It was time to count all the votes. By the end of the day they would know who the winner was. The winner would be crowned that night at the Great Ball.

This ceremony was one of the most famous balls—huge and

beautiful, bright and shiny like a star. And only the most important people in the city were invited to attend. The media would be there with photographers.

The party started with music and appetizers and all the fabulous people started dancing. Angelina's and Jasmine's family members were also there. The master of ceremonies was about to announce the winner with a small speech. He said, "This city needs someone to rule it, but really, you the people rule it. And you voted for your new princess. The city goes to… Angelina!"

You could barely hear over the people's shouts of happiness. "Hurray!" The master of ceremonies put the crown on her head and gave another speech. He told her, "We give you all the rights to make changes for the best. We hope you open your heart to the entire city."

Jasmine was so upset, she didn't even congratulate Angelina! She and Kathy only stayed at the party to mess it up and get Angelina mad. But Angelina ignored them and tried to have fun as everybody congratulated her.

One of Angelina's family members took Angelina out to dance. While they were dancing, Kathy stuck her foot out and tripped Angelina. When Angelina fell and broke the crown, Kathy and Jasmine laughed so hard. Luckily, it wasn't the real crown.

Jasmine and Kathy planned to do something else too just to ruin the lovely time Angelina was having. They both thought of dropping paint on Angelina's face while she took a picture. So they put paint in a fake camera and it squirted on her. Again, Jasmine and Kathy laughed.

Even though Jasmine and Kathy hurt her feelings, she knew she should ignore them. Angelina washed her face and changed into a nice red dress that made her look beautiful. Everyone was shocked because she looked so pretty. No one could keep their eyes away from her. This got Jasmine mad because she wanted all the attention. Angelina was getting to know a lot of people, and she danced all night with handsome guys. All of this was getting Jasmine so upset that she wanted to do something else to her, but she and Kathy had run out of ideas. They left the party mad.

The next morning Angelina had to be at the palace for a meeting where she was going to present herself to the city. They also needed to measure her head to fit the crown. Angelina picked out another nice red dress for the announcement she was going to make. All you could hear were the noise and cheers of the city outside the palace balcony. Angelina stepped out, happy to see the excitement. She could also see Jasmine and Kathy among the people. She didn't care, but she knew that they were up to no good. Angelina gave her speech to her people.

After she was done, Jasmine and Kathy yelled out loud and said that they had seen Angelina pick her nose! They were both laughing. Angelina ran off the balcony and went inside to cry on her bed. Everyone outside looked at Jasmine and Kathy and said that they were mean. That's why they didn't think Jasmine was the right candidate to be princess, and that's why she didn't win. They yelled to Jasmine, "That's why we didn't vote for you! You're so mean!" At that moment, Jasmine felt like Angelina had felt. She wanted to cry and went running home.

Two days passed and neither of them came out of their rooms. Jasmine was at home thinking of everything mean she had done to Angelina and she realized that if she hurt someone it was going to come back to her.

The next morning, Jasmine got up and went to the palace to talk to Angelina. Angelina received her, but with a sad face. Jasmine told

RYAN JACOBS
PATRICK HOFFMAN
SIMONE WELKS
AZSA WEST
JEFF CHILDS

CAMERON STONE
KIM CLARK
STEVEN SNYDER
JASMINE BROOK
KEITH RITCHIE
GABE TUCKER
DAMON BUTTS
DAVID KRAMER

her that she was very sorry, that jealousy had made her act that way. They gave each other a good hug and Angelina forgave her. Angelina told Jasmine that there was a position open for secretary, and she should apply for it before someone else did. Jasmine applied for it and got the position because there was nobody else running for it. Kathy came to congratulate Jasmine and apologized to Angelina.

When Jasmine got the secretary position, she had to take a picture for her palace ID. Angelina accidentally picked up the fake camera from the Great Ball, and as she snapped the photo, the camera splashed paint onto Jasmine's face. She laughed and so did Angelina.

After that, they both worked hard to improve everything that had to be done. Angelina made an arrangement that said if you went to school and did well, then Friday and Saturday would be goof-off days. This arrangement worked for everyone! The school grades improved so much that everyone got to goof off. After that, everything went well between them. Angelina, Jasmine, and Kathy were best friends. Every Friday and Saturday the girls goofed off together. ✳

SCOUT IN SEARCH OF SCOUT

by Devon Barnett

ILLUSTRATED BY MICK WIGGINS

Scout grew up knowing he looked different from every dog in his family. Scout had fur as white and as pure as the snow while his mom, dad, brothers, and sisters had blue fur with red spots. He felt all alone in the world. His mom and dad noticed that he never left the doghouse so on his birthday they bought him a blue sweater with red spots. Scout was so happy about it that he wore it everywhere even as it grew old, faded, and full of holes.

One hot summer day while playing tag with his brothers and sisters in the forest he took off his sweater and set it down on a rock. While they were playing, a sneaky wolf came up and stole it. Afterward, when Scout went to look for his sweater, he couldn't find it. Scout asked his brothers and sisters to help him search but they couldn't find it either. He started crying and ran home to his mom. She promised him that she and his dad would find him another sweater just like his old one. The next day, his parents went in to town to find another sweater. They searched high and low but they couldn't see another one. Back home, Scout's mom even tried to make him a new one, but the sleeves were not even, there was no opening for his head, and the spots turned out lopsided.

Scout started staying home all day long. His brothers and sisters would invite him out to play but he'd say he didn't feel good. They got tired of waiting around for him to get better and once again they started teasing him and leaving him out of their games. So Scout decided to run away from home.

One snowy winter night he waited until everyone was asleep. He tiptoed out the front door, looking back at his family one more time before leaving. Then he ran quickly and happily tumbled in the snow. As he grew tired he needed to find a nice warm cave to sleep in.

Scout awoke the next morning and noticed that he was not alone in the cave. He saw Mrs. Cottontail and her five children staring at him with wide eyes and open mouths. They feared he was a young wolf.

"Hey," said Scout. Startled by his words, the little rabbits ran around in a panic.

"Wolf! Wolf!" the five of them screamed.

"Wolf?! Where?" screeched Scout as he pawed his way under a pile of leaves.

After Mrs. Cottontail calmed her children and eased Scout out of hiding, she offered him some breakfast. Mrs. Cottontail asked Scout what such a young puppy was doing all alone in the forest. Scout told his story.

Mrs. Cottontail listened and replied, "Even though you don't look like them, they are still your family and they're probably worried about you. Stay close to the ones who love you the most, like your family and friends."

Scout missed his family after seeing how happy Mrs. Cottontail and her children were, so he decided to go back home. While walking he saw kids playing in the forest, and they too had left someone out of their games. He remembered what it felt like to be left out and he began to cry. He ran in the opposite direction from home. Scout ran and ran, ending up even farther away from Mrs. Cottontail's home, near the tall trees.

Sitting upon the lowest branch of a tree was Snowy Owl. He had seen Scout running and crying.

"Whooo goes there?" asked Snowy Owl.

Scout sat down in the snow and started crying. Snowy Owl saw that he had scared the poor little puppy and he flew down to the snow where Scout was sitting.

"Please don't hurt me," pleaded Scout.

"I would never hurt yooou," whispered Snowy Owl.

After a while Scout calmed down and was ready to tell the owl his story.

"Don't yooou think your family is worried about yooou?" asked Snowy Owl.

"They probably don't even know I'm gone," said Scout.

"Well, whooo do yooou think yooou are going to live with if not your family?" asked Snowy Owl.

"I might go and find myself another doghouse to sleep in," said Scout.

"Can yooou take care of yourself?" Snowy Owl asked.

"No," said Scout.

"See, yooou need yooour family. Yooou have tooo go back home," said Snowy Owl.

The next day Snowy Owl and Scout headed toward Scout's home. When it became night, Snowy Owl told Scout they'd better rest because they were going to go twice as fast tomorrow. As Snowy Owl fell asleep, Scout was thinking once again about his brothers and sisters and how they left him out of their games. Soon the tears came back to his eyes and he began to run.

He kept running until he tripped over a branch and stumbled into Polar Bear's giant cave. Startled by the visitor, Polar Bear suddenly jumped up.

"Aaghh!" he hollered.

Scout just looked at him with wide eyes.

"W-w-who are you?" Polar Bear managed to stutter.

"H-h-how did such a little puppy make it all the way out here by himself?" asked Polar Bear.

Scout then told Polar Bear his story. Polar Bear insisted that Scout have some food and offered him some advice.

Polar Bear said, "T-t-there are families all around the world with members that look different from each other. Your family doesn't even have to mean just your actual family. Many families include friends too."

The next morning, after Scout ate breakfast, Polar Bear walked Scout to the end of his cave and they said their good-byes. Scout began walking toward his home but then he took off in the opposite direction again, past Polar Bear's cave, coming to an empty part of the forest where there was a huge mountain. Scout climbed up the side of the mountain, pulling himself up with his paws. Once on top, Scout walked down the other side. On his way down, Scout spotted some animals who looked like him and he thought they were other dogs, although they were actually wolves. He was so excited that he almost fell down the rest of the mountain. When Scout got to the bottom, he walked up to them as if he had known them his whole life.

"Hey, guys," said Scout, but the wolves weren't as excited to see Scout as he was to see them.

"*What do you want?!*" Ears, the leader of the group, demanded.

Scout was scared by his words and began to cry. While he was crying he noticed that a wolf who was wearing a sweater had come to the front of the pack.

"Hey, that looks like my sweater," said Scout.

"You wish," said the wolf.

"I lost a sweater that looked just like that one," said Scout.

"Yeah, well, finders keepers," growled the wolf.

Scout was about to apologize to the wolves for intruding on them. As he was turning away he noticed that the sweater had holes similar to the holes in his sweater.

"You found that sweater on a rock, didn't you?" asked Scout.

"Yeah, so what? It's mine now," snapped the wolf.

"I want my sweater back!" screamed Scout. Scout was so angry he was about to jump on the wolf and start a barking feud.

"Calm down, everybody," said Ears. "Just give him the sweater back before he goes crazy."

"Fine," said the wolf.

"Go home and don't you ever think about coming back or you'll be sorry you did," Ears threatened. Scout gladly agreed and ran off.

Scout didn't stop running until he got back home. He was surprised that nobody was there. He went to sleep outside of his house and was still asleep when his mom, dad, brothers, and sisters all walked up to the doghouse. They were in tears because they hadn't found Scout, but they stopped in their tracks and stared when they saw him sleeping. Then they all rushed toward him. Scout opened his eyes but just thought he was dreaming. He gave his eyes a good rub and realized that he wasn't, it was his family!

"Mom! Dad!" Scout shouted excitedly as he ran toward them.

They all hugged, glad that he was back home. Then they noticed that he had found his sweater but wasn't wearing it. They asked why this was so. He told them about his journey and that he learned that he didn't need the sweater to make him feel like he belonged in the family anymore.   ✻

POE LOSES HIS PAINTBRUSH

by Annie Wong

ILLUSTRATED BY ANNA URA

P oe had two good friends: his canvas and his paintbrush. The canvas was his blank sheet of paper, his white wall, his freshly paved cement sidewalk. The paintbrush created life and chaos. Poe loved to paint. His imagination was as wild as horses and pigs escaping from their farms, and it made him a good painter. He painted a house in the middle of a purple lake. He painted the sun riding a skateboard. He painted a bed with wings, flying to the moon in the middle of the night.

Poe painted in all his free time. His dog, Pabe, usually had paint all over his paws.

Poe's teacher hung his paintings all over the classroom. His parents entered him in art contests, and Poe usually won first place.

However, Poe was not popular among his classmates. He often criticized their artwork. He even painted over their works. "You drew that all wrong! It's supposed to look like this!" He would say that their paintings were ugly compared to his. He boasted that he was the greatest painter in the universe. Poe thought he was doing his classmates a favor by giving them his honest opinion, but he wasn't well liked by them. Painting was his only priority; friends didn't matter to him. Poe usually spent his days at school by himself or with his lone friend, Pete.

One afternoon during art class, Poe approached his classmate Pamela. She was painting a picture of her family. Poe just stared at it with bulging eyes. Then he opened his mouth.

"Wow! I never thought it was possible, but someone finally painted the ugliest painting ever. I mean, look at your mom. You made her look like a horse. And your dog reminds me of a soggy pile of beans with a pair of eyes!" Poe sneered with a pleased grin on his face.

Pamela dropped her paintbrush on the floor. Sobbing, she fired back, "This is my painting, not yours! Why do you always have to be such a jerk? Did you ever stop and think about why you only have one friend in this entire school?"

No one had ever stood up to Poe. It took a long time for him to think of a good comeback. "Who needs friends when you're the greatest painter in the world? I'm going to be rich and famous! While I'm painting masterpieces, you're going to sit here for the rest of your life painting ugly pictures of your family," Poe spat out.

Pamela's eyes were a pair of water balloons; Poe was determined to pop them both. But that was the last straw for Pamela. She ran to the girls' bathroom and remained there for the rest of art class.

Poe continued on his insult rampage. "Penny, I can't tell if that's a dog or a cat or you in the picture! Paul, I think your picture needs a little black!" Poe painted a black slash across Paul's painting of tall buildings and skyscrapers.

"Poe! You're really gonna get it one day!" Paul screeched angrily.

"I don't think so!" Poe sang.

Poe's friend, Pete, was the only one who could stand Poe's attitude. The two had been friends since the days of preschool and alphabet soup. They met when Poe became curious about the covers of the picture books Pete was reading. They read and looked at the pictures together. This sparked their friendship and Poe's interest in art.

However, Pete was a shy person. It was difficult for him to chat with other kids and make friends. Poe was Pete's only friend. Pete was a writer, an eager reader, and the worst artist in the world next to Pabe the dog. He didn't participate in art at all, so he didn't have to take Poe's nitpicking. Whenever Poe painted, Pete usually sat next to him and read.

"Poe! I've been reading this book about strange bugs. Have you ever heard about a Painter's Block Creepy Crawler? It's shaped like a block, and it has all the colors of the rainbow on its body, like an art palette. It has seven legs; each leg is a different color. The book says the bug bites kids all over the world, and one bite causes them to lose their ability to draw or paint well. It also says it causes them to lose all their ideas for future paintings. Are you scared yet?" asked Pete.

Poe replied, "That's just silly talk! How can one bite do all that

harm? I'm not scared at all. Plus, does the book mention where that bug lives?"

Pete flipped a couple pages in his book, took a deep breath, and exclaimed, "They live everywhere in the world! It could be in your backyard, your laundry basket, even your bed! Be very careful, Poe. Don't say I didn't warn you, because I just did."

"Pete, nothing ever happens in this town we live in. If the Creepy Painting Block Crawler, or whatever it's called, decides to come live here, it'll be a huge celebrity," Poe joked. What Poe didn't admit was that he was scared out of his mind. The bug was all he thought about for the rest of the day.

That night, Poe put on his thickest sweatshirt and sweatpants, three pairs of socks, and a scarf. He told himself it was just a silly story and none of it was true. But he stayed awake in bed for a long time before he finally drifted off into the land of snoring and fantastic dreams.

Poe was awakened the next morning by a ray of sunlight that shot through his window. Since he didn't feel any pain or tingling or any different at all from the night before, Poe felt like he had outsmarted the Painter's Block Creepy Crawler. He got up to brush his teeth. In the mirror, he noticed a bright pink circle on the palm of his hand. Poe thought it was paint that he had not washed off. He scrubbed at the pink mark, but it would not come off!

In art class that afternoon, Poe began a new project. He started to paint a straight line, but it turned out curved. He tried to draw a triangle, but it turned out as a circle. His circles turned out pointy, and his squares only had three sides. Frightened, Poe tried to paint a spider, but it ended up looking like a huge black dot. After that, he gave up and put away his art supplies.

When Poe was washing his hands, he noticed the strange pink

mark on his hand again. Then it hit him like a ninety-mile-per-hour fastball.

"Could it be the bite of a... Painter's Block Creepy Crawler?" Poe wondered.

That night, Poe tried again to revive his failing painting skills. He held up the paintbrush, but his mind went blank. No ideas came through his head. Then Poe remembered what Pete had told him: First, you lose your ability to paint. Then, you will form no new ideas about anything related to art. Poe rushed back into the bathroom and tried again to wash away the bright pink mark.

The next morning, Poe searched frantically for Pete. He found him in the library.

"What's up?" Pete asked.

"The bug... the Painter's Block bug... it bit me! I tried to paint, but I couldn't put anything on paper!" Poe ranted.

"That's so bizarre! I'll try to find a cure for you. It'll take three weeks, though. I suggest you find a new hobby for now, so you don't strain your brain thinking about anything artsy."

"Why would it take three weeks?" a puzzled Poe asked.

"Somebody checked that book out, the one that I was reading to you yesterday. Whoever has it, has it for three weeks," Pete informed Poe.

Defeated, Poe trudged into art class. He felt he had to do something with art. He took out black paint and splattered it over a blank canvas. His classmates thought his behavior was weird. His black-splattered painting was the simplest thing they'd seen Poe do.

One classmate, Preston, approached Poe and said meanly, "Hey, Poe, seems like you lost your great artistic skill." Poe heard Pamela giggling behind him.

Poe muttered, "You've got that right."

When Poe got home from school, he thought hard about finding a new hobby. He decided to try reading like Pete. He picked up the *New York Times* and he read the headline out loud, APPROVAL RATE OF PRESIDENT DROPS FORTY-EIGHT PERCENT! What does that even mean? Poe wondered. He kept on reading anyway. The sentences in the article didn't interest him or make any sense to him. All of a sudden, the words in the article started crashing into each other and melting. This melted blob formed two booming sentences: *You are not a reader, Poe. Stop now.*

Next he tried bike riding. It took Poe a while to get balanced. When he finally did, he started pedaling as fast as his legs would go. Flying down the street at 115 miles per hour, Poe thought he was doing well. However, he did not see the red fence in front of him until it was too late.

He decided ten scrapes, five bruises, and a bunch of red splinters stuck in his face were enough for one day. He walked his bike and himself home.

Poe limped into the kitchen. There, he spotted a cookbook on the table. I could be a baker! Poe thought. Poe gathered the ingredients for cupcakes, mixed them, poured out the cupcakes, and stuck them in the oven.

As the cupcakes finished baking, Pete arrived.

"Whoa, that is one mangled bike outside! Anyway, what's that awesome smell?"

"I just made cupcakes. Here, have one!" Poe handed Pete a steaming hot cupcake.

Pete took a bite. He realized the taste did not match the awesome smell and swallowed with a frown.

"Hey… Did you forget to take out the eggshells or what?" Pete asked.

"Oh! I had a bite earlier, but I couldn't figure out what was wrong with it! Don't worry. I won't forget next time!" Poe promised.

Poe began inspecting his cupcakes for eggshells. Pete tossed his cupcake in the garbage and then announced, "This is the first thing you've ever given me. Even though it was the worst cupcake I've had in my life, I still appreciate it."

What Pete said sent a shock through Poe's body. He realized that he'd never thought about anyone but himself. He never cared about his classmates' feelings when he hurt them. Even though Pete was his best friend, Poe had never showed his appreciation for their friendship.

Poe's mind had been set on painting mode twenty-four hours a day, seven days a week. But now that his painting skills were totally kaput, he had time to think about making things right with his classmates.

For the next couple of days, Poe baked and baked. He didn't forget to take out the eggshells. He iced the cupcakes with strawberry and chocolate frosting. His cupcakes filled every inch of the kitchen. Even his hair smelled like cupcakes. Poe showed up at school with all the cupcakes he had baked. He handed them out, greeting each classmate cheerfully.

Then Poe saw Pete. "Hey, Pete! I followed your advice, and here you go!" He handed Pete two piping hot cupcakes.

Pete took a small nibble. "This is so good! I hope everyone else thinks so too," Pete said.

"Thanks for the encouragement. I appreciate it," Poe replied.

"One for you, Patrick. That cap suits you well!" Poe said, with joy oozing from the corners of his mouth.

"Hey, thanks!" Patrick said, waving good-bye as he ate.

"One for you, Peggy. What a smashing outfit you're wearing!"

Poe placed the cupcake in Peggy's hand. She beamed at Poe and then took a bite of if.

"Wow, this is delicious! I never knew you could be so nice, Poe. This is the biggest surprise of the century!"

"This last one's for you, Phoebe. I really like that pencil you're holding." Poe gave Phoebe the cupcake.

"Thanks, Poe. I always thought you were a jerk, but I guess not." Phoebe swallowed the cupcake in one bite and nodded approvingly.

During art time, Poe did his usual inspecting of his classmates' paintings. But now he complimented them. Because he could not paint, he began to see the beauty in everyone else's paintings. With every compliment he gave, Poe included an apology. His classmates were confused by Poe's new attitude, but they preferred it.

The next day at lunchtime, Preston and Patrick stopped him.

"Hey! There's a baseball game after school, and we need a second baseman. Are you in?" they chimed.

Poe was surprised. No one but Pete ever wanted Poe to do anything with them. "I don't know much about baseball, but I hope you guys can teach me. Pete, come here!" he yelled across the cafeteria.

"Pete," Preston yelled across the cafeteria, "you should join us and Poe in the baseball game after school. We can have two second basemen. I'm sure the other team won't mind!" Preston laughed and patted Pete on the back as Pete sat down.

"Sounds good, you guys!" Pete could feel his shyness start to fade away.

The three-week mark came three days later. Poe met up with Pete on the playground.

"So, did you get your hands on the bug book yet?" asked Poe.

"Sure did," Pete replied and handed the book to Poe.

Poe peered at the first page. He noticed that the due date was that day's date. "Hey! You've had this book all along!" Poe yelped in confusion.

"True. The only cure was to wait three weeks. I knew to you that would seem like a lifetime and a half, and I didn't want you to worry," Pete explained. He then handed Poe a paintbrush, paint, and a blank canvas.

Sure enough, waiting three weeks cured Poe. His straight lines were straight again. His circles were round. His triangles had three sides. And he had more friends now. He looked at the palm of his right hand, and the bright pink mark had vanished.

"Thank you so much, Pete. I've got something for you too." Poe then brought Pete to his house. He gave Pete the once-mangled bicycle, which was now fixed, and the three-week-old copy of the *New York Times* that he had once attempted to read. ✳

DAISY THE SHOPPING SQUIRREL

by Stella Chin

ILLUSTRATED BY HELLEN JO

This little town's nickname was "The Big Acorn" and every squirrel that lived in it always had something to do. The town had a lot of tiny schools, a neighborhood, and a business district. Tall trees were skyscrapers and the squirrels worked inside them. Redwoods were schools that looked big outside but were small inside. The smallest trees in the forest were their homes and pine trees were the shopping malls.

In the Big Acorn, a squirrel named Daisy, who was about eight squirrel years old, shopped all the time. She loved shopping. She would buy clothes, shoes, and many toys. She loved the feeling of having new things. And she was the most spoiled squirrel in the school because her mother always bought her what she wanted.

Daisy's friends loved to spend most of their lunchtime playing games like ring-around-the-rosy or hopscotch. But Daisy never played with them anymore because she was busy going shopping.

One day during lunchtime, Daisy walked by her friends, and they said, "Daisy, you're always going shopping instead of hanging out with us! We never play together anymore!"

Daisy didn't have anything to say because she knew they were right. But after school, she went shopping for more toys. At the mall, she saw a beautiful acorn that had sparkling pink and gold diamonds all around it. The acorn cost about ten squirrel dollars, which sounds like very little but in the squirrel world it is actually a lot. Daisy walked around the mall into other stores but only thought about buying that beautiful acorn. She didn't have enough money, so she went home and begged her mom to buy the acorn for her.

"Hey, Mommy! I saw this great acorn and it was so pretty! It is pink and gold and it has sparkling diamonds on it and I want to get it! Can I get it?" asked Daisy.

"No! You have too many things already. I am not getting it for you!" said Daisy's mom.

"Please, Mommy?! I want it and I want it now!" Daisy became so upset that she cried.

Her mother felt guilty so she said, "Fine! I'll get it for you, but this is the last thing I buy for a while. You have too many useless things!"

"Yay, I get to have the pretty acorn! Yippee!" Daisy yelled.

The next afternoon Daisy was walking home after shopping when she bumped into her friends.

"How's it going? Are you still mad at me? I'm sorry that I don't

play with you anymore. You want to play at my house tomorrow?"

Her friends were surprised by what Daisy was saying.

One of them said, "It's OK… Yes, we should play. I'm having a party at my house tomorrow—I forgot to tell you. Come to the party! It's going to be fun. We'll get to play with each other again!"

"OK! I'll be there!" said Daisy.

Daisy was bored the next morning, so she decided to go shopping in town. She was shopping for some clothes and toys when suddenly she realized that she forgotten about her friend's party.

"Oh, my friend's birthday party! I feel so bad. I think I need to go shop for more toys to make myself feel better," said Daisy.

Meanwhile, her friends waited for her to arrive and were angry when didn't show up.

"Where is Daisy? I really hope she doesn't forget about the party. I really want her to come," one of Daisy's friends said.

"Me too. She hasn't been with us in so long. I miss her!" exclaimed another. When Daisy went to school the next day, she tried talking to her friends, but they ignored her

Back at the mall, Daisy was thinking, I feel so bad for what I did. I should have gone to the party even if I was late, but instead I've been so selfish. I need to stop this right now.

She promised herself that she wouldn't buy any more things. Whenever Daisy was in town, if she saw something she wanted, she wouldn't purchase it.

One day while Daisy was walking around, she had a great idea to combine her love for shopping and her love for her friends. She went into town to buy some party supplies. She bought balloons, paper plates, streamers, confetti, and banners. Afterward, she went home and decorated her house.

The color theme of the party would be pink and silver because of the pink sparkling acorn she loved so much. The dining table was full of fruits and nuts and the pink, sparkling, and beautiful acorn was placed in the middle of the table. She set up paper plates and cups on the dining table with the colorful streamers lying next to the plates. Meanwhile her mother was baking a yummy homemade acorn pie.

"I'm so excited about this!" said Daisy.

Daisy called her friends to come over to her house as soon as they could. They didn't want to at first, but they finally decided to come over since they were curious about what she was doing. When Daisy's friends arrived, Daisy's mother invited them inside. The room was dark. Then Daisy popped out of nowhere and yelled, "Surprise!"

They put on music and played fun games such as duck-duck-goose and hopscotch. Daisy and her friends ran around the yard like it was a little carnival. They laughed and jumped with joy. All of her friends enjoyed the party and they were finally playing together again.

"Daisy, this was a great surprise! I will never forget this!" said one of Daisy's friends.

"This party is great! I'm glad you did it!" another one of Daisy's friends called.

"We should have done this a long time ago!" said Daisy. "I know I have been so selfish lately—not caring about anything else except shopping, but I must change for you. I'm really sorry for what I have done. I want to put the pieces of our friendship back together."

"Yeah, it's been a while but we forgive you. The only thing that you need to do is just spend time with us!" said her friends.

Daisy realized that didn't need to buy everything she wanted in order to be happy, and that her friends were what really counted. And they were all so glad that they played all day long, which is what little squirrels do best. ✳

IT'S OK TO HAVE MORE THAN ONE BEST FRIEND

by Vera Lee

ILLUSTRATED BY JOEL SMITH

La La woke up with a big yawn. She looked at the clock. "Oh no!" she said. "I'm late for school." She jumped out of bed to get ready. She ate a big bowl of oatmeal for breakfast. It was hard to swallow and felt like it got caught in her throat. She ran out of the house without combing her light brown hair and as the cold air hit her face and her chubby cheeks, she felt a little unsure, like she was forgetting something. But she couldn't wait to get to school and see her friends.

At school she played with her good friends Li Li and Lu Lu. Li Li was about six inches taller than La La and had dark brown hair. Lu Lu, on the other hand, had blond hair. Even thought they all looked so different, everyone still thought they were sisters because they were always together. They loved to play with each other.

They played hide-and-seek in the schoolyard. Li Li was the best at hide-and-seek. She always found the best hiding places. One time when they were playing she hid right in the middle of the tube slide. La La and Lu Lu couldn't understand how she managed to stay in there so long.

They also played princesses. They would pretend that the play structure was the castle and beneath them was a moat full of croco-

diles. Lu Lu loved to pretend that she was being rescued by a prince and that a witch had cast a spell on her. She would hop like a frog, or moo like a cow, or even bark like a dog. La La would laugh and say that it was cute. Li Li and La La liked to pretend they were warrior princesses and to fight crime. La La's favorite game was to pretend that they were on the moon, and to jump around as if they were in space. They would pretend to shoot aliens and space monsters.

But today it seemed different when they were playing. They were playing hide-and-seek, and, like always, Li Li got to hide first. But before Li Li left, Lu Lu said, "Why can't we play princesses first? It's so boring playing hide-and-seek. Li Li always finds the best hiding places; it's not fair."

"I'm just good at it," said Li Li.

They started to argue, and La La didn't know what to do. "Stop arguing and just pick a game. We can play hide-and-seek first, then play princesses. Tomorrow we can play princesses first."

"No!" cried Lu Lu. Her dark eyes started to tear up.

"Well, which one do you want to play?" Li Li asked La La. "My game or Lu Lu's game?"

"I don't know," said La La. "I like both of the games."

"Well, then, who's your best friend?" asked Lu Lu, wiping tears from her eyes and pushing her hair out of her face.

"You are my best friend," said Li Li to La La.

La La smiled. "You are my best friend too," she said.

Lu Lu started to get jealous. "What about me?" said Lu Lu.

"You are my best friend too," said La La.

"You can't have more than one best friend," said Lu Lu.

"Yeah," added Li Li, "you have to pick one." She glared at her.

"I can't," said La La. "I don't know."

La La didn't know what to do. She didn't know she couldn't have more than one best friend. Li Li and Lu Lu walked away leaving La La there alone. Then she walked home really bummed and didn't eat dinner that night.

"You're so quiet, honey," said her mom.

"I know," said La La.

"You know you can tell me anything," said her mom.

"I know," said La La.

In her room she tried to decide whom she would pick. She thought about how she loved playing hide-and-seek with Li Li and she loved playing princesses with Lu Lu. They all had fun playing any game together.

The next morning La La woke up late again. This was because she could not sleep during the night. She was still sad. She ate her bowl of oatmeal and got ready to leave. She thought maybe they were just going to be mad for a little while and that they would play with her today, but she was still scared to go to school.

When La La got to school, she saw Li Li and Lu Lu. They didn't talk to her. La La's heart started to race as she went up to them. "You want to play hide-and-seek?"

"No," they said.

"How about princesses?" La La asked.

"No," they said again.

She could feel her face turning red. This was her last hope. "How about pretending to be on the moon?" she asked. Again they said no.

"We don't want to play with you," said Li Li.

"Yeah, you're not my best friend anymore," said Lu Lu. La La started to cry.

Li Li and Lu Lu walked away and played together. La La watched as they played together. They played a game she had never played before. She was so sad, mad, and jealous. They looked as if they were having so much fun without her.

La La tried to play with her other classmates, but they didn't want to play with her either. One boy named Ki Ki said, "I don't want to play with you. You're a girl. Plus, Li Li and Lu Lu told me about how you're not a good friend."

La La tried to play with two other girls, Mi Mi and Mu Mu. They said, "Lu Lu and Li Li told us about you. We don't want to be your friend."

La La started to cry again. No one wanted to be her friend, and she couldn't understand why. She sat on the bench in the yard by herself.

That night La La went to her mom. "Mommy? Can I talk to you?" La La asked.

"Of course," said her mom.

La La started crying. "Li Li and Lu Lu don't want to be my friend anymore because they say I can't have more than one best friend," La La said, looking down.

"Why, of course you can," said her mom. "I have a lot of best friends. My best friend Di Di, she's the best. She listens to me and has the best cheesecake recipes. My best friend Co Co is so much fun to go shopping with, plus she gives me great advice."

"But you can't," said La La. "You can only have one."

"Yes, you can," her mom said. "I love doing different things with all of them, and we always have fun together."

"Me too," said La La. "I love playing hide-and-seek with Li Li, and I love playing princesses with Lu Lu. We always have fun together."

"Well," said her mom, "sounds to me like you have more than one best friend." Her mom smiled and kissed her. She winked as she walked out of the room.

The next morning La La woke up early and wasn't late for school. She ate her oatmeal and left. She saw Li Li and Lu Lu but was scared to walk up to them. They looked at La La and just rolled their eyes. La La felt like just giving up and turning around, but she didn't. She remembered what her mom had said.

"Hi," she said. Li Li and Lu Lu looked at her but didn't say anything. "I know who my best friend is now," said La La.

"Who?" they asked.

La La looked at Li Li and said, "I love playing hide-and-seek with you. It's so much fun. Remember the time when you hid in the slide and Lu Lu and me couldn't find you the whole recess until Ku Ku slid down the slide and screamed? That was so funny." Li Li smiled and couldn't help but laugh too. La La then looked at Lu Lu and said, "I love playing princesses with you, and I have a lot of fun too. Remember when you pretended to be under a spell by an evil witch and acted like a frog?" Lu Lu smiled and giggled. "I love playing different things with both of you," La La said.

"Yeah, me too," said Li Li.

Then Lu Lu said, "Yeah, I love to pretend to be on the moon."

"Well," said La La, "you know it's OK to have more than one best friend." They all smiled and went off to play together, just like old times.

That night La La ran up to her mom and hugged her. "Mommy," she said, "you are my best friend."

"But I thought Li Li and Lu Lu were your best friends," she said.

"Didn't you hear, Mommy? It's OK to have more than one best friend," said La La.

That night La La realized something. It's not that you can have more than one best friend. It's that everyone is unique in their own way. They all have special qualities. Now she understood what her mom was trying to say. ✳

NEVER BE LATE

by Anderson Lam

ILLUSTRATED BY LAURA PARKER

Angelica was the wealthiest girl in the city. She lived in a mansion surrounded by golden gates and beautiful lawns and trees, perfect for playing tag and having picnics. Her family was so rich that they could buy her anything. She had almost everything in the world—everything except an alarm clock.

School started at eight o'clock in the morning, but Angelica always woke up at eight-thirty. Each time Angelica was late, the teacher would take five points away from her grade. After just a few weeks, her grades dropped very low. Angelica didn't care at all.

But the funny thing was, school wasn't too bad. All the teachers were nice, they always gave out good snacks and had free time, but best of all, the playground was enormous. The students had enough space to run around and play kickball.

Snack time followed recess and Angelica's teacher would hand out treats for the students to munch on. But Angelica was always late for snack time too! By the time she showed up, all the good snacks were gone. Nothing was left but the nasty yellow chewable candy, which Angelica hated. If she had arrived on time, she could have gotten a Snickers bar, her favorite.

"You need to come on time in order to get the snacks you want, Angelica," said the teacher.

"Yeah, yeah. I'll be on time tomorrow. But why don't you save something for me in case I'm late again?" replied Angelica.

"No, you have to come early to get it yourself. It wouldn't be fair to the other students. I know the yellow Starbursts aren't your favorite, but they're better than nothing."

Angelica tried really hard to get to there on time, but she either ran into a problem on the playground or lost track of time.

Every day after school, Angelica went home to take care of her pony, Chloë. Her daily shores included feeding, bathing, brushing, riding, and playing with Chloë. Angelica's family had a huge stall and a wide-open field for Chloë to run around in. Everything sounded perfect for Chloë, but there was one problem—Angelica was always late. Chloë got so mad at Angelica for not feeding her on time that she didn't play with her anymore. Whenever Angelica came by, Chloë would completely ignore her. Eventually, Chloë ran away and found a better owner that took much better care of her.

"Oh, don't worry about Chloë, Angelica. We can always buy you

another pony. It doesn't even have to be a pony. Anything you want! Just name it and it's yours," said Angelica's dad.

"Thank you, Daddy! But I don't really want a pet anymore. Let's go to Great America!" exclaimed Angelica.

"Sure, anything for you, my dear."

One day, her parents lost their jobs. They were spending too much money on Angelica and their debt piled up. They had to think of something quick or else they'd have to move out of their mansion. Not wanting to leave her beautiful estate, Angelica decided to help solve this problem.

"Mom, Dad, I've decided to get a job so we don't have to move away," said Angelica.

Her parents agreed. "That's a wonderful idea. We're proud that you're taking on this responsibility."

Angelica went out to find a job as quickly as possible. She found a few job openings in the newspaper. She scheduled all her interviews on different days. Unfortunately, she wasn't able to get to any of the interviews on time. One after another, she was late. For the thirty-seven interviews she had, she was late thirty-seven times. Finally, one manager at a restaurant needed waitresses so desperately that he quickly hired her on the spot.

Angelica showed up late to her first day of work. And the next day. And the day after that. She was very slow and clumsy at work. She kept mixing up the orders and gave out the wrong food to the wrong people. She also broke a countless number of dishes. The manager couldn't take it anymore and told her to leave.

Feeling sad, Angelica went home and collapsed on her bed. Then she began to think, Why does my life stink? Why doesn't anyone like me?

Then she slowly fell into a deep sleep. That night, a fairy came to her in a dream.

Angelica asked the fairy, "Why doesn't anyone like me?"

"Because you're always late to everything," replied the fairy.

Angelica then realized that this was true. She had never noticed it before. All her life, she had been late to everything. That was the reason why her life was so miserable.

"What can I do to change this?" she questioned.

"I will grant you one wish. You name it, and it shall happen," said the fairy.

"I never want to be late again. I want to do everything on time!" exclaimed Angelica.

"Very well, your wish is my command."

As these last words echoed away, Angelica woke up again. It was seven o'clock in the morning. Even though it was just a dream, she knew the fairy was right. She promised herself that she would never be late again and bought an alarm clock. Not just any alarm clock but one that let everyone in town know when Angelica was supposed to be awake.

The morning after she bought the alarm clock, she decided to get ready to go back to work. She got there fifteen minutes early and waited for the manager. The manager was shocked to see her again. Not because he had fired her, but because she was there so early. Angelica asked him for one more chance at the job. He agreed and Angelica started working again.

After only a few months, she earned enough money to keep her parents from selling their home. Like any other average person, she was never late again, never late for work, never late for a meal, never late for anything.   ✳

MAX LIGHTSPEED

by Jon Dowell

ILLUSTRATED BY JOEL SMITH

Max Lightspeed was a twelve-year-old boy who lived in the space station Zeus, located above Mars. He owned his own spaceship like all the other kids in Zeus did. Max liked his spaceship because it was fire red, which made it different from other kids' spaceships.

Max was a good student and hung out with his friends after school. Everything about him made it seem like he was a normal boy. But at night, when everyone was sleeping, Max fought evil. He flew around in space looking for evil people who did nothing but cause trouble. Max liked to help humankind because it felt good. Everyone in the universe thought Max was a special kid, and everyone depended on him.

Max had an evil twin brother, Bob, who lived all alone in a separate part of the space station. Bob liked to do evil things because he didn't have any friends. Bob caused the typical troublemaker kind of crime: he stole space pants and moon shoes, and removed parts of spaceships at night so that they would not start in the morning. One time Bob broke Max's spaceship on purpose, and Bob never apologized. The two no longer got along.

One day while Max was flying in his fire red spaceship, he turned around the corner of a large chrome meteor and saw Bob trying to rob an elderly lady of her space money!

"Give me your money, old lady," said Evil Bob.

"No, it's for Space Bingo!" said the old lady.

Max quickly said, "I will save you!" as he shifted the gears in the spaceship and flew at light speed.

Evil Bob saw Max coming to the rescue and got into his spaceship. He attacked Max with a huge spit-wad gun that covered Max's windshield with a gigantic wad of wet paper. Evil Bob then shot one of Max's wings with his atomic spit wads, and Max flew out of control. Meanwhile, the elderly lady entered her granny ship and puttered off to Bingo Night. Bob decided to return to his space station because he thought Max was out of his way forever, but Max was still spinning in space. "Oh no! The only thing I can do is land on that unknown planet," Max said out loud.

When Max landed, he realized everything was different from Mars. All the colors were different, and the creatures looked very strange. Some had hair, some had scales, some had feathers, and some had all three. The trees were rubber and the leaves were different shades of blue, red, orange, and yellow.

Although the changes were all distracting, Max had to find a way off this planet because he had a mission. He had to stop Evil Bob. He thought this was a test to see how well he could do.

While he was trying to fix his ship, some aliens come up to him. One of the aliens was fat and green, and had three eyes. His name was Blob. The other alien was skinny with one big eye in the center of his head and called himself Toothpick. They both had chalky green skin.

"Do you need any help?" Blob asked.

Max realized he did and said, "Sure. Why not?"

The three worked together to fix Max's ship. When they finished, Max asked the aliens if they wanted to help him look for his evil twin Bob. The aliens thought about this for a few minutes and then responded, "Sure. Why not? We are always looking for an adventure, and besides, you are our new best friend. Let's go get him!"

As the three entered the ship, Max closed the hatch door and said, "Hang on, guys, this is going to be a bumpy ride. Three… two… one… blastoff!" Blob and Toothpick were not wearing their seat belts, so as they took off, they flew to the back of the spaceship.

Max and his new friends searched for days for Evil Bob. But space is just so big. It seemed it was going to be hard to find him anytime soon. Max decided to try to find Bob on the planet Nacho Cheese. This planet had rivers of cheese, huge tortilla chip buildings, and busy streets of dip. The people of this planet were made out of chips. Max thought this might be the one place where Evil Bob was hiding, because Bob loved nachos and cheese.

They landed on Nacho Cheese and the three started to search. They searched every cheddar corner store and every food store with plastic chip-and-dip containers, but they could not find Bob.

Max was very sad because he didn't know what else to do. Blob suggested they search the space station above the sun. "That's the place where all the bad guys hang out these days," he said. Max's eyes lit up. That was the place where they would find Evil Bob!

They all ran to the spaceship, closed the hatch door, and took off at the speed of light. Max said, "Hang on, guys, it's going to be another bumpy ride! A few hours later, they arrived at the space station. Blob had been right! Every person and alien there was evil. And even Evil Bob was there!

Max didn't know what to do because there were so many people around. He knew he couldn't fight them all even with the help of Blob and Toothpick.

Max and the two others needed to come up with a plan that would not fail. Their lives depended on it.

Max decided to capture all the evil space beings, but he needed bait. Max thought for a few minutes—he would use Toothpick. Toothpick would anger all the evil space beings, and then he would run down the hall. As the bad guys ran after him, Blob and Max would enter the room and drop a net from the ceiling, catching every last one. It was a perfect plan because Max wouldn't catch just Bob but *every* evildoer in space! Max, Blob, and Toothpick would be space heroes.

Toothpick casually walked into the bad guys' hangout, so casually that no one noticed him. He looked around and tried to think of something to say or do that would make all the bad guys chase him. He thought and thought and finally came up with a scheme to spill a drink on one of them. That should do it, he thought, and he started looking for the right target. After a while he found one. The guy was huge but he had two very, very small eyes, so Toothpick thought he could easily hide from the guy's view. Toothpick snuck up, spilled the drink on the guy, and ran! He took one look behind him and saw the whole crowd running after him.

Toothpick ran into the room where Blob and Toothpick had set up the net, and the bad guys ran in right after him. Max and Blob dropped the net. All the bad guys were trapped, even Evil Bob!

Max loaded them up and threw them into the back of his humongous, fire red spaceship. He thought, What am I going to do with all these bad people? He pondered a bit and then snapped his fingers, saying, "I got it!"

Max decided to put all the troublemakers in one room with smelly socks. He then locked the door and decided to leave them locked inside until they promised to become space do-gooders.

About three hours later, the bad beings gave in and agreed to become good. They never wanted to deal with those smelly old socks ever again.

Max had helped all the troublemakers in space turn good. ✳

THE SHOE THAT TRAVELED THE WORLD

by Gabrielle Ho

ILLUSTRATED BY LISA BROWN

There was once a shoe that lived in a shoe box. His name was Converse. He was always trapped in his box with nowhere to go. His box felt really rough because it was made out of cardboard. It smelled of cardboard. He hated his box! He did come out once in a while, but only when people would try him on. When he was first being tried, he felt stretched and stomped on. But after they walked around with him a bit, he no longer hurt. He actually liked being on someone's feet because he felt that he was helping them and keeping their feet warm and protected. He even felt like a hero. But Converse wished that he could have more freedom to explore the world and see what was out there.

One day, Converse decided that he couldn't stand living in his box anymore. He saw a man pass by so he jumped out of his box and into the stranger's backpack, leaving his empty box behind! This man with the backpack was actually a traveler visiting from China and he was on his way back to his hometown. Converse's ride in the backpack was dark and bumpy. He started feeling queasy so he decided that it was time to get out of the backpack at the next opportunity.

When Converse hopped out, he discovered that he had arrived in China. The busy streets amazed him. He had never seen anything like it. There were more people, stores, factories, and buildings in one big place than he had ever seen! Converse even saw a very big wall. He was fascinated by it and wanted to learn more. He overheard some people calling it "The Great Wall of China." They said the wall was built to protect China from outside intruders. Converse hiked along The Great Wall the whole day.

When he reached the very top, Converse was tired and he returned to the city. Since it was becoming nighttime, Converse started to look for a shoe box to sleep in. He walked the busy streets of China but he soon realized that he wouldn't find one and that he would need to find his own shelter. Converse found a giant trash bin with many garbage bags in it. That was his shelter for the night. He smelled spoiled food and felt many bags of garbage beneath him. He heard cars and people passing by the whole night and he saw blinding lights on the buildings above him.

This was Converse's first night spent somewhere other than his box or the backpack. He was really scared and started to miss his shoe box back home. But despite the noise and lights and his fear, Converse was able to fall asleep quickly because of his tiring hike.

The following morning, Converse woke up and decided to leave China to explore a different place. So, like the first time, Converse jumped into a traveler's open backpack. This time, the traveler was headed toward Africa. During the trip to Africa, Converse faced a ride bumpier than the first! Converse peeked out of a hole and realized that he was on an extremely steep mountain inside a hiker's backpack. Feeling queasy, Converse decided to hop out and start exploring.

Converse soon discovered that he was in Nigeria. It was a lot different from China. There weren't busy city streets; instead, it was a desert. As Converse explored Nigeria, he saw many big creatures that he'd never seen before. These creatures were animals and they were very exotic. One of them was big, black, and very hairy. It seemed to have some of the same characteristics as humans, like hands and feet with fingers and toes, and the features of its face resembled those of humans too. He found out that this animal was a gorilla. He saw another animal that was really fat. It lay in a swamp all day and it was called a hippopotamus. Last, he saw a very fast, skinny, furry, black and orange catlike animal. It was a cheetah. He had never seen anything so fast in his life.

Converse continued to explore Nigeria, but became quite tired when the sky started to grow dark. Since Nigeria was desertlike, it didn't have many shelters to sleep under, not even trash bins, but he found a little spot under a tree and he made a bed of dried grass. It was prickly, but luckily it didn't smell. As he lay under the tree, all Converse could see was darkness and, for the very first time ever, the moon.

Converse began to think about his shoe box again. Each night he spent away from it, he began to miss it more and more. Soon after all his thoughts of home, Converse fell asleep.

The following morning, Converse woke up to a lion trying to eat him. Converse jumped up and ran away fast. He wanted to leave Nigeria that instant. So, he set out to look for another traveler once again. It took him a long time to find anyone because in the desert there aren't many people. Luckily, Converse found another backpack to hop into. This traveler's backpack was really small and Converse couldn't wait to get out of it. After a long trip, it finally came to a complete stop. Converse peered out and realized that he definitely was not in Nigeria anymore. Converse had arrived in Europe.

Converse found out that he was in a place called Paris. Paris was beautiful. He saw a tall structure shaped like a pyramid. He later learned that it was called the Eiffel Tower. As Converse continued walking through the streets of Paris, he came to another interesting structure. It looked like the front of a tunnel, but it wasn't. It was called the Arc de Triomphe. He also noticed that the Arc de Triomphe was covered with engravings. Converse also saw a big stone church. It was called Notre Dame. By the time he finished looking at Notre Dame, it was night. After his long walk, Converse was tired and wanted to sleep. But once again, he had to look for shelter. He walked through the streets of Paris and saw beautiful lights. There were still a lot of people strolling around and many people eating in restaurants. But Converse missed his shoe box and he wished he could go home at once. But as much as he wished and hoped, he was still in Paris. Converse ended up finding shelter underneath the Eiffel Tower. It was cold and the ground didn't comfort him so he vowed that in the morning, he would make his way back home to his shoe box.

As soon as the sun rose, Converse awoke. Right then and there,

he began to walk out of Paris. He passed many backpacks but he was scared to jump into one because he didn't want to be transported to anywhere other than home. But Converse was a slow walker and he wanted to get home so badly that he decided to risk jumping into the next backpack he saw. This traveler was traveling right back to China, his original stop. When the traveling stopped, Converse climbed out onto the busy streets of China again. This time, Converse went in search of other shoes because they might be able to help him find a way back home.

As he was walking down a little street, Converse found a shoe factory. He entered it, and inside he met many shoes. As he approached, one of them came walking toward him.

"Hi, my name's Nike, what's your name?"

"I'm Converse, it's nice to meet you," he replied. As they continued to talk, two more shoes approached them.

"Hi, I'm Puma."

"And I'm Adidas."

They continued to talk and Converse found out that they were all headed for America and they were set to leave the next day! Nike and Puma were nice enough to find a new box for Converse and he slept soundly that night. When the next day came, they all stayed in their shoe boxes and they were put in an even bigger box and then on a ship.

During this journey back to America, Converse was happy to be in a shoe box because he hadn't been in one for so long. He almost forgot how cozy, warm, and safe it felt in there—much better than a backpack! When they finally arrived in America, Converse had a stoke of luck—he was shipped back to the shoe store where he originally lived.

Back home, Converse returned to the box he had spent every day, month, and year in. He was home. Content in his shoe store, Converse began to appreciate his life and he now knew not to compare it to anything or anyone else's. He was grateful and thankful for what and who he was and for the comforts of home. He was happy to be back in his own cardboard box and he was happy to feel cozy again. ✳

PANDA BARRY

by **Wayman Ng**

ILLUSTRATED BY LART COGNAC BERLINER

O nce upon a time, there lived a family of eleven pandas in a small forest deep in the mountains. The family lived together in harmony for a very long time. Barry, the youngest, was no ordinary panda; he was about the size of your palm but ate much more bamboo than anyone in his family. Barry's appetite was so huge that he never grew. His brothers, sisters, and even his grandparents began to resent him for eating so much. For years Barry was eating up all the food he could lay his paws on, sometimes even his parents' paws. Yet even after all this eating, Barry barely grew an inch.

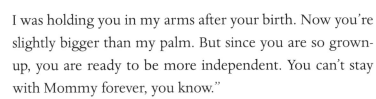

Although the rest of the family didn't like Barry, his parents still continued to love and spoil him. Barry had no problems with his gigantic appetite or his unusually small size. He grew up thinking that his brothers and sisters were just jealous that they weren't spoiled by their mother and father.

In the days when Barry wasn't able to wander around by himself, he stayed close to his mom for warmth and the supply of food. Barry liked the feeling of doing nothing and just eating the food his mother fed him. But one day his mother said to him, "Barry, dear, you're getting quite grown-up now! It seems like only yesterday that

I was holding you in my arms after your birth. Now you're slightly bigger than my palm. But since you are so grown-up, you are ready to be more independent. You can't stay with Mommy forever, you know."

With that said, Mama Panda walked off while Barry chased after her. He couldn't catch up because for every step Mama took, Barry needed to take ten. Sad and alone, Barry sat there looking at the spot where he and Mama used to sit. After a couple of minutes, Barry felt hungry. Since Mama wasn't there, Barry had to get food for himself. After he found bamboo growing a couple of yards away, Barry gathered his first meal alone.

As night came rolling in, Barry heard footsteps. At first he was frightened, but then he saw that it was actually his mama coming to spend the night with him. When their eyes met, his mother said, "Barry, I'm so proud of you! You spent your first day alone, and I saw that you were gathering food for yourself. Well, Barry, since you're so grown-up now, I'll tell you a story only for grown-up boys like you. Legend has it that there is a Forest of Dread. This special forest has a limitless supply of bamboo." Barry got hungry and his stomach growled. Mama Panda continued, "But to get this limitless supply of bamboo, legend tells us that you have to get through a great mythical beast. Nobody knows any more than that because those who enter the forest never return."

A few days after Barry was left to fend for himself, he went to the family's bamboo reserve for a quick snack. When he got there, he saw that it was completely empty. The only things left were a few leaves from the bamboo sticks. Barry ran frantically back home. As he ran up to his family, he could see that they were seated in a circle, having a heated argument. Not wanting to intrude, he stayed back and listened quietly.

"Barry hasn't gained a single pound nor grown a single inch, yet he is eating more food than me!" his eldest brother exclaimed.

"Peter's right. If Barry stays the same size and never helps the family, he will eat up all the food and drag us all down with starvation," said another brother.

In defense of Barry, Papa Panda explained, "It isn't Barry's fault for not growing. Give him more time. I am sure Barry will pull through this stage and help out the family when we need him to."

With that, the youngsters went into a panic. "We're starving!" "He's too small to even pick up one bamboo shoot!"

Finally, the wise grandparents spoke up. "We have no choice," said Grandpa Panda.

"Either we starve," said Grandma Panda, "or we send Barry off to live by himself."

Mama Panda burst into tears. Seeing her cry broke Barry's heart. He knew what he had to do. With the determination to right his wrongs, Barry had to journey through the Forest of Dread to search for the endless supply of bamboo. Only after doing that could he prove himself to his family.

At first the journey in the forest wasn't so bad. But as he entered deeper into the forest, the trees covered up much of the sunlight. Sometimes when Barry walked around a tree, it would howl and whip its vines on the floor next to Barry. Although it frightened him, he continued on with his journey to find the bamboo hill. Deeper in the forest there was a powerful scent in the air. It smelled like a dangerous animal that was ready to kill anyone who entered its lair. Barry's instincts told him to turn around and run, but his love for his family drove him to move deeper into the forest.

As Barry reached the interior of the forest, he saw a dusty, gigantic mountain. As he approached, he heard the mountain snore. He whimpered in fear, waking the mountain from its slumber. As he took cover behind a pile of leaves, the mountain started to unravel into a dragon with claws and fangs the size of trees. Its brown, filthy body was jagged and rough to the touch. Its head was big enough to swallow Barry's entire family in one bite. The intimidating dragon had enough power to cause tsunamis and earthquakes with one shake of its tail.

"Who dares enter my territory?" it asked. Barry had to devise a plan or the dragon would surely discover him and devour him. He gathered rocks to cause a diversion while he crept closer and closer to the bamboo hill. Before he made his way toward the dragon, he rubbed dirt all over himself to mask his scent.

Every time the dragon looked in his direction, Barry would throw a pebble to deceive it. As Barry slipped by over the dragon's scaly tail, the dragon gave a loud and thundering roar. It yelled, "I swear I will find you, even if I have to tear through every tree and bush." With a great flex of his powerful muscles, the dragon flew into the sky. As it slowly rose, it searched the bamboo hill for intruders.

With a deep breath into the dragon's lungs came a great flame that burned down the trees of the forest surrounding the bamboo hill. Safely amid the bamboo shoots, Barry watched this amazing display of the dragon's might. Thinking that he had burned down the intruder with that powerful blast, the dragon slowly settled back down onto its cozy bed and fell into a slumber. The dragon's body turned back into the mountain Barry had seen when he first entered the forest. Now that Barry was inside the bamboo hill, away from the dragon's suspicion, the only way to transport the bamboo without waking the dragon was to dig his way out of the Forest of Dread.

Meanwhile, back at Barry's home, Mama Panda worried about her youngest son. She thought that she wouldn't see him again and was concerned about how he would take care of himself in the wild. Barry's brothers and sisters spent the day searching for more bamboo, but they came up empty-handed. The family decided to rest for the evening and begin another search in the morning.

Back at the Forest of Dread, Barry dug until he reached the edge of the forest. He then turned around and, one by one, dragged the bamboo through the tunnel. Once he had gathered enough, Barry ran home to tell his family of his good fortune.

By the time he arrived at home, he was exhausted from all the digging and running he had done. After regaining his strength, he told his family of his encounter with the dragon and how he had managed to steal bamboo for them. At first Barry's family doubted him, even his mother. But he offered that if he had indeed lied to them, he would leave the family forever. He led his family to the bamboo heap next to the entrance to the tunnel.

The family was shocked. Barry, the weakest and smallest member of the family, had done something they could never do. His brothers and sisters wanted to hear more about his encounter with the dragon. The grandparents and parents were so proud that they told neighboring families of his great deed.

From then on, Barry was able to feed his family by sneaking bamboo out of the Forest of Dread and dragging it through the little tunnel. Because nobody but Barry could fit through the tunnel, he had become a legend to all the families in the region. Because he had redeemed himself, his family proudly accepted him and loved him with all their hearts. ✳

IN GREEN BEAN TOWN

by Kalena So

ILLUSTRATED BY RACHEL LYON

In Green Bean Town, on a street called Wonderful Street, where many gardens bloomed with colorful flowers, there was a red house and a green house. They were separated by a row of bean plants. People in the neighborhood were friendly and caring. When they saw neighbors walking down the street, they stopped to say hello to one another.

In the red house lived an eight-year-old girl named Mindy and her parents. Mindy was short and chubby. She loved to eat bananas so much that everyone called her Mindy the Monkey. She had long brown hair and big blue eyes. She always wore a pair of star-shaped red earrings. She had not taken them off since she got them on her birthday almost six months ago. Red was her favorite color.

One day, a new girl moved into the green house next door. Her name was Kelly. She had just moved to Green Bean Town from a faraway city—Peanut Union. Kelly was a tall girl. In her old school in Peanut Union, she had been the tallest in her class. She tied her ponytail up really high, which made her look even taller! There were four people in Kelly's family: Kelly, her dad and mom, and her little sister, Viccy.

Toward the end of August, the weather was getting windy. Leaves began to turn golden and started to fall off the trees. On a rainy day, Mindy and her mom went to a local store to buy colored pencils, an eraser, glue sticks, and several notebooks for school. In the green house, Kelly tried on her new uniform. She couldn't wait to meet some new friends in Green Bean Town.

On the first day of school, Mindy put on her uniform and walked to school with her mother. When they passed by the green house, Kelly walked out in her uniform. Kelly waved at her, but Mindy was nervous and shy. She blushed and looked away quickly.

In school, their teacher, Ms. Pineapple, introduced Kelly to the class. "Class, let's welcome our new classmate, Kelly. She just came from Peanut Union." The whole class looked at Kelly and clapped their hands to welcome her. She felt nervous but still had her bright smile on. Mindy recognized Kelly from the morning. Now as Mindy looked more closely, she noticed Kelly also wore a pair of red, star-shaped earrings. They had the same earrings!

Mindy wanted to become friends with Kelly—but she was too shy. What if I scare her? Mindy thought. She was afraid Kelly might run away when she started talking to her. Mindy didn't know what to do. Luckily for Mindy, in music class Ms. Pineapple assigned Kelly to be her singing partner.

"Hi, I'm Kelly! I'm new to the school. What's your name?" Kelly asked.

"Hel—hello. I am… Monkey! I mean Mindy!" she said, surprised that Kelly had talked to her.

She and Mindy soon became best friends. They were so close that teachers and classmates thought they were sisters. They loved going to the park on sunny days. They liked to sing on the swing and seesaw. When they got tired, they went to the fish pond at the park to feed the fish. Mindy and Kelly both liked ice cream a lot. They would eat it every day they were together. They both had a bad tooth on the right side. When they smiled at their classmates, the others would laugh at them and make fun of their black little teeth. "Brush your teeth!" some classmates said.

Everything was going well for Mindy and Kelly until one week before Thanksgiving. Kelly's parents told her they were moving back to Peanut Union. Her grandpa was sick and he needed the family to take care of him. Kelly loved her grandpa very much but she didn't want to leave. She cried for the whole night in her bed.

The next day, she decided to tell Mindy what was going on. She went to Mindy's house in the morning. For a very long time, she just sat there and kept quiet.

"Mindy… are we best friends?" Kelly asked.

"Of course! And we will always be!" Mindy was surprised by Kelly's question.

Then Kelly started crying. "Are you OK, Kelly? Who is being mean to you?" Mindy asked. "I will punch him in the face and throw ice cream at him!"

"My dad, mom, Viccy, and I are moving back to Peanut Union. Tomorrow will be my last day here!"

"Are you ever coming back?" Mindy asked.

"I don't know… " Kelly looked down at the floor. She couldn't stop her tears.

That night while eating dinner, Mindy's mom noticed Mindy wasn't eating and that she looked very sad.

"Are you all right, honey?" Mindy's mom asked.

Mindy didn't reply but shook her head.

"Share it with Mommy. Tell Mommy what is wrong."

"Kelly is leaving tomorrow… I don't know what to do… " Mindy started to cry.

"Why don't you give her a gift so whenever she looks at it, she will remember you?"

"But… but I don't know what to give her." Mindy sounded disappointed.

"I suggest something memorable for both of you girls—maybe something that only you and Kelly will know the meaning of."

On Kelly's last day, they went to places they had always loved to go to. They went to the park and sang on the swing and seesaw. They fed the fish. They ate ice cream at Uncle Berry's ice cream store. They watched cartoons together and laughed until their stomachs hurt. They were having so much fun that they forgot it was their last day together.

When Kelly finally had to leave, they gave each other gifts. Mindy gave Kelly a picture that they'd taken while feeding the fish at the park on a sunny day. Kelly gave Mindy a picture in a frame she'd made in art class. The picture was taken when they were eating ice cream and their mouths were dirty. They both laughed at their pictures. Then they gave each other a last hug and said good-bye.

That same night, around nine o'clock, when Mindy was usually sleeping, she came downstairs, where her parents were watching the news. Her face was streaked with tears and she was holding the picture Kelly gave her.

"I will never see her again," Mindy said as her finger traced across the picture.

"Oh, Mindy…" Her mom gave her a hug. "You know you two can keep in touch by writing and calling each other. Don't worry. She will always be your friend."

"But… but I don't have any friends here anymore," Mindy said.

"Maybe it's time to make some new friends. Remember how easy it was to make friends when you met Kelly?" Her mom gave her a warm smile.

During lunch the next day, Mindy was sitting in the corner of her classroom eating her sandwich, looking sad and lonely. Two girls named Twinkle and Shiny walked past.

"Mindy, can we join you for lunch?" Twinkle asked.

Mindy nodded nervously. She was surprised that these girls wanted to eat lunch with her.

"Mindy… are you all right? What's wrong? You look sad," said Twinkle with concern.

"Nothing… I just don't feel well," Mindy lied.

"Where's Kelly? How come you guys aren't hanging out together?" asked Shiny.

Tears dropped down from Mindy's eyes. She missed Kelly so much. She felt so lonely and sad. She was a loner!

"She… she went back to Peanut Union…" said Mindy tearfully.

The two girls looked at each other then back at Mindy. For the next few minutes, they sat there silently. Nobody knew what to say. Finally, Shiny said quietly, "Mindy, you are not alone. You have Twinkle and me as your friends…"

And Mindy said quietly back to them, "Really?" Tears still kept dropping down, but now she was smiling. Mindy was thankful to have Twinkle and Shiny. Now when she was in her loneliest and hardest time, they were there to be with her and cheer her up.

During the rest of lunchtime, they sat laughing and giggling while sharing their sandwiches and cookies. They soon became very close to Mindy, and Mindy didn't feel as sad and lonely anymore. Every month, she talked on the phone with Kelly about their schools, friends, and other things. They missed each other a lot. Mindy was happy to hear that Kelly had made new friends back in Peanut Union. Mindy and Kelly were not as close as before, but they enjoyed being with their new friends, and they knew in their hearts that they would be best friends forever. ✳

SOPHIE BLOOM

by Victoria Lee

ILLUSTRATED BY JEN WANG

They call me Sophie Bloom and I write my name on the wall of my room every day. Some days I use a different color just to be a little different. Still, every day is the same routine. I wish the walls of my room would call me by some other name.

I live in a house not too big and not too small that is surrounded by many other houses that are not too big and not too small. School is the same old thing over and over. I see the same students and teachers every day. I do the same math problems and read the same textbooks all the time. My life is just a routine.

And come summer, my family usually goes on vacation to get away from our boring lives.

But this summer Mom said, "I'm sorry, I have been doing a lot of thinking. I have just started my new business and I need more time to get it working. Your brother decided to go away for summer camp, and Dad wants to stay home and spend more time with you, Sophie, so you can stay home to take care of the dog."

"But the Bloom family always goes on vacation during the summer, Mom. This isn't fair!" I yelled. I felt like I wasn't part of the decision. "You guys don't even care!" I said.

Mom said that I must stay at home and finish my summer homework. What am I supposed to do now?! I don't understand. Why can't Dad take care of the dog? I hate this! I wish I were somewhere else and someone else!"

Before my brother Jason left for camp, I told him, "Come back soon. It's not fair that you get to go and I'm stuck here with nothing to do."

But then Jason gave me his backpack. It looked old, had a lot of holes in it, and people had written all over it. And it had shiny glitter all over. He said, "Take good care of this, and don't lose anything. I'll miss you a lot."

"I'm giving you this heart patch like a trade for the backpack," I said. "It means a lot to me. "

I spent each day moping around waiting for something exciting to happen. I sat near the window and watched people walk by. I glued fake coins on the sidewalk so I could see people try to pick them up.

Mom was always on the phone. She was so busy every day that she forgot to feed Jeff. She was typing, or just at work. I missed Mom, and I wanted her back to normal.

Dad said he wanted to spend time with me this summer, but he spent more time with the television. Ever since we got the upgrade with two hundred more channels, he feels that he must get what he is paying for. I wished that I could tell him to turn it off and have lunch with me. Every day when I came home, I saw him sitting on the right side of the red couch. In one hand he held the remote and in the other a can of soda. I wished that I could be the TV so he'd finally spend more time with me.

The summer was so boring. I did the same thing every day. I wished for something to happen. Every day I got up early. While I watched cartoons, I would eat my favorite cereal—that sugary cereal my family doesn't like. Then I would walk Jeff to the park so he wouldn't start to bark. We would play catch and run around in circles until we got dizzy. Then I would come home and have lunch. For a whole week my parents didn't make time for lunch with me. I didn't even want to come home after that. For the rest of the day, I would read, write in my journal, sing and dance, or just imagine what I could be doing next.

I missed my brother. He taught me everything I know—how to tie a bow and how to make snow angels. He taught me how to add tax to what I want to buy. Now I know to look at the price and buy something that costs a little less than what I have. Summer was not the same without him. I wished he were here. He could have been sitting here being bored with me.

Suddenly I remembered his backpack. I saw it in the corner of my room under a pile of clothes. I picked it up, wondering what he might have left me… candy, or some of his cool magic items. When I put my hand in the bag, I felt something hard, with a lot of pages. I took it out and saw that it was a book. It looked like it was a thousand years old. I was not too happy to have another book to read in addition to the ones for school. I took an extra look in the bag to see whether there was more. I found a wand and a note too.

The note said, *Here's something that helped me. But be careful what you wish for.*

I opened the book to the first page and noticed an odd-looking picture. It looked like a picture of an imaginary perfect land. There were animals everywhere and delicious-looking food. There was also an unusual empty cage in the middle. The directions read, *Close your eyes, use your wand, touch the cage, and make a wish.* Then a warning said, *You can never escape from reality.* I didn't know what that meant, but I knew I had to escape.

I took the wand and I made a wish. I wished for some candy. Then I looked and saw some lying on my chest of drawers. Then I wished for some clothes. I looked in the closet and saw several cute outfits. I couldn't believe it. I was sick and tired of staying in the room. I took the wand and swayed it around like a magician, wishing to be by myself. I wished to be somewhere I could eat candy without getting sick, somewhere I could sing loudly and become a beautiful animal and not have to listen to anyone! I could be a butterfly and show off my beautiful wings, or a giraffe and have a long neck. I waited and waited, but nothing happened. I went downstairs and still saw Mom on her phone and Dad on his couch watching television.

I didn't understand and tossed the book under my bed and lay down. I thought about the phrase *Be careful what you wish for* over and over again.

Suddenly, I was in another world. I was in an identical town with many people. The people all looked a bit strange. They all seemed like they were being controlled. There were many people, all wearing the same thing: shirts and pants all the same color. I looked for my parents and Jeff, but I couldn't find them. At home, the phone was back on the holder against the wall and the TV was off with the remote on top. I couldn't believe it! Was this really happening? Once, I saw a kid pinch himself to make sure he wasn't dreaming. Ouch! I guess hurting meant I wasn't dreaming. It was a dream come true. For a good laugh, I raised the volume on the stereo and had a party of my own. I danced and changed my clothes. I didn't even have to clean up. I was getting hungry. "What should I have?" I asked myself. "I think I should have ice cream! And candy!"

I got out of the house and went to the store. I picked up the candy and ice cream and walked out. *Beep! Beep! Beep!* What was that noise? I heard someone coming.

"Excuse me, young lady, you have to pay for that. Where are your parents?" said the man behind the cash register.

I didn't know what to say. "My parents are in the car. Can I pay you back?"

"Sorry, I don't think that's possible. Please put those items back or I'll have to speak with your parents," said the man behind the cash register.

I had to find my parents. I wanted to look over the whole town from above. It would have been the easiest way to find my parents. So I became a butterfly soaring over the people. Butterfly wings are awesome! While flying I saw my mom and dad. Mom looked different. She usually wears a business outfit, but I saw her wearing a summery flower dress. Dad looked like he had lost some weight, and he was out of the house! I flew over and transformed back into a young girl again. Mom and Dad looked at me and asked me what my name was. I was confused. Then I realized that I was not their daughter anymore.

What did I do? I never meant for this to happen. All I wanted to do was get away. It's not fair that we're not on that cruise. I was being good, so we all could've gone on the cruise.

I went over to park where I usually go every day with Jeff. When I got in trouble in school, everybody was mad at me except Jeff. I love Jeff; he is always here for me. The park was lonely. I didn't see anyone who I recognized. The sky looked so gray. Is this how it is to live on your own? To pay bills every day and work? I looked around and saw my brother. He looked a little different. Maybe it wasn't my brother. I jumped and walked right over anyway just to make sure. It was him! I remembered those dorky glasses and the huge coat that he always wears. His skin was slightly darker and it looked like he had gotten a haircut. Other than that he still looked like my cool brother.

"Hey, Jason, is that you?"

He looked at me up and down and still didn't recognize me. He wondered how I knew his name and said, "I don't talk to strangers."

He seemed so different. He was always nice to everyone, even people whom he didn't know. He may have looked like my brother, but I knew for sure that it wasn't him.

I wanted to run after him and tell him what had happened. But I figured that it would be useless because he doesn't even know who Sophie Bloom is. Suddenly I felt tears roll down my cheeks. I felt a frown come down and the whole world seemed to close up.

What had I done? My older brother, who had taught me everything he knew, who had paid attention to me, didn't even know I existed. I didn't want to be there. I wanted to be back in my cozy room watching Dad watch TV and Mom talk on the phone.

I cried and ran back home. I went under my covers and wished to be back in my real home. I wished over and over again. I fell asleep hoping to be back home. I rolled over and closed my eyes for

a second and fell asleep. I woke up because I heard noises. I quickly ran downstairs but couldn't find Mom or Dad. It was probably the wind. I went back to my room to think. I remembered that I had thrown the book under my bed. I ducked my head under and did not see the book anymore. All I saw were a couple of dust bunnies. I started to scream, cry, and throw everything everywhere. I tried calling my relatives but the phone was disconnected. I was so alone. This wasn't how I wanted to spend the rest of my life.

I really missed my mom even though she had canceled our trip. I missed my dad even though he sat and watched TV all day. I really missed my brother, Jason. I didn't want to be alone anymore! I would rather have been a daughter, a sister, a friend, and a student. I wanted to be Sophie Bloom! I wished to be me! I wanted to see my name written on the wall again! I wanted to play with Jeff! I didn't want to be far away, I wanted to be right where I was! Please. Is anyone there? Is anyone listening? It was hopeless. I didn't know what to do.

I suddenly felt the sun against my cheek and heard birds chirping outside. I woke up and had a huge headache. I couldn't remember when I had gone to bed. I looked out the window and saw people moving and wearing different clothes. I looked at the chest of drawers and saw the candy that I'd wished for, and I still saw the new clothes in my closet that I'd wished for. I ran downstairs and saw Mom on the phone wearing her normal business clothes and Dad on the couch with that belly he has. What had just happened? I realized that it all had been just a dream.

I smiled and went to give both my parents a long hug and say I love you and thank you for everything they had given to me. They hugged me back so tight I couldn't breathe. They looked just as happy as I was.

Mom and Dad asked with wonder, "What happened, Sophie? Is everything OK?"

I said, "I'm the luckiest girl to have a mom and a dad. I really hated you guys when you said the trip was canceled. I was so sad to hear Jason wasn't going to be here. It wasn't fair. It's like everybody forgot about me." Tears built up in my eyes, and I started to taste the salty teardrops. I felt a little sick, but I was happy to be here.

Mom said, "We never knew you felt this way, Sophie Bloom. I'm sorry I have been so busy and that this wasn't the summer you planned. I felt bad that the trip was canceled, so I wanted to surprise you. I left you some candy on your chest of drawers and a couple of new outfits in your closet. I was just so busy and only thinking about myself that I forgot about how you were feeling."

Dad shut off the TV and let go of the remote.

He got off the couch and said, "I think we all haven't been enjoying this summer with each other. I've been so focused on this television, I almost forgot what was real. But summer isn't over yet. How about we hurry and pack our belongings and go on a family camping trip? This will be the best vacation yet."

I was shocked. I couldn't believe what my parents were saying.

I asked, "Before we go camping, can we go pick up Jason? The trip won't be the same without him."

I ran back to my room, took a look at the book, and realized my happiness wasn't far away. It was at home with my family.   ✳

BARRY AU has twelve hamsters and a goldfish. He has a Chinese and Cambodian background. "Remember," he says, "to be cool and stay in school. School gives you an education and education opens doors for opportunities."

 DEVON BARNETT loves to play volleyball, goes to tutoring after school, is an obsessive gum chewer, loves to shop, and has sixteen pairs of shoes. Devon's advice to young readers is: don't roll down grassy hills in your favorite pair of jeans.

 CASSANDRA BEUTLER has three rabbits, four dogs, and six cats. She thinks everyone should have fun, play games, play in the mud, and be themselves. And remember, don't cut your own hair.

 MICHAEL BURA loves to sing, dance, play video games, and listen to music. He advises his young readers, "If you ever get the chance to be a pirate… *take it!*"

 MONICA CHAN loves to laugh and sing and eat KFC biscuits, which are delicious, even without margarine. She wants children to know: it's OK to act crazy and to be yourself, because people will love you for it. Also, although adults seem like very tall, serious robots, they're crazy too. So, be yourself all the time!

 ROGER CHAN has two older brothers. He loves video games, likes to play sports, and can move his shoulder blades without moving his shoulders. His advice for young readers is: being weird isn't bad, it's what makes you *you*.

 ADDISON CHEN can make a strawberry wild smoothie in less than a minute but can't finish his physics homework! He says to his young readers, "Learn to swim!"

 BRENDA CHEN has been playing the guitar for three years. She enjoys listening to all kinds of music, but mostly rock. She also likes to volunteer in honor of cleaning up the environment and helping people because it makes her really happy. She plans to adopt many cats when she grows up. Her advice to kids is: be creative and make friends because that will be helpful in life.

 VICTORIA CHEN plays the violin and loves eating. When she was in first grade she pulled out one of her teeth by eating beef jerky on picture day! Victoria thinks children should eat healthy foods and take good care of their teeth. She says, "Remember to brush!"

 CONNIE CHEUNG is on the volleyball and badminton teams at school. Her advice to young students is: make good friends you can keep. Connie's inspiration for her

story came from two kids she met while teaching at a day camp in Arizona.

 STELLA CHIN loves to challenge herself and to try as hard as she can to achieve what she wants. Her advice to kids is: never give up. Try your best at everything!

 MOLLY CHU likes to sing in the shower when no one else is home, even if she's singing off-key. She would like kids to know: stay strong even in the tough parts of your lives. When you stay strong, you help not only yourself but also the people around you.

 MICHAEL CHUNG speaks English, Cantonese, and Mandarin. Michael is an immigrant from Hong Kong and when he came to this country he didn't speak a single word of English. He says, "Read! Cherish what you have, and live life the way you want!"

 JENNY CHUNG still reads children's stories because she thinks they're more interesting than any other type of book. Jenny would like young children to just have fun.

 JASMINE CRISS has taken filmmaking and graphic design classes and she likes to play sports. She would like kids to know that they should enjoy childhood while they can.

LEHA DANG plays volleyball and basketball. She's an A student. She also used to be a ballet and hip-hop dancer. She lived in Paris when she was little. Leha advises, "Friends matter because of how they are deep inside, not how they dress. You can be popular by being yourself."

 JON DOWELL is on the Pacific Rowing Club team. He likes to do extreme sports. He has been racing BMX for eight years. His advice to young readers is: try new things.

 JAYE EVANS is a beginning horseback rider. She loves to dance and do water aerobics. For her young readers she recommends, "Be yourself. Don't be someone you're not. When you work hard to please others, you forget about pleasing yourself."

 LESLIE FRANCO enjoys hot summer days and traveling. In fact, she was inspired to write her story during her Costa Rican vacation, when she woke up to find two anteaters in her hotel room. She advises her readers, "Have fun enjoying the good times now."

 Whenever RONNEY FREEMAN gets in trouble he always blames his twin brother, Rodney. You can catch Ronney in a good mood at night; he is not a morning person. He says, "Never lie to your parents."

 GABRIELLE HO loves to play sports. She is on the volleyball, basketball, and softball teams at her school. She is also involved in student council and is the secretary of her class. In the future, she aspires to become a successful journalist. She would like everyone to remember to be active and to always smile.

 TAMOOJIN JANG, aka T.J., comes from a Korean background. He enjoys playing golf and basketball with his friends. T.J. believes that "winners will do what losers won't."

 JONATHAN JEUNG is one of the weirdest people you could ever meet and he's proud of it. He wants his readers to know that "trying new things can change your life. Everyone has something special about them."

 BRITTANY RHYNEA JONES is the only girl of six children. She was inspired to write her story by her six-year-old cousin who wants to be a princess when she grows up. Always remember that, according to Brittany, "there is nothing wrong with being independent."

 ABE JUE lives with his parents and his dog, Taka. He enjoys traveling and playing baseball. He rides public transportation daily. His advice to young readers is: swing for the fences, but if you get a single, that's OK too!

 ANDERSON LAM doesn't enjoy reading and writing during his free time. But he advises you to give it a shot. Maybe you'll be published someday, just like him!

 ALLISON LEE enjoys playing on the playground with her friends. She loves swimming in the pool and pretending to be a mermaid. As a child, Allison's classmates were very mean to her and always made fun of her. She would like everyone to know "that being yourself is very important. Don't try to be someone you're not or change yourself to be included in a group. Act like yourself and people will like you."

 VICTORIA LEE is an artist like no other. Her imagination is uncontrollable. She paints and draws to make you laugh. She wants people to "be creative! Use all your senses and talents!"

 TIFFANY LEE likes to travel to many different places. Her cousins Colin and Darren inspired her to write her story. She wants young readers to know that everyone is different, but being different doesn't mean anything bad. It is what makes you unique and special.

 VERA LEE was born on the seventh month, on the seventh day, at seven o'clock in the morning, and she weighed seven pounds. One time Vera tried to walk her pet fish and she advises her readers, "Don't ever try to walk your fish; they don't swim well on land."

 VIVIAN LEI likes to eat. She loves Italian food the most. Vivian would like kids to know: you should take very good care of your pets because they won't be around forever.

 MIN LI is an interior designer and a creative person. She expresses crazy ideas through drawing. Even when people think Min's ideas are crazy they turn out to be helpful.

So Min says, "You should start creating your crazy ideas, now!"

ALEX LIM is a hip-hop producer and lyricist. He is also a photographer and a graphic artist. Alex Lim wants children to know that "being different isn't weird; it takes difference to make a change."

JESSICA LO loves to jump into pools and eats lots of cheese. She thinks kids should know that it's important not to be shy, because if you show your true colors, people will love you for your great personality! Don't be afraid to act weird in front of your friends.

KAREN LUU's nickname is Care Bear, of which her favorite character is Wish Bear. Her wish is to swim with a whale in the ocean. Karen's advice for young readers is: you can wish for anything and keep your dreams big—it makes things more possible!

JANIE LY loves to watch TV. Her favorite hobbies are eating and sleeping. She also enjoys playing softball and hanging out with her friends. Her advice to young readers is: never stop doing what you love to do, because no one can stop you except yourself.

RICHARD McKNIGHT enjoys underground hip-hop from artists like Zion I, Livin Legend, and Hieroglyphics. He is ready for life as it comes to him. He lives in Hunters Point, San Francisco, and understands what it's like to live in a tough area. For the children of the world he says, "Become your own person and be strong. Enjoy yourself and worry about no one but your family and close friends. Concentrate and break free from stereotypes… live life to the fullest."

JULIAN MERINO loves kids! He works, tutors, mentors, plays video games, dives, laughs about the stupidest things, sings to music, and dances all the time. He would like his young readers to remember that "there is a little of Matt and Jack in all of us. So keep on searching."

TENISHA D. MILLER is a young poet. She likes to play basketball and softball in her spare time. She advises, "Always be friendly and get to know a lot of nice people."

ALDO NAVARRO loves mountain biking, playing paintball, and doing crazy but fun things. Aldo wants kids to remember to "play as much as possible, because if you don't you will get old and wrinkly in your head. Don't forget to eat healthy or you will be old and wrinkly as well."

WAYMAN NG lives with his family of eight. Wayman wants little children to help their families. Even if they don't, he hopes they can be useful in other ways—like getting good grades.

SANDRA ORTEGA is a fun, active young woman who likes to goof around like a little girl. She says, "It's important to have fun when you're a little kid, because you need fun in your life. As you get older you can't goof around because you're too busy studying."

KSENIA RAKITINA loves sports. Since she was three and half years old, she's enjoyed skiing, and at the age of seven her dad taught her to play tennis. For her young readers she recommends, "Study in school. Remember, being the smartest means being the finest."

TAMICKA PRICE-BAKER is the oldest of seven children. She loves to volunteer for programs that deal with children. Her goal in life is to own a day care. Tamicka's advice for her readers is: it takes more muscles to frown than to smile.

LA SHANNA SMITH is a very active person. She loves to put herself out there and try new things. She tries to be as outgoing as she can. A bit of advice from LaShanna: live your life to the fullest because you never know what's out there and what can happen. Every day is a new day… just live it up!

KALENA SO moved to San Francisco from Hong Kong six years ago and she still keeps in touch with her friends. She says, "Distance doesn't matter in friendship as long as there is a way to keep in touch—email, write letters, and call on the phone. Learn to write!"

REGINA TAM likes to draw, sleep, and play games during her spare time. She especially enjoys watching cartoons and reading stories. She thinks you should be a kid as long as you can and have fun because that's what it's all about!

One of ERIKA TANG's weird quirks is that her tongue can touch her nose. Erika believes that "everyone is weird in one way or another so accept yourself for who you are."

 HECTOR TRASVINA really hopes that children love his story and the creativity he put into it. Hector loves to skateboard and enjoys writing. He is part African American, Native American, and Mexican American. He thinks young kids should be open and creative to themselves and open-minded to everyone else.

 GIA TRUONG really treasures peace and quiet. He would like to let his young readers know that "you should never stop reading or going out." Also, he believes that you should not stress yourself out too much when you get older.

 KAI-FAN TSANG enjoys writing music, listening to music, drumming on the desk, and shooting hoops. A good piece of advice for Kai's young readers is, "Remember to chill with your friends."

 ALLEN WONG enjoys playing *Counter-Strike*, *StarCraft*, and all kinds of games. He thinks games bring fantasy to life and let you enjoy it. Allen says, "Use this fantasy to bring out the creativity within you. But don't forget to do all your homework because that will help you bring your fantasy to life."

 ANNIE WONG and her iPod are conjoined from earphone to ear. Watching movies and re-runs of TV shows take up most of her free time. She prefers to be antisocial, but would like all boys and girls to know that being a bully doesn't pay off.

 KURTIS WONG has been a resident of San Francisco for seventeen years. His interests are card games, cooking, and basketball. He loves to go out, be adventurous, and do wild things. As a bit of advice for his young readers, Kurtis says, "You sometimes fall so you can learn to pick yourself up."

 KEVIN YU is the only child in his family and doesn't think it is fun. He wants kids to know: you should stay in school, enjoy the fun, don't do drugs, and shine like the sun. Express your love, keep your memories, and be faithful to your friends and family.

 ALLAN XUE's name is misspelled by almost everyone. He would like to tell his young readers that television shows and video games are fake, they are not real. They only show the good things without any of the hard work behind them.

 In a group of friends, MONA ZHAO is always considered "the crazy one." She is the type of girl that will dance in the street even though there is no music—the music is in her heart. By writing this story, she hopes to inspire kids everywhere to love and be themselves.

JON ADAMS has just released his 112-page graphic novel, *Truth Serum: The Lonely Parade.* Character bios, revealing the secret names and secret origins of such figures as The Barnacle and Unicorn Princess, as well as comics themselves, are available at his website, *theuniversityofmyopia.com.*

SCOTT BARRY works in a wide variety of media. His work can be seen at *birdstand.com.* He is currently working and living in San Francisco.

LART COGNAC BERLINER aka Sarah Lannan is an itinerant artist of the world. She has worked on projects with San Francisco–based publishers Little Otsu and McSweeney's Voice of Witness series. She has designed covers and T-shirts for bands such as Macromantics and Tussle, and she plays in the band Coconut.

LISA BROWN is the writer and illustrator of the Baby Be of Use books, a series of board books for busy parents (including *Baby, Mix Me a Drink*), and *How to Be,* an instructional picture book for children. She is also rumored to be Sarah "Pinkie" Bennett, who has illustrated a book called *How to Dress for Every Occasion by The Pope.* Her next book is tentatively titled *Sometimes You Do… and Sometimes You Don't.* Lisa Brown lives in San Francisco with her husband and a young son who makes a mean martini.

CARLA CALETTI is a self-taught San Francisco artist. In her paintings, she explores the female form and the evolution of women expressing themselves in the world. Inspired by folk art, her figurative style is representational with an emphasis on bold color. Some of her paintings are portraits of women from her imagination. Other paintings take on more narrative, juxtaposing the female figures with other elements that begin to tell a story. Carla is involved in curating group shows and is also a former board member of WidowSpeak, a nonprofit literary project and humanitarian effort benefiting widows worldwide. You can view samples of her work at *carlacaletti.com.*

EVAH FAN lives like a vampire and is very afraid of the sun. Her artwork reflects nonsense and mystery, and is sometimes overcast.

MARIA FORDE graduated from the University of Iowa with a writing degree before completing her masters degree at the San Francisco Art Institute. She is perhaps best known for her Pickpocket series, which was shown along the kiosks that run down Market Street in San Francisco. Recently she exhibited her life in drawings titled *A Strange 31 Years.*

MATT FURIE received a BFA from Ohio Wesleyan University. He currently lives in San Francisco and likes to have fun, dance, and draw. His medium of choice is colored pencils. Matt's influences include animals, Audubon, comix, video game instruction booklets, Flemish painting, Richard Scarry, stuffed animals, toys, street sharks, Aphex Twin, sci-fi, dinosaurs, and more.

ELIZABETH GÓMEZ is a Mexican painter currently residing in the San Francisco Bay Area. She received an MFA from San Jose State University and a BFA from the San Francisco Art Institute. She specializes in oil painting on a variety of surfaces. Her work has to do with animals, women, and personal history.

JOSHUA GORCHOV is a full-time illustrator, drawing and painting every day. He graduated from the California College of the Arts with a Bachelor of Fine Arts in graphic design, and is currently working on both editorial and commercial illustration assignments. His work responds to a broad range of subjects with a distinctive graphic language that is both vivid and conceptually concise. His work has appeared in a host of publications and he has received honors from *Communication Arts, American Illustration,* and the New York Society of Illustrators.

LANCE JACKSON has worked in journalism since 1984, so he has taken part in the use of early and current incarnations of digital media in the great Bay Area visual experiment. As a digital artist, he has worked with diverse clients ranging from *Time* magazine, the *Washington Post,* the *Los Angeles Times, Sports Illustrated,* the MacWorld Expo and, Dominican College. Lance exhibits nationally and works on a commission basis. Examples of Lance's work can be viewed at *lancejackson.net*.

HELLEN JO was born one cold afternoon in Starkville, Mississippi. She then promptly vanished and was quickly forgotten. She mysteriously resurfaced twenty-four years later in San Francisco, as a stapler of comics and a drawer of squirrels. To this day, she cannot recall what happened and states, "I don't know where I was, but I'm here now, so who cares?"

RACHEL LYON grew up in Brooklyn, New York, with a swing in her living room. She went to school for nineteen years and then moved to San Francisco, where she soon became a frequent loiterer at the 826 Valencia Pirate Store. She likes to wander and to draw.

PAUL MADONNA is a San Francisco artist, former *Mad* magazine intern, and a cartoonist for the *San Francisco Chronicle* ("All Over Coffee"). He earned his BFA from Carnegie Mellon University in 1994. In 2002 he began his website, *paulmadonna.com,* where he posts a new cartoon each week. City Lights is about to release an anthology of his work titled *All Over Coffee Collection.* Paul is also the illustrator of 826 Valencia's *San Francisco Literary Map.*

JACOB MAGRAW-MICKELSON lives in California and sometimes on an island. He paints. He feeds the cat.

SETH MATARESE is an East Coast transplant who has been living in San Francisco for seven years.

He learned most of his technical skills at Syracuse University, where he studied illustration. He also spent a summer in Florence, Italy, studying fine art. He paints because he loves to paint and he likes how his feelings at the moment dictate his painting.

ADAM McCAULEY draws all the time. Luckily, he enjoys it. You can see his work in magazines such as *Time, Los Angeles,* and *Nickelodeon,* and in recent advertisements for United Airlines and the Kentucky State Fair. He also illustrates children's books, most recently *Mom and Dad Are Palindromes* by Mark Shulman (Chronicle Books), and *Oh No, Not Ghosts!* by Richard Michelson (Harcourt), both designed by Adam's wife, Cynthia Wigginton. You can view his work at *adammccauley.com.*

DAN McHALE is an animator and illustrator living in San Francisco. He recently painted a series of pictures called *36 Views of the Hamm's Brewery.* You can take a look at *36views.moonfruit.com.*

BRENDAN MONROE lives and works in Berkeley with his girlfriend Evah Fan and a cat named Jalapeño. Mostly he makes paintings of smaller organized lifeforms. Once in a while he'll sculpt with wood and in his spare time do some gardening and furniture building. His work may be viewed at his website, *brendanmonroe.com.*

AVERY MONSEN is living the dream. All he does is make comics and T-shirts on his website, *BigStoneHead.net.* He should probably get a real job soon.

SARAH NEWTON is a San Francisco–based artist who graduated from the California College of the

Arts in 1997. She works primarily as a printmaker, making etchings and also drawings. She is represented by the Dolby Chadwick Gallery in downtown San Francisco.

LAURA PARKER is an interdisciplinary artist living in San Francisco. Her work focuses on agriculture and the environment and includes drawing, painting, artist books, and installation. Her work has been exhibited nationally and internationally.

CHRIS PEW merges the dynamic, and often polar, worlds of science and art by examining ideas of an abstract cosmos and different trajectories for the unobservable universe, all from his home in Oakland, California. Chris interprets speculative scientific theories that only take place if a certain condition exists, or are impossible to prove in the foreseeable future, and his work portrays these conditions.

LARK PIEN paints in her studio in San Francisco and draws comics (*Long Tail Kitty, Mr. Boombha*) at home in Oakland. Her contributions include stories for *Blood Orange* (Fantagraphic Books), *Nickelodean Magazine,* and *Flight Volume 4* (Random House), and she is the colorist of Gene Yang's *American Born Chinese,* recipient of the 2006 Printz award. For gallery and show dates please visit *larkpien.blogspot.com.*

MARTHA RICH, formerly a pantyhose-wearing cubicle worker from Philadelphia, is currently a Pasadena, California–based artist obsessively painting wigs, undergarments, lobsters, and Loretta Lynn.

ZACH ROSSMAN moved to Berkeley in 2006, shortly after graduating from Art Center College of Design. His influences include natural history museums, found photographs, and poorly recorded music. Most of his drawings are made very late into night because that's when he can focus and things become more clear. His work can be seen at *www. zacharyrossman.com*

JOEL SMITH currently enjoys drawing animals that feel like people, as well as taking long walks by the river with his lovely girlfriend. He practices freelance illustration and works on inspiring his students with freedom through creativity.

HANNAH STOUFFER is a San Francisco–based illustrator and designer who constantly strives to define *classic* and explores how the term relates to our modern attractions. She draws inspiration from traditional notions of elegance and always tries to engage them as the basis for her work. More of her work can be seen at *grandarray.com*.

RACHELL SUMPTER is a native Californian who studied at the Amerian Academy in Italy before receiving her BFA from the Art Center College of Design in Pasadena, California. Exposure to her grandmother's illustrations of children's books led to an early understanding of art, design, and the desire to create poignant visual narratives. Her imagery explores ironies inherent in our society, and in her work she both records and projects her perception of the human condition—its sweetness and its pathos.

DETH SUN received his BFA from the California College of the Arts in 2002. He now resides in Oakland, California.

ANNA URA received her Bachelor of Fine Arts degree from the School of the Art Institute of Chicago. She has exhibited work in galleries in Chicago; Philadelphia; Los Angeles; San Francisco; Telluride, Colorado; Ljubljana, Slovenia; and Florence, Italy. Her work has been featured in *Ten by Ten* magazine and on the online gallery The Beholder. Anna currently resides in San Francisco, where she can be found painting and working as the director of events and retail at 826 Valencia. To see more of Anna's work visit *annaura.com*.

JEN WANG has contributed work to several publications including the *Flight* and *You Ain't No Dancer* anthologies and *ShojoBeat* magazine. She just finished college in San Francisco with a degree in social science and she plans to start working on a graphic novel soon.

MARCI WASHINGTON grew up moving all over the Bay Area. In 2002, she received her BFA from the California College of the Arts and Crafts, where she is currently pursuing her MFA. Her work has been shown nationally as well as abroad.

JANE WATTENBERG nests in San Francisco with her husband, a flock of sons, and a flock of hens. She is a photographer and the author-illustrator of *Henny-Penny* and *Never Cry Woof!* among other yowza books! You might know her also as Mrs. Mustard, author of *Mrs. Mustard's Baby Faces* and *Beastly Babies*. Jane is a bee-keeper and the bees make magnificent San Francisco honey.

MICK WIGGINS is a freelance illustrator who has lived and worked for the past twenty years from his home in Berkeley. He has contributed to most of the country's major publications at one time or another and has received his share of professional accolades.

JUSTIN WOOD was born in Berkeley in 1977 and he's lived around the Bay Area up until the turn of the century. The places that he called home included a house without a floor, a converted chicken coop, an enormous glowing white ranch house on an apple farm, and finally a school bus rescued from a church group and fixed up. His mom is a fine artist, and his dad is a software engineer. He credits those two influences with helping shape what kind of work he does today. He graduated from the Art Center college of Design in 2001, and is now living in Sacramento, California, enjoying life as an illustrator and gallery artist with his fiancé and their nefarious cat. He's done work for the *New York Times,* Sony, W+K Tokyo Lab, the *Progressive,* and *Wired,* among countless other publications and companies. His gallery work has been shown in Los Angeles, San Francisco, Portland, New York, Tokyo, and Hong Kong.

For a few years now, 826 Valencia tutors have been clamoring for return trips to Jacqueline Moses's and Guilan Sheykhzadeh's classrooms at Wallenberg Traditional High School. Our tutors fell in love with Jacqueline's presentation-based lessons and Guilan's creative methods for tackling college entrance essays. It was clear that the students wanted to produce their best work for their teachers. We felt fortunate to work alongside these talented and innovative educators who got the room laughing, debating, and writing.

At the end of last year, when planning for this unique book (and the slightly different process than that of the other books in our Young Authors series), we knew that working with these two creative teachers would be not only a productive partnership but also an absolutely joyful one. When both teachers agreed to take this project on, they accepted a tremendous amount of work on top of their already exhausting responsibilities. It was their commitment and support that made this children's book possible.

At the inception of this project we also knew that we would need to bring in some experts on the topic. Our dear friends Lisa Brown and Keisa Williams ("Ms. K") offered their help. Both women brought unique insights: Lisa, a children's book author and illustrator, brought her creativity; Ms. K, a children's librarian, brought her background in the history and variety of children's literature. Lisa helped us compile a reader to prepare the students

and gave us countless ideas on how to make this book a stunning success. We invited them as guest stars for the launch of the project and they were both hugely inspirational hits!

Once the students had been inspired, they were ready to write. During the next six weeks, they worked on their stories with the help of volunteer tutors who went to their school to meet one on one and help craft these tales. These tutors provided undivided attention to the students' stories and pushed them to make every description vivid, every character memorable, and every detail colorful. Often the tutors took drafts home to continue reading after classes were over and stayed tuned to their email, eagerly anticipating rewrites and additions from the authors as the stories grew closer to the final pieces.

These volunteers are the most important resource 826 can offer: a connection between young people and helpful professionals from the community. We are very proud to partner San Francisco's students with volunteers in such a large variety of fields. The tutors who participated in this project were an exceptional bunch, and we're grateful to all of them: Osama Aduib, Kathy Cohn, Laurie Doyle, Maureen Evans, Suzanne Ginsburg, Tina Harrington, Bonny Hinners, Dylan Houle, Emily Jocson, Keren Kama, Sasha Kinney, Luke Lambert, Zoë McCann, Reese McLaughlin, Jesse Misslin, Lindsey Pace, Alex Palhegyi, Ben Palmer, Michelle Quint, Shannon Rice, Nancy Stait, Jennifer Tanguay, Chris

Tillisch, Liberty Velez, Amethyst Ware, Dan Weiss, and Daniel Worden.

The students encouraged each other, too. They pushed each other through the many, many drafts even when they had a lot of other important things going on: college applications, after-school jobs, play rehearsals, and sports practices. The students approached this project as their most important job this year.

To complement the efforts made by the educators and the student authors, 826 Valencia invited professional artists from the community to illustrate the students' work. We were totally amazed at the incredible response from these local, and sometimes traveling, luminaries. Thirty-seven generous illustrators each spent a month working on the gorgeous pieces. They held meetings with their partner student author and then painted, drew, photographed, and collaged scenes from the story. At a special presentation breakfast held in the high school library, each artist shared his or her work with the students and everyone celebrated the images. Thanks so much to the participating artists: Jon Adams, Scott Barry, Lart Cognac Berliner, Lisa Brown, Carla Caletti, Evah Fan, Maria Forde, Matt Furie, Elizabeth Gómez, Joshua Gorchov, Lance Jackson, Hellen Jo, Rachel Lyon, Paul Madonna, Jacob Magraw-Mickleson, Seth Matarese, Adam McCauley, Dan McHale, Brendan Monroe, Avery Monsen, Sarah Newton, Laura Parker, Chris Pew, Lark Pien, Martha Rich, Zach Rossman, Joel Smith, Hannah Stouffer,

Rachell Sumpter, Deth Sun, Anna Ura, Jen Wang, Marci Washington, Jane Wattenberg, Mick Wiggins, and Justin Wood.

After all the writing was completed, a student editorial board took the individual stories and collected them into a cohesive book. Tutors and students volunteered time on top of what they'd already invested to come to 826 during the evening in order to edit stories and discuss their content. There was much hard work put into bringing the fun within these stories to the forefront, and the editorial board never backed away from the challenge of making that happen. Or from admitting when it was time to stop for a short break and eat some pupusas. This group also wrote the introduction and gave the book its structure. This board, to which we're profoundly thankful, included Sona Avakian, Justin Carder, Monica Chan, Victoria Chen, Jaye Evans, Lara Fox, Ellen Goodenow, Bonny Hinners, Keren Kama, Sasha Kinney, Victoria Lee, Vivian Lei, Min

Li, Alex Lim, Jessica Lo, Karen Luu, Zoe McCann, Reese McLaughlin, Felipe Motta, Aldo Navarro, Rosey Rouhana, Victoria Sanchez, Kalena So, Regina Tam, James Warner, and Mona Zhao.

826 Valencia interns were also instrumental in making this project happen, we're especially indebted to Keren Kama, Emily Kaplan, Zoe McCann, Reese McLaughlin, Jessi Misslin, Felipe Motta, Michelle Quint, and Dan Weiss.

This project involved many members of our community, and we would like to acknowledge the following contributions. For invaluable editorial support we would like to thank Lara Fox, Sasha Kinney, and Caitlin Van Dusen. For assistance in recruiting artists to illustrate we thank Lisa Brown, Paul Madonna, and Rachell Sumpter. For help with the production of the book, we thank Pedro Ferreira. We would also like to thank Jasmine Kitses for partnering her English 678 course with this project and lending us the great minds and talents of her stu-

dents, future English teachers, who joined the ranks of our tutors. And we could not have done this book without the help of Wallenberg principal Aileen Murphy and her staff: Helen Flynn, Harry Huberman, Pat Nishimoto, Michael Reimer, and Susan Warner.

We hope that, when you pick up this book to read it for yourself or to someone even younger than you, the students' visions shine through as they share their words and their ambition to teach and inspire. And we hope you have fun too, getting a sense of what joy it was for them to write these stories. We're so proud to have been a part of this process, to have worked with the students and watched as they transformed into authors and editors who brought this project to its stunning conclusion.

We would like to leave you with the words of one of our young authors, Temo Jin Jang: "I will show this book to my kids and pass it down for generations." We hope you will, too.   ✳

THE STAFF OF 826 VALENCIA

Founding Executive Director: **Nínive Clements Calegari**
Development Director: **Leigh Lehman**
Programs Director: **Erin Neeley**
Director of National Programs: **Joel Arquillos**

Retail & Special Events: **Anna Ura**
Programs Coordinator: **Jory John**
Programs Coordinator: **Daniela Bazán**
Design & Publishing Director: **Alvaro Villanueva**

Programs and Administration Coordinator: **Lauren Hall**

THE BOARD OF DIRECTORS OF 826 VALENCIA

Barb Bersche, Jennifer Bunshoft, Nínive Clements Calegari, Dave Eggers,
Bita Nazarian, Alexandra Quinn, Vendela Vida, Richard Wolfgram

ONE-ON-ONE TUTORING

Five days a week, 826 Valencia is packed with students who come in for free, one-on-one, drop-in tutoring. Some students need help with homework. Others come in to work on ambitious extracurricular projects such as novels and plays. We're particularly proud of our thriving services and support for young students learning English.

WORKSHOPS

826 Valencia offers free workshops that provide in-depth instruction in a variety of areas that schools don't often include in their curriculum. We've had workshops on writing college-entrance essays and on writing comic books, on preparing for the SAT, and on producing films. All of the workshops are taught by working professionals and are limited in size, so students get plenty of individual attention.

FIELD TRIPS

Three or four times a week, 826 Valencia welcomes an entire class for a morning of high-energy learning. Classes can request a custom-designed curriculum on a subject they've been studying, or choose from one of our five field trip plans. The most popular is the Storytelling & Bookmaking Field Trip. In two hours, students write, illustrate, publish, and bind their own books. They leave with keepsake books and a new-found excitement for writing. Other field trips allow students to meet a local author, to learn the basics of journalism, or to work on a student publication.

IN-SCHOOLS PROGRAM

826 Valencia coordinates an in-schools program that sends tutors directly into classrooms throughout San Francisco. Throughout the year, 826 Valencia's tutors were found at Everett Middle School helping seventh-graders create a guidebook for travelers in the Sahara Desert, working with third-graders at Bryant Elementary helping who wrote stories about dragons and vampires, and at Leadership High School encouraging seniors through the process of composing speeches based on Hamlet's famous soliloquy. In the fall, tutors guided students toward compelling essays for their college applications at several local high schools.

826 Valencia runs one full-time in-school project at Everett Middle School: a classroom that has been turned into a pirate-themed Writers' Room. The room is staffed throughout the school year by 826 tutors and volunteers who help students at Everett work on researching, writing, and perfecting their writing assignments. In its fourth year, the Everett Writers' Room is so successful that every single student at Everett receives one-on-one attention there throughout the school year. In 2008, 826 Valencia will open a similar satellite room at James Lick Middle School.

STUDENT PUBLICATIONS

826 Valencia produces a variety of publications, each of which contains student writing from our various programs. These projects represent some of the most exciting work at 826 Valencia, as they expose and enable Bay Area students to a publishing experience otherwise not available to them. Students of 826 Valencia wrote for the following publications:

I Might Get Somewhere: Oral Histories of Immigration and Migration emerged from 826 Valencia's ongoing work with local public high schools. This book exhibits an array of student-recorded oral narratives about moving to San Francisco from other states in the U.S. and from all over the world. Acclaimed author Amy Tan wrote the foreword to this compelling collection of personal stories on the problems and pleasures of life in new surroundings.

Waiting to be Heard: Youth Speak Out about Inheriting a Violent World—thirty-nine students from Thurgood Marshall Academic High School wrote about the themes of violence and peace, through perspectives that are personal, local, and global. With a foreword by Isabel Allende, the book combines essays, fiction, poetry, and experimental writing pieces to create a passionate collection of student voices.

Talking Back: What Students Know about Teaching is a completely student-produced book that delivers the voices of the class of 2004 from Leadership High School on the relationships students want with their teachers, how students view classroom life, and how the world affects students.

826 Valencia also publishes scores of chapbooks each semester. These are collections of writing from our workshops, in-school projects, and class projects from schools that team up with us.   ✳

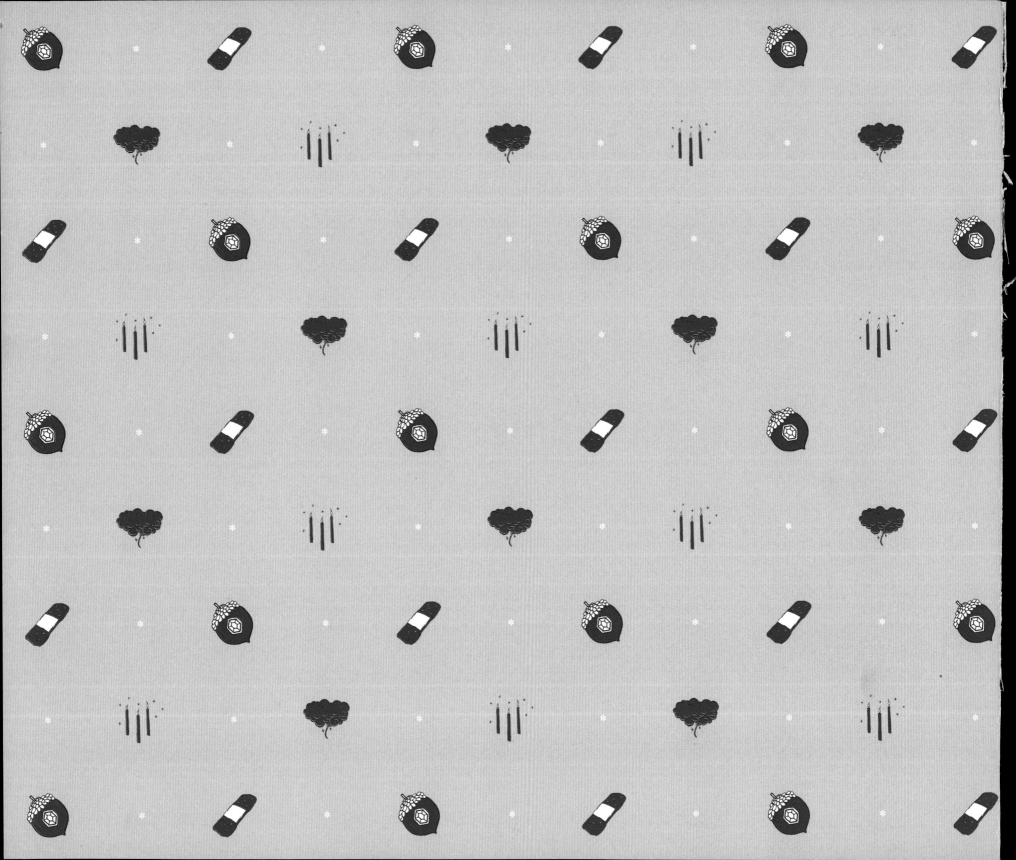